IF I DIE BEFORE I WAKE

The Better Off Dead Series Vol. 8
TALES OF HALLOWEEN HORROR

IF I DIE BEFORE I WAKE

The Better Off Dead Series Vol. 8
TALES OF HALLOWEEN HORROR

Foreword by **Nick Roberts**, author of *The Exorcist's House*

EDITED BY
R.E. SARGENT & STEVEN PAJAK

IF I DIE BEFORE I WAKE
The Better Off Dead Series Volume 8
Tales of Halloween Horror

Edited by R.E. Sargent & Steven Pajak

Foreword by Nick Roberts

SINISTER SMILE PRESS

Published by Sinister Smile Press, LLC
P.O. Box 637
Newberg, OR 97132

Copyright © 2023 by Sinister Smile Press, LLC

"Accidents Happen" © L.P. Hernandez, 2023
"Edna, Edna" © G. Nicholas Miranda, 2023
"Haywire" © Kevin M. Folliard, 2023
"Dead Runners" © Mike Marcus, 2023
"The Pack" © Bryan Holm, 2023
"Stomper-Screamer" © Jason A. Wyckoff, 2023
"The Night Train" © Alexandr Bond, 2023
"Witch Hunt" © David Anthony, 2023
"Fun-size Traci" © David Rider, 2023
"Blind Date" © Sarah Cannavo, 2023
"Slaughterhouse X" © DW Milton, 2023
"Little Miss 666" © Scotty Milder, 2023
"Night in the Lonesome" © Richard Chizmar & W.H. Chizmar, 2023

All rights reserved. This book or parts thereof may not be reproduced in any form, stored in any retrieval system, or transmitted in any form by any means—electronic, mechanical, photocopy, recording, or otherwise—without prior written permission of the publisher.

This is a work of fiction. Names, characters, places, and incidents either are the product of the authors' imagination or are used fictitiously, and any resemblance to actual persons, living or dead, business establishments, events, or locales is entirely coincidental.

Trade Paperback ISBN – 978-1-953112-56-9

www.sinistersmilepress.com

"Anyone could see that the wind was a special wind this night, and the darkness took on a special feel because it was All Hallows' Eve."

-*Ray Bradbury*

CONTENTS

Foreword Nick Roberts	xv
ACCIDENTS HAPPEN L.P. Hernandez	1
EDNA, EDNA G. Nicholas Miranda	13
HAYWIRE Kevin M. Folliard	41
DEAD RUNNERS Mike Marcus	57
THE PACK Bryan Holm	79
STOMPER-SCREAMER Jason A. Wyckoff	109
THE NIGHT TRAIN Alexandr Bond	127
WITCH HUNT David Anthony	155
FUN-SIZE TRACI David Rider	181
BLIND DATE Sarah Cannavo	201
SLAUGHTERHOUSE X DW Milton	223
LITTLE MISS 666 Scotty Milder	243
NIGHT IN THE LONESOME Richard Chizmar & W.H. Chizmar	275
About the Authors	303

FOREWORD
NICK ROBERTS

In the year 2021, I sold my first short story. Until then, I had only submitted stories for the publishing credits. Getting selected to be in an anthology where someone (other than my mom) would read my work blew my mind. I was chasing that insidious notion of *exposure* and even paying "reading fees" to enter my stories into contests. After I landed a few and got a little confidence boost, I decided to only aim for paying markets, even if it was just a nominal fee.

I didn't have a backlog of stories, so I got online and searched for open calls. I ran across SSP's call for an anthology called *A Pile of Bodies, A Pile of Heads (Let the Bodies Hit the Floor Volume One)*. The title kind of tells you everything you need to know about what they were going for, right? Anyway, I sat down and cranked out a 12,000-word story called "The Devil's Road," which was about a college kid who uses a girl to get close to her dad because he suspects that this man is a long-dormant serial killer. Needless to say, some bodies hit the floor.

Fellow West Virginia author and brilliant short story writer Bridgett Nelson worked with SSP at the time, and I'll never forget the acceptance email she sent stating that they loved the story. Not only that, but they paid me. Holy shit! No, it wasn't thousands of dollars, of course, but it was enough to make me an Active Member of the Horror Writers Association. And if you think it's easy to get someone to pay you a dime for your art, whether that be writing, drawing, painting, music, or online feet videos, give it a go. See how long it takes to not only create the finished product, but to earn money for it. You'll quickly realize that fifty bucks for something that your imagination birthed into this world will make you feel like a millionaire.

Since then, SSP has published two of my other stories, "Sally Under the Bed" and "Percepto!," and I hope to collaborate with them again in the future. I highly encourage you to go through their catalogue and dive into tales of madness, murder, and mayhem. Not only do they give shots to new voices, but they bring in the big names as well. As you will see in this anthology, they just put out quality work.

Now, in what could be their best anthology yet, *If I Die Before I Wake (The Better Off Dead Series Volume Eight): Tales of Halloween Horror*, SSP has assembled a killer cast of authors to serve up some pumpkin spice–flavored gore. And what better time to sit down and crack open a new collection of spooky stories than Halloween? If you're lucky, your autumn gets chilly with the changing of the leaves from green to orange, yellow, and brown. Perhaps you live on a street where every other house has a jack-o'-lantern on their porch or a giant purple spider in their yard. The local haunted houses and hayrides are in full swing, and Spirit Halloween has possessed the corpse of a former K-Mart.

Yes, there is no greater time for the horror fanatic than the Halloween season. And it truly is a season now. We used to be limited to thirty-one days of spookiness (which I kind of prefer), but now the candy corn and cheap rubber masks start getting pumped into CVS in early August. For me, I start to get the ghostly butterflies in my belly on October 1st. A horror movie is on every other channel and streaming platform and on full display in the electronics section of major retail stores.

FOREWORD

I like to say that, like Bane from *The Dark Knight Returns*, I was born into darkness. October 17th is my birthday, so I naturally looked forward to this month as a child. Birthday parties and presents were precursors to All Hallows' Eve. There are those who enjoy Halloween while it lasts and then move on to the next part of the year. You might be one of them, and that's all well and good. We thank you for your support and look forward to seeing you next year. But for the diehard horror fans, we are October people, and Halloween is a state of mind.

They say that the veil between the worlds of the living and the dead is at its thinnest on Halloween. Light a few candles, curl up in your favorite chair, and read some stories that'll have you seeing odd shadows in the corner and second-guessing every floor creak or curtain flutter. The boogeymen, monsters, killers, witches, ghosts, and goblins are just waiting to come to life with each line that you read. Maybe they're already there with you right now, looking over your shoulder, breathing down your neck as you read this very sentence. Don't look! Just keep turning pages, and you might make it out of this alive.

Halloween is here, my friends, and you found it.

ACCIDENTS HAPPEN
L.P. HERNANDEZ

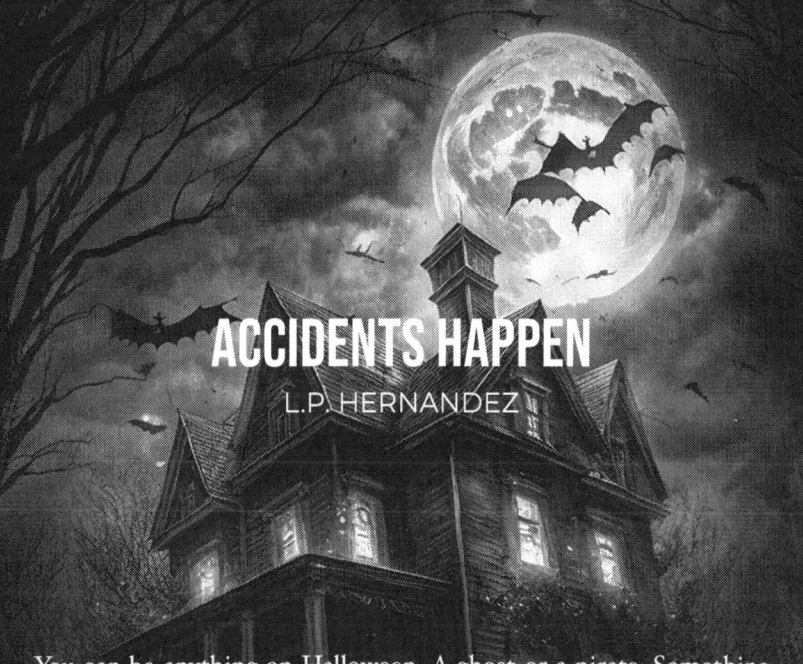

You can be anything on Halloween. A ghost or a pirate. Something scary or fun. It's my favorite holiday, 'cept I'd be lying about that come Christmas Eve, thinkin' about all the presents in Santa's sack and all the space under the tree. It's my favorite holiday 'cept during December. I think that's about right.

Ma thought it was silly. A boy my size getting excited to tromp around the neighborhood with a dirty pillowcase beggin' for candy. I didn't have no say in how big I was, and a pillowcase can hold more than one of them plastic pumpkin pails anyway. Ma thought a lot of my ideas were silly. And I don't think she liked that I was so big for a boy who just added *teen* to his number. She said I looked like Dad, but not in a way that made it seem she was happy about it. I don't know what he looks like, so I don't know if it's a good or bad thing myself.

Her husband, Wayne, got a new look in his eye lately. Used to be he could stand over me when he was tryin' to make a point. Didn't say nothing usually, just let that beer gut touch my cheek with his fists tight like he was trying to squeeze water outta granite. It's different now. He gives me the same look, makes the same fists but from across the room. That's okay. I like him better across the room.

My little sister, Darcy...that's Ma and Wayne's daughter together, so I guess she's half, she's been walking for about six months. Not good enough for trick or treatin'. She still falls some, but I wanted to take her with me still.

I'm big as a man now even if I don't feel like one. I knew this Halloween might be my last time trick-or-treatin', and I wanted to do it with Darcy. Ma and I fought about it something awful. She said Darcy was too small and I was too big. Her little steps couldn't keep up with mine. She said, *Remember what happened to Sofia?* and I told her that was an accident like I do every time.

Sometimes I think Ma doesn't like me. She loves me. I know that like I know what a Snickers tastes like before I bite it. But I don't think she likes me. When she holds Darcy, she looks...I guess I don't know the word for it 'cause I've never experienced it myself. It seems nice, though. I bet it's nice to be looked at like that.

Ma stopped arguing with me, oh I guess a couple days ago. I don't know if I won. I just know she stopped talkin' about it. Giving me the quiet treatment, or whatever that's called. I figured if she ain't saying *no* that means it's okay.

Me and Darcy trick-or-treatin' together for the first and last time. I'll probably take her next year but will be too old for candy myself. I was so excited when Ma stopped sayin' *no,* I got right to work on our costumes. Well, I guess Darcy's ain't so much a costume. It's just messin' up her baby clothes some, scuffin' 'em and tearing little holes here and there.

"Come here, baby girl," I say and lift her out of her crib.

Ma's right next to us in the rockin' chair giving me the quiet treatment. You can say *no* more ways than with your mouth. I know that for sure. But if it ain't said, I'm not changing my plans. Darcy's clothes are already a little messed up, like she mighta not liked the last thing Ma fed her. It's kinda smelly, but it's got the look I'm goin' for. Green and black like camo paint on her shirt, some brown crusted on her mouth. I find a coupla loose threads and tug 'em. I think it looks okay now.

"In you go," I say and pull her arms through the holes in the baby backpack-thing. Ma has a word for it, but it's not one that can stay in my head long. I walk us to the bathroom, or try to. I'm so excited I get lost in my own house. Takes two wrong doors to find the right one.

"Look at us," I say to the mirror. My zombie makeup is perfect. It's just like the movies. I wipe a bit off on my thumb and smear it on Darcy's cheeks. They feel like pizza dough that got left out too long. Right under my nose, she doesn't smell so good, but I can't change a diaper (I'm not allowed) and Ma ain't gonna help me do it. It'll be a nice surprise for when we get back. Here ya go, Ma, a nice, full diaper. Probably all smeared and such.

In the mirror I can see a window to the outside behind me. It's not dark, but dark enough for trick-or-treatin'. I'm so excited. My belly feels like it's got spiders in it. Sofia used to eat spiders. I remember that. Sometimes she'd just bat 'em around a bit, snap a few legs off. Does that make her bad just 'cause she hurt a few bugs? Does it, Ma? I miss Sofia.

"Zombie dad and zombie daughter. Look at us."

Darcy isn't excited and that's okay. She won't make a memory of tonight. I'll have to tell her about it when we're older. I take another wrong turn lookin' for my bedroom, but the pillowcase in Ma's room works just as good as mine. It'll probably break her out of her quiet treatment when she sees I used it for candy.

"I'm goin', Ma!" I yell and clomp down the stairs holding Darcy's head to my chest.

Ain't seen Wayne in I don't know how long, but he's not in my path to the front door. He and Ma are probably fightin', which I like better than Ma pretendin' to love him. The way she touches him like I don't notice, pinches and such. I see it, Ma. I see what you are.

I step outside and fill my chest with smoke and cider. I don't know if that's what I'm smelling exactly, but it's good. Better than Darcy's diaper.

There's kids on the sidewalk across the street swingin' pumpkin pails. I wanna run to show off my costume, but I can't with Darcy. Gotta keep her head from movin' too much. *Remember Sofia?* That's what Ma would say if she wasn't giving me the quiet treatment. Of course I remember her, Ma. Accidents happen. Instead, I walk fast.

One thing I don't like about Halloween is how most folks don't let you trick-or-treat no more. They just leave the candy outside in a bucket or a bowl, usually with a sign sayin' *take just one*. I always obey the sign. It's easy to obey somethin' that's written down. It's tougher when it's just me and my own head.

Three houses in a row with just a bowl outside. One of 'em was empty, and I knew it had to be bad kids doing it, cause trick-or-treatin' just started. I hope they get caught. I hope they get in trouble for it. Bad kids don't deserve a fun Halloween. That's what Ma says. *Remember what happened to Bella?* Not really, if I'm telling the truth about it.

"Oh, there's a person!" I say to Darcy as I cut through the yard to the next house. The lady's just about to close the door as a bunch of little kids rush back to their parents on the sidewalk. The door shuts before I get there, and that's okay. It feels more like Halloween when you have to knock.

BAM BAM BAM

I don't try to be loud, but it happens sometimes bein' so big. I take a step back. Oh, I can't wait. Them spiders are crawlin' all over themselves in my gut. The lady opens the door, and her eyes are lookin' too low, like she's expecting kids half my size.

"Trick or treat!" I yell.

She jolts, and the candy in the bowl jumps with her. A couple pieces fall on the floor like teeth. No. Not like teeth. Why did I think that? Her face! Look at her face! She looks scared for real, like Ma does when we get to squabblin' and I use my outside voice. She shrinks a bit, like she's trying to hide behind the door.

"Braaaaiiins," I say, holding the pillowcase out.

It's a joke, but she doesn't laugh. She's lookin' at Darcy like she's a rattlesnake instead of a baby, like she might get bit. She tries to close the door, but it bounces off my knuckle.

"Trick or treat," I try again.

She looks behind. I can see a picture in the hallway. A man and two kids about halfway in age between me and Darcy. I bet they're out trick-or-treatin' right now. I bet she's alone.

"I..." she starts, but the words take a wrong turn.

Her hair's not the same color, and her face is a little rounder, but she looks like Ma. Maybe a little. Maybe it's just the way her eyes are all big and her mouth is open like her heart might jump out of it. I wonder if she touches her husband like Ma does with Wayne. Maybe they're the same like that, too.

She grabs a handful of candy and throws it at the pillowcase. Some makes it inside. Some falls on the patio like teeth.

No. Not teeth.

I bend down to pick them up, forgetting about Darcy, but that's okay. She can sleep through anything. The door slams shut, and the porch light goes out. That's funny. She had plenty of candy in her bowl.

"Lots of people are like that, Darcy. You probably won't have to worry about it 'cause you're so cute and small. People like cute and small things."

I stand on the porch for a moment. It's not the Halloween I was dreaming about. Not like Halloweens from when I was small. I had to fight with Ma and Wayne about it. Maybe that's why Wayne left. I guess that's a good thing, at least. There ain't many people answering doors, and the one that did was so scared I almost felt bad. The kids don't seem to know any better. They're still runnin' around like ants on a griddle. Maybe it's just about candy for them.

I shake my head. It's my last Halloween. Last time trick-or-treatin' at least. I head back out thinkin' about how heavy my pillowcase will be by the end of the night. Maybe I could use it as a pillow! No. I don't think that would work. I think the chocolate would melt, or maybe I'd wake up at night and eat some. Ma says no candy after I brush my teeth. That's fine, Ma, I just won't brush 'em.

I hold my arms out and groan as a group of princesses and fairies comes toward me. They giggle and scream, and I can't help smiling too. A couple of their dads are right behind 'em sippin' beers. Not the kind Wayne used to drink. They both give me a nod, and I nod back. That feels better. Halloween is supposed to be fun. Right, Ma?

I tried to tell Ma I would be careful with Darcy. I'd be safe. *Remember what happened to Mr. Bill?* How do you know, Ma? You weren't there.

There's a group of teen boys coming at me now. One's wearing a football costume, which isn't really even a costume. The others are just carrying masks. I don't like teen boys. Never have. They do mean things on purpose instead of on accident. Make fun of someone just for bein' big.

We don't say nothin' to each other. They walk off the sidewalk onto the grass. But I hear 'em a few seconds after.

"Fucking sick. Did you see that?"

I want to turn around and get 'em. It'd be easy to do. Snatch 'em up and squeeze like how Wayne squeezes his fists, like how I did when Mr. Bill peed on my bed. But that was an accident. And I got Darcy with me.

I reach to lift her head and it feels like I'm touchin' a caterpillar.
"Uh!" I make a sound like someone punched me in the belly.
It's flies. They must like the throw-up on her chin.
"Shoo!"

There's an old man sitting in his driveway up ahead. I can see he's not givin' out the good candy, but it would be mean to walk past and not take it. I wave a hand in front of Darcy's face to keep the flies away as I walk over to him.

"Trick or treat!" I say, makin' my voice a bit higher so maybe I won't spook him.

He holds out a Tootsie Roll, just one. His eyes are kinda foggy, kinda cloudy like Mr. Bill's were. Or was that Bella? I don't think he can see too good, so I hold the pillowcase right under his hand. The Tootsie Roll falls, and he smiles, and I'm glad I didn't skip him.

"You have a good night," I say, and he taps a finger to his forehead.

Two more houses with just bowls out front. At least the candy's good.

"Shoo!" I say. The flies really like the throw-up on Darcy's face. I guess it kinda makes her look more like a zombie, but I don't think flies are good for babies.

There's more kids out now. It's easier to blend in when there's a bunch of 'em together. The parents are all staring at their phones or drinkin' outta those metal cups with the lids. I don't think it's orange juice by how big they're smilin'. There's a whole buncha kids running around. Feels nice to blend in.

"See, Darcy, this is what Halloween's about. Dressing up and havin' fun. Filling your pillowcase up with enough candy to last 'til Christmas," I say.

I still say, "Trick or treat," even if I'm in a big group. Gotta teach Darcy the right way.

I'm at a house with lots of decorations and spooky music. There's fog comin' from somewhere and a green light in it. Now this is Halloween! I bet they give out good candy. A little girl turns around too quick and bumps into me. She falls, and her candy scatters over the concrete like teeth. Darcy sleeps right through it. Good girl, Darcy, not like Bella.

"Sorry 'bout that," I say, and the kid's looking at my hand meant to lift her up and then at Darcy. Her eyes move over to the side, and

I turn to see what grabbed her attention. There's red and blue lights. A police car parks next to a house with its lights out. I think not celebratin' Halloween should be against the law, too, Mr. Cop-man.

I help the girl up, and she scoots away without picking up the candy that spilled outta her pail.

"Trick or treat!" I say, using my high voice again.

It's a bit darker now, and the light in the fog turns my skin green.

"Happy Halloween, brother!" the man says. He's dressed like a zombie, too. And I was right, they give out the good candy. A full-size Snickers and I know just what it will taste like.

I guess the day isn't ruined after all. I like it better in the dark, and I can see lotsa people handing out candy down the street. I start heading that way, walkin' fast to catch up with the group I was with. One of the dads on the sidewalk has a big gut like Wayne used to. I wonder if he bumps his kids with it to make a point. I wonder what his teeth would sound like falling on the concrete.

The farther away from home I walk, the better it gets. In about fifteen minutes, it's all the way dark, and it makes the spooky houses stand out more. I don't waste time with the bowls and buckets on porches. There probably ain't no candy in 'em anyway. The bad kids had too much time. That's not what Halloween's about, after all. It's about spookin' people and not just cause you're big as a man. I didn't have no say in how big I was, Ma. I came from you, didn't I? You made me this way.

Maybe it ain't a bad thing if Ma keeps givin' me the quiet treatment. Sometimes she doesn't know when to shut up.

The pillowcase feels like its full of bricks after an hour. I shoulda just waited 'til it was dark out, 'cause people treat me better in the dark. They think I'm just a good dad takin' his little girl out trick-or-treatin'. Well, that's not exactly true, but we can pretend, can't we, Darcy? Maybe I can be a dad again next year.

I walk for a while, not really payin' attention to where I'm heading. Once the porch lights start going off, I'm pretty lost. The houses seem the same out here, the same parts just rearranged to make 'em look different. My feet hurt, too. Wayne's shoes feel tight on all sides.

I head back in what I think is the right direction. There's a few spooky yards I'll know for sure when I see 'em. It's mostly dads following behind their tired kids now. They nod or tilt a beer can at me, and I nod back. I wonder if I've ever seen my real dad before and not known it. Maybe he would look at me the way Ma looks at Darcy, like I'm somethin' to be proud of, like it's okay if I make mistakes 'cause we can always get a new cat. They're all over the place. You don't even have to buy one.

My socks feel wet, and I don't know if it's sweat or blood 'cause they hurt so bad. Sorry about the boots, Wayne. You weren't around to ask if it was okay.

"What do you think, Darcy, a good first Halloween? I don't think you can eat the candy yet. I'll eat it for you."

I comb her hair and brush the flies off her face. Darcy can sleep through anything, not like Shadow. It must be nice to be a baby. You're carried everywhere. People bring you food when you cry. You can use the toilet in your pants even! Is it a toilet if it's in your pants? I guess I don't know the right words for it. I don't remember being a baby. Seems like I've been big forever.

The sidewalks are empty 'cept for teenagers that are probably waiting 'til it's midnight to do something awful. Maybe after I put Darcy in her crib I'll come back out and do something awful to them before they get the chance.

Finally, I see the spooky yard with the green light. Next time I need to remember the numbers on the houses. I head to my house but stop. There's a hummin' sound somewhere, like someone far away is out with a weed-whacker, but it's too dark for that. There's no one on this street, not even teenagers.

"Do you hear that, Darcy?"

I move to comb her hair but then figure out where the hummin' sound is coming from.

"Ew!"

There's so many flies it's like fur. Like Mr. Bill when I was running my fingers through his hair tryin' to tell him he was okay. I give her head a thump and the flies buzz off all mad I spoiled their dinner. It's okay, Darcy can sleep through anything.

"Let's get you back inside, Darcy. I bet Ma's been worried sick about you," I say, then laugh.

I drop my treasure just inside the front door. The house is still, a little chirp from a smoke detector begging for its batteries to be replaced. Isn't that the *man's* job, Wayne? Or whatever your name is. I flip on lights as I navigate through the house. The houses are the same, after all, just the parts rearranged, and there have been too many to remember.

The stairs squeak like mice under my feet. I don't need to have memorized my way to the baby room. I can smell my way there just fine. At the head of the stairs, I catch a glimpse of myself in the darkened bathroom mirror. Just the crown of Darcy's head is visible. Her arms and legs are slack like a rubber doll.

"Look at us," I say and push her forehead back a little. My finger leaves a divot. The skin isn't quite sure what it's supposed to do in its current state. That's so interesting. Reminds me of Bella, much more interesting when she stopped fighting. "Well, time to get you to bed."

You can be anything on Halloween. That goes for the woman in the rocking chair as well. Tonight, she is my mother giving me the *quiet treatment*. I tug Darcy, or whatever her name is, free and it feels like her skin might slough off the bones.

"Here you go," I say, depositing her in her mother's stiffened arms. There are still a few flies on her face, exploring moisture where they find it. One settles on her mother's breast, a single drop of yellowed milk frozen on the nipple like pudding. I bet that's a treat for a fly.

"Happy Halloween!" I say in my high voice, my *don't scare the neighbors* voice.

The cop car had me worried, but it's a pretty ridiculous story to convey. A giant man dressed like a zombie with a dead baby going trick-or-treating. It's Halloween, after all. It was probably just a prop or a doll. She would have struggled to convince them otherwise. Sometimes women just know. Intuition. My mother had it. She understood the connection between a missing cat and a locked bedroom door, a shovel not in its usual place in the garage. So why was there a Bella after Sofia, a Mr. Bill after Bella?

Feed the monster so he doesn't go hungry.

That's what Wayne said.

I close the door behind me. It's been a long day, a long couple of days, actually. I'm not hungry anymore. I'm ready to go home. Just have to figure out where that will be.

Downstairs, I open the door to the basement. There's a single bulb burning in the middle of the room. I can only see an arm in its light, a cold hand with fingers curled into a fist. Beside it, a few teeth catch the light. My knuckles hurt, remembering.

"Happy Halloween, Wayne," I say. I know that's not his name. I saw it on the mail on the kitchen table. To me, he is Wayne. The next one will be as well.

I remember overhearing a conversation between Wayne and my mother. He whispered in such a way it was louder than talking. Yes, I was eavesdropping, but I probably could have heard it across the house.

"It's not safe! You know it's not. We have to find a place for him or he's going to do it to her, too."

My mother's voice didn't carry as far. When it was quiet, I knew she was speaking.

"We have a chance to be a family. A *real* family."

So it wasn't a *real* family with me in it? Well, I had a few thoughts about that, Wayne. And you were right. It wasn't safe.

There is one thing left to do before I leave. I pop the can's lid and hear the tinkling of the bell on its collar. Cats are so interesting. It could have been in the room with me and Wayne, this version of Wayne, when I broke the teeth out of his mouth, and still, a hint of fish in the air and it comes running...

"What's your name?" I ask.

I am careful, scooping the cat into my arms after it has eaten its fill. Accidents happen, after all. Especially to cute, small things.

"I think you look like a *Darcy*."

You can be anything on Halloween. A ghost or a pirate. A teenager. A son. A big brother.

I wonder what I'll be next year.

EDNA, EDNA

G. NICHOLAS MIRANDA

Edna, you are so wise.
Speak. Speak, and utter no lies.
Tell us, tell us, which of us dies?
Edna, Edna, open your eyes.

Dana came out of the house, and Ray frowned. At twelve, she was shedding her childhood like it was wet clothing that awkwardly clung to her developing frame. Her hastily assembled "costume" consisted of a baggy hoodie and jeans and a cat-eared headband to keep her sandy brown hair out of her eyes. She hadn't even bothered to streak some face paint on her cheeks for whiskers. In the weeks leading up to Halloween, Dana had vehemently repeated that this would be her last year to trick-or-treat, and that she was going out with her friends. The whole thing, she explained, was for kids, like her six-year-old brother, Peter.

"You look...normal," Ray said.

"I'm comfortable." She shrugged, looking for her friends among the blobs of kids that had started to gather up and down the street.

"Your brother about ready?"

"Grandma was finishing his makeup." Dana's arm shot up, flailing as she signaled to a girl walking down the sidewalk toward them. "That's Maddy." Ray saw that the girl wore the same standard-issue tween uniform as Dana, except her headband sported a tiny witch hat. The two girls might have been sisters; both were about the same height and of similar body structure, and they shared that annoyed expression that would soon mature into pure disillusionment by the time they hit high school. "See ya," Dana said. She sauntered up to the girl, and they leaned close, giggling in mouselike chirps.

Suddenly, the front door banged open. Ray whipped around to see a zombie charging at him, arms outstretched and mouth hanging open in a starving moan.

"Wait a second, honey. Let Mommy get in front so I get pictures of you coming down the porch steps." Ashlee appeared behind the little monster, holding her phone high for a better angle. She wore shimmering black tights netted with silver spider webs that seemed painted on to her slender legs. Her loose black t-shirt showed the original movie poster for *Halloween*—the hand clutching the kitchen knife and the fang-toothed Jack O'Lantern. She pranced on the balls of her bare feet, her toenails painted metallic black.

Peter was loving every second of the attention. "I'm gonna eat your brain, Daddy," the boy said.

"You might starve, kiddo," Ray said, smirking.

Ashlee slid around her zombified son and padded down the steps. She stood next to Ray. He smelled the floral deodorant she wore and the tropical scent of the products she used to keep her shoulder-length black hair looking its best. She smiled at Ray, quizzically. Her burgundy lips hitched in one corner. The sapphire eyeshadow glinted, making her dark eyeliner look like liquid night. "What?" she asked, noticing his stare.

Ray shook his head, smiling nervously. They'd been married for almost fifteen years, and it was difficult not to need the constant reassurance that she loved him. He was a pudgy nerd and she was a sultry Goth princess. Nothing about them being together made sense, and he was afraid that he would wake up and realize their life, their love had all been a fever dream.

"Okay," Ashlee said, raising the phone. "Give us your scariest zombie."

Ray's mother had definitely improved her makeup skills since his younger days. The mixture of color and shadow gave Peter's naturally round face the appearance of being sallow and sunken. Much better than the smear of red she'd applied on Ray's forehead, cheeks, and nose when he had gone trick-or-treating as the devil or the amorphous squiggles of green and black when he'd dressed as a soldier.

Slowly, Peter lumbered down the steps, head cocked to the side.

"He looks great," Ray admitted to his wife.

"He should," she whispered. "Your mom watched that YouTube tutorial video a hundred times, I swear."

He slung an arm around her waist and let his hand drift under the loose-fitting shirt. He found the small of her back and strummed her warm flesh like guitar strings. Goose bumps rose under his caress. His fingers brushed the elastic waistband of her tights, and he dipped a finger under the material.

"Later," she mumbled out of the side of her mouth, then bumped his hip with her own. She cast him an agreeable yet exasperated grin. The dying light caught a kind of purple-pink glow mixed into her makeup as though some magic, inner light was radiating beneath.

"Better hurry," he said to Peter. "You've only got two hours, and it's a big neighborhood."

It was one of those perfect Halloween nights. Not nearly cold enough to be forced to wear a coat—which always ruined the look of a costume—but not too warm as to make those in costumes uncomfortable as they marched mile after mile for their treats. The air smelled of sweet earth, woodsmoke, and scorched pumpkin guts. Screams and shouts floated through the neighborhood. The throbbing tempo of music stalked the streets from many of the houses. Ray followed Peter, the boy toting his pillowcase at his side.

The neighborhood really hadn't changed much over the decades, but Ray's perception of it sure had. He remembered the vivid colors of paint and siding, lawns that were tended to. True, some people had moved out. That happened in every neighborhood. But it was strange seeing Mr. Hawkner's house left to the elements. The man had been emphatic about keeping his white siding as flawless as cake icing and his yard as manicured as a golf course. Now, the white aluminum was as gray as cold bones and small patches of mildew and moss grew near the downspouts. From the awnings, cancerous splotches of rust chewed from the edges inward. The yard had become gnarly lumps of grass spotted with choking patches of clover and spots of bare earth. If he wasn't already dead, seeing his property in its current condition would likely do Mr. Hawkner in.

It was still a lively grid of streets, though; that's the reason Ray and Ashlee brought the kids over for Halloween. Their plat was smaller, stuffed with cramped little houses. Their neighbors either didn't give out candy or they too left the neighborhood to seek better goodies elsewhere.

Peter shifted his laden pillowcase onto his other hand. "What time is it, Daddy?"

"It's not even seven. Why? Are you done?"

"No!" Peter took off up a driveway, brandishing his sack. "Trickertreat," he yelled, smearing it all into one word.

Ray stopped and waited. Looking around, he saw a familiar pair of cat ears among a bouquet of heads tromping down the sidewalk.

He was going to ignore them and let Dana have her independence, but then he saw the look on her face.

"Dana," he called.

The group stopped. Besides Dana and Maddy there were two boys and another girl whom he'd never seen. All were dressed in the same attire of their age group.

They turned inward, looking at Dana, then parted. Silent.

Dana emerged from the group, head lowered, hugging herself.

"You okay, sweetie?" Ray asked, his voice lowered to keep her from being further embarrassed.

She nodded.

Maddy appeared next to Dana. She had removed her little witch hat. "It's okay if you want to skip out," she said to her. "I'll stay with you."

"Thanks." Dana's voice was barely audible, and it was quickly stolen by the October wind.

"Everything okay?" Ray eyed the two boys and the other girl. They instantly lowered their heads and marched on.

Peter popped in between them, grinning. "You forgot your candy bag," he said, thrusting his bulging pillowcase at his sister. "But you can have some of mine." He rattled the contents.

Dana gave her brother a weak smile. "Thanks, Pete." She ruffled his hair. "You know what you need to look like a *real* zombie?" She bent over and came up with some dead leaves and smashed them onto his head. "There. Now you really look like you crawled out of the grave."

Peter laughed. He dropped his pillowcase and began chasing Maddy down the sidewalk, moaning.

"What's going on?" Ray asked again, gently nudging her shoulder with his elbow.

Dana shook her head. "Spooky Old Edna."

Ray's mouth went dry. He forced a laugh. "That lady's still alive?" Of course he knew that she was but felt it best to play dumb.

"Kaleb saw her before we met up. Just sitting on her porch," Dana said.

"You guys weren't going to go mess with her, right?" Ray hoped his disapproving dad tone overpowered his panic.

"No." She watched Peter and Maddy, her tongue playing along the corner of her bottom lip. Then, "Well, Toby went ahead of us to see if he could get a Halloween selfie. We were going to meet him on the corner by her house and see if he'd been brave enough."

Ray gently took her by the shoulders. Dana looked up at him with little girl eyes that were bracing for a stern beratement. "I want you to promise me that you'll stay away from her."

"Who?" Peter appeared at their side and picked up his candy bag.

"Spooky Old Edna," Maddy sneered, coming up next to Dana. "The witch."

Peter's smile vanished. He stepped back until his spine was pressed against Ray's hip.

"She's not a witch," Ray scolded. He dropped his hands onto the boy's shoulders and squeezed, assuring. "Just a blind lady who is really, really, really old."

Edna, Edna, you are so wise.

Ray coughed away the crazy giggle that had been boiling in his throat.

"We weren't going to *do* anything," Maddy said.

"She's not hurting anyone, and she doesn't deserve to be harassed."

"Dad?" Peter whined. "You're hurting my shoulder."

Ray released his grip and flexed his sore hands. "Sorry, pal."

"Is she really a witch?" Peter asked.

Speak. Speak, and utter no lies.

The girls eyed him, waiting on his judgment. He felt their tension, saw them fidget. Ray sucked in his bottom lip and peeled off a thin sliver of dead skin with his teeth. The bright sting of tearing flesh and the salty tang of blood on his tongue kept him quiet for a moment. Long enough to gather his thoughts. Superheroes and monsters passed around them.

Tell us, tell us; which of us dies?

"No, Peter. Edna isn't a witch." He left it at that and motioned for the kids to keep going.

Edna, Edna, open your eyes.

The sun was dropping fast. Trick-or-treat was going to end soon, but Halloween would keep going until the night had had its fill.

Edna Schantz had not been born the cursed monster of neighborhood legend that she became.

Her family had owned a large farm on the outskirts of Woodburn, Ohio, and thanks to some shrewd business dealings, as well as some simple luck, the Schantz family saw practically no hardships during the Great Depression, earning them not only vast wealth, but also the ire of their neighbors. They built themselves a large house as most in the community were having their homes foreclosed. People didn't understand how one family could be immune to the struggles facing the rest of the country.

And that's where the stories began.

Whispers snaked through Woodburn. The gossip wound and threaded through the town until it formed a twisted knot of speculation and nonsense. And by then, it was too big to untangle; it was just easier to accept it.

The truth became whatever came out of someone's mouth.

When Edna fell ill in 1937, just shy of her tenth birthday, more knots were added to the story thread. The Schantz family kept their family ordeals within their walls, and all that anyone knew for sure was that the little girl was now totally blind and deaf, and that every day, regardless of weather, her mother wheeled her out onto the front veranda. Edna's body had withered due to the sickness, and she could no longer move under her own power—except her mouth and her eyelids.

Just as the nation began to turn itself around, the Schantz family experienced the opposite. For whatever reason—most likely due to Edna's medical bills—they were forced to sell off all their land to the city for a housing plat to be developed. Though they were able to keep their home, they lost everything else.

Through it all, Edna sat on her veranda, unable to hear the houses being built. Incapable of seeing the neighborhood starting to strangle the home she had lived in her entire life. It was a housing boom, as men returned from the war to a country desperate to kickstart its greatness again. Young families moving into the new neighborhood saw the old mansion as an oddity. Their children saw it as big and forgotten, like every haunted house ever portrayed in cartoons and movies. And as often happens, they invented an explanation for what they did not understand: the sad old lady who was blind and deaf, who lived in the creepy old house, became a witch. And the only way to get her attention was to recite the magic words.

In any case, every kid in the neighborhood knew to avoid Edna's house. Parents warned of bothering helpless old woman, but children warned of darker things.

While he explained some of this to Dana and Peter, Ray was aware that Maddy knew exactly what he wasn't saying. She'd grown up on these streets, same as he had. She lived with the same fear. It only made sense that as she, along with her friends—which included Dana—grew more mature, they needed to confront the ridiculous childhood terrors, proving they were past that stage in their lives.

Ray hadn't been so brave.

House after house, they made their way down the street. Closer to the looming blackness at the end of the street. The angular frame of solid shadow. The trees were taller now, their upper limbs doing their best to shield everyone from having to look at the decrepit monstrosity, but everyone knew it was still there.

Dana, Maddy, and Peter cut across the street and started up the other side, heading away from the moldering carcass of the Schantz house, but Ray could feel its icy existence pressing on his back. He knew that Spooky Old Edna was sitting in her wheelchair on the front veranda, letting the evening's air pet her waxy, translucent flesh.

The girls took Peter up to a house. The woman on the porch, slightly older than Ray, was dressed in a white blouse, pink poodle skirt, and patent leather saddle shoes. A worried expression cracked the thick makeup around her eyes and mouth. Maddy and Dana either nodded or shook their heads in unison as the woman spoke, but each gesture only deepened the creases in the lady's visage.

"He was supposed to meet up with you," she said as Ray came up to see what was going on. The woman looked up at him and offered a slanted smile.

"Is everything all right?" Ray asked.

The woman cleared her throat and adjusted the plastic bowl of miniature candy bars she rested on the crook of her hip. Peter eyed them, transfixed by the temptation. "I was just asking Madison if they were having a good time." Then her smile faded. She looked back at the girls. "My son, Toby, was supposed to be going out with their group tonight. But she said they haven't seen him."

Ray put his hand on Dana's shoulder. "The girls were with some other kids," he explained, "but broke off a while ago. She and my daughter have been with me for the last forty-five minutes or so."

"And I didn't see Toby at all," Maddy added.

"They might have met up with him after we left," Dana said.

The woman looked at Ray and smiled again, weaker than before. "You know how it is. You give them an inch and they take a mile."

Ray gave her a knowing, parental nod.

The woman gave the kids extra candy for troubling them and sent them off.

They were reaching the end of the street when Maddy raised her hand and pointed. "There's Kaleb." A pause, then. "No Toby."

Ray saw it was the same group Dana had been walking with. They moved down the middle of the street to avoid the crowds on the sidewalk, and while they weren't running, their strides were hurried and determined.

"Kaleb!" Maddy yelled.

If he heard, the boy showed no signs of it.

"Are they going back?" Dana asked.

Maddy turned and glared at Dana, eyebrows raised in warning. She flicked her gaze at Ray, then back. "Probably just being dumb," she said. "Finding houses with good candy and hitting them a few times."

Ray clenched his teeth. He was old, but he knew the look, the tone. He hadn't forgotten being twelve—desperately trying to convey one message disguised as another.

He stepped between Maddy and Dana and looked his daughter in the face. "What does she mean?" Dana tried to look at her friend, but Ray slid over, blocking her view. "Going *back* where, Dana?" Neither girl volunteered an answer, though Ray was sure he knew.

"Daddy," Peter whined, looking at all the houses they had yet to claim their candy from.

"Just a minute." To the girls he said, "Somebody talk. You aren't in trouble."

"They might be going back to look for Toby," Maddie said reluctantly.

Edna, Edna, you are so wise.

Ray sighed. "Look, I know taking a picture isn't the worst prank in the world," he said, "but it is still mean if you're doing it to make fun of her."

"She's deaf and blind," Maddy groaned. "She probably wouldn't even know he was there."

"That's exactly my point," he snapped.

"Dad," Dana barked. "Maddy and I weren't going to do anything.

Kaleb said Toby was acting all brave and stuff, so he dared him to take a selfie with the old witch. He was supposed to meet us on the corner and show us. That's where we were going when you made me come with you and Peter."

"I didn't *make* you. You looked totally miserable."

Speak. Speak, and utter no lies.

"Yeah, because I didn't want to go see the witch."

"She's not a witch." Ray felt his frustration bubbling like a shaken soda can.

"Daddy, do we have to go see the witch?" Peter asked softly.

"No, buddy. You and Dana are going back to Grandma's."

Both Dana and Peter deflated with audible sighs. "But trickertreat isn't even over yet," Peter whined. The heavy bag of candy sank onto the sidewalk.

"Just take your candy back for a deposit and then, if you want, you two can go get more, okay?"

Dana folded her arms, her face pinching into a scowl. "Babysitting. Again."

"Just walk with him," Ray instructed.

"Fine," she spat. "But there's a fee." She grabbed Peter's pillowcase and, despite his cries of protest, reached in and pulled out a dripping handful. She stuffed it in her pocket, save one that she started unwrapping. "Let's go," she ordered her brother while maintaining sour eye contact with her dad.

Tell us, tell us; which of us dies?

When they were on their way, Ray turned back to Maddy. A normal twelve-year-old girl testing the waters of maturity to see how deep she could go before she found herself in over her head. But she was someone else's child.

"You're not in any trouble," he told her. "And I promise I won't tell your parents, but were you and your friends *planning* on pulling some prank on Edna Schantz? Is that why you all looked so nervous?"

"I was telling the truth. Toby went to take a selfie with her."

"Did you tell Dana the stories?"

Maddy squinted at him, judging, debating with herself. "It's Halloween," she said, her lips cracking into a wicked smile. "We told all of them."

"I'm going back to talk to Toby's mom," Ray said. "You..." He swallowed the lecture he was about to give. "You have a good rest of the night. And stay safe."

He walked away, leaving the girl to the night and whatever fate she had brought upon herself.

And he had no intention of talking to Toby's mom. Especially now that he recognized who she was.

Edna, Edna, open your eyes.

Ray couldn't do it. He'd thought that maybe this year he could.

The sun was gone, and the cold shadows had swallowed all of Woodburn. Younger trick-or-treaters had already gone inside to have their candy checked, and only the diehards, the true champions of the holiday, were left. Ray and his friend Ben Russo had covered the inner streets of their neighborhood in the first hour and a half, leaving only the outer ones. There was no way they could do the full two-mile circuit in thirty minutes.

They would try, though.

They were ten. Ben wore jeans, a flannel shirt, and a werewolf mask. The mask was huge and refused to stay in place for Ben to see out the eye holes. The elephantine snout flopped flaccidly with every step. Ray's costume was a bright blue pair of sweatpants and matching sweatshirt, bright red socks pulled almost to his knees, and an old, red tablecloth safetypinned to his sweatshirt. On the chest he'd used yellow puff paint to draw a large "S" inside a diamond. Sure, it wasn't as nice as a store-bought costume, but homemade was always better.

As they hurried, they saw that many of the homes they'd previously visited had already turned their porchlights off. They also kept their eyes out for the bigger kids, the ones who stole bags of candy, or hid in the shadows with an ample supply of water balloons. Though he was wearing a sweatsuit, Ray's mother had insisted on him donning long underwear under his costume since he strongly refused her request to wear a coat. The underwear was hot, and it chaffed his inner thighs. The chilled wind that blew cut through them anyway and attacked his damp skin. He ignored the discomfort for the sake of Halloween and ran, flew through one yard and on to the next.

They hit a dozen houses. Twenty. Time was ticking. Porchlights were winking out and parents were calling out names to summon children home. Twenty-five houses. Still barely halfway done with a single street.

A police car rolled by, its lights dark. Ray recognized it as one that had been passing out Smarties earlier that night. Any second they would flash the lights and the siren would blare, signaling the end of trick-or-treat.

How much time was left? Superman didn't wear a watch, so Ray had taken his off. Ben never wore one. They could stop and ask, but that would take time.

"Trickertreat!" they shouted, leaping on and off porches, barely waiting for the candy to fall into their bags before they were off.

And then, *BWOOP!* The street was doused in red and blue.

"The time is now eight o'clock." The policeman's rattling voice roared from the squad car's loudspeaker. "Woodburn trick-or-treat has ended. Please be safe as you return home."

Ben and Ray stopped, defeated. Seconds later, the announcement was repeated.

"Next year," Ben groaned, ripping off his rubber face. "I think if we skip half of Redstone we could do it. Those lame-wads give out crap anyway. And half the street had their lights off. It's bogus, man."

"We could start on the outer streets," Ray offered. He scooped up his dangling cape and wiped sweat from his face.

Ben shrugged. He looked up and suddenly went rigid. "I'll see you at school," Ben said. The words darted from his mouth as though they were racing to see which could enter Ray's ear first. He took off running, his heavy candy bag swishing against his hip.

They had been moving so fast, so resolute in their goal that they hadn't really paid attention to where they were. Ray turned.

Spooky Old Edna's house sat across the street from him. Though it was the biggest house in the neighborhood, it looked smaller in the dark. Compressed. It hunkered like a stalking cat about to pounce. No lights shone from inside—Edna was blind, so what use did she have for light? The infected yellow glow of a nearby streetlight splashed on the front of the house like slimy mold, and Ray saw Edna, right where she always was. Her wheelchair had been pushed almost up to the railing that rimmed the veranda, just to the right of the steps. But no one had ever seen anyone push the old woman into this position. It was as though she would just appear in that spot, then fade away, back into the shadows of her house.

Ray began to back away. Though she was deaf and blind, some people swore that Edna's face would follow them as they passed.

Hushed, rapid tones drew Ray's attention to the dark space between Edna's house and the brick ranch home next door. A large privacy fence had been erected between the two and the wood was warped and gray. A head popped up and surveyed Edna's yard.

Ray crouched behind a parked car.

"Looks like most people are gone," a young man's voice said.

"Careful, Johnny," a girl said. "Getting a nasty splinter would be a bummer."

From the side of the smaller house, four figures peeled away from the shadows and stepped into the pale light. The two boys were dressed in black leather jackets and had their hair slicked back like John Travolta in that movie with all the singing that Ray's mom and aunt liked. The girls wore poodle skirts and pink satin jackets. One had red hair that curled like soft springs; the other had a blond ponytail.

"Relax," Johnny said. Ray recognized him as Johnny Ring, a high school sophomore who would patrol the neighborhood streets on his BMX bike looking for young kids to bully out of their quarters so he could ride over to the Krazy Kat's arcade. And if that was Johnny, then the other boy must be Jason Russo, Ben's older brother. Jason was pretty nice when he wasn't with Johnny.

"This is gonna be totally awesome." Jason snickered, looking over his shoulder at the old lady sitting on her porch, oblivious.

"You remember what you gotta say?" one of the girls asked.

Johnny nodded. "It's a stupid rhyme. We all know it." He cleared his throat and sang out in falsetto: "Edna, Edna, you are so wise."

"Shhh," the blonde hissed, checking to see if faces were peering at them from neighboring windows.

"So lame," Jason said. His laughter had transformed into a shattered sound, something sharp that made Ray want to run away.

"I don't get it," the redhead said. "She's blind and deaf. How's she supposed to hear you? And what does opening her eyes have to do with anything?"

"Don't be a toad, Mandy," Johnny scolded. "Edna's pop went totally loco. The family did some sick, Satanic shit to try and get their fortune back. Ripped her eyeballs out when she was a kid—right before her momma plunged knitting needles into her ears—so that the kid couldn't see or hear any of it."

"They were trying to save her soul," Jason said, wiggling his fingers as he spoke, his voice rising and falling in a mocking, spooky tone.

"Well, I'm totally against this," the blonde said. She slid up next to Johnny and took his hand. "What if she's, like, got a nurse or something? What if they call the cops?"

Johnny pulled her close. "Like Mandy said, she's deaf and blind. She'll never know I'm there."

"I don't know," Jason said. His fingers fumbled with the zipper on his jacket. "What if she's got super-senses, like Daredevil?"

Johnny punched him in the arm. "Don't be a spaz, Jay."

BWOOP!

The police car turned the corner and flashed its lights at the teens.

"The time is now eight ten," the cop said. "Woodburn trick-or-treat is now over."

Johnny nodded and ushered his group to the sidewalk in front of Edna's house. As the squad car passed, Johnny flipped the bird and stuck out his tongue.

They were too far away for Ray to hear their hushed plans. He couldn't step out from behind the car now. They'd see him and know he'd been there, listening.

He watched. When Johnny had finished explaining the plan, they all turned to face the house. Johnny opened the gate to the front walk.

Ray slunk away from the car. Cape curled around his arm, he moved low and fast, ducking and pressing himself against trees the way he did when he played war with Ben. Stealthy, heroic theme music pounded in his head. When he was sure he was in the clear, he stepped onto the sidewalk.

"If there's something strange," he sang, "in your neighborhood..."

The dark had given everything the appearance of being damp. The wind, which had recently burned with cold, now barely moved the dead leaves that were too stubborn to let go of their branches. Ray looked in the front windows of the houses he passed. In some he saw kids, now out of their costumes, watching their parents sift through a mountain of candy as they hunted for razor blades, needles, or other deadly treats. In others he saw the blue-white flicker of television sets, and he couldn't remember if this was a

Knight Rider or an *A-Team* night. Dinner smells began to take over the night. His heart slowed, and he wondered what his mom was going to cook. Hopefully cheeseburger macaroni.

This, Ray thought, was the scariest part of Halloween. The fun was over. The darkness would get stronger, more oppressive. The night would put its spidery finger to its lips and hush the world. This was the time when the real monsters came out—the ones who took wandering little boys and girls and made them cry in all manner of ways—or so his mother had said.

He felt something pull at his cape. Thinking it was caught on a branch, Ray turned. His cape fluttered but was not hooked on anything.

He heard screams coming from the direction of Edna's house. Just staccato noises, really. Shouts of warning or surprise.

The wind picked up. But it wasn't like the *real* wind. The real wind would have come from his back and felt like it was pushing him. No, this sensation was like when he'd held the vacuum hose close to his face and felt the fine hairs lift and pull at his skin.

He stepped back reflexively as the gusts grew more insistent. Bullying.

The screams were louder now, too. Ray saw flashes of pink at the end of the street. The blond girl darted into the street and started running, her arms waving. She ran the direction the police car had gone. Mandy soon after, her red hair bouncing like the rubbery strands on a Koosh ball. Jason chased after both of them. He made it a few steps past Edna's front gate, then stopped and doubled over, his hands on his knees.

The feeling of being reeled in like a fish eased, and Ray felt cut loose.

He broke for home. Somewhere along the way, he dropped his bag of candy but couldn't have said where. His mother wouldn't care. It meant that he couldn't gorge on sweets for the next week.

Ray kept running, flying, his cape billowing out behind him. He did not stop until he reached his front door.

Ray came into the house to find Ashlee sitting on the floor, Peter's pillowcase draped across her lap, and its contents heaped between her splayed legs. From deep in the house came low, sobbing moans and the hiss of running water.

"Here," Ashlee said. She tossed Ray a pink Starburst, then popped a dark red one into her mouth. "That face paint isn't as 'washable' as the package says." She smiled and chewed, wiggling her bare toes. "So what's the Mommy-Daddy tax going to be this year?" Her hands dropped into the pile of glittery wrappers. "I'm thinking Milk Duds and Reese's Pieces." She came up with a tiny orange bag of the peanut butter candies. "I know how much you love them." She winked and slowly slid the wrapper down her neck and let it fall beneath her shirt. "Oops."

"Where's Dana?" he asked, ignoring Ashlee's playfulness.

His wife frowned. "She dropped Peter off and said she was going back out with you." She got to her feet. The bag of Reese's Pieces dropped atop the massive pile. "Did something happen?" Ashlee's hand crawled up her chest to the neck of her shirt.

"Not really," he said, shaking his head. "The friends she was with, they were heading toward that old house, and she looked... nervous."

Ashlee pinched and plucked at the neckline, toying with the elastic. "And?"

"She didn't want to go, so she and that girl, Maddy, came with Peter and me." Ray rubbed his face. Dana wasn't at home, and he hadn't passed her on the street. She could be out looking for him, or —and this was his biggest fear—she had defied him and went to meet her friends at the Schantz house. Unjustified anger had already rooted itself in his mind.

"So why did you send her home?"

"I didn't know what else to do." He sighed. "Something about some boy named Toby; he was supposed to do a simple dare. The girls were just acting shifty, and I was getting frustrated. I wasn't getting a straight answer." He rubbed his chin. The stubble made his skin feel like sandpaper. "It was easier to just stop and sort it all out later. But she was supposed to stay with Peter. I told her she had to go back out with him if he wanted to trick-or-treat more."

Ashlee touched his shoulder. "She's stretching out of her kid-skin. I did the same things."

Ray took her hand and brought it to his lips, gently kissing her palm. "I know." The cool skin felt nice against his rage-hot face. He let her paint his cheeks with her touch for a moment. Then he turned and opened the front door.

Ashlee followed him onto the front porch, her bare feet making dainty slapping sounds on the concrete. "So what are you going to do?"

"Not sure. Find her. Apologize? Promise to stock the cupboard with those snack cakes she loves?"

Ashlee hugged herself to keep warm, shifting her weight from foot to foot to limit contact with the chilled concrete. Her exposed arms were already turning red. "Try not to embarrass her too much," she ordered. She gave him the same smile that he'd fallen in love with decades before: pinched lips that made her round cheeks rise and her nose scrunch.

"Any minute now the cops will be rolling down the street to end trick-or-treat. I don't want her caught up in something if they come by."

"It's, like, almost nine," Ashlee said, checking her watch. "And I don't think the police do that anymore."

Ray was already crossing the street. It had taken him a lot longer to get home than he'd thought.

Time was the villain. Not only because each second could bring Dana closer to trouble, but also because it allowed his mind to conjure those troubles. Injuries. Misdemeanors or felonies.

The night was fully birthed, its blue-black shroud tucked neatly at both horizons. Without the sun, the air had cooled rapidly. The darkness tasted of slick dampness, and a skein of moisture had started appearing on car windows. Ray was in no shape to run, or even walk fast for that matter, but he hoofed it down the sidewalk with urgency anyway. His well-maintained gut flopped with each anxious step and he felt all that extra weight slam down. He could have driven the short distance, but in his haste to locate Dana, it hadn't even occurred to him.

Ray turned the corner and saw the jutting outline of the Schantz house rising above the other homes in the street. He slowed his pace, huffing. His face burned. His eyes couldn't focus. His hands felt like inflated rubber gloves. He ached everywhere, as though he'd been trampled by a herd of stampeding cows.

As a boy, the house had appeared massive, like a skyscraper set at the edge of the neighborhood. But now, it seemed somehow bigger. He had avoided looking at it for so long that not seeing it was easier than acknowledging it was there in the first place. Ray repeatedly passed the house whenever visiting his mother, and it had always been just a crumbling old structure in his periphery, collapsing in on itself a centimeter at a time.

Tonight, though—Halloween—the house looked stoic. Puffed and proud.

It was a tombstone commemorating a bygone era that had never really existed. When it was new, it was an ostentatious slap in the face to those who were suddenly facing the fear that there might not be another meal for days. It was designed to reflect the glorious architecture of the nation's history: a broad, rectangular front with the door in the middle like colonial estates; a wrap-around veranda supported by columns that called back to the spacious plantation homes of the antebellum South; a large, rounded turret and intricately detailed woodwork around every window, under every eave, and across the roofline like all the great Victorian mansions.

Edna sat in her wheelchair on the porch, as she always did, hearing and seeing nothing. The old sodium vapor streetlamp had been replaced by a more powerful halogen bulb years ago, and the crisp, blue-white light landed on every rotting detail, making the shadows deep and sharp.

For the first time in ages, Ray looked up at the house—really observed it for what it was. He saw the drooping eaves and the pillars and posts that bowed under the weight they supported. There were shutters and shingles missing. Paint was peeling like psoriatic skin. While the child in him had feared ghosts and monsters and witches, he was now terrified of the cost of needed repairs.

"Toby?" a woman's voice called. It echoed off the houses on the street. Ray turned and saw the woman in the pink poodle skirt hurrying toward him. When she neared and saw that he was not her son, she frowned. "Have you seen a boy dressed like—oh, I forget the name—some famous wrestler?"

"No," Ray said. He doubted she recognized him from earlier. But, with that skirt and her blond hair pulled back into a ponytail, he knew he'd been right about seeing her when he was a boy.

The woman looked up at Edna. She grimaced. "I wish I could ask her. But she's blind and deaf."

"I know."

The woman stared at Ray, her eyebrows mashing in a lump of skin above her nose.

"I grew up in this neighborhood," he explained. "Mom still lives over on Danube. I came to your house with my son; my daughter and her friend, they know Toby."

The woman's face eased, and she nodded. She turned toward the house again.

"They said he was supposed to come here and take a selfie with Edna," Ray continued.

Her face flushed. She started across the street, whispered fears leaking from her mouth.

Ray followed. The sidewalk in front of Edna's house was carpeted with dead leaves and discarded candy wrappers. They crunched under his shoes like whispered warnings.

The woman reached for the gate and pushed it open. Ray caught it as it swung back on its ancient spring. The wood was smooth and spongy.

"Wait," he called, grabbing for her arm.

"Toby!" The lady flinched from his touch.

"You can't just barge on to her property."

All sense had left her eyes, and she glared at him with wet marbles. "My son. He doesn't know. I didn't tell him." She fixed attention back to the poor old lady on the porch.

Ray skirted around, blocked her path. "Johnny Ring," he said.

The woman's mouth fell open, and she took a reflexive step back as if he'd just pulled a weapon.

"What happened to him?" he asked.

She shook her head. "He dropped out and ran away." She sidestepped one way, then the other. Her eyes wouldn't let go of Edna.

"I know you were here," he said, splaying his arms to keep her from passing. "Halloween. Something happened to him."

The woman shook her head again, kept shaking it. "No. No, he ran away. He dumped me and ran off. West." She did not try and make another move around him.

"I saw him and Jason Russo and you and another girl, Mandy. You were right here." He pointed to the spot on the sidewalk where they stood. "I saw the four of you. But only three of you left."

The woman went pale and began to rub at her temples with the heels of her palms. She closed her eyes. Her words were mumbled, but Ray could make out the sound of her son's name.

"My daughter may have come here," he insisted. "She might have been looking for Toby, too. Whatever happened to Johnny may have happened to them."

EDNA, EDNA

As though a switch had been flipped, the woman raised her head and squared her shoulders. The look of confused terror had been replaced with a mask of determination. Again, she locked on to Edna.

"Edna, Edna, you are so wise."

Ray stepped back, hands raised as if she'd just become a jolting, sparking live wire. "Whoa. What the hell are you doing?" He had not heard those words spoken aloud in almost thirty years and never anywhere near Edna's house.

"Speak. Speak, and utter no lies." She shoved past Ray and started up the steps.

Ray looked up at the porch.

Edna's head had turned, her face angled toward them. Deep shadows pooled under her sagging skin around her eyes and lips. Perhaps she'd felt the woman's footsteps on the stairs?

"Tell us, tell us; which of us dies?"

"Stop!"

"Edna, Edna—"

He reached for her, his hand clawing at the slick fabric of her satin skirt. He managed to grasp the hem in his fist.

"—open your eyes."

Edna did.

The sensation was a familiar one: looking into the hose of a vacuum. The air around him slithered across his face and over his shoulders, through his hair. Upward, toward where Edna sat.

The woman in the poodle skirt screamed, but the sound was yanked away, the wind reaching into her throat and drawing it from her lungs. Ray felt her moving toward the porch and held on to her skirt, tightening his grip. The rush of wind racing over his ears became a constant roar. He fought to breathe, fought to keep his share of oxygen. Things began to swirl around them, debris and dust and little bits of flaked paint from the side of the house.

He looked up.

Edna Schantz's eyelids were open. Ray stared into her skull—

into twin swirling vortexes of gray-black smoke that were expanding from her eye sockets like blooming roses. Spider legs of orange lightning walked between the rotating clouds.

"Marilee Compton."

The words from Edna's mouth were raspy and harsh, like a saw chewing through a dry, hollow log.

Marilee screamed again. He felt her being pulled away from him. The sheer force tugging on her combined with his sweaty hands made holding on impossible. He felt her slip free.

Ray grabbed the post at the bottom of the steps to keep from crashing backward. Marilee was lifted off the ground and slammed into the railing next to Edna. He could hear the wood creak and crack under the strain. At least he hoped it was the wood.

Marilee's hair arced toward Edna's face, toward the center of those smokey hurricanes that leaked from her eyes. Jagged lines of deep red appeared on her forehead and cheeks, and teardrops of blood were sucked from the openings and disappeared into the vortexes. The woman thrashed and kicked, fought the incredible power that was sucking at her. The scene reminded Ray of sci-fi movies where a spaceship's hull had been ruptured and the force of the suction was so strong an entire person could be slurped through a hole the size of a marble.

The leaves and candy wrappers from the front walk skittered their way toward them like mice on a feeding frenzy.

The rips in the flesh of her face widened, opening cracked and bloody mouths. Her face was painted crimson in seconds. Ribbons of skin curled away from her skull and fluttered in the wind like streamers in a storm. The fabric of her blouse gave way, as did her skirt, and the material was compressed into the nothingness inside Edna's head, leaving Marilee clothed in her mismatched bra and underwear. Ray saw a small blue-black flower tattooed on her hip.

The hungry power increased, greedily pulling at Ray. He felt lighter and found it difficult to keep his feet braced against the sidewalk. The heels of his shoes skated across the pavement. His feet began to rise off the ground. Grunting, he hooked his arm around the wooden post and hugged it as though it was Dana. He prayed she was okay. He pleaded with whatever deity would listen that she had not been subject to this horror.

Marilee's scream became a constant tone of pain and fear. Ray squinted through the tiny bits of swirling debris and saw that her right arm was bent at a startlingly wrong angle, and it flopped like a confused windsock. The rends in her skin extended from the center of her bicep to the edge of her wrist. Misting blood formed a pink fog in front of the rotating smoke, which had grown so large that Edna's face was completely hidden.

With a wet pop, a sleeve of skin slid off Marilee's arm, vanishing into the unknown. The exposed muscles and tendons began to snap and wave like sauced pasta being slurped into a child's mouth, leaving only the wet bone.

The sucking roar of wind overpowered any dying sounds Marilee might have whimpered as her brain went into overload and simply shut down. She was probably dead when the torn meat that flopped against her face broke free. Ray averted his eyes, but not before seeing her slick skull flash its revolting grin.

His arms were aching from holding the post with all his strength. It had begun wiggling in the earth like a loose tooth, threatening to be plucked out. One of his shoes was yanked from his foot. Though his eyes were shut, his ears could make out the snapping and slurping, the ripping and the rending and the popping of Marilee's remains being gobbled up by the incomprehensible hunger that existed inside the head of the old woman.

Suddenly, the wooden post snapped. Ray was hauled backward, toward Edna. His shoulders crashed into the wood railing, and he felt the hot, wet smear left by parts of Marilee. The strength of the suction drew his cheeks back like the pilots and astronauts who train at immense speeds. Blindly, he reached out to find something to hold on to. His hand slapped against the cold meat of one of Marilee's legs. The appendage dislodged from where it had been caught between the railing and instantly flipped into the air. It was gobbled by the dark vortex.

Then everything went silent.

Gravity regained its dominance. Ray tumbled down the porch steps, feeling every impact as though he was being struck with a sledgehammer.

Stillness. Silence.

He coughed and clawed at the grass, pulling himself toward the front gate. He simply did not have the strength to get up.

He managed to roll onto his back and lift his head. Edna was gone. He caught the glint of light reflecting off the glass in the front door as it slammed closed with the echoing hollowness of distant thunder.

Above, a starless sky hovered.

"She's not there? That's bullshit." It was the voice of a boy.

"Could be worse." The girl's voice was familiar.

"How?"

"She *could* be there."

Laughter trickled from several young mouths.

"What the—?!" This voice might as well have belonged to an angel. "Dad?!"

He heard the gate open. Dana's confused face looked down on him. Ray suddenly broke out in a fit of giggles.

"Oh my God, Dad! Are you okay?"

"Is he wasted?" the unseen boy asked.

"I don't think I've ever seen you from this angle before," Ray said, overcome with the absurdity of his perspective: looking up her nose, seeing the speck that remained of a small birthmark he'd forgotten she had under her chin.

Dana helped him sit up. The group of kids from earlier had gathered at the gate. He forced a stern expression and shook his head to clear it.

"What are you doing here?" Dana asked.

"I was looking for you." He got himself on his knees and

brought his feet under him. Upright again, he towered over the kids. They seemed so small. "What are *you* doing here?" he demanded.

"Heading home," one of the boys said.

"Did you ever find Toby?" Ray investigated each face.

Silence. They looked at each other.

"We never met up with him," Dana said. "Trickertreat's over, so we figured he went home."

Relief filled his trembling gut.

Ray limped onto the sidewalk. The cold of the cement soaked into his one sock. He let the gate slam shut behind him. Putting his arm around Dana, he squeezed, not caring if she was embarrassed or not.

She squeezed back.

"What happened?" she asked.

"I'm old and fat. Might have gotten woozy," he said, sighing. "Practically ran over here hoping you weren't up to something." He grunted with each step.

"I told you we weren't. We were just out walking."

He hugged her again. "You're a good kid, honey."

Dana said her goodbyes to her friends, and she and Ray started back home. It was slow. Ray hurt in so many places, and the loss of one shoe made his stride awkward.

Edna, Edna, you are so wise.

"What were you *really* doing at Spooky Old Edna's?" Dana asked.

"I went there to save you from the witch."

"Dad," she whined with a smile.

Speak. Speak, and utter no lies.

"I'm not going to lie to you, kiddo. The police are going to ask us questions."

"About what?" She didn't sound surprised by his statement.

"Well, they're going to want to talk to anybody who might have seen or talked to Toby and his mom tonight."

"Because they're gone?"

Ray nodded. Dana understood, though she might not fully comprehend yet.

"What should I say?" she asked, quietly.

"The truth. Tell them about the dare and not being able to find him later."

"And what are you going to say?"

They were not that far from his mother's house. He could see the Dodge Caravan parked in the driveway.

"The truth." And he left it at that.

Tell us, tell us; which of us dies?

A car rolled past, the pizza delivery sign on top shining like an illuminated shark fin.

"Hey, how about some pizza?" Ray asked as they turned into the driveway.

"Don't we always get pizza? Like, as a Halloween tradition?"

Ray laughed, holding his ribs. "Well, what if we get something really scary?"

"Scary pizza?"

He opened the front door and let Dana go first. "What about... Hawaiian pizza?"

Dana's face scrunched, and she made a retching noise. "Oh, sick!"

"With anchovies."

Peter was sitting on the floor sorting his candy hoard, chocolate candies on the right, fruity treats on the left. Everything within those categories was also divided into individual piles by name. As he sorted, he was hum-singing.

The words stabbed into Ray with icy daggers, and he nearly collapsed again.

"Edna, Edna, open your eyes."

Outside, tree branches snapped and groaned. Fallen leaves hissed as flocks of them tumbled and danced down the street and through the grass. The wind began to pick up.

HAYWIRE

KEVIN M. FOLLIARD

On October 20th, 1987, a school bus bound for Preston Powell's Prestigious Pumpkin Patch suffered a terrible accident.

Eleven-year-old August Andrews sat in the back of the bus, practicing lines for drama club. "You all call me monster. But it is not I who am the monster," he whispered. "You who steal and murder and commit..." He strained for the next word. "Atrocities..."

The bus rumbled and thumped.

"You people are the monsters. I am but a..." *A what? A vehicle? A...*

August sighed; he slid the folded-up piece of paper with his monologue from his pocket and read the last few words. "A harbinger of retribution."

He read it over a few more times. When he'd first struggled to sound out "harbinger of retribution," he asked his teacher Mr. Sonnet what it had meant. With a flourish of his scarf, Mr. Sonnet proclaimed: "A vehicle of destruction! An agent of justice! A lord of punishment!" Since then, August had all of those alternate lines jumbled in his head.

August had never wanted to get into acting, but his parents forced him to choose one extracurricular activity, and drama club sounded fun, like playing pretend in front of an audience. When he was chosen to play Count Dracula, excitement soured into anxiety.

The lines were tough to remember. If he could get them down, he'd be the star. But if he messed up...

An explosive pop startled everyone. The right side of the bus slumped, and they careened across wide country road.

Wheels squealed. Rubber burned pavement. Two dozen fifth-graders shrieked as they cut across the emergency lane and thumped offroad. The bus crunched through rows of gray corn. Snapping stalks crackled. He jolted, thumped, and slammed against the vinyl seat in front of him.

At last, the bus lurched to a stop. The entire vehicle tilted right as tires sank in soft soil.

Kids gasped and shouted. Mr. Sonnet and the four parental chaperones were already on their feet as the bus settled at a queasy slant. They began checking on the students. The bus driver, a heavy-set young woman, exclaimed, "Lord Almighty!" as she fanned herself with her cap.

Mr. Sonnet stood at the front of the bus and told everyone to remain seated over the loudspeaker. "We appear to have suffered a blow out. Remain seated. Remain calm." The chaperones went row by row to check on each kid.

One of the four chaperones happened to be August's mother. She had brought her second born—August's one-year-old brother Bobby—on the field trip and dressed him proudly in an orange pumpkin onesie. Baby Bobby seemed strangely calm in her arms, alert but tranquil, as Mom hurried to August.

August's stomach was still somersaulting when Mom approached. The Fruit Loops he'd had for breakfast crept up his throat. He lurched and puked onto his shirt and pants. He faced the window in embarrassment. Stalks and leaves pressed against the glass. The slant of the bus was stark enough that he felt gravity tugging him toward the window.

"You okay, honey?" Mom massaged his shoulder.

"I threw up," he muttered.

"Oh sweetheart, are you hurt?" Mom dug into her purse for a wet nap. She dabbed at his shirt.

"I'm okay."

Mom hooked Baby Bobby in one arm and dribbled her water bottle down August's shirt.

"Mom, that's cold!"

"It's all right." She helped him wipe his clothes, leaving a long, wet stain. "Watch your brother for a minute while I help check on everyone. I'm going to talk to the adults, then I'll be right back."

August groaned. As soon as Mom handed Bobby over, the kid wailed like a banshee. August had thought it would be fun to have a brother. But Bobby only liked Mom. He screamed or puked every time August tried to hold him.

"Just a minute, baby." Mom went row-by-row, checking on each kid.

Oliver Tonka leaned into the aisle. "Can't tell who's the bigger baby, you or your brother." He looked August up and down, then smirked. "You *must* be the bigger baby. You wet yourself!"

A few of Oliver's friends snickered, but most of the kids were still too panicked to care.

"I did not," August snapped. "I puked."

"My mistake. Just a little spit-up."

"Shut up!" August shouted over the noise of his wailing brother. "People could be hurt."

Oliver scoffed. "Nobody's hurt. I mean *I'm* fine."

A loud thud sounded, and kids were gasping at the front of the bus. August leaned out and saw their driver collapsed in the aisle.

Mr. Sonnet, Kyle Callahan's father, and Grady Mitchel's father propped the driver up and tried to rouse her.

Baby Bobby fidgeted and cried louder. August couldn't hear what anyone was saying. "Hush!" Bobby screamed.

August tried to run his Dracula lines under his breath, but he couldn't hear himself think.

Jenny Castle leaned over her seat. "Is the baby okay?"

"He's always like this." August bounced Bobby on his knee, but he only bawled harder.

Jenny rounded the seat. "Let me try."

"Good luck. He only likes my mom."

The instant Jenny lifted Bobby into her arms, he calmed and cooed. Jenny made a silly face, and Bobby giggled. "He was just scared. But it's okay, baby! You'll be okay!" Bobby squealed.

August sighed.

"Attention, please!" Mr. Sonnet shouted. "Let's have quiet!" The chatter died out. "The bus's radio is malfunctioning, but our driver is okay. Just light-headed. The pumpkin patch should be just up the road. I want everyone to wait with the chaperones while I get help."

August peered out the window. A gray signpost poked over the corn. "Mr. Sonnet, I think this might be the same farm." He peered closer. The words *Henrietta Haymitch's World Famous Hayride* dripped in red paint. "There's a ride that goes past here." August pointed out the window, and his classmates chattered in agreement.

"Brilliant!" He tossed his orange-and-gold striped scarf over one shoulder. "I shall cut through the cornfield. Remain calm. I'll make haste and return in ten minutes' time."

"See that, baby Bobby?" Jenny said in high-pitched baby-talk. "Maybe we can ride the wagon to the pumpkin farm? Won't that be fun?" Bobby cooed.

Mr. Sonnet's ten minutes turned to twenty, then thirty. The kids grew restless. Although the air outside was crisp and cool, the midday sun baked the slanted bus like a greenhouse. Kids started opening windows, and clouds of gnats streamed into the bus.

"Mom, how much longer is this going to take?"

"That farm might be farther than we realize," Mom said. "Be patient." Bobby giggled and squirmed in her arms.

August watched a black beetle crawl up a long, dry corn leaf, then flutter onto the windowpane. Its antennae twitched. He stared at its beady face and yellow markings and recited lines under his breath. "You people are the monsters. I am but a heartbreaker of retribution." He groaned. That was definitely wrong.

A tan, gloved hand reached up and smacked the glass. August flinched. The beetle flew away. Jenny screamed in the seat in front of them.

"Hey, y'all!" A pale, painted face sprang into view. The woman had rosy cheeks and a triangle nose like a Raggedy Ann doll. Scarecrow stitch-marks draped beneath her eyes. "How y'all doin'?"

August scrunched away from the window as her clownish face pressed against the glass, leaving smudges of white makeup. The woman wore overalls, a checkered shirt, a crooked straw hat, and a wig of wiry hay that poked in every direction. Her makeup ran with sweat from her brow.

Jenny screamed again. More kids on their side of the bus started shouting.

Mom passed the baby to August and ushered them toward the aisle. Bobby let out staccato yelps of distress. Mom hushed the other kids and gestured for them to move to the opposite side of the bus. She approached the stranger in the window. "Hello. Do you work at the pumpkin farm?"

The woman grinned, waved at Mom, and proclaimed, "I run the hayride!"

"Well, as you can see, we had an accident, but everyone is okay."

Henrietta did a strange little jig. She pointed at her dark-circled eyes. "I *can* see!"

Mom scrunched her face in concern. "Our teacher Mr. Sonnet went to get help, and we thought he'd be back by now."

"Mr. Teacher? Goodness. He's who sent me to check on y'all! See, I run the hayride, and it goes right past these parts."

"He sent...you?" Mom exchanged uneasy glances with the other parents. Grady Mitchel's dad was already outside the bus, approaching the woman.

"Mr. Teacher telephoned for help, but it's going to be a long, long time for another bus," Henrietta said. "Some trouble about something with the bus company. He's sorting that out, but in the meantime, I have cider donuts and water, and I can drive y'all to meet him. Plenty of room on the hayride." She applauded, her gloved hands making muted thumps.

Grady's dad started talking with Henrietta in quieter tones and guided her away from the bus.

"Sit tight, kids," Mom said.

Bobby whined until Mom took him back in her arms. She headed toward the front of the bus and convened with the other parents.

After Grady's father finished talking to her, Henrietta Haymitch skipped through the path in the corn. August spotted a train of wagons, and blocks of hay that blended with the crops. He heard the faint rumble of an engine.

"Everyone," Mom announced. "Line up. We're getting off this bus." The kids cheered.

They exited single-file and carefully navigated through a filthy puddle. Mud tugged at August's shoe as he trudged toward dry land.

Brittany Jenkins's mom groaned and laughed. "All these kids are going to need new shoes!"

In the cornfield, past the signpost, Henrietta had parked her green tractor, which was hooked to two wagons, lined with blocks of hay. Henrietta stood at the back end of the second wagon and passed out paper cups of water from her orange cooler and donut holes to each kid as they boarded. "Donut panic! Henrietta's here to help," she repeated ritualistically to each kid who boarded.

August accepted a donut and a cup of water as he climbed onto the first wagon behind the tractor. Jenny sat next to him. Mom bounced Bobby on her lap and sat at the front of the wagon. The chaperones sat one at the front and back ends of each wagon, and they started counting off kids. The bus driver gulped down water next to Mom.

"Do you want your donut?" Jenny asked. "They're really good."

"I'm still kind of queasy," August said. "You can have it."

Henrietta mounted the driver's seat of her green tractor and hefted a megaphone: "Greetings, y'all! Welcome to Miss Henrietta Haymitch's World Famous Hayride! Every good ride has a story, and I've got a humdinger of a tale to tell, but first there are some safety rules to review. All arms and legs must remain inside the ride at all times. There are no seat belts, and it can be a bit bumpy on this bumpkin's backroads, so hold tight! The most important rule is to respect your neighbors! Okay, time to tour this mysterious world of corn!"

"Yeesh, nobody wants a tour. Just take us to the farm," Oliver muttered.

"Be on the lookout as we make our way to our final destination," Henrietta's voice rang. "There could be strange, colorful characters along the way!"

They hit a big bump in the road, and the wagon wobbled. August's water sloshed onto his shorts.

"Hey, look!" Oliver shouted. "August wet himself again!"

"He did not," Jenny said. "Don't be a jerk, Oliver."

"Now you folks might not realize, but this land hosted several generations of sordid history. One hundred and fifty years ago, the Haymitch family settled here and grew the finest crop of corn known to these United States. But shortly after, the Powell family slunk over to these parts with a great big bag of money. The Powells tried to buy the land, and there was an ugly property dispute."

"What kind of story is this?" Jenny popped August's donut hole in her mouth.

They rounded a bend in the corn, and the ride slowed. A judicial bench towered alongside the road. "Oh look!" Henrietta proclaimed. "There's old unfair Judge Croakus!" A skeleton had been propped up behind the bench, dressed in a black robe with a white wig. Its gaunt fingers had been wired around a gavel.

"See Judge Croakus settled the land dispute in favor of Preston Powell's family, so the Haymitch clan only got a fraction of their God-given land. One year later, the judge's daughter married into the Powell family, and they *all* got rich. What do y'all suppose happened next?"

The tractor lurched forward. August spotted more figures poking out of the corn. Scarecrows.

"Excuse me," Mom turned and shouted. "These kids had a traumatic accident. Can we skip the story and just enjoy the ride?"

"Stay seated, ma'am!" Henrietta snapped. They rolled past a mean-looking scarecrow clutching bags with dollar signs on them. "In the generations that followed, the Powell family grew stinking rich, while the poor Haymitches scraped by. Preston Powell III opened a gaudy pumpkin patch and invested in big commercial farms, and the poor Haymitches couldn't compete."

"Hey! Enough!" Mom snapped.

"Where is this ride going?" Kyle Callahan's dad shouted.

They thumped and bumped faster, past a happy family of scarecrows—a mother, father, and little girl in overalls and a plaid shirt. "Preston Powell's Prestigious Pumpkin Patch grew in popularity. Every fall it attracted scores of screaming children and vulgar tourists. The operation swelled like a prize-winning pumpkin. And Preston III tried to buy out the Haymitch farm so he could build dumb rides like the one y'all are on now."

Kyle's dad stood and moved toward the front of the wagon. "Where are you taking us..." He held his stomach. His face blanched. Kids started shouting. August noticed some of his classmates had also gone pale. They started leaning over the wagon. Vomiting.

Kyle's dad doubled over.

The tractor picked up speed. "Preston was a sick, sick man. And he made all his neighbors sick. As sick as y'all are now!"

"Stop this ride!" Mom shouted. But she too had grown pale as bone.

"Then one day, Preston's neighbor Henrietta snapped. She took a shotgun to a school bus tire, jammed its radio, and did something unspeakable."

August looked down in horror at his spilled water.

They had all been so thirsty when they got off the bus.

Jenny suddenly slumped against him, unconscious.

"Preston was a snake, you see. When Henry Haymitch III refused to sell his land, that snake poisoned Henry and his beautiful wife Marlene. He made it so that their sole surviving daughter couldn't keep the farm going. He made her crack like an egg. Made her want to punish him and the little children who make him his money."

Everyone was screaming, retching against blocks of hay as the wagon thumped along the rocky road. Mom's face twisted with illness. She clutched Bobby against her chest. She tried to move toward August but slid onto the floor of the wagon. August lay Jenny down on the hay and moved toward Mom.

"Preston thinks he can pay me to abandon my family's legacy. But if we can't have this land, I will curse it with the blood of his precious pumpkin patrons."

Baby Bobby smiled complacently in Mom's arms as her eyes shut.

"Mom!"

The tractor came to an abrupt stop. August tripped forward. He clocked his head on the wood floor.

"Look everybody," Henrietta announced. "It's Mr. Teacher!"

August glanced up, rubbing his throbbing skull. Mr. Sonnet was wired to a fencepost, soaked in blood. His eyes were missing, the sockets stuffed with hay. His striped autumn scarf flapped in the breeze.

"Take your brother," Mom rasped. "Run... Find the road..."

The engine cut out. Henrietta stood on the seat and faced the wagons. Her scarecrow makeup ran with lines of sweat. In each hand she raised a sharp, curved sickle.

August scooped up his brother. Bobby cried. Kyle Callahan's father attempted to climb over the side of the wagon, but he fell and collapsed in mud. Grady Mitchel's dad was deathly pale, but on his feet. He approached Henrietta with both hands outstretched. "Stop what you're doing. Nobody has to be hurt."

She leaped from the tractor, then in one swift burst of speed, she ran to him and sliced his throat. A jet of red shot into the air. Kids screamed, but his son Grady's voice cut through the noise. "Dad!" Grady's voice came ragged as a sawblade. "Dad! No!"

Half the kids who weren't deathly sick were scrambling over the sides of the wagon, rushing into the corn.

August's heart slammed his ribcage. He couldn't leave Mom. He couldn't let that happen to her.

Grady screamed for his dad. August caught the glint of Henrietta's sickle in the sunlight as she raised it over her head and swiped down again.

Mom's fingernails dug into his ankle. "Run! Protect your brother!"

August ran to the back of the wagon. Bobby wailed against his chest. He leaped and thumped into wet mud. He followed his classmates into the corn. Stray kids retched in the road behind him.

He wanted to help them, but he couldn't. He couldn't save Bobby *and* Mom *and* his classmates.

But he *could* get to the road.

He could get help.

He pushed through stiff, feathery cornstalks. Dewy leaves slapped his face, and he nearly tripped into a long empty row where several of his classmates cowered. He couldn't see what direction the road was in, but it had to be away from the hay wagons.

After a long, breathless moment, Bobby screeched like a baby eagle.

"Shh, please, please." August bounced his brother. Rubbed his back. "Please, shush, please."

Bobby gasped and wailed.

"Where y'all headed?" Henrietta Haymitch shrieked. "I haven't finished my story!"

"Keep that baby quiet!" Mitch Huggins whispered. "She'll find us."

"We have to get to the road." August searched the tops of the corn for a telephone pole, some sign of direction.

"I hear that little crybaby!" Henrietta sang.

August's classmates scattered farther into the corn in every direction, abandoning them. Within minutes, Mitch returned with a long, red gash running down his arm. "There's barbed wire," he cried. Blood trickled down his arms. "It's everywhere. Can't go that way."

"Ollie Ollie Oxen Free!" Henrietta's blades hacked the corn: *chuff, chuff, chuff!*

August raced down the row of corn, clutching his screaming brother. *Follow the path,* he thought, *back to the bus. Find the road there.* But he stopped dead in his tracks when he spotted silvery lines coiled across the path. Circles upon circles of razor wire, blocking his escape.

More screams echoed. He turned to find Henrietta slashing toward his classmates. Bobby's wails pierced his eardrums. He wormed his way through the corn again, back toward the tractor, hoping there was no wire leading back toward the farm road. He slipped onto the main access road and fell knees first into mud, keeping Bobby upright. Just up the road, many of his classmates remained slumped, sick by the wagons. Mrs. Jenkins—Brittany's mom—had her arms wrapped around her daughter at the end of the back wagon. Her bloodshot eyes slowly opened and shut.

August couldn't save everyone. But *his* mom was still on the front wagon.

If they could drive away, he could save her. Get her to a hospital.

August rounded the other side of the wagon train and nearly stopped dead in his tracks when he spotted poor Grady Mitchell and his father, side by side in the wet, red mud.

Bobby's shuddery gasps gave way to a deep inhale and a fresh shriek. August bolted along the side of the road, cradled his brother in one arm, and climbed onto the tractor. He searched the ignition, the seat, the floor. But, of course, Henrietta had taken the keys.

Tears burst from August's eyes.

Why had he thought he could just drive away?

Bobby screamed.

August pushed his brother against his chest. Muffled him. "Stop crying," he sobbed. "Stop."

Through blurry eyes, he saw Henrietta emerge from the corn, face streaked with white and flesh and smudges of blood. Overalls speckled red. "No more tears, babies," she hissed. "It's almost over."

August held his brother over his shoulder and climbed down from the tractor. Bobby's infant screech pierced his ears. Henrietta lurched onto the tractor and swung her sickle. He let go, but the blade grazed August's sweatshirt sleeve. August shouted, backed away, and checked to make sure his brother hadn't been cut.

Henrietta leaped at them when suddenly Mom sprang over the edge of the wagon and grabbed the crazed woman by the strap of her overalls. She pulled her back over the tractor seat and yanked at her hat and straw wig, exposing a bird's nest of filthy gray hair.

Henrietta snarled.

Mom's face was pale as a ghoul, her jaw clenched tight, as she yanked their attacker's hair and attempted to choke her. "Run... boys! Run!" Her voice scratched. "Run now!"

August bolted down the road. Bobby's cries drowned out more screams from behind. He did his best to block it out, but sure as he could pick out Grady's cries for his father, he heard his own mother's bloodcurdling howl. He knew. He knew it was her.

He just knew.

Don't think about it.

His heart shattered. Temples throbbed.

Just run and run and run.

In the distance, a gray farmhouse loomed beyond the cornfield.

There's got to be a phone, he thought. *Get there.*

Bobby's cries rang in his ears. August's legs seemed to move on their own. Everything felt like a slow motion dream. Dracula's words flowed through his head as the gray house drew closer.

It is not I who am the monster.
You who steal and murder and commit atrocities.
You people are the monsters.
But I am...
A vehicle...

The horrible green tractor flashed in his mind.

Of punishment...

Henrietta's hideous face flashed in the window of his mind. She grinned through a swarm of gnats and black-yellow beetles.

August tripped on a stone. He managed to flip himself, roll onto his back. *Protect Bobby!*

Everything was white for a moment.

Then he gasped. His brother's eyes peered into his. A sapphire sky and puffy clouds floated behind him. The sun beamed over them.

Baby Bobby was dead quiet. Innocent eyes bored into him.

"Bobby," August said. "I'll protect you. But you have to stay quiet. Please, please, not a sound."

In the distance, Henrietta's tractor rumbled.

"The bad woman is coming, Bobby. We have to get to the phone. Then hide. But we can only hide if we're quiet."

Bobby's eyes scrunched. He pawed at August's face with a chubby pink hand.

August turned his head. The green tractor rolled up the road; the wagons kicked up dust behind it. He got onto his feet and raced toward the farmhouse, up the porch. The front door hung open a crack. Its hinges squealed like angry hogs when he entered.

The stench of decay smacked August in the face. Buzzing flies droned. He winced, shifted Bobby in one arm, and yanked his sweatshirt over his nose. A cloud of flies floated around two dark figures across the living room, backlit by morning sun.

An old man and woman sat in twin rocking chairs. Their skeletal hands reached over a side table, fingers overlapping as if they had been holding hands. August pulled the green hood of Bobby's pumpkin outfit as much over his face as he could.

He felt his brother's steady breaths against his thundering heart as he approached the couple. Their skin sagged, pale as paper. Their eyes were rolled pink slots.

An empty pill bottle sat between them, and a note. In large pen strokes it read:

Henrietta. Take the offer.

Her parents killed themselves, he realized. *But she thinks the Powell Family poisoned them.*

Bobby started to cry, soft at first. The stench was unbearable. August headed into a white kitchen in search of a phone. He laid his brother on a cracked tile counter, atop a pile of unopened mail, and rested his head on a faded floral-print potholder. Bobby gave a cranky yelp. August lifted a yellowing receiver off the wall phone. He started to dial 911, but there was no dial tone. He flicked the light switches and realized there was no power.

Outside, Henrietta's tractor rumbled up the driveway. Bobby cried harder.

"Shh." August scooped up his brother. "I'll keep you safe if you can stay quiet." The baby calmed.

He found a sharp butcher's knife in a kitchen drawer and stuck it in the loop of his belt. Then he carried Bobby up a creaky, winding staircase.

The front door squealed open.

"I saw you go inside, little boy. You see what he did to my folks. The Powell family can't get away with this injustice. I'll poison all this land with blood before they can have it!"

August hurried up the steps. The wood creaked. He slipped into the first bedroom he found. A frilly pink comforter draped the mattress of a queen bed with a gold-barred bedframe. The wallpaper was plaid pink with white flowers, and on the mirrored bureau, a pyramid of dolls was stacked with precision. The black button eyes of a Raggedy Ann glared at him atop the pile.

On one shelf, a series of colorful blocks spelled H-E-N-R-I-E-T-T-A.

Boots thumped up the steps. August set his brother on the edge of the bed and attempted to open the window. But the frame was old, warped.

"It had to be done," came Henrietta from the hallway. "Sorry, but they left us no choice."

August wiggled his brother under the bed. He locked eyes with him, put his finger over his lips. Bobby stared curiously from the shadows. "Please," he whispered.

The door opened, and Henrietta stood, caked in blood, hands clutching her sickles, face a mess of red-and-white makeup and rivulets of sweat.

"If you're sorry, let us go," August said.

"Not sorry enough, I'm afraid. See, I'm just getting started. Scores of school buses head to that farm every day, all season long, and I can only pick 'em off one at a time."

She stalked toward him. Raised her sickle.

August burst into tears.

Then Bobby cried too.

Henrietta glanced at the bed. Smiled. "Don't worry about the little pumpkin," she said. "He won't remember any of this. So I have no reason to kill him. He's a lucky baby, isn't he?"

"Please, let me take my brother and go," August sobbed. He reached for the handle of the butcher knife tucked in the belt behind his back, but he'd never get it out in time.

"Close your eyes."

Bobby screamed louder.

August blurted out, "They think you're a monster, but you're not."

Henrietta cocked her head in confusion.

"They call you...a monster. But it is not *you* who is the monster. It's *them*. They who..." August sniffled, shook. "They who steal and murder and commit atrocities. Those people. *They* are the monsters."

Slowly she nodded.

"You're better than that, Henrietta. You're...you're..." He took a deep breath. "You are a harbinger of retribution."

Henrietta's jaw dropped. She shook her head. "I'm a *what?*"

"A harbinger," he said slowly, steadily. He gripped the handle of the butcher knife. "Of retribution!" August pulled the blade free, rushed forward, and plunged it into Henrietta's stomach. She gave a stilted gasp. Her sickles clattered to the floor. Then she fell.

She convulsed on the floor as blood seeped under the frilly edge of her bed. She rasped, cried, "Momma." Her chapped lips twisted. Her fingers curled toward the knife, but she swiftly lost the strength to grasp.

Her eyes went slick as morning dew, and then she stopped moving.

Blood oozed toward the green pumpkin booties of his brothers' squirming legs. August pulled Bobby from under the bed and held him close. He rubbed his back. Hushed him.

Within moments, Bobby grew content in his brother's arms. His breathing steadied, and he slept. A tapping, buzzing sound interrupted the stillness. August held his brother and watched a metallic green housefly batter the bedroom windowpane over and over.

DEAD RUNNERS
MIKE MARCUS

"I think that's the last of the trick-or-treaters," Susan said, closing the front door and hanging her witch's hat on the nearby coat hook.

"How many did we get?" Dale asked from the living room sofa, his right leg propped on a stack of pillows. A heavy brace immobilized his knee, a white plaster cast enclosing his calf and ankle.

"About a dozen. Better than I expected," she replied, dropping the empty candy basket on a nearby table. When they lived in Mount Moriah proper, a hundred kids visited their townhouse on Halloween. They didn't expect many trick-or-treaters at the old farmhouse they bought outside of town. "I gave the last of the candy to Cindy Everhart's kids. We may be responsible for their dental work for the next five years. Cindy asked how you were doing."

Three weeks ago, Dale took a distracted step off the high school gym bleachers, shattering his ankle and tearing knee ligaments, putting the art teacher out of commission for his favorite holiday. The only upside were the goblins, devils, and witches covering his cast, courtesy of his advanced drawing students who visited last week. Cindy Everhart was the school nurse who called 911 and tended to Dale while waiting for the ambulance.

"What did you tell her?"

Susan smiled at her husband as she turned off the front porch light. "That you're a giant pain in the ass and as needy as a toddler."

"She already knows that." Dale laughed, scrolling through the horror movies available on streaming, remote in one hand, the other petting Harold, their orange tabby curled up in his lap.

Susan paused at the bottom of the steps leading to the old farmhouse's second floor. Plastic sheeting and crisscrossed yellow caution tape billowed in drafts blowing through the upstairs windows and splintered clapboard siding. Vinnie, the general contractor overseeing the remodel, warned them against using the worn steps. There was no reason for them to venture upstairs.

"The contractors are back on Monday, right?" Susan asked. "Are they sure they can get the windows replaced and siding installed before it gets cold?"

Dale glanced back over his shoulder to where Susan stood, hands on her hips, gazing up at the closed-off second floor. "Yep. The roof is done. The new windows and siding are supposed to arrive this week. Vinnie promised me as soon as the truck arrives, they can seal everything and blow in the new insulation," he said. "I see you staring, like you're going to go fix everything on your own. Forget it, honey. I know you're good with your hands, but there's a reason we're paying the contractor."

The middle-school vice principal and part-time furniture refinisher tucked her hands into the hoodie's kangaroo pouch and sighed. She loved the old farmhouse, and the inspector said it had great bones, but she hadn't realized it would take months to make the home livable. The summer flew past as contractors made the first floor habitable, though it was still questionable at times. A week after they moved in, they awoke to a raccoon rooting through the kitchen trashcan after sneaking in through a gap in the siding.

Sarah flopped into the living room's overstuffed chair cattycorner to the sofa. "I feel like Vinnie is stretching this out to surprise us with more bills."

Dale sat up, gingerly lowering his cast-covered foot to the floor. "I know, but we needed him to focus on the first floor so we could move in before summer. We couldn't afford to rent the townhouse and pay the mortgage, plus the remodeling costs, all at the same time," he said, rubbing his knee. "Don't worry about that right now. The trick-or-treaters are done. I'll make some popcorn and we can curl up on the couch and watch a movie."

Susan took her husband's narrow, long-fingered hand and kissed his palm as he hobbled past her chair. They could have been pianist's hands except he had no rhythm. She knew he was a klutz but didn't realize how bad until the dance class ahead of their wedding reception. He hurt himself learning the Macarena.

"You're going to make me watch one of your horror movies, aren't you?"

He laughed. "Yep. We're going old school tonight. The original *Halloween* from 1978, with Jamie Lee Curtis."

"You know I hate horror movies. They scare the shit out of me," she complained as he threw a bag of popcorn into the kitchen microwave and punched the button. The microwave hummed as the bag turned, and Dale took two beers from the fridge.

Knock. Knock. Knock.

Susan spun in the chair toward the front door.

Knock. Knock. Knock.

"Is that someone at the door?" Dale called from the kitchen. "I thought you turned the light off."

Susan stood and glanced out the front window into the darkness. The farmhouse stood at the end of McIntyre Lane, that last vestige of the old Brookins farm. Two miles in the distance, house lights from Brookins Manor flickered. Developers built the housing plan after subdividing the farm.

She couldn't see anyone on the front porch, though if they were right up against the door, she wouldn't be able to see them from her vantage point.

Knock. Knock. Knock.

"Are you getting the door?" Dale called out over the steady rat-a-tat of the popcorn popping.

"I've got it," Susan replied, turning on the porch light and unlocking the deadbolt. *I wish we'd already put the video doorbell in*, she thought, though she knew Vinnie recommended waiting until the new front door arrived. It was supposed to be on the same truck as the windows and siding.

"Trick or treat," the three kids on the front porch yelled in unison as Susan opened the door.

Susan froze. The oldest couldn't have been more than eleven or twelve, but they wore old Halloween costumes like she'd seen in black-and-white photos online. The girl, the tallest of the three, wore a long black dress that dragged the ground and a tall, pointed witch's hat. The middle child wore a skeleton costume, off-white bones painted on worn black pants and a black button-up shirt. The smallest of the children wore shorts and an oversize coat, his hands hidden within the sleeves. All three held out old pillowcases to collect their candy.

The costumes were unusual, but it was the masks that set Susan's nerves on edge. The two older children wore papier-mâché masks that hid their features. The featureless masks were flat and white, as though intended to disguise the wearer, but were not part of their costume. The youngest child's mask was different, painted and detailed with hair and skin texture and oversize human features with bloody edges that glistened as though wet. In the porch light glow, the mask's red edges looked like someone peeled an adult's face from their skull and slapped it on the child.

"Trick or treat," they repeated.

"Oh my, aren't you a scary bunch," Susan responded, her voice cracking as her throat tightened. She cleared her throat, wishing she had one of the beers Dale just opened. "I don't think I've ever seen costumes quite like yours."

"Trick or treat," they responded with the same fervor as though it was their first house of the night.

Susan glanced up the driveway to McIntyre Lane. No parents waited at the yard gate; no car idled in the driveway or at the road.

"Do you guys have an adult with you?" she asked. "We're a pretty far walk from Brookins Manor. I doubt your parents want you this far away from the development, especially without streetlights or sidewalks out here."

The kids were silent, their eyes locked on Susan. She shuddered again at the youngest child's horrific mask.

"Trick or treat," they said again, their voices grating her nerves like fingernails on a chalkboard.

Susan turned to grab the candy basket from the landing and remembered it was empty.

"Let me check if we've got any more candy," she said to the kids. "I thought we were done for the night. Hold on."

Susan stepped back from the door, careful not to turn her back on the three kids. "Dale, do we have any more candy? We've got three late trick-or-treaters."

Cabinets banged in the kitchen, Dale's faint swearing echoing in the background as items fell from the shelves. He stuck his head out of the kitchen and whispered. "No candy. I've got a few old fortune cookies, some little boxes of raisins, and a half-dozen apples. Give 'em the apples."

"I'm not giving them apples," Susan whispered through gritted teeth, turning to give a forced smile to the kids on the other side of the screen door. "Their parents will think we're creeps who put razor blades or sewing needles in them or something."

Susan stepped back over to the door. "I'm sorry, guys, we're out of candy. I thought the last of the kids came earlier, and we gave them everything we had left."

The kids looked at each other for a moment, then turned back to Susan. "Trick. Or. Treat," they repeated with a sharp edge, as though demanding payment.

Susan backed up a pace, her hand reaching for the door handle.

"Again, I'm sorry. We don't have any more candy. It's time for you to leave."

The kids hesitated, staring up at Susan before the witch turned and stomped down the steps, followed by the skeleton boy. The boy in the skin mask, as Susan thought of it, stared up at her, bright blue eyes glaring out through the jagged eye holes, then turned to follow the others. He paused at the top of the three steps leading down to the flagstone walk and looked back over his shoulder at Susan in the doorway and growled, "Trick," before kicking each of the four jack-o-lanterns lining the steps. The pumpkins ruptured as his bare foot smashed into each, slimy orange chunks splattering on the walk before he jumped off the last step and followed the other two children into the darkness. Susan hadn't noticed until then that all three kids were barefoot, their feet covered in dirt and grime.

Susan slammed the door and turned the deadbolt, stepping back from the door as Dale hobbled into the living room, a bowl of popcorn in one hand, two beers clutched in the other. "The kids gone?"

Susan's hands shook as she double-checked the deadbolt, then turned to Dale. "Is the back door locked?" she asked.

"What?"

"Is the fucking back door locked?"

"I don't know. Yes. Maybe. I don't know," he replied as she rushed into the kitchen.

The deadbolt wasn't locked. Susan turned the kitchen door deadbolt and flipped the light switch, two security spotlights mounted on the home's back corners flooding the backyard with hot, white light. A previous owner installed them after coyotes attacked the henhouse at night. Susan wished they had similar lights out front, where twenty feet beyond the front porch there was nothing but inky darkness.

"What's wrong?" Dale asked, leaning against the kitchen counter.

Susan hurried to her husband, wrapping her arms around his

thin waist. "Those kids freaked me out," she said, her head against his chest, his heart thumping in her ear. "There was something about them that wasn't right."

Dale wrapped his arms around her and pulled her tight to him. "It's okay. It's Halloween. Kids do stupid shit because they think they can get away with it. They were little kids, right?"

Susan nodded and clung to him.

"I'm sure they'll go home. High school kids are the ones who like to raise hell on Halloween, but little kids can be creepy as fuck sometimes," he said, rubbing her back in slow circles like he did when she awoke from a nightmare.

"They didn't have parents with them. It was just the three of them. The oldest couldn't have been more than twelve; the youngest was maybe six or seven. He had this horrible mask that reminded me of someone, but I don't know who."

"It's okay. They're gone. Let's have a beer and watch our movie. I'm sure in an hour you'll have forgotten about them."

Dale pointed her to the sofa as he hobbled to the front door, peering out the side window as she had done. The front porch was empty, the walkway strewn with exploded pumpkin and smoldering candles. "Assholes," he muttered, double-checking the front deadbolt before turning off the light.

"Do we really have to watch *Halloween*?" Susan asked as they settled onto the couch, the bowl of popcorn in her lap. Harold leaped onto the couch and curled up at her feet, his tail swishing back and forth over the edge of the cushion.

Dale took a swig of his beer and picked up the remote, starting the movie. "Trust me. It will help you get over the jitters from those kids. Focus on the movie and forget about them. It's a classic. John Carpenter is a genius."

The first egg splattered against the front window, followed by two more hitting the screen door.

"Those bastards," Dale growled, pausing the movie and pushing himself up from the sofa as Sarah flinched at the noise. He pushed the curtains aside and glared into the darkness. "God damn it, I can't see a fucking thing out there."

Susan climbed from the couch and hurried to the front door, turning on the porch light. "Can you see them now?"

"No. They've got to be in the bushes," he said, stepping next to her and carrying one of the heavy flashlights they kept handy. Power outages were commonplace so far out from town, or when Susan used her hairdryer and the old wiring gave up.

Dale unlocked the front door and swung it open, stepping onto the front porch and shining the flashlight out into the brush. The brilliant white beam of light cut through the darkness and the fog beginning to roll across the ground as the temperature dropped.

"Where are you, assholes? I know you're out there," Dale yelled into the darkness from the front porch as Susan watched from behind the screen door. Another egg sailed through the air, illuminated for a moment by the flashlight before breaking against the wall next to Dale. "Sonofabitch! Try that shit again!"

The next egg landed at his feet, bursting over his cast. Dale teetered on his bad leg, pinwheeling his arms to maintain his balance. The next egg hit him in the chest, splashing green, stinking slime with bits of eggshell across his t-shirt.

"Dear god, that stinks." He coughed, stepping back awkwardly and slipping on rotten egg on the wood plank front porch. Since the accident, he didn't always need his cane, but moving quickly was out of the question. Dale gasped in pain as his shoulder slammed into the porch as he fell, twisting his broken ankle and injured knee.

Susan grabbed the flashlight and swept it across the yard as Dale sat up, his shirt caked with mucousy egg.

"There," she said, steadying the light on the maple tree next to the driveway. The witch girl and skeleton boy stood in the flashlight beam, still wearing their costumes and masks, an old metal basket of eggs on the ground between them. Their giggling carried across the yard. "Where's the third one? The little boy in the skin-mask?"

"We're calling the police," Dale growled, pulling himself to his feet with the porch railing. "You hear that, you little shits? We're calling the police, so if you know what's good for you, you'll get out of here before they arrive."

Dale limped inside, waited for Susan to follow, then slammed the front door and clicked the deadbolt into the locked position.

"Are you okay? You twisted your knee and ankle pretty good."

"I'm fine, just pissed off. I'm sure it'll hurt more later, but I'll just take an extra oxy tonight."

"I didn't see the third kid," Susan said. "Where was he? Did you see him?"

"It doesn't matter. Egging the house is one thing, but hitting me with rotten eggs is different," Dale said, grabbing a clean t-shirt from a basket of laundry he'd folded earlier. He threw the egg-covered t-shirt into the corner, pulled on the clean one, and picked up the landline telephone from the end table. He held it to his ear and pressed the button twice. "The phone is dead. No dial tone."

"It's probably the wiring again. It didn't work the other day, either. Vinnie said the wires were ancient. Just use your cell," Susan said. "Where'd you leave it?"

Dale looked around the coffee table littered with art supplies and empty soda cans. "It should be right there. I left it on the coffee table earlier."

Susan piled drawing tablets and shoveled pens and charcoal pencils into their storage box, but there was no phone amongst the clutter.

She reached into her back pocket for her own cell, then looked around. "My phone is missing, too."

"Fuck," Dale said, stepping back to the window and shining the flashlight through the glass, trying to find the source of the giggling they still heard. "Those little fuckers are still out there. It's like they're taunting me, knowing I can't chase them."

Susan started toward the kitchen. "Stay here. I'm going to check the kitchen for our phones. There's no way we both lost our phones in the last hour."

"I'm tempted to get the shotgun out of the bedroom closet and see how they like some birdshot in their asses," Dale grumbled.

Susan flipped the kitchen light switch and froze, staring at the open back door.

"Dale," she yelled. "Dale, get in here."

"What?" he asked, hobbling into the kitchen and pausing, following Sarah's outstretched arm pointing at the open back door. "Why did you open the back door?"

"I didn't. It was open when I came in. We locked that door. I remember locking the handle and the deadbolt," she said, then pointed to the line of muddy footprints on the linoleum kitchen floor. The tracks led from the door into the living room, then back outside. "That kid, the one with the skin mask. He got in here while the two out front distracted us. He took our phones."

Dale trudged across the kitchen, looking at the footprints before staring out the open back door into the darkness. "I don't see anyone now."

"I'm telling you. I locked that door. We need to get out of here. Can we just go into town? I'm sure there are rooms available at the motel."

Dale turned on the flood lights, bathing the back yard in white light.

Susan gasped and pointed past him out the door. The smallest of the kids knelt next to the tree stump near the old chicken coop, a hammer in his hands. He looked up at Susan, his bloody mask grinning at her, and slammed the hammer down on the two cell phones on the stump. He smashed the phones until the screens shattered.

"Trick or treat," he growled, looking off into the dark as the other two joined him from around the side of the house. The girl carried a large pillowcase that wriggled and squirmed as she gripped the bag in her fists. A cat's screams and cries echoed across the yard.

"Harold!" Dale yelled. "How the hell did they get the cat?"

Susan fell against the doorjamb as Dale pushed past, hurrying into the house toward the bedroom. The witch carried the squirming pillowcase to the tree stump, adding it to the shattered cell phones and holding Harold in place through the fabric.

"No," Susan ordered, stepping out onto the small back porch and starting across the short yard toward the kids. She swallowed her fear, putting on the vice-principal voice she used when confronting kids who wouldn't listen. "I don't know who you are, but this stops right now. Let that cat go, or I swear there's going to be consequences."

The kids paused, looking at each other as though they'd never been talked to in that manner before. Susan strode across the wet grass, the fog swirling around her ankles. She stopped an arm's length from the kids, the witch holding Harold steady within the pillowcase as he hissed and howled, the smallest child still holding the rusty hammer over his head.

"Let the cat go. *Now*."

Susan reached for the bag, hoping the kids' silence was a sign she'd gotten through to them. Her fingertips grazed the fabric as she hushed Harold.

The blade glinted in the light a second before slashing the back of Susan's hand, bright red blood filling the wound and trickling over her wrist as she pulled back. The skeleton boy stared at her through his mask, brown eyes filled with rage as he stepped forward and slashed the blade in her direction again, grazing her arm as she stepped backward.

"What the fuck?" Susan cried out, stumbling backward as the

boy advanced, swinging the knife like a sickle. The folding knife held a fresh razorblade. It was a knife Vinnie's guys used regularly around the house, swapping out used razor blades and dropping the dull ones in a bucket in the back of one of their trucks.

The skeleton boy paused as she fell backward on the small porch, blood trickling down her hand from the cut and her sleeve in tatters where the blade missed her flesh but sliced through the fabric.

"Let him go, please," Susan cried, her eyes falling from the knife to the kids holding her cat in the pillowcase. Harold's screeches and hissing ripped through the night as he struggled to escape his captors. The skin mask boy dropped the hammer into the grass and picked up a red-handled machete hidden next to him. It was the blade Susan used to clear overgrown brush from the yard and had been in the small shed around the side of the house, along with any number of other yard tools.

The boy raised the sharp blade, looking up at Susan, his blue eyes shining across the yard. Through the mask she could see his excitement at the thought of killing the defenseless cat trapped in the pillowcase.

The machete was about to come down on the cat when the shotgun blast erupted behind Susan. Her ears rang from the explosion and her eyes swam in and out of focus, the concussion of the gun firing nearby echoing in her head. She'd been to the gun range years before with her brother, but that was with hearing protection.

"Let the cat go," Dale yelled, loading two fresh shells into the shotgun's breach before slamming it closed and clicking back both hammers. Dale's grandfather passed the gun down after he couldn't hunt anymore, and until that moment, Susan wasn't sure it still functioned.

The kids stood stone still, staring at Dale as he lowered the side-by-side double barrel in their direction. After a momentary standoff, the witch whispered something to the others and released the pillowcase. The fabric fell from her hand and Harold burst from the bag at a full sprint, disappearing into the darkness behind the house.

"I don't know who the hell you are or what you want, but this is over. You leave and there won't be any trouble," Dale yelled. "You keep playing games and things are not going to end well for you."

The skeleton boy walked backward toward his compatriots, his eyes never leaving Susan. The bloodlust was palpable, his eyes locked on her bleeding arm. As he reached the other two, the boy in the skin mask rose to his feet, the machete still in his hand.

"Trick or treat," they called out, their voices taunting, as though daring Dale to fire on them before they turned and sprinted into the darkness.

Dale released the shotgun hammers and lowered the gun, his hands shaking. "What the fuck is going on?" he said, leaning against the doorjamb. "You're bleeding. Are you okay?"

All four tires on both cars were flat, cut by knives or stabbed by screwdrivers left on the ground next to the vehicles.

"What now?" Susan asked, raising her flashlight from the flat tires to the shrubs in the yard. The wind was rising and the temperature dropping, the blanket of fog crawling along the ground growing denser with every moment.

Dale held the shotgun at the ready. "I can't walk the two miles to the houses for help, and I don't want you out there on your own. We should probably go back inside and figure out a plan."

Susan checked every door and window, Dale hobbling behind her with the shotgun. She blocked the back door with the small kitchen dining table and jammed the heavy coffee table against the front door. Curtains were drawn and shades pulled.

"What about the basement? Is the outside storm cellar door padlocked?" Susan asked, searching for any other access point to barricade.

Dale glanced at the kitchen door to the basement steps. "Vinnie's plumber was down there yesterday, but I don't know if the outside door is locked."

Susan picked up a flashlight and opened the inside door to the cellar, revealing the narrow wooden steps. She turned on the lights, and three bare lightbulbs hanging from the low ceiling cast a weak yellow light throughout the flagstone-floored room.

"I can't get down the steps like this," Dale said, gesturing to his right leg.

"We need to make sure that door is barred. The padlock is on the outside, but there are no lights on that side of the house. There are brackets on the inside to bar the door. I saw a board for it the last time I was in the cellar," Susan said. "I'll go down, put the board in place, and come right back up."

Dale hesitated. "Are you sure? Can't we just block this door?"

Susan shook her head. "I can't have them in the house, not even the cellar if I can help it. I'll be quick. You keep the shotgun."

Dale nodded and positioned himself in the short hallway where he could see both the front and back doors as Susan descended the creaking steps.

The cellar was cool and damp, harking back to its days as a root cellar. Thick, rough-cut timber framing sat on field stone walls. The furnace stood in one corner, two pipes leading outside, one to pull heating oil from the tank at the back of the house and a second venting the system. A few random dressers, a moldy dress form, and a broken butter churn lay against one wall, remnants of the previous owners that they hadn't cleared out yet.

Susan hurried to the double-doors opening outside. She slipped the boards into the brackets and pushed the doors to confirm they were secure. As she turned to head back upstairs, she paused by one of the old wooden dressers.

"Everything okay down there?" Dale yelled from above.

She walked to the bottom of the steps where he could see her. "Yeah, I'll be up in just a second. I need to look at something."

"Don't mess around. Come back up."

Susan walked back to the dresser and pulled out the top drawer, rummaging through old, mildewy clothes. The second drawer was empty other than an old, broken mousetrap. The bottom drawer contained the boxes she remembered when they were cleaning out the first-floor bedroom. Susan pulled the top off the box and found handfuls of old black-and-white photos, the paper yellowing with age, the corners curling from moisture. She shuffled through the photos until she found the ones she remembered and tucked them into her back pocket.

"Are you okay down there?"

"I'm fine. I'll be up in a minute," Susan replied, clicking on her flashlight and shining it into the shadowy, cobweb-filled corners. Spiders and millipedes scurried away, seeking shelter as she poked through the piled trash and debris with an old broom.

"Susan, where are you?" Dale called out. "Please come up. I don't like this."

Susan was halfway across the cellar when the double doors she barred rattled against the bracing. She paused, turning her flashlight against the far wall as the doors rattled again, the boards holding firm as someone outside pulled and fought against them.

"They're around the side of the house," Susan yelled, sprinting up the steps, nearly knocking Dale over. "They're trying to get into the basement."

She dragged the kitchen table away from the door and snatched the shotgun from her husband.

"What are you doing? I thought we were going to try to wait them out," Dale whispered.

"We can't," she said, unlocking the back door and throwing it open. Susan grabbed the shotgun in one hand, the flashlight in the other, and ran around the dark side of the house. She rounded the corner, her heart pounding as she lowered the shotgun, attempting to aim both the gun and flashlight at the same time.

The flashlight beam bounced and swung wildly, seeking out anyone near the doors, finding only overgrown scrub grass. Susan spun, shining the flashlight around the yard, walking toward the cellar storm doors. Bloody handprints covered the door like an insane child's art project, the chain and padlock that previously secured the doors laying in the grass nearby. Dale called for her from the back porch, his own flashlight shining around the yard.

"I'm coming," Susan yelled, stomping through the ankle-high grass, entering the wide cone of light cast by the security lights on the back of the house. In the yard, a faint line of red across the grass led to the chicken coop and the extra vehicles and equipment Vinnie's team left onsite. Susan turned to Dale standing on the porch. "I need to see something. I'm walking to the coop."

The man lay against the far side of the chicken coop, hidden in the shadows. Susan recognized the t-shirt as the same Vinnie's employees wore, but she couldn't say who he was. She'd seen him earlier that day working on the plumbing. He'd worked until dark, and she'd offered him a soda, but he turned it down. He said he was just leaving to get home and take his kids trick-or-treating. He'd been the last worker to leave, though obviously he never made it off the property. Susan gagged as her flashlight traveled up his prone body. The man's face was missing, the skin sliced and peeled away, his brown eyes and bloody skull grinning up at her.

Susan dropped the flashlight and shotgun, vomiting undigested bits of pizza mixed with warm beer. Bile and bits of pizza ran down her chin and dripped from her nostrils as she retched into the grass at the dead man's feet. Susan panted and picked up the shotgun, afraid every creaking branch or blowing leaf were the kids sneaking up on her. A moment later, she picked up the flashlight and ran back to the house, pushing Dale inside and locking the door behind her.

"What is it? What happened?" he asked as she gulped air like a fish out of water, trying to catch her breath.

"One of Vinnie's guys…behind the coop…dead," she panted, hands on her knees, head hanging. Vomit soaked her t-shirt, and her empty stomach lurched again at the thought of the faceless man, though there was nothing left in her stomach to expel.

"Dear god. How?"

Susan shook her head, catching her breath. "They took his face. The smallest of the kids…that's not a mask. He's wearing the guy's face. They pulled it off his skull like an orange peel."

The living room window shattered as a fist-size rock rolled across the floor. Dale grabbed the shotgun from Sarah and hobbled into the living room, aiming into the darkness, searching for a target as Sarah followed him, falling on the sofa.

"What did you find in the basement?" he asked, the shotgun raised to his shoulder and aimed at the window.

Susan reached back and pulled the photos she gathered in the cellar from her back pocket, wincing as the bandages around her arm pulled tight. She handed two to Dale as he settled on the edge of the sofa, the shotgun handy as he rubbed his sore knee. "I saw these when we cleaned things out but didn't realize what they were."

The first black-and-white photo depicted three kids standing in front of the house wearing the same costumes as the kids tormenting them, except the smallest child wore a featureless mask like the other two.

"This has got to be a hundred years old," Dale said, holding the photo up to the light for a better view.

"Keep going," Susan replied.

Dale swapped photos, his eyes growing wide. The same three kids stood on the farmhouse front porch, the plain white masks replaced with drooping, dark-skinned human faces. Three dead black men lay on the ground in front of them, their faces peeled away. The men were shirtless and wore rough pants held up by a length of rope around their waists. Their feet were dirty and bare, with rough iron shackles around their ankles.

"Did they...?" Dale asked, unable to finish the question, looking between the two photos in his hands.

Susan dropped eight more photos in his lap. "There's more. All the photos have jack-o-lanterns on the porch and they're different, so it had to be different years. I don't know who—or what—they are, but I think they hunted men on the farm as some demented Halloween tradition. The men in the older photos are either black or Latino, but some of the newer ones have white men as well, and a couple of women," Susan said, pointing at one of the photos.

Dale finished the half-empty warm beer he'd left on the table earlier, dropping the empty bottle to the floor. "What the fuck is going on? We own the house where this happened? What do they want with us?"

"The real estate agent said it was a farm, but I think it was a plantation. Tobacco used to be a big deal down here. The men in the older photos were probably slaves. But there are newer photos, too. There are fucking Polaroids with almost identical photos. Polaroids. They aren't that old. The kids hunted those people, killed them, and ripped off their faces."

Movement out the front window captured Susan's attention. She hurried to the window and pushed back the curtain. "And I think we're the prey this year," she said, staring into the darkness.

A flash of sparks erupted outside as the old phone pole that carried power and telephone lines crashed onto the cars parked in the driveway, shattering windows, and covering the driveway with glass. The house plunged into darkness, revealing a faint red glow outside the windows. Susan peered into the darkness as the children, in their garish costumes, ran around the house, giggling as they carried burning road flares, the bright red light burning like July Fourth sparklers.

"What can we do?" Dale asked, slumped on the sofa. "I don't know what to do. They won't stop."

Susan knelt on the floor next to him. "We can't give up," she said. "We have to..."

Her words were interrupted by breaking glass and the clatter of feet on the wooden floor above them. The kitchen and living room doors crept open, the tables blocking them scraping against the floor as the doors pushed against them, fog rolling into the house from the darkness outside, illuminated by road flares' red glow.

Susan picked up the shotgun, stepped toward the front door, and raised the wooden stock to her shoulder. The witch child floated through the door with a wave of fog, and Susan squeezed the trigger, the double-ought buckshot ripping through the witch's dress and embedding itself into the wall behind her. The girl wavered for a moment, then continued into the living room as though the shotgun blast was nothing but a stiff breeze. Susan aimed at the girl's forehead and fired the second barrel.

The papier-mâché mask shattered, bits of old plaster and paper crumbling to the floor. Susan dropped the shotgun barrel to the floor, staring at the dead girl's face. Her skin was a sickly blue gray, her brown eyes bulging from the sockets. A trail of black, dried blood ran from one nostril, ending at a mouth filled with jagged, broken teeth. The glowing red flare she carried revealed hand-size bruises around a delicate, blue neck, her throat caved in as though a man's strong hands crushed her larynx and squeezed the life from her. A beetle crawled from her hair and made the mistake of approaching her mouth. A long, forked tongue flashed out to snatch the insect and draw it into the dark void where she chewed and crunched it. She swallowed and grinned at Susan like a shark watching a seal foundering in the water, unable to escape the bloodthirsty predator. The girl took a step forward, the burning flare in one hand, a knife in the other.

"Dale, do you have any more shells?" Susan yelled, afraid to turn her attention from the girl as she advanced, licking her dark blue lips. "Dale?"

Susan turned and stumbled over the coffee table, dropping the shotgun and falling to the floor. Dale was dead, his throat sliced, bright red blood running down over his shirt. The skeleton boy sat astride his chest on the sofa, slicing the skin around Dale's face. The boy pulled at Dale's scalp while cutting away with a small knife, skinning Dale like an animal he was preparing for taxidermy. The skeleton-boy slid the knife over Dale's nose and pulled the Dale-mask off his skull, removing his own plain white mask and pressing Dale's face over his own dead blue visage. The boy's neck bore hand-shaped bruises and damage identical to the girl's.

Susan skittered backward into the corner as the smallest of the children leaped from the closed-off stairs, still holding the machete. The three approached as one as Susan cried out and raised her arms to fend them off. The last thing she heard was their giggling.

"What should we do with them?" the deputy asked, nodding to the three bodies laid out on the front porch of the old Brookins farmhouse. Each was missing their face, the skin sliced and peeled away. Two were the new owners—Dale and Susan Carey. The third was an employee of the contractor working on the house.

The sheriff pulled off his hat and wiped the sweat from his brow with an old red handkerchief, blew his nose into it, and shoved it back into his pants' pocket. He glanced at the bodies on the porch like they were an annoyance before turning his attention to the distant housing development. "Can't believe they sold the Brookins homestead and split it up. Just erasin' our history one farm at a time. Gotta know your history, livin' in these parts."

The deputy nodded, staring at the faceless corpses, his Adam's apple bobbing in the open collar of the shirt as he swallowed. "I guess they didn't."

The sheriff shook his head. "Outsiders and undesirables. It used to be everyone knew their place, but not anymore," he said, removing his sunglasses and spitting tobacco juice into the leaves littering the yard. "I guess we can't just throw 'em in the crick or bury 'em out in the field like we used to do. Someone would start asking questions."

He patted the heavy wooden banister running along the front porch. "It's a great old home. The Brookins family used to have big Halloween parties. I came when I was a boy, but they'd been going on for a long time before me. Great memories here. My first kiss was with Shirley Snyder during one of those parties. A couple years later, I got to third base for the first time in the hay loft of the barn that used to be over there. Just a grand old time. They don't do stuff like that anymore. And of course, the chase. The party stopped when it was time for the chase," he said, a look of nostalgia washing over his face.

The sheriff stared at the massive oak tree near the wood line, thinking back to the Halloween parties. When the three barefoot kids in their costumes and white masks walked out of the woods, the music stopped, and everyone grew quiet, the only sound being the kids' giggling.

They would knock at the front door and yell, "Trick or treat." The eldest Brookins would release the prey, sometimes their ankles bound to make the chase more interesting. A couple years, the sheriff won quite a bit of money betting on which kid would kill which runner. He also had a knack for guessing which runner would last the longest, though they were always caught and skinned by midnight. The kids liked to mess with the runners sometimes, disappearing into the darkness to make the runners think they had a chance to escape before the trap was sprung and they died like all the runners before them. The entire time, the giggling continued.

He sniffed and rubbed at his nose, returning to the moment, and turned to the deputy. "They put a new oil furnace in the cellar, right?"

The deputy nodded, his head bouncing up and down on a long, skinny neck. "Oil tank is around back, near the cellar storm doors."

The sheriff stepped off the porch. "Drag 'em into the cellar, douse 'em with fuel oil, and light 'em up. Make sure their faces burn good. It'll look like something went wrong with the furnace."

The deputy called out to the two men leaning against a nearby rusty pickup truck, a Confederate flag hanging in the back window. The three started to drag the bodies around the house to the cellar back door as the sheriff started across the side yard to the big old oak tree.

He paused and called back to the deputy. "Make sure you don't burn the house down."

The portly sheriff circled the oak and knelt next to three small headstones. Most of the engraving on the headstones was worn away, the names once etched into the granite forgotten to history. Only the date carved into each stone was still readable: October 31, 1851. Legend had it the kids met a violent death that night, and while no one knew exactly what happened, three slaves were strung up from that very oak tree a few days later. Three kids died on Halloween, and three slaves hanged for it. No one knew why the family buried the kids beneath the lynching tree or what brought them back every year.

The sheriff swept the leaves and dirt off the headstones and leaned on one to stand, his knees aching in the autumn weather. He stared across the empty fields at the housing development two miles away. If there was no one living at the Brookins farmhouse next year, he'd have to round up some runners like his uncles, county sheriffs before him, did previously. He couldn't have the kids wandering over to the housing development, stirring things up. He was certain he could find three undesirables nobody would miss.

Maybe he'd invite a few close friends to restart the Halloween parties. Someone had to make sure they remembered their history.

THE PACK

BRYAN HOLM

If you lived in Minnesota during the Halloween of 1991, you already know what I'm going to talk about, and you're probably already rolling your eyes a little bit. The state experienced a once-in-a-century storm, a colossal blizzard that came roaring in on All Hallows' Eve. When all was said and done, it left over three feet of snow and drifts over ten feet tall. Roads were impassable. Thousands were without power. Businesses and schools were closed for days. Over a hundred people were injured, and twenty-two people died.

It was a rite of passage for anyone who lived through it. When the major anniversaries roll around, all the old stories get retold, seemingly every citizen in the state with a badge of honor to recount, whether it was helping a baby to be born in a stuck car, or skiing across town to get Grandma her groceries.

The deaths are recounted on the anniversaries as well, the victims recast as heroes, whether it was warranted, like a State Trooper giving his life for his job, or not, the drunk uncle who had a heart attack shoveling. Either way, they're honored by friends and family.

A handful of deaths from that fateful storm are rarely discussed.

Those deaths are better left forgotten, reduced to a footnote in a local newspaper, an opaque reference on the nightly news. If anything, they're whispered about in drunken circles in dingy bars, out of earshot of any outsiders. Those deaths are just too disturbing to revisit, and the tragic questions surrounding them can never be fully answered.

Elise sized herself up in the full-length mirror nailed to her closet door. Her grandpa's striped sweater was too big, the colors weren't quite right, and his fedora was much too nice, but the mask sealed the deal. It was a legit, New Line Freddy Krueger mask, costing a small fortune at Spencer's. Her mom didn't know the price, thank God. Elise hoped for her father's sake she never would.

Her dad was a horror fiend like her, and it drove her mom crazy. She would go to bed early, and Elise and her dad would stay up late with a stack of fresh VHS horrors from the video store. They would consume obnoxious amounts of popcorn and soda, and bask in the bloody glory of 80s' horror cinema.

Elise was a junior, which meant she was in the constant pull between childhood and adulthood, between staying home and going out with friends. There had been less and less movie nights with her dad, she'd blown him off three weekends in a row, and she felt bad about it. They had seen Freddy's Dead at least, a Sunday matinee the previous month. Her dad loved it. Elise wasn't so sure. She appreciated a few of the kills but thought the 3D sucked shit. At least she was able to use her dad's enthusiasm to steer him through the mall to the sweet mask she was currently wearing.

Her bedroom door flew open. Kate, her best friend, seductively danced her way in, wearing a faded, cracked, child's Cabbage Patch Kid mask.

"If you're going for a sexy Cabbage Patch Kid, that's not it."

Kate snorted, tossing the mask on the bed, lying next to it. "You're actually dressing up?"

"It's Halloween! Do you know me at all?"

"You're right, I shouldn't be surprised." Kate rummaged through her purse, pulling out a pack of 120 Virginia Slims. "Ta da! I scored a pack of my mom's smokes."

"Inside voice," Elise hissed as she sprinted to her bedroom door, shutting it quietly. She took off her hat and mask and laid on the bed beside Kate.

Elise pointed out the window. "You realize it's snowing, right?"

Kate stared at the light flakes whipping against the glass. "So?"

"You've only got a windbreaker, and you're wearing Chucks?"

Kate looked down at their feet. Elise wore her dad's old combat boots from Vietnam and a pair of ancient cords. The boots looked gigantic next to Kate's fading yellow Converse. "If you're going for a sexy Freddy, that's not it."

The girls broke into laughter, the unguarded, obnoxious laughter that can only be shared between best friends. Elise pretended to shove Kate off the bed.

"Oh, wait until you see the rest of my costume!" Elise jumped up and grabbed it from her nightstand, tossing it on the bed beside Kate.

"Holy shit, Elise! Where did you get this?"

"My dad made it."

Kate held a homemade Freddy glove in her hands. The glove itself was nothing special, a brown leather gardening glove. But using superglue and thick baseball glove thread, her father had sewn in steak knife blades on the four fingers.

"This is badass!" Kate put it on, flexing the knives in and out. She touched the tip of one with her index finger. The blade pierced her skin, a drop of blood forming on her fingertip.

"Careful, they're real!"

Kate made a face, sucking on her finger. "No shit!" They broke into laughter again.

Headlights flashed in the windows, followed by five loud, long honks.

Elise sighed. "He knows that pisses my dad off."

Alex and Scott were waiting in Alex's old pickup, its Swiss-cheese muffler echoing down the block. Kate slipped on Elise's front steps; there was already an inch of slushy snow on the sidewalks. That didn't stop the kids though, and Elise took a moment to take it in, the trick-or-treaters running up and down the block, the jack-o-lanterns burning on the porches, each one already wearing a small crown of snow. Even though there was a biting wind, the fluffy flakes made it feel even more magical than usual. It was still Elise's favorite night of the year.

"C'mon!" Alex, Elise's boyfriend, yelled through the open passenger door. "We got a tight schedule this evening!"

Scott, Kate's beau, stepped onto the boulevard. He had a Michael Myers mask on top of his head, pushed up like a hat. Elise brushed past him and climbed into the cab. "C'mon, man, no jumpsuit? Do you even have a knife?" Elise slid down the bench seat, getting cozy with Alex as Kate and Scott piled in behind her. Alex gave her a sloppy kiss.

"So what do you think of my costume?" Alex asked. He wore a black leather jacket and blue jeans.

"Uh, Danny Zucko?"

"What? Who's that?" Alex was dumbfounded.

Scott burst out laughing. "Yes! Zucko, that's his name! Ha! I told you, man. Travolta in *Grease*!"

Alex shook his head, embarrassed. "Not you, too." Alex grabbed a pair of sunglasses off the dash. "Does this help?"

"Not really, sorry."

"The Terminator?" Kate guessed.

"Yes! Thank you! I knew I should have stolen my dad's shotgun."

Elise leaned into his shoulder, stifling her laughter. "I'm sorry. It's your hair; it's your beautiful, luxurious, black hair." She ruffled it like he was five years old.

Alex mimicked a pouting child and put the truck into drive. "Whatever."

Scott burst out laughing again as Alex squealed down the street, fishtailing in the snow.

Alex drove way too fast, up the steep hills away from Elise's neighborhood. The snow was getting heavier. The cracked windshield's defroster had trouble keeping up.

"Alex, slow down," Elise pleaded.

Alex gunned the engine in response.

"Don't be a dick. There're kids out here!"

Alex reluctantly applied the brake. "You're no fun."

"So any hints on this *amazing* plan of yours tonight?" Kate asked.

"Shit, he won't even tell me," Scott replied.

"Don't worry, my darlings, all will be revealed soon enough. But first on the agenda, we trick or treat."

Kate sighed. "Are you serious? We're too old. No one's giving us any candy."

"We could have done that by my house," Elise added.

"No, this is on the way, and even better, it's the rich neighborhood, and you know what that means?"

Scott did. "Full-size candy bars!"

Alex slapped the dash. "Yes! My man! And we only need to hit a few blocks. I mean, how can we not? It's free munchies!"

Kate was relieved. "Thank God, does that mean weed is part of this master plan at least?"

"It is. Your patience will be rewarded. The Pack rides again!"

Kate elbowed Elise in the ribs, and Elise bit her tongue. When Alex got this way, all unearned cockiness and adult posturing, she wondered why she dated him.

The snow was heavier on top of the hill, but the streets were busier. It seemed Alex wasn't the only one thinking about full-size candy bars. Elise watched multiple families drive into the neighborhood, park, and join them in the hunt.

With Elise, Kate, and Scott in masks, most folks just shook their heads and gave them candy. Some would either shut the door in their faces or not answer at all. After being ignored by the second house in a row, Alex scooped up their pumpkin from the steps as they walked away.

"What are you doing?" Elise asked.

"Those bastards, a bunch of grinches up here if you ask me."

"Wrong holiday, dude," Scott quipped.

Alex bolted out into the middle of the nearest intersection and smashed the pumpkin against the curb. It split open down the middle, its candle snuffed out by the snow.

"Alex!" Elise fumed.

He jogged back to the group, a shit-eating grin on his face. "It's Halloween, man!"

"Some kid made that, you know."

"Whatever. I think he can afford another one."

"That's not the point."

Alex continued past her, joining Kate and Scott a few feet ahead. Kate rubbed her shoulders, trying to stay warm. "How much longer?"

Alex checked his stash, an old pillowcase. "Let's see. How about one more block? Here." He took off his leather jacket, draping it over Kate's shoulders. As he did so, Scott slowed down, walking in step with Elise behind them.

"Having fun yet?" Scott asked.

"I am, actually, besides that little prick up there."

Scott snickered. "I dig the costume, by the way. And that glove, man, it's killer."

"Right!? Thank you. At least someone appreciates fine art."

"You see the new movie?"

"Of course. You?"

"Opening night."

"What'd you think?"

"It was all right. 3D sucked, though."

"That's what I said!"

Elise nodded ahead. Alex whispered something to Kate, and she snorted in response. "Aren't you worried about that?" Elise was joking, but the look on Scott's face made her regret saying it.

He leaned in toward her. "What do you remember from last weekend?"

"What do you mean?"

"The woods, the kegger."

"Not much, to be honest."

"You didn't hear anyone talking this week?"

"About what?" Elise remembered a few double-takes in the hallway Monday morning, but she did wake up Sunday with a bruised knee, so she just assumed she had put on a good show, falling flat on her face by the bonfire or something.

Scott leaned in closer. "I was passed out in the woods by ten."

"No surprise there, lightweight."

"Whatever. Anyway, rumor is that maybe Alex and Kate made out, just a little bit."

Elise stopped, her heart beating fast. "What? No way. Who told you that?"

"I can't confirm it, at least from anyone who saw it with their own eyes."

"Then it's bullshit."

"That's likely, but is it so farfetched?"

They watched them up ahead, laughing together. Alex must have said something purposely shocking because Kate playfully punched him in the shoulder.

"No way, she wouldn't do that to me."

Scott laughed. "Maybe not sober, but an annihilated Alex, on the other hand..."

Scott had a point there, and Elise was trying to figure out if she even cared. On the one hand, it was betrayal, but on the other, it was an easy way out. And if Kate had been as drunk as she was, Alex would for sure be more to blame.

As she mulled this over, Scott leaned in even farther, whispering in her ear. "I have an idea on how we could get back at them." He grabbed her hand and squeezed it.

Elise pulled away. "What are you doing?"

"Just something to think about."

Alex turned back, realizing they had stopped. "What are you two conspiring about?"

"About how fucking cold it is. Can we go?" Elise pleaded.

Alex checked his bag. "Hold on."

Alex sprinted ahead, cutting into a front lawn behind three boys. He aimed for the smallest one, shoving him into the snow.

"Jesus Christ, Alex." Elise ran toward him.

"This, my friend, is called a trick!" Alex ripped the kid's bag of candy from his hand. The kid rolled onto his back, tears running down his beet-red face. Alex made a dramatic bow, and the kid flinched. "Thank you, kind sir!"

Elise was livid. "What the hell?"

"It's a Pine Haven rite of passage!"

"You're an asshole!" Elise stormed past him, taking off her hat and mask.

"C'mon! I had my candy stolen."

Elise ignored him and helped the kid up, brushing the snow off his back. "I'm so sorry." She turned back to Alex. "Give it back!"

"No way!"

"I'm serious!"

"So am I. You're messing with a time-honored tradition here. This is more important than you or me or one weaselly little shit. This is the very fabric of this town we're talking about here, of America itself."

They stared at each other, a standoff, and one she knew she wouldn't win. Alex wouldn't back down, he couldn't, not in front of his friend or the handful of kids who had stopped and were watching this play out, waiting for more fireworks.

Elise bent down, wiping tears from the boy's cheeks. She handed him her candy, a plastic gas station bag from the floor of Alex's truck. "You can have mine."

Alex looked on, shaking his head. "Oh, come on."

Elise motioned to Kate. "Yours too."

"What? No way."

"Kate, bring it here."

Kate reluctantly made her way over, rummaging through her bag. "Sorry, kid, but you can't have my Skittles. I have to draw the line somewhere."

The storm had intensified, rolling in more quickly and with much more force than anyone had anticipated. Alex's truck was having trouble finding the pavement, sliding in and out of icy ruts on the road. His headlights barely penetrated the wall of snow coming down.

"Maybe we should call it a night," Elise said.

"We're almost there," Alex replied.

Elise glanced at Kate and Scott for backup. No one took the bait. "The roads are bad."

"We're all good. I threw extra sandbags in the cab." Alex caressed the dashboard. "And you're offending Sheila here. When has old Sheila ever let us down?"

Elise gave up. Her mind kept going back to what Scott said. Was he really into her? She wasn't exactly sure how she felt about it. He was a nice guy, and funny, and she certainly had more in common with him than Alex. Still, there was the Kate factor, but what if she had really made out with Alex?

Alex took a right on a county road, and Elise's stomach dropped. There was only one destination out this way that made any sense. "The cemetery?"

"Yes! Elise gets the gold star!"

"C'mon. For real?" Kate whined.

"I have a big surprise. It's gonna be epic. A new benchmark for the Pack."

The "Pack" was Alex's stupid name for their group of friends. It had started years ago, pre-girls, and had gradually faded away as the guys grew up, made new friends, and started dating. It was an embarrassing reflection of childhood for everyone except Alex, who still invoked the name anytime he wanted to do something extra dumb, or illegal, or both.

The cemetery was on top of the hill overlooking town, surrounded by neighborhoods on two sides. Alex parked a block away, and they headed the rest of the way on foot, trudging through the deepening snow, the wind whipping at any exposed skin.

"We can't be out in this for too long, man," Scott warned.

"Oh, not to worry. We'll be inside," Alex replied.

"Inside?"

"You'll see soon enough."

They ducked under a low-hanging pine, where two sections of the wrought-iron fence met, leaving an opening just large enough for a scrawny high school kid to squeeze through. It was well known by those under the age of eighteen.

As the four of them snuck through the fence, Elise tried to keep calm. Even though she loved all things horror, cemeteries—and the no-fun, real-life death they represented—were a different story. They scared the shit out of her.

Once they were well inside and away from houses on the street, Alex took off his backpack, his "bag of tricks" as he liked to call it, and pulled out a flashlight and a map. "Hold on." He studied it, getting his bearings. He pointed to their left. "This way. It's pretty close, actually."

Alex led them toward the rear of the massive cemetery, up a hill. Behind them, down at the main entrance, the caretaker's house glowed, mostly obscured by the snow.

Alex caught Elise looking that way. "Don't worry. Pretty sure the old man's not doing any rounds tonight, even if it is Halloween."

At the top of the hill was a mausoleum, the largest in the cemetery by far. Its entrance was an arched door made of black walnut wood, framed by wide granite pillars. Its roof was half-domed, large green tiles made from clay, with a large stone cross adorning the top. Over the doorway, spelled out in stained glass panels, was the name "Crawford."

Alex turned back to the group. "We have arrived."

Kate read the name above him. "Wait, this isn't..."

"It is. The final resting place of the notorious Anton Crawford, the infamous town *murderer*." Alex drew out the last word, attempting a Transylvanian accent, before cracking himself up.

Anton Crawford was a one-time pillar of Pine Haven, a mining baron who built half the town himself. In the forties, his wife and child drowned in a suspicious boating accident, and a few days later, he was seen kissing his long-time assistant, twenty years younger than his recently deceased spouse. Murder charges were filed, but the best Chicago defense attorney money could buy ripped the small-town prosecution to shreds, and Anton walked. A town pariah, he lived the rest of his days behind the walls of his estate, dying in the eighties.

Alex set his backpack in the snow and removed a tire iron. "We are going to smoke a joint with old man Crawford."

A booming sound cracked above them and everyone flinched.

"What the hell was that?" Scott asked.

"Thundersnow! Holy shit! I couldn't have planned this night better if I tried!"

"Thundersnow? That's a real thing?" Kate wondered out loud.

The sky roared again in response, and the wind picked up. Elise looked down at her boots, a tiny drift of snow blowing up against them. There was already six inches on the ground.

Alex went to the door and slammed the tire iron into the seam. He cranked on it, and the weathered wood gave way, splinters falling to the ground as he broke off the iron latch. He yanked on the door several times, and it finally broke free from the frame, sliding toward him in the snow, the rusting hinges shrieking in the night.

Alex turned to Elise and Kate, extending one arm and taking a bow. "Ladies first."

The inside of the crypt was cold, dark, and smelled like a jar of pennies, but it was still a welcome respite from the storm. They huddled together, stomping snow off their shoes, while Alex pulled a camping lantern from his bag. He lit it and set it on the marble slab containing the remains of Mr. Crawford. Elise removed her mask. She had left it on for the added warmth, but it was hard to see through in the dark. She set it on the slab with her glove and put the fedora back on, slipping the tips of her ears underneath its brim.

As their eyes adjusted to the darkness, Elise saw that the inside was even more ornate than the exterior. As she took in the etched marble walls, a baroque statue of the Virgin Mary, and jade vases filled with fake flowers, she couldn't help but laugh at the pointlessness of it all. All this money spent on a tomb that no one ever saw. And for what? A piece of shit's dying ego.

Alex scanned the small space with his flashlight, erasing any shadows made by the lantern. "Holy shit."

They followed his beam of light to the floor. In one corner of the marble slab housing Anton's corpse, a small trickle of moldy, green slime oozed from the seam, forming a tiny pool.

"Oh my God. Gross!" Kate exclaimed.

Scott knelt down, examining it. "What the hell is that?"

"Probably embalming fluid, mixed with a little old man corpse?" Elise answered.

"Should we dip our joint in it?"

Everyone stared at Alex. "Isn't formaldehyde supposed to fuck you up? Make you trip?"

"I'm gonna puke," Kate half-whispered, turning away.

"I'm kidding! Jeez, lighten up, guys. This is fun! Right?"

"It's still really cold in here. Let's do this," Elise said.

"All right, all right." Alex rooted around in his backpack and pulled out a pint of cheap whiskey. "This will help."

Elise took a long slug. She didn't want to get drunk on a school night, but it warmed her up, and it was looking more and more likely that tomorrow would be a snow day anyway.

"We ready?" Alex sat up on the marble slab and smacked it. "This one's for you, old timer. Hope you're having a blast in hell." He lit a large joint, took a long drag, then another. He was notorious for smoking more than his fair share. He finally passed it to Elise.

They smoked for a few minutes, and when it was nearly a roach, Alex lit another. It was good shit, and it smoothed out the rough edges from earlier in the night, recalibrating the equilibrium of the group. Soon enough, everyone was laughing and passing around the whiskey and candy they'd collected, fighting over the Butterfingers. They made plans for the next day. It was a Friday, and if they didn't have school, it was going to be a three-day weekend.

"Word is Mel's parents are out of town, so I think we can hang there," Scott said.

"Perfect. She's only two blocks from—"

Alex cut Kate off. "Did you guys hear that?"

"What?" Kate asked.

"I don't know, be quiet."

They stood still in the smoky tomb, the wind whistling outside. A muffled wailing rose, echoing around the chamber.

"That! What's that?"

It was coming from the slab. Suddenly, Alex began shaking, like the stone beneath him was moving. His eyes went wide, then rolled up in his head. "Help me!"

Kate shrieked, stumbling back into a corner, falling on her ass. "Oh my God, oh my God!"

Alex leaped off the slab, revealing a small tape recorder playing a Spooky Halloween Sounds cassette. "Ha! I got you good!"

Kate sprang back up, tears on her face. "You asshole!"

"I can't believe you fell for that!"

"I'm way too high for you to pull that shit!"

Elise shut off the tape. "Way to kill the vibe."

"C'mon. Scott, back me up here, it was pretty funny, right?"

Scott was stuck between his girl and his friend. "Let's just finish that and get out of here."

"Fine." Alex sheepishly handed Scott the joint.

Elise took Kate by the arm. "How about a smoke outside?"

"Great idea, thank you."

Elise pushed on the door, but it wouldn't budge. "Uh, guys?"

Scott tried, but it barely moved. He shouldered it again and again, gradually pushing it open. The storm had become a full-fledged blizzard while they were inside. The marble entrance was covered in ice, with deep drifts already building up against the mausoleum.

Elise and Kate squeezed through the door out into the elements. Elise yelled back inside. "Hurry up, guys. This is getting nasty."

Elise and Kate made their way around the mausoleum, leaning against the back wall, sheltered from the wind. Elise always felt stupid smoking the long, thin, 120 cigarettes, but the added buzz felt good.

"You okay?" Elise asked.

Kate exhaled a large cloud of smoke. "I'm fine. Just a little fucked up and really cold." She rubbed the arms of Alex's leather jacket.

"So I don't think I even care anymore, to be honest, but last weekend, did anything weird happen?" Kate stared straight ahead, silent. "Kate?"

Kate pointed at the tree line ahead of them, a large grove of pines that bordered the north end of the cemetery. "What is that? Do you see that?"

Elise followed her hand, trying to see through the lashing snow. "See what?"

"There's something out there."

"Nice try, but I'm not falling for it."

"No, I'm serious. There!"

Elise squinted. A pair of eyes stared back at her, a flash of yellow. "What is that?"

Two more pairs joined them, and three wolves emerged from the trees. The one in the center was massive, clearly the alpha, a long pink scar running across his snout to his left eye, which drooped slightly from the badly healed wound. He sniffed the air and snarled, fangs shining in the moonlight. They didn't move any closer, just watched, fierce gargoyles guarding the forest.

"C'mon," Elise whispered. She walked backward slowly, staying against the mausoleum walls, never breaking eye contact with the alpha. Kate was frozen in place, shaking. "Kate, c'mon, *now*." Kate finally listened, scurrying around the building.

The wolves began to creep slowly, carefully, through the snow. The other two fanned out to the sides while the alpha moved straight toward them.

Elise took a chance, raising her voice. "Kate, run!"

They turned and booked it toward the mausoleum door. Flying inside, Elise tried to close it, but it was embedded in the snow, the bottom of the door encased in a thick ridge of ice.

"What the hell?" Scott asked as Kate flew into his arms.

"Wolves, fucking wolves!" Elise shouted.

"Bullshit," Alex replied.

"No bullshit! Three of them!"

Alex squeezed out the door to see for himself. He was back in a second, his face pale. He kicked the door, trying to get it unstuck. It wouldn't budge.

"What do we do?" Elise asked.

"The house!" Kate exclaimed. "The caretaker's house!" Kate ran outside, stumbling through the snow.

"Kate! You won't make it!" Elise yelled.

Scott sprinted after her.

Elise looked at Alex. "What do we do?"

"We can't stay in here."

They went outside. Scott was several yards away, completely still. The wolves were already ahead of him, slowly following Kate as she trudged through the drifting snow. The wolves were in no hurry; she was clearly easy prey. Kate tripped over a grave marker hidden in the snow, letting out a cry as she briefly disappeared beneath the surface. The wolves pounded ahead, leaping effortlessly through the snow.

"Kate!" Elise yelled before Alex clamped his hand over her mouth.

One wolf stopped. Turning back, it eyed the three of them. It rushed at Scott.

Alex shouted, "The roof!"

Elise didn't understand at first, but then he was scrambling up a mausoleum pillar and swinging over to the wrought-iron bars covering the side window. He was up on the roof in seconds, reaching for her hands. "Come on!" He pulled her to safety.

Scott raced back as the other two wolves pounced on Kate, her blood-curdling screams echoing through the cemetery. The third wolf was only a few yards behind Scott and gaining ground fast. Scott slammed into the side wall, reaching up for their hands. The wolf leaped into the air, its claws ripping into his jacket as they hauled him up, down feathers intermingling with the snowflakes floating to the ground. The wolf clamped down on the heel of his right shoe, but he kicked it off. Elise and Alex yanked him the rest of the way up. They collapsed onto their backs, the wolf still below, growling, jumping up the wall, unable to reach them.

They tried to catch their breath, tried to ignore the horrible screams coming from Kate. Elise sat up, peering into the snowy dark. The two wolves fought over Kate's body. One of them shook something, a dog shaking a favorite toy.

Kate's screams stopped.

The wolf below them gave up. Whimpering, it jogged off to join the others. Elise, Alex, and Scott could only look on, helpless spectators.

"What are they doing?" Scott asked.

Elise couldn't figure it out at first, the wolves' movements, but as they got closer, her fears were confirmed. The alpha was dragging Kate's body through the snow toward them. It stopped in the clearing outside the mausoleum entrance, a sliver of moonlight cutting through the snow, shining a spotlight on Kate's mangled body.

Elise choked back bile. Kate's face was gone, most of the skin anyway. It hung to the side, a serrated flap, exposing the bone around her left eye, the socket a dull ivory against the fresh white powder.

What was the purpose of dragging the body to them? Could wolves really be that sadistic? Were they really forcing them to watch the all-you-can-eat human buffet that used to be Kate? The alpha placed a massive paw on Kate's chest and howled into the darkness.

As he went to work tearing apart Kate's shirt, two cubs, only a few weeks old, stumbled out of the woods, struggling in the snow, following the cry. The alpha tore Kate's stomach open, a jagged laceration bisecting her belly. Her intestines spilled out into the snow. As they steamed in the icy air, the cubs pounced on them, eagerly devouring the soft fleshy coils. Scott leaned over the roof and vomited, a mix of candy and whisky landing in the snow with a wet thud.

Elise, Alex, and Scott sat in silence, their stoned brains attempting to process the current situation. The wind had worsened as the full force of the storm hit, creating near whiteout conditions in the cemetery.

Elise stood, pressing the fedora tight to her head. She could barely see the lights of the caretaker's house through the heavy snow. She screamed at the top of her lungs until she was hoarse. It sounded like a whisper against the squall. As if mocking her directly, the thundersnow began again, bellowing crashes above them, echoing through the trees.

"No one's hearing us way back here. Not in this," Alex said.

"At least I'm trying!"

"He's right. Save your energy. We might be up here all night," Scott said.

Elise sat back down. "I don't think we're going to make it up here all night. We'll be blocks of ice before morning."

Scott rubbed at his back, wincing. Elise leaned over. "Let me see." He lifted his shirt. His back was red with scratches, but the claws had barely broken the skin. "It's not horrible. You got lucky."

The wolves, done with their feeding, turned their attention to the remaining three meals staring down at them. The two cubs, soaked in blood, their bellies full, played in a snowbank. The alpha sat next to what was left of Kate, staring at them. The other wolves paced back and forth, eyeing them, whimpering. One took off in a sprint, leaping up the wall beneath their feet but coming up short of the roof. It stayed there briefly, on its hindquarters, its breath whisps of smoke at their feet.

They slid farther up the roof.

Elise peered over the edge. "I hope that snowbank doesn't get much higher." It was gradually growing, encasing the open door, snow spilling into the mausoleum. The wolf finally gave up, rejoining the others.

Elise looked at the boys on either side of her. Alex, shaking, his eyes completely bloodshot, couldn't take his eyes off the alpha. Scott's eyes were in his lap, hiding tears.

"All right, guys, we need a plan. If we stay up here all night, we're getting frostbite, hypothermia, probably both."

Alex nodded toward the ground. "If we go down there, we're dead."

"Thank you, Alex, that was very helpful."

Elise scanned the cemetery. "What about that tree?" There was an old, massive oak tree thirty yards away with low-hanging branches. "Is it close to the tree behind it?"

"What do you mean?" Alex asked.

"The branches intertwine I think, and that second tree might be close enough to the fence. Maybe close enough to get over it?"

It was hard to tell through the snow. Elise wasn't sure she could trust what she was seeing, the accuracy of her depth of field.

"It's a stretch. And you'd have to make it to the tree first," Scott said.

Elise was annoyed. "Any other ideas, then?"

"If we can get inside the mausoleum, we can wait until morning, until the wolves leave."

Alex stared at the entrance below them. "That fucking door. We can't close it."

"My glove!" Elise exclaimed.

"Where is it?" Scott asked.

"It's inside."

"Shit."

"It's a weapon, though, four knives. Might be worth the risk. If you guys distracted them, maybe I could grab it, make for the tree."

Scott shook his head. "No way. You're not going." He looked at Alex.

"Fuck that. I'm not doing it."

"One of us has to try. We can't stay here."

"Be my guest."

"This whole thing was your idea!"

Alex reached into his pocket and took out a quarter. "We'll flip for it."

Scott shook his head. "No. Fuck it. I'll go. And for the record, you're a pussy, man, always have been."

Alex twisted, raising a fist. Elise gripped his wrist. "Let it go."

Alex turned away from them both, a petulant child.

Scott stared at the tree, then the house. "I think it makes more sense to go for the house."

Elise wasn't convinced. "Are you sure? It's farther."

"It is, but I don't know. I mean I'm not a fricking gymnast. Swinging through trees seems like a stretch."

"You really think you can make it that far?"

"If I'm gonna have any chance at all, you're right, you guys need to do something to distract them, force them to move."

Elise made a snowball, packing it tight. She threw it at the cubs. It landed between them. They both jumped back, then crept forward, sniffing the spot where it disappeared, wagging their puffy tails. Elise made another and tossed it. She hit one of the cubs in the ribs. It flattened against the snow, letting out a yip. The alpha stood up, staring up at her, a guttural growl.

Scott joined in, and they kept pummeling the cubs. Alex reluctantly began to help, still pouting. The adult wolves were agitated, their protective instincts kicking in. They paced, growling, their fangs shining in the moonlight. They took turns running and hurdling against the wall, but the roof was just out of their reach. The cubs scurried to the alpha, weaving in and out of his legs, scared.

The wolves headed toward the mausoleum, then around it. Elise shimmied over to the other side. The alpha was nudging the cubs along, toward the safety of the treeline. Elise was elated. This was even more than she hoped for; were they actually leaving?

They were not.

Once they hit the treeline, they stopped, turning back to face their adversaries.

Scott whispered, "I'm going."

Elise gave him a tight hug. "Good luck." Alex refused to make eye contact.

Scott smiled. "You two just make as much noise as you can, bang on the roof, keep throwing snow, whatever you can. I need a head start."

Alex positioned himself on his knees, and Elise chucked snowballs at the treeline. Alex banged his hands on the roof, slapping the clay squares. It didn't produce as much noise as they'd hoped, so he began to howl. Elise joined in. The wolves' ears went back, their growls increasing at the perceived mockery.

Scott slipped over the edge of the roof in front. He planned to hang, then drop lightly, but the tile on the edge cracked from his weight. He lost his grip, his shoulder bouncing off the open door as he fell. The snow was deep, but not deep enough. His right foot pierced the fluffy snow, hitting the ice-covered marble underneath. He rolled his ankle as he landed and let out a grunt as he fell onto his back.

Elise heard it, and so did the alpha. She watched its head tilt, its ears pointing forward, listening. It was no longer paying attention to them, no matter how much noise they made. He trotted forward, leaving the treeline. The adult wolves followed.

Elise scrambled to the front. "Scott! Run! They're coming!"

Scott's eyes were wide as he clambered to his feet. He winced in pain as he bolted into the mausoleum and grabbed the glove. The wolves were picking up speed, spreading out. Scott stumbled out of the doorway.

Elise laid on her stomach, reaching down. "Come back up!"

Scott tried to jump up, to reach her hand, but his ankle was useless. The first attempt worsened the sprain, the second jump tore the swollen muscle.

He bolted for the tree, tripping through the drifting snow. The wolves separated as they flew past the mausoleum, flanking him. Even in the madness, Elise was in awe of how well the wolves worked together. Centuries of instinct was on display in front of her, cunning killing machines hunting together seamlessly without so much as a glance between them.

And what were they doing? Just trying to eat, just trying to feed their young. The senselessness of it all crushed her, and she realized, in that moment, that there was probably no way out of this. They were all going to die in the cemetery that Halloween night, either from the wolves or from the storm. She thought of her poor parents. Tears filled her eyes.

The alpha stayed back, letting the other wolves go in for the kill. Scott wasn't even ten yards from the mausoleum when they took him down. One wolf leaped onto his back, its claws on his shoulders as it slammed him down into the snow. The other wolf went to work on his legs, tearing apart his calf muscles, severing his Achilles, putting him down for good.

Scott screamed, a high-pitched wail. The wolf on his shoulders flipped him onto his back. It clamped down on Scott's neck with snarled fangs. As it tore away his flesh, blood spraying the snow, Scott shot his hand up, burying the glove in the wolf's neck. It squealed and jumped back, taking the glove with it. The glove dangled from its neck, three of the four knife blades buried deep.

The wolf whimpered, confused, blood pooling at its front paws. It lurched toward the alpha, looking for help.

It collapsed, its whines becoming a shallow wheeze, its breath fading. The alpha trotted over, sniffing it. He nudged its head, licking its snout, trying to wake it up. Once the wolf was completely silent, still, the alpha howled, long and loud, an anguished echo amongst the trees.

The alpha turned to Scott, his eyes wide, his teeth bared, growling. He slowly moved up Scott's body, sniffing it, finally stopping at his face. Scott closed his eyes, his body trembling. As the other wolf gnawed on Scott's leg, the alpha bit into Scott's nose, pulling away most of the flesh from his face. Elise turned away after that. She covered her ears to drown out the wails.

It didn't work.

Elise and Alex sat down on the edge of the roof. The wind was blistering, and the snow hurt, blowing sideways from the gales whipping out of the west. Even with the clamor of the storm, they could still hear the tearing of flesh, the crunch of bone. The cubs left the safety of the trees, rejoining the adults to feast.

Alex broke the silence. "There's something I need to tell you, if this is really it."

"Don't, Alex."

"I need to. Last weekend..."

"Don't. It doesn't matter, and honestly, I don't care. Whatever that says about us, I don't know."

That shut him up. She didn't buy his attempt at an apology, and she didn't want to hear it. It was for his benefit, not hers. He was a child pretending to be a man. She saw that now, painfully laid bare.

He put his arm around her, and she let him. She didn't have it in her to fight anymore, and they needed to stay warm. They huddled together in silence.

A moaning rose, faintly, underneath the wind. Elise broke away from Alex. Was it the tape recorder? Did he still have it? Was he still playing fucking games, Halloween pranks?

"Really, Alex?"

"What? It's not me!"

"Help me." The moaning became words, muffled, wet.

It was Scott. He raised one hand in the air, a bloody stump with only two fingers left. One of the cubs licked it. "Help me!" His voice was a hissing squeal, a mouth forming words for the first time without lips.

The alpha licked Scott's exposed, bloody skull clean, his drool pooling into Scott's mouth. Choking for air, Scott's tongue left the safety of his teeth. The alpha clamped down on it, snarling, and ripped it out. He tossed the tongue to the cubs. They pounced on it with glee, playing tug-of-war. Scott's throat quickly filled with blood. He was silent after that.

Alex stood, pacing the edge of the roof.

"Careful," Elise said.

He rubbed his hands together. They were bright pink, raw. His fingertips were white, frostbite already taking hold of his extremities. "You're right. We're dying up here if we don't do anything."

"Yes, we are. I just can't decide what's a better way to go, being eaten by wolves or freezing to death."

Alex shook his head. "Fuck that. Neither." He stared at the nearest tree. "Maybe you were on to something, with the trees. If I could climb out far enough on that one branch, I could drop down on the other side of the fence. Even if I broke a leg, I could be at a house with a phone in minutes."

Elise was impressed that Alex was actually stepping up, but she feared it was too little, too late. "What about them?" She pointed at the wolves. "Scott didn't make it very far."

"Scott fucked his leg up, stopped for the glove. If you can distract them again, and I just run straight for the tree. Maybe..."

"That's a big maybe, Alex."

"It is, but like you said, either way we're dead. If I don't make it, I guess I choose the *eaten by wolves* option."

"Okay, but what can I do to make a big enough distraction?"

"You're going to have to trust me on this."

"That sounds promising."

Alex went to the side of the mausoleum. "What if you hung over the side, on the window bars? Just long enough to get them to come to you."

"What?"

"Come over here, look."

Elise followed him, peering over the edge. "So I'm the bait? I don't know if that will work."

"You're probably right."

Alex embraced her in a tight hug, whispering in her ear. "I'm sorry."

Alex shoved Elise as hard as he could, launching her off the roof.

Elise gasped as she floated in the air, her mind unable to process what had occurred before slamming into the ground below. She landed on her back, the wind knocked out of her, plumes of snow rising around her. She tried to get up, to find her breath. The wolves heard the impact. They were up and moving swiftly.

Alex watched the wolves round the corner of the mausoleum, and then he leaped off the other side, landing in a snow drift. He lurched through it, losing a shoe. He stumbled toward the tree.

The wolves circled Elise, taking their time, sizing her up. The smaller wolf pounced first, landing on Elise's chest. She gripped its face, digging her thumb into an eyeball. It jumped back, yelping in pain. As it backed away, Alex's pitched movement registered in its peripheral vision. Sensing easier prey, it left Elise for Alex, bounding through the snow in pursuit.

Elise, finally able to draw a breath, scrambled through the snow on all fours. The alpha tilted his head, watching her struggle to flee. She made it to the dead wolf before the alpha took off, soaring onto her back, flattening her in the snow. She felt its massive claws digging into her back, shredding her sweater. She squirmed beneath him, twisting onto her side. She kicked him hard in the belly, shoving him back with her hands at the same time.

The alpha sucked in breath and backed away, its mouth a vortex of snarling fangs drenched in blood. Elise ripped her glove from the dead wolf's neck, and crawled toward the mausoleum. The alpha leaped again, slamming into her, shoving her headfirst into the door. Her forehead split from the impact, blood streaming into her eyes.

The weight of their two bodies dislodged the door, breaking it free from the icy rut that held the bottom in place.

Elise crawled inside backward, on her haunches, the alpha attacking her, clawing at her chest, arms, face. She fought back, punching it, kicking it as she pulled on the glove. The wolf caught her hair in its teeth and yanked back, tearing part of her scalp away from her skull. It ripped open her cheek with a paw. She felt a claw inside her mouth, tearing at her tongue.

The alpha opened wide for the kill. Elise reached up with one hand, digging into his neck, holding him back. His snout was inches from her face, his nostrils expelling hot, rancid vapor. He inched forward, his strength slowly overpowering hers. Elise slammed the glove deep into its belly, all four blades tearing into the soft flesh. The wolf wailed as she wrenched the glove upward, disemboweling him. She felt his hot intestines spill onto her legs.

Outside, snarls rose beneath the wind, and Alex screamed. Elise shoved the wolf aside, crawled to the door. Alex was sprinting back to the mausoleum. "Help, Elise! Help!" The third wolf, chunks of Alex's back dripping from its mouth, was in pursuit, toying with its prey. Elise pulled herself up by the jamb of the door. Alex was almost to her, only a few feet away.

Elise slammed the door in his face.

She heard Alex crash into it, felt the door vibrate on its hinges. She planted her feet against the wall and held onto the handle, keeping the door from opening. "Elise! I'm sorry! Let me in!" He banged on the door with his fists, yanking on it. "Fuck you, you goddamn—"

The door buckled as the wolf smashed into him. Elise shut her eyes and listened to the roars and screams on the other side of the door. They gradually faded away. She couldn't tell if Alex had died quickly or if the wolf had dragged him somewhere to feast. She hoped it was the latter. She hoped he was out there somewhere, still alive, in as much pain as Scott had been.

She let go of the door, slid down the wall on her back, and gently touched her scalp. She screeched in pain. The long flap of skin was loose, much of her hair torn out. The gash on her cheek was blazing fire, a sizzling hole in her face. She poked it with her tongue, her eyes watering as is slid through the wound and out the other side.

The mausoleum provided shelter from the wind, but little else. The temperature was dropping quickly, and her body shook from the cold. She knew she was stuck there for the night. There was no way to know if the last wolf was still out there or if it retreated to the woods with the cubs. She crawled to the back corner, curling into a fetal position.

The alpha stared back at her, his eyes a milky yellow in the moonlight streaming through the stained-glass window. "I'm sorry," she whispered. She pulled the body of the wolf toward her, on top of her. She buried her head into the warmth of his furry neck. She pushed her arms into the wound she had opened in his belly, feeling the warmth of his organs penetrate her freezing skin. Within seconds, she passed out.

"My God."

Elise woke with a jolt, blinking her eyes in the bright sunlight. The caretaker, a heavy-set man in his sixties, stood over her.

"Miss? Are you okay? What the hell happened out here?"

He leaned over, gripping her shoulder. Elise screamed, tossing the wolf's cold, stiff body aside. She shoved the man, and he fell backward onto the stone floor. He raised his hands. "It's okay! You're okay."

Elise stumbled out of the door into the cemetery, clutching her Freddy mask and her glove. The sun was blinding off the fresh snow, over three feet of it blanketing the rolling hills in front of her. She squinted, scanning the ground. Much of the blood was still visible, her friends' frozen bodies jutting out of snow drifts.

Alex was only a few feet from the mausoleum, on his back. His clothes had been torn away. He lay naked in the sun, his chest a gaping cavity. There was only a pool of thick blood between his pale legs, a nightmare Ken doll on display. Elise wondered if the cubs had eaten his balls and if he was still alive when they did. The wolves were gone, fleeing with the dawn.

She made her way through the deep snow, toward the old man's truck. A rusty plow blade was bolted to the front grill; the narrow-paved road behind it had been cleared. Elise followed it.

The old man hollered after her. "Miss. Stop! You need an ambulance!" Elise ignored him.

Her head pounded. Her first steps had reopened her scalp, warm blood trickling down her back. It would require four dozen staples. Frostbite had taken hold of her overnight. She would lose four fingers and six toes in the coming days. The wound on her cheek would become a deep, crimson scar, a haunting reminder tattooed on her face for the rest of her life.

Elise left the entrance to the cemetery, heading into the neighborhood. It was a post-apocalyptic scene, abandoned cars, toppled trees, downed powerlines. Dozens of neighbors, digging out with shovels and snow-blowers, stopped to stare at the blood-drenched girl weaving down their street, grinning maniacally.

Elise dropped to her knees in the middle of the road. An older couple rushed to her aid. They asked her questions, yelled for a neighbor to call 911.

Elise didn't hear them.

Something shiny blew by her feet, a candy bar wrapper. She watched it blow into a yard, underneath a porch. On the front steps, a row of three jack-o-lanterns stared back at her, half buried in the snow. One was carved with the face of a werewolf, grinning at her, its fangs long and sharp. Elise began to laugh, a shrieking cackle, rising from deep inside her.

She wasn't sure if she'd ever be able to stop.

STOMPER-SCREAMER

JASON A. WYCKOFF

I wanted to kill the little witch as soon as she stepped in the door. I know I shouldn't say that, but I want to be completely honest about everything.

And if I'm being honest, no, I didn't much care for the other girls, either. Thirteen-year-old girls are the *worst*. I know they're dealing with massive insecurities about their bodies, and their hormones are poking hot irons into the darkest corners of their anxieties, but damned if they haven't developed the perfect evolutionary response: they have a devastating ability to make any person, regardless of age, gender, or achievement, feel "uncool." Of course, that shouldn't bother me. A man of my age should be immune from such considerations. But they twist "uncoolness" like a kris into your soft white underbelly, and the more they hurt you, the more you crave their approval. Oh, you try to tell yourself that they're not laughing at you, because that would be the height of absurdity and narcissism. Why should they care about you at all? But that is another trick they play, making their giddy secrets seem naïve or innocent, when in truth they *are* laughing at you. It's bewildering how their opaque in-joke taunts and their badly stifled laughter can even sever the spine of a man who is father to one of their number.

I suppose much of my distaste with Madison—ugh, and the rest of her retinue, Hailey, Kaylee, Hannah, and Grace—had to do with my disappointment with my daughter's choice of friends. Neveah is an intelligent and, thank God, *strange* child. She should have strange friends—outsiders, freaks, smart and independent girls like her. But instead, I discovered she was trying to curry favor with the "in" crowd. As much as I might not want that life for her, I can understand her motivation. No matter how amazing a young lady she might appear in her father's eyes, she must still suffer those same insecurities and anxieties of her age. But what startled me, even more than the acceptance of the invitation, was the affable way the girls interacted. Madison didn't slouch petulantly like she was doing Neveah a favor. No, she seemed genuinely happy to be there. *That* was a shock. It meant my daughter didn't have weird friends at all; it meant she was *part* of the "in" crowd. Whom had I raised?

Oh, yes. There was another girl who stayed over. Big girl, quiet. Laura? Cara? I don't remember. And of course, the Nguyen twins, but their mother picked them up at eleven thirty sharp as promised.

As for the Queen Bee—imagine if they had heard me use that term!—it wasn't enough that Madison was the prettiest and most confident, whose pronouncements on celebrities whom I'd never heard of held the most sway, and who was always fastest with a retort laden with vernacular I could understand only enough of to feel bloodied by the barb; but to rub salt in the wound, her father was a successful producer! Of all the insults for me to bear, that was the worst. I know his product well: box office pabulum. Movies with five names credited for script rewrites that end up on the cutting room floor anyway, because the leads who command the biggest part of the budget decide they're "serious" enough about their craft to improvise themselves straight into gaping plot holes. If I had access to *his* kind of financing, I could create something of real substance. But of course, I will never see that sort of capital, because subtlety and real artistry go forever unappreciated.

I know my track record isn't stellar, but I've never had the right support. I've directed three movies. The first was an arthouse thriller called *The Fire Pit*. I wrote a clever script about a cop whose partner turns out to be the serial killer they're investigating—not bad for a first go, right?—and I had enough second unit work on my résumé to lock down what I *thought* was legitimate financing. The project was low-budget, but the finished product was good for what it was. Not that you can find a copy anywhere except the occasional punch-out DVD at a flea market. The production company collapsed and swallowed the rights amid allegations of money laundering. At least *The Fire Pit* brought me to the attention of the producers of *The Bog Beast II*. The Louisiana location shoot was hell, but I delivered on time and under budget. The first *Bog Beast* was exactly the craptacular man-in-a-suit drive-in fare you might expect. I delivered a sequel superior in every way, even down to the practical effects. I should have guessed my sober, atmospheric film wasn't what the producers wanted. Since they couldn't afford to reshoot (except to insert a scene in a strip club that didn't serve the story at all), they just cut up my vision into an eighty-minute monster romp. They added stingers onto inexplicable jump cuts to try to manufacture scares! Well, it made money, anyway. Enough that I got the third movie, one I didn't want, but which I took on because I had a family by then. *Camp Super Rock* flopped. But it was a big-budget flop, so it had notoriety—enough that I haven't worked since. The studio continues to re-sell streaming rights to try to make up the loss; the result of which is that it is the only movie of mine anyone, including Neveah's friends, have heard of. And if I didn't know already how "lame" they thought it was, Madison made it painfully clear when she entered my house repeating the film's unfortunate tagline, "Let's make this party heroic!"

Though I would never put it in those terms, I certainly didn't need Madison's encouragement to make my daughter's birthday party the best it could be. Neveah had had a hard year. Her mother died last November. She was driving along the bluffs above the quarry. She missed a tight turn. There were no skid marks, as though she hadn't even tried to stop the car. She punched through the guardrail and went over the cliff. The cops suspected it might have been suicide; luckily they called it an accident officially, otherwise we couldn't have claimed the insurance money. There were witnesses who saw her pounding on the windows as the car sank, so we know she was there. I mention this because when they pulled the car from the water, she wasn't in it. And though they dredged the quarry for two days, they never found my wife's body. I think that made saying goodbye even harder for Neveah. She didn't have closure. And to make it worse, she and her mom had begun arguing a lot right before the accident, so she couldn't resolve that, either. Poor girl.

As Neveah's birthday is October 30th, and as she is intelligent and strange and every bit her father's daughter, her birthday celebrations have always been Halloween-themed. This year, I decorated with the usual cotton cobwebs and plastic bats and things, severed limbs, and Styrofoam chains and such. In addition, I had been fortunate to recover several of Rip Steeger's wonderful creations for *Bog Beast II* from his estate following his untimely death in the spring (the result of an accident involving hot latex). I didn't have the Bog Beast suit itself, and I didn't really want it. Rip had made considerable improvements to the original costume—essentially an upright boar with claws and prominent forehead ridges—but there was only so much that he could do with it, and I had no attachment to that memento even if I knew where it was. No, what I had retrieved from Rip's studio space were several panels covered with Spanish moss and tufty lichen to which we attached thick, automated vines and bark "faces." They were quite eerie-looking and most of the controls were still functional: eyes lit up with red bulbs; vines twitched and coiled; mouths gaped in anguish. You see, my idea for *Bog Beast II* was that the bog itself was the root of the evil, and the lumbering beast was only its caretaker. I hung the panels on three walls of our sunken family room at the back of the house, where the girls would spend the night, and added the other touches to tie it all together. The girls ooh'd and ahh'd in appreciation. I think Laura or Cara was actually a little scared. I was happy I could show them I'd done more than just *Camp Super Rock*. Feeling proud, I expounded a bit on the creative origin of the effects and downplayed the missing rubber suit, explaining—just as any other horror aficionado will tell you—that it's often best to leave the creature *unseen* to maintain suspense.

At which Madison laughed.

"You find that funny?" I asked.

"Oh, I'm sorry," she said, clearly not sorry at all. "It's just that my dad says he hears that all the time in pitches and his response is always the same." She imitated an alpha male's voice: "'You know what's scarier than *not* showing the creature? *Anything!*'"

At which the girls *all* laughed, even my Neveah. The spell was broken. Even Laura or Cara stopped being bothered by the decorations. I left the robotics on, flashing eyes and twitching vines and all, but the props no longer held their interest. Flush with embarrassment, I muttered something about leaving them alone and did just that. At some point later I checked in on them and the panels were turned off. I expect it must have been Neveah who did it. Maybe Madison asked her to.

The reason I went to check on them was that it had gotten suspiciously quiet. Up until then it had been a screeching dance party, with only a brief respite when I was cajoled into buying far too much pizza. I remember hearing the latest single by that redhead guy—what's his name—like, six times, including twice in a row. Then I didn't hear anything. It must have been ten thirty or so; the Nguyen twins were still there. I peeked around the corner into the family room and all the lights were off. The girls were sitting in a circle and Hannah was holding a flashlight under her chin. Despite her sparkling bubblegum lip gloss and button nose, the streaking shadow effect still did its work as she whispered something I couldn't hear and then cried out, "In the back seat!" The girls screeched appreciatively.

I should have expected: they were scaring each other with spooky stories. Hannah passed the flashlight to her left, to Madison. But instead of commencing her tale, Madison flashed the cone of light to the entrance to the hallway where I was lurking. Hailey screamed, and then they all laughed. I apologized for frightening them and turned to go, but Madison stopped me.

"Come join us, Mr. Milton. We're telling ghost stories. And since you directed a horror movie, you should be able to tell us the *best* story."

It wasn't an invitation so much as a challenge—a challenge with an implied expectation of failure: "You *should* be able to tell us the best story."

Of course I decided she wouldn't get the better of me. If she wanted a scary story, I would oblige her.

They expanded their circle, and I sat. I snatched the proffered flashlight. I gazed around at the expectant faces of seven teenage girls and the dubious face of another...and as I gazed at Madison, my mind went blank. I had nothing. I sputtered, "Let me see...let me see..." but the delay tactic soon wore thin. All I could think of were bad creature costumes. So I told them the story of a nervous flier on a stormy flight who sees something on the wing. Yes, I regaled them with *Nightmare at 20,000 Feet*. Where does it say that my scary story had to be original just because I was an adult who made movies? Besides, I figured none of them knew it. But I could tell from Madison's half-smirk, that, yes, she was familiar with the old *Twilight Zone* episode. Of course she was.

I thought I told it well, though a faulty memory and translating from screen to speech might have hindered the impact, and Madison's damnable nonchalance flustered me. Perhaps the girls were taken aback by my enthusiastic performance, or perhaps because teenagers are always so wary of responding too earnestly lest they be labeled a "spaz," I received only polite applause at the end of my tale, such as that reserved for "honorable mention."

I reminded myself yet again that Neveah's was the only opinion I cared about, and I was ready to retreat to my den and lick my wounds, but then Madison chirped up, "My turn!" So I decided to see just what sort of story *she* thought might be scariest. I handed her the flashlight and waited. The other girls squirmed uncertainly, but Madison seemed to think nothing of it that I remained in their circle to be entertained.

Her features split the light from below into austere shadows. Her eyes twinkled with hidden knowledge. "Have any of you ever heard of the Stomper-Screamer?" she asked.

The whistle of anticipatory inhalation followed by stunned silence was clearly meant to indicate that no, none of them had heard of such a thing.

"I wish I never had. Because now I can't stand to be alone this time of year. Nobody knows where he comes from, but he shows up where it's *too* quiet. That's why there are so many Halloween parties. That's why kids make so much noise running around, getting candy." Her voice became more hushed. "The Stomper-Screamer walks the earth on the three nights of Halloween. In the middle of the night, when you can't get to sleep, do you ever hear the floor creak?"

Again, none of the girls answered, but I saw that Hailey and Kaylee and the Nguyen twins were both huddled into fearfully clutching pairs.

"Well, that's not him. Because *he* doesn't make any sound at all... at first. Because *he's* listening to hear someone listening for *him*. That's what draws him in. When you're awake too late, and you're tucked in tight with your covers up to your chins, trying not to make any sound, and scared, so scared, that you might hear something in the quiet...when everything is totally still..." She paused to lean forward ever so slightly, and then whispered, "That's when you hear him."

Suddenly she smacked the base of the flashlight against the floor and screamed.

Thunk! "AAAH!" *Thunk!* "AAAH!" *Thunk!* "AAAH!"

The flashlight's beam careened around the room with each blow. The third scream was inaudible under the responding chorus. And then the screams became fits of laughter and congratulatory cheers. Madison gave me a mocking look—*how did I do?*

I did not handle it well.

"That's not even a story!" I shouted. Everyone fell silent and stared at me. "There weren't any characters or plot! And 'the three nights of Halloween?' What does that even mean?"

"Dad!" Neveah whined. The sting of that word pronounced that way is a terrible thing to hear, because you know you've failed her. The worst thing a girl can do is to acknowledge her embarrassment, whatever the cause.

I looked at their blank faces, and I understood: they knew what the three nights of Halloween were, even if such a concept had never existed until five minutes before, and the only character they needed mentioned was the titular boogeyman. "You didn't even say what he looked like!" I added lamely.

Madison giggled. "But Mr. Milton—don't you know it's better to leave the creature unseen?"

And so she effortlessly diffused the tension in the room and eased Neveah's shame. Everyone laughed. And when I hurried away in a huff, the laughter trailing after me only grew louder.

I stormed out to the garage. I was unassailable in my sanctum. Perhaps I did not often take the tools from the shelves to use on my workbench, but I had selected and bought them and put them there. They were mine to use when I needed them. And the heavy, acrid, vanilla smell from half-used oil containers was a satisfying aroma. Centered against the back wall was the refrigerator where I kept my beer. I sat in a green and orange-striped folding chair, chugged one bottle start to finish, and then opened another.

After I'd downed the second, I saw lights pull into the drive, and

I remembered Mrs. Nguyen was coming for the twins. So I rushed back inside the house to answer the door. She must have smelled the beer on my breath, because she wrinkled up her face and poked a finger at me while she barked some kind of warning. Like I know Cambodian. I ignored it. I went and announced to the girls that it was time for the Nguyens to leave. No one looked at me—in fact they all seemed to be avoiding eye contact—but they acknowledged the message and the twins departed. I went back to the garage.

Fifteen minutes later, Neveah stood at the door.

"You embarrassed me," she said without preamble.

I started to apologize, but she held up a hand to stop me.

"You can make it up to me if you really want to."

I told her I'd do anything. Of course I would. She was all I had.

Neveah cast a glance in the direction of the refrigerator. "The other girls want to try beer."

Now, I try to be a responsible parent and set boundaries. So I opened my mouth to object, but again she stopped me, this time not by expressing disappointment, but by pleading for help.

"Please, Daddy? Just one beer each, that's all. *All* the girls want to do it."

Several things occurred to me simultaneously: If I allowed them to have their first beer in a safe environment, then I *was* being a responsible guardian. And at one beer each as per Neveah's request, the boundary was set. Plus, the likelihood of any of them not being so disgusted by the taste that they actually finished seemed scant. And most importantly, I'd redeem myself in my daughter's eyes.

I affected sternness as I agreed, "*One* beer each."

Neveah jumped and giggled. She ran over and hugged me and said, "Thanks, Daddy!"

I grabbed the depleted twelve-pack from the fridge and said, "I'd better open these in the kitchen." She tried to not appear over-eager when I brought in the beer and popped the tops. I handed four bottles to Neveah, who struggled to get her fingers around the necks. "Be careful," I advised. Then I held up two more bottles.

Indicating the left, I said, "This one will be yours." Then I held up the right and said, "And I'll give this one to Madison. I want to apologize to her." Neveah looked at me questioningly, but I told her, "You'd better pass those out before you drop them," and off she went.

I went into the family room and presented Madison with her beer. "This is for you," I said. "Sorry about earlier."

Madison grabbed the bottle as though its feel was quite familiar to her.

She smiled coyly. "That's okay, Mr. Milton," she said. "You're cool."

And so I learned that the only thing more hurtful than being told by a thirteen-year-old girl that you were uncool is being told you *are* cool when the sentiment is clearly not intended.

I went back to the kitchen and desultorily drank my beer. Neveah came in and looked at me with wide-eyed disbelief. It took me a second to realize what the problem was: I'd absconded with the bottle I'd meant to give her. I promptly opened another and handed it to her before I retreated once more to the garage.

I sat down in my chair again and looked around, wanting nothing more than for the night to be over, as I was starting to feel tired. I happened to gaze over at the dusty bench and weight set in the corner. And then I looked at the supplies on the shelves. And I came up with a wicked little idea. I would become the Stomper-Screamer. I would give them something they would remember forever. Anything Madison could do, I could do better; I could be scarier. I would bring her stupid little "story" to life!

I gathered six five-pound metal disks and put them on the workbench. I grabbed the duct tape off the shelf and fished out one of Neveah's old jump ropes from the "sports locker." I cut the handles off of the rope and threaded the disks. Normally, the weights would lock together on the bar, but I tied knots between them to keep them slightly separated on the line. I took my shoes off and I taped the top disks to the bottoms of my shoes. I didn't test them because

STOMPER-SCREAMER

I didn't want to give away the surprise, but I was sure my contraptions would have the desired effect. Of course, I couldn't wear the shoes walking into the house. I'd wait until later, when they'd all gone to sleep, and then I'd slip the shoes on when I got to the hallway. The "stompers" weren't pretty, but they didn't need to be. Satisfied that they would do the job, I sat back down and finished my beer while I waited.

I woke up to my daughter pummeling me on the chest and screaming, "How could you? How could you?" She called me a monster and said that she hated me.

I was groggy. I grabbed her wrists so that I could think. I pushed her away as I stood up from the chair. I was wobbly, so I took a step. My foot was heavy, and I nearly toppled forward. When my shoe came down I heard a loud, metallic *clunk!* and then I slid forward a few inches. I looked down. I was wearing the "stompers." And I slipped because I stepped in a smear of blood.

There were roundish tracks leading from the interior door.

Neveah was still screaming at me and crying. I sat down again and removed the jerry-rigged footwear. I know my heart was pounding and my extremities were tingling with adrenaline, but I was still trying to blink myself fully awake. Finally I stood and went to the door, careful not to step in blood. Neveah had stopped screaming, but she was still crying, watching me.

I told her, "Stay here."

I went inside the house and walked down the hall to the family room. I don't...I don't want to say what I saw. You saw it. You don't need me to describe the horror of what happened to those girls.

"What *happened* to those girls," growled Detective Randolph. "That ain't the way I'd put it."

"So that's the story, beginning to end." Detective Frohm raised a hand from the referenced manila folder in front of him and scratched at the stubble on his fleshy cheek. "Hey, Randolph. You're a bit of a movie buff, right?"

His partner answered, "Yeah, sure."

"Wouldn't you say that the 'interrogation room flashback' is a bit of a cliché?"

Randolph pushed off from the wall where he was leaning and stepped over toward the table where Frohm sat facing Milton. "I sure would, partner. Far too trite a device for an artiste like Mr. Milton to use."

Milton tried to wave his cuffed hands around the white-walled, green-tiled room, but the chains running through the table restricted his movement. "But we're not in a police interrogation room," he complained. "We're in a psychiatric hospital."

"A psychiatric hospital for the *criminally* insane," specified the bespectacled Dr. Harris, sitting in the corner and scrolling on his smartphone. His interjection was the first indication he was paying any attention to the proceedings.

Randolph lunged forward and slapped his large, tanned hand on the file in front of Frohm. Had it been any other interrogation, he would have opened the folder to spread out the crime scene photos in front of the accused to get a reaction, but he had no desire to gaze again at the carnage documented therein. "*This*," he said, "would have caused a hell of a racket. You expect us to believe you slept through it in a lawn chair—even four or five beers deep? Nuh-uh. I don't buy it."

Milton dipped his head and looked at his wrestling thumbs. "Well, it's possible...it's possible that I roofied myself."

"Come again?" Frohm asked.

Milton explained, "When Neveah asked for the beers, I saw an opportunity to embarrass Madison: what if she got shit-faced drunk off of one beer? She'd never live it down. So I put, like, less than half a roofie in her beer. Or at least, I thought it was her beer."

Randolph knocked back the sides of his jacket to put his hands on his hips. "Hold up: you're admitting that you tried to give a date-rape drug to a thirteen-year-old girl?"

"No! I would never do anything like that!" Milton protested. "I mean, yes, I tried to give her the drug, but I wanted to give her just enough that she'd act stupid and sloppy. I would never..." He shook his head, unwilling even to utter the word.

"Oh, so you draw the line at slaughter!" Randolph shouted.

"Easy, partner," Frohm advised without moving his gaze from Milton. Randolph cursed under his breath and turned to smack the wall.

Frohm asked, "So why exactly do you keep a supply of Rohypnol in your house?"

Milton winced. "I work in the entertainment industry," he said. "People give you pills and things all the time that you don't even want. I'm not sure what all I've got in my medicine cabinet."

Frohm chuckled and raised his eyebrows. "Well, I've never heard *that* excuse before," he said. "But even if *you* don't know what's in your medicine cabinet, *we* do. Because we would have searched it even if you hadn't—*allegedly*—dumped half of Grace Carson's body in the bathtub. Guess what we found in there? Haloperidol, an antipsychotic. And Fluoxetine, used to treat intermittent explosive behavior."

Milton shook his head. "I don't know how they got there. They're not mine."

"Maybe forgetting to take your meds made you forget whose name was on the prescriptions?" Randolph hissed.

Milton looked at him, confused. "That's not possible. I've never had prescriptions for those drugs."

Still locked onto his smartphone, Dr. Harris opined, "Sounds to me like he's building a defense."

Frohm snapped his fingers. "You're right, doc, it does sound like that, doesn't it? Like he's trying to make us think he was completely dissociative when he went on his rampage and that, even when he's cognizant, he's not aware he's sick. Pretty keen stuff, Milton. Maybe you do have a creative mind, after all." He leaned forward. "Ah, but there's two big problems with that scenario. Firstly, you've already described, in disturbing detail, your lurid hate and jealousy of young Madison Wiles. Goes to motive. Secondly, if you only roofied one beer, then *you* couldn't have been the one to drink it, because a test has already indicated traces of Rohypnol in your daughter's blood. *She* was the one you roofied—intentionally—to keep her out of the way while you massacred her friends. And *that* means planning and premeditation, and *that* makes what you did mass murder and not some extemporaneous, uncontrollable spate of violence."

"No!" Milton shouted. He jerked indignantly against his chains. "I didn't do it, I swear! I'm being...set up..." His voice faltered as the words left his mouth.

Randolph laughed bitterly. "By who? There's only one person left!"

"That's true," Frohm said. "So that must mean your thirteen-year-old daughter slaughtered her friends and pinned it on you—and made it to look like you took inspiration from her dead friend's story when you did it. Does that sound about right to you?"

"No, no, she wouldn't," Milton breathed to himself. "The 'evil innocent?' Not my girl. That would be beneath her."

"Is this psycho still focused on plot points?" Randolph howled.

"Could be the dead wife, back from the grave," Dr. Harris observed.

"Yeah, yeah, sure, could be," Frohm said. "I mean, Milton *swears* it wasn't him, and if it wasn't him and it wasn't his daughter, then who else could have killed those girls? A restless spirit, back for revenge? That's not bad. Makes you wonder exactly what happened with her 'accident,' doesn't it? Or maybe it was the effects guy; didn't he also die in an 'accident?'" He snapped his fingers again. "Unless of course, the Stomper-Screamer is *real*."

Milton sank back in his chair. He had to admit, it was better. A bit of a twist. But still unsatisfying. He looked up; they were all staring at him. "I wish I could believe that," he said.

STOMPER-SCREAMER

Milton's cot was bolted to the floor. There was a toilet and a sink of white ceramic streaked with brown stains against the back wall. Otherwise, his cell was empty. Light spilled from the hallway through the small, wire-checkered window set eye level in the door. The air was clammy and cool, though frustratingly not chilly enough to rebel against with a shiver. The springs under his lumpy mattress creaked in protest as Milton turned to face the narrow room. Wall-dulled shouts and cries from the other inmates, mostly unintelligible, peppered the drone of the fluorescents in the hall.

Sleep was impossible. That time the night before, Mrs. Nguyen would have been pulling into his driveway. It seemed like the event occurred in a different world with different rules; there were no rules in his world anymore; the unimaginable seemed possible—so that every possibility must be entertained. What had truly happened? Too many questions remained unanswered. A vague ending might have fit his aesthetic sense, but encountered in real life, he found it unendurable.

Milton's breath whistled lightly in and out of his nose. It was so very quiet in his cell.

So very suddenly quiet.

The other inmates had fallen silent to a man. Even the constant hum of the lights had faded. The world seemed frosted still. Milton was afraid to move lest he break the silence, lest he draw attention to himself...in case there was anything waiting in the too-quiet gloom to hear...perhaps just outside his door. He listened. He *stretched* his listening into the empty spaces, wondering: Was anything there? Was anything reaching back, searching its unknowable sense for a hushed, bed-laden soul stiff with apprehension, the too-awake wonderer plumbing the dark for what may lurk there, hidden, unguessed?

Thunk! "AAAH!" *Thunk!* "AAAH!" *Thunk!* "AAAH!"

The sounds were not staggered as Madison had performed them, but simultaneous. And the impact was not one of a girl hitting the floor with flashlight, and the scream was not a playfully scary screech. Each footfall reverberated through the cement and shook the bedsprings. Each scream was anger and agony, human and animal, predator demon and pleading captive giving and receiving pain in unison. Milton's body went rigid with fright. He did not want to raise his eyes to the small window, but the sway of shadows inexorably drew his gaze. From the cot, he couldn't see anything beyond the blot of a shape moving in and out of view. He did not want to, but he had to see. Every muscle trembled nearly to spasm; the hands he used to push himself to the end of the bed resisted his order to unclench. He rose uncertainly and staggered to the door. His knees refused to straighten of their own accord, so that he had to pull himself erect with his fingertips on the narrow ledge of the window. And he didn't want to, but he looked:

Thunk! "AAAH!" *Thunk!* "AAAH!"

Two couples danced to the infernal rhythm. Neveah was perched on Detective Frohm's toes and holding his hands, as a younger, smaller girl might, daddy-daughter style. They rocked slowly and gazed at each other's smiling faces. Randolph scowled and cursed; he was having a rougher time of it. Madison's mangled corpse, besides being limp, had several crushed joints, so that her body flopped like a hopelessly snarled marionette; her lifeless feet would not stay atop his, and the weight of her blood-matted hair pulled her face to the side, so that they could not share a loving gaze. Milton could not see was what was displayed on the screen of Dr. Harris's smartphone, which both enthralled and demonstrably aroused the doctor, and so did not know whether he was recording the dancers on video or staring at other recreation far removed from the present revelry. And the sight of the horror around which they lazily twirled gave cause to the origin of its stomps and screams by its very existence: an enormous, foul bulk of gray-fleshed limbs, human arms and legs, and extra arms and extra legs, twined with creepers and vines above bone-studded tree-stump hooves, each crash of which forced a horrid wail from the drowned woman's mouth and the burned man's half mouth and a piercing squeal from the malformed boar's head to which they were grafted.

Milton leaped back to his bed and spun to face the wall. He covered his shut eyes with his arms and matched scream for scream in equal measure, hopeful it might drive the creature back into the silence.

But the terrible stomping drew louder and closer, into his cell, next to his cot, and the screams bore into his head and echoed:

Thunk! "AAAH!"
Thunk! "AAAH!"
Thunk! "AAAH!"

THE NIGHT TRAIN

ALEXANDR BOND

I've never been one others would call brave. In fact, I was bullied heavily throughout my adolescence, being the butt of practical jokes, malicious pranks, and downright cruel scares. It was as though I had some invisible sign that read "easy target, come and get me." Frankly there were times when I wondered how I survived.

Because of this, I was usually in a constant state of anxiety, always looking out for that next attack. Some days were worse than others though. And the worst by far was Halloween since everyone in my small town decided to scare the living crap out of each other —especially those of us with anxiety issues. Six years ago, back in 2002, I was seventeen and trying to enjoy a quiet Halloween. Of course, I should have known such things were out of my reach. All I wanted was to listen to Nickelback and watch Charlie Brown. Instead, the power went out around eleven. I was the only one home—my parents and sister were out enjoying the evening. It took everything for me to head to the circuit breaker box in the basement and turn the lights back on. When I returned upstairs, I literally stumbled upon the mutilated remains of my family in the living room. Before I could even react, they lunged at me, nearly sending me to the emergency room. I hyperventilated while they laughed.

"Oh, it was just a joke," my mom said.

"Don't be such a baby," my dad added.

"You should have seen your face," my sister concluded.

So to say I'm not a big fan of Halloween is an understatement. Don't get me wrong, I'm not against every aspect of it; I just prefer the more cutesy parts, the animated specials or shows one would let a child watch.

Eventually I found my way to Tokyo about a year and a half ago. I grew to love the city, the people, and the culture. It was a chance to reinvent myself. Of course, you can't always run from your problems if you are one of them. Even so, I enjoyed myself and started to let my guard down. To make it all the better, Halloween wasn't treated the same way as it was in the States. And for that, I was grateful until Craig, one of my roommates, heard about the Halloween Train.

"We have to do it this year," he said as he heated up some miso soup. "It sounds awesome." If I ever had an image in my head of the perfect surfer dude, that was Craig. California-born, Hawaii-raised, he still held a tan upon his skin somehow despite spending most of his time indoors since coming to Japan.

"Will there be booze?" Marcy asked, yawning, her sandy blond hair still tangled from sleep. She usually worked nights, and when she didn't, she liked to drink. Some might use the term "functioning alcoholic."

"Totally," Craig said, then moved toward the table once his food was ready.

Marcy slunk beside him, draping an arm over his shoulder. "Sure." She plucked a piece of fried tofu from his bowl and popped it into her mouth.

I gritted my teeth as I looked up from my laptop. "I'm not really one for parties," I said. I hadn't truly confided my feelings toward Halloween or what I went through. It really didn't concern anyone else, and I didn't like to dwell on it.

"Come on, it will be totally fun and chill. Just a bunch of us good ole boys and gals dressing up and drinking." He slurped his food as he spoke.

"Who should we go as?" Marcy asked.

They discussed costumes until I left for work.

I didn't bring it up and hoped it would be forgotten. But like a bad penny, it came up twice more in the days leading toward Halloween. By the third time, when it was just Craig and me in the apartment, I admitted my apprehension toward the holiday and shared a minute example of why I disliked it: including the time my parents decided my babysitter should let me watch *Halloween* when I was seven.

"Dude, that is some harsh shit. But that's why you have to come with us."

"I just told you—" I started, but he interrupted me by clapping me on the back.

"My dude, you don't have to be scared. It's just a bunch of idiots getting drunk, listening to music while in silly costumes. Nothing serious or scary." He saw me hesitate and continued. "Just do the loop. One full rotation and then if you aren't having any fun, you can head home. No stress, no mess." He grinned at me.

Maybe it was the way he spoke, his voice always bereft of worry or seriousness, or perhaps it was the big dumb grin on his face. I didn't know but I finally agreed figuring I'd do as he suggested: stay an hour, then go.

How wrong I would be.

As Halloween approached, my anxiety rose, and I wanted to back out. The stress of having to get a costume and buy alcohol coupled with the fact what we were going to do wasn't strictly allowed made me regret the whole idea. That being said, I should mention I have an issue confronting others, especially when that deals with breaking arrangements. A therapist told me I have a fear of disappointing others. I knew that. What I needed was a way to get over it. That was never said, though. So while I didn't want to go, I didn't want to disappoint Craig, who was a decent guy when it came down to it.

I can't believe I'm doing this, I thought as I headed toward the crowded train station that Halloween. The Shinjuku Train Station was one of the busiest in all of Tokyo, a hub for travel throughout the central parts of the city with dozens of platforms and numerous sights to see. So many trains flowed through the station day in and day out, I wouldn't have been surprised if it was the busiest in the world. At least it seemed so to me. I used it twice a day, going to and coming from work. It was the life's blood of the city. I moved with the throng of commuters, trying to appear as though I wasn't in too much of a hurry. My heart pounded when I slowed to let an older Japanese man get ahead of me. *I know I'm going to get caught. How could I let Craig talk me into this?*

As I approached the way to the Yamanote Line, I stole a moment to catch my breath, slipping beside a kiosk display across from a ticket counter. The station was a veritable market of goods, snacks, and supplies while still containing the numerous trains and platforms that served the people of Tokyo. In some ways it reminded me of an airport.

As more people strode past me, mostly paying me no mind, I collected my thoughts. I hadn't celebrated Halloween in a long time, even before moving to Tokyo. I think I grew accustomed to the fact it wasn't so front and center here. It had been a moment's weakness to agree. I clutched my bag tighter. Inside was my laptop, a few snacks, some water, a bottle of whisky, and a Halloween mask. At that moment, I just wanted to head back to the apartment and watch *The Halloween Tree*.

Instead, I sighed and peered around before continuing my way toward the right platform. A female voice made announcements overhead, first in Japanese, then in English while soft music played here and there. I pulled out my cell phone and glanced at the last text from Craig giving me the details. It was just after seven p.m., and the party would begin soon on Train 24, car #10.

THE NIGHT TRAIN

Where are they? I wiped my brow and pulled at my collar. Despite the cool October evening outside, the train station was humid thanks to the crowd—or maybe it was just me. I hoped the inside wouldn't be too crammed. At its worst, we could be packed in there like sardines.

As the announcement of the upcoming train began again, I fumbled with my bag. I wasn't paying attention and bumped into an older Japanese man who was heading away from the Yamanote Line stairway. Startled, I dropped the bag. While I tried apologizing, my Japanese nowhere near proficient, I noticed the man looking down in my bag at the very visible Dracula mask. I could see the old man making the right connections as he glanced back toward the way he came, then at me. This was what I was worried about. Ever since Craig mentioned it, I knew it was a bad idea. The trains were sacred in Tokyo, and the *Gaijin* train on Halloween was deeply frowned upon if not outright despised by numerous people, including police officers and the railway's operators. There were even online forums where people complained about it bordering from idle displeasure to downright threats. From where I stood, I could see three officers standing at the base of the stairs keeping an eye out.

My heart thundered once more, the throb of it compressing my head. I snatched my bag and started down the stairs. The old man yelled after me, speaking quickly. Between the blood rushing through my ears and my lackluster mastery of the language, I only caught snippets of the man's words, equating to something about a night train. It made no sense. I didn't care. I descended quickly but stopped short when I reached the platform.

People swarmed around me. Salarymen, trendsetting women, and tired-looking commuters mingled with costumed figures, some wearing masks and robed in black while others were dressed as more recognizable characters from various anime and manga. Excitement filled the air, as did sweat and the slight scent of alcohol. A row of police officers lined the edge of the platform talking with one another while a few costumed commuters held professional-looking cameras, filming the whole event.

Honestly, the amount of people in costume surprised me. I stared at the police and clutched my bag. They didn't seem as bothered by the gathered revelers as I thought. From what I read online, it seemed like the police were out for blood. Maybe believing everything you read online was really a bad idea. More people moved past me, some of whom were dressed up. Most were foreigners like me, but I saw a handful of Japanese men and women, some wearing masks, hanging out beside the majority of the revelers.

A strong hand gripped my shoulder, and I nearly yelped.

"Sorry, dude," Craig said, his eyes wide before his face contorted into a big smile. "Look at all this." He gestured at the crowd. "Totally awesome, huh?"

"Totally," I said, though I didn't completely feel it. I looked Craig over. He wore cowboy attire, hat and fake brown mustache included. He gripped a beer bottle in his other hand.

"Where's your outfit?" Marcy asked from behind me. I turned to see her dressed as a very typical nurse in white with red accents. Her opened bottle of beer was half empty.

I pulled out the Dracula mask from my bag.

"Cute," she said in a way that indicated she thought the opposite. I ignored her and put it on. Two others stood beside her, a man and a woman, both Japanese and neither in a costume. They grinned as their eyes washed over the revelers dispersed through the crowd. Marcy glanced at the two, then blinked. "Oh yeah, this is Sora and Ayane. They work at the toy store across from the restaurant."

They offered a quick bow that I returned as I introduced myself.

"Come on," Craig said as he pulled me toward the edge of the platform, the others following behind. As we moved through the crowd, Craig explained to Sora and Ayane that another larger group had set the whole thing up and this group would merge with them eventually as they changed trains.

"I've never done this before, have you?" Ayane asked as she fell

THE NIGHT TRAIN

in step beside me, a smile on her angular face.

"Oh, no," I said and was about to add, "Halloween isn't really my thing," but decided against it.

"Last year the whole station shut down," Sora said. Like a coatrack, he stood out amongst us as the tallest. He said something under his breath in Japanese to Ayane, then brought out a small bottle of beer. She shook her head, and he shrugged before taking off the top. He glanced at the gathered police, hesitation in his dark eyes, before shrugging once more and taking a sip.

From what I gathered as we waited near the edge of the platform for the next train, the police were watching the group but not interfering. A buzz of anticipation grew as the moments ticked by. We wouldn't have to wait long. The transit system in Tokyo was quick, and dozens of trains were on the track at all times.

Cheers bellowed through the platform as the train roared along the tracks, coming to a gradual stop beside us. The gathered revelers waited for some of the commuters to disembark before heading inside. I watched a few hurry off the train, scowls upon their faces. An attractive Japanese man with jet-black hair and deep set eyes met my gaze, and I nearly blanched from his baleful expression. It was only in passing, but his look lingered with me as I hurried toward the door, slipping past the large advertisements and into car #10.

People crammed the benches while others gripped the handles that hung from above. More filed in, and soon we were wedged together like it was morning rush hour. Ayane, shorter than me by three inches, stood almost on my feet while Craig breathed down my neck. The group with the camera moved closer to the rear of the car, sweeping it back and forth as conversations filled the air like the buzz of locusts. The announcer from the PA system could just barely be heard over the din, and as the six doors closed, a cheer rose up, and the train began to move.

The Yamanote Line was divided into the outer circuit going clockwise and the inner circuit going counter-clockwise and cut a loop around central Tokyo, stopping every few minutes at each station. We were on the outer circuit, and it would take nearly an hour to make one complete rotation back to where we started. While we all worked in Shinjuku City, we lived closer to Ebisu to the south. My intent was to stay on the train until we reached that station, then get off.

Things rarely go as you plan them.

As the train made its way, Craig and Sora chatted while Marcy drank, twice spilling her beer on some random passerby. The first, a young German man dressed like the Phantom of the Opera, laughed heartily. The second, an uptight-looking Japanese woman in a navy blue pantsuit, glared daggers and beat a hasty exit once the train reached the next station. I kept my drinking to a minimum, mostly passing around the bottle of whisky I brought to whoever could grab it, which was a feat in itself. The revelers didn't seem to mind the crowded conditions as they shouted and laughed and chanted the names of the upcoming stations. There were twenty-nine stations so the thought of everyone chanting each's name was a bit grating.

Ayane wanted to know all about Halloween in America. She had never been, never left Tokyo aside from a trip to Okayama to visit family. I should have told her I was the last person to ask, but that would be confronting, wouldn't it? Plus, I found it difficult to resist her smile. It came easy to her, crinkling her cheeks and making her eyes squint.

"Well, a number of Halloween stuff comes from Europe," I said in answer to her question. "The only real American ideas I know of are the Headless Horseman and maybe razorblades in candy." I never ate much candy on Halloween because of that. My friend Hector swore his cousin cut his mouth on a blade in a candy bar when he was five. Not sure if I believe him, but why take the chance?

"I heard of that," she said, moving even closer so she could be heard over the multitudinous conversations around us. "We don't have things like that here but there are a lot of ghost stories. A few of my friends thought they saw the *Kuchisake-onna*." She made a slicing motion by the edges of her mouth. "And one time, when I was taking the train, I thought I heard the Teke Teke." The vibrations of her shiver rattled through me.

I didn't recognize the name, but I decided I wouldn't investigate. Japanese legends could get gruesome; between the plethora of ghosts and demons, it was not for the faint of heart, particularly mine.

By Tabata Station, more people disembarked and the car felt a bit less claustrophobic. I was able to extend my elbow a bit. Most of the people who stayed celebrated the evening with the other revelers and a general sense of amusement permeated the car. Craig and Ayane moved toward the group recording while Marcy acquired another bottle and Sora flirted with a girl from Toronto.

"Anata wo koroshitai, Gaijin," a voice whispered near me. I turned to see the attractive man from earlier. He stood a hair's breadth away, his eyes locked on me. His blank expression chilled me more than his previously malicious one.

"What?" I stammered. I didn't quite understand what he said.

He leaned closer. "I want to kill you."

I backed up quickly, bumping into Sora. He turned and looked from me to the man and asked what was going on in Japanese. I tried to explain, but my mouth didn't seem to work right. My heart felt like it sank into my liver, and beads of sweat, already present, began to dampen my palms further. Sora grabbed my shoulder to steady me and said something else I couldn't quite catch. Craig did, however, and came back, placing himself in front of me.

"Hey, bro, I think you need to back off." Though he said it in his usually polite way, I could hear an unfamiliar edge in his voice, though he didn't look as intimidating as he probably expected in his faux cowboy chaps and plastic hat. The man stood his ground for a few moments until the train began to slow as it closed upon the upcoming station. Then, once others started to come in, he shifted into the crowd but remained on the train. Craig and Sora drew me away toward the other side of the car where Ayane and a visibly drunk Marcy conversed with a couple from England.

Craig shoved a bottle in my hand, and I took off my mask to drink from it, wincing when I realized it was the whisky I brought and had passed around.

Marcy eyed me then spoke, her words an approximation of, "What's wrong with you?"

"One of those internet fools," Sora said.

"A few of the others mentioned some forum jockeys were out on the trains making threats. Looks like we got one here," Craig added.

The train started to move on and with it my desire to remain. As we moved to the next few stations, I felt the man's eyes upon me, lingering like smoke in the air. I tried to ignore him, to keep my attention on the others or on one of the various advertisements on the windows. Still, I sensed him there, his poison radiating through the car like burned coffee in a small room. The acrid touch of his presence brought back bad memories, spreading a bright light on the emotional stains I longed to cover up.

Suffice it to say, I was done for the night.

I lost sight of him by the time we reached Hamamatsuchō Station, but that didn't mean he wasn't on the train. It was still crowded, and the revelers seemed in no hurry to call it a day.

"Anyone hungry?" Craig asked as though he sensed my unease. "There's a Denny's near here." Ayane and Sora nodded in approval while Marcy just blinked while holding one of the handles. I suspected if she let go, she'd end up on the floor.

"Okay," I said. Food was second to my longing to be away from that man. As the train came to a halt, we got off. I paused to see if I could catch a glimpse of the little peeing monk, a favored statue in the station, but it was at the other end of the platform. Slightly disappointed, I followed the others, staying close to them.

Without warning, Marcy pulled away from the crowd. We paused and shared a look before hurrying after her. She staggered toward the nearest bathroom, barreling inside. The four of us stood outside, an awkwardness encircling us. The sound of vomiting, though muffled, wafted toward us, and I frowned at Craig, who sighed. Sora and Ayane wore uncomfortable expressions. After a few minutes, the retching passed, but Marcy didn't come out.

"Could you check on her?" Craig asked Ayane, who offered a stiff smile before heading into the bathroom.

As we waited, I noticed something strange. A stillness had crept along my skin, an itch like spiders' legs climbing up the wrist. I shook my hands thinking that was the issue but soon started to move from one foot to the other, this nagging sense of restlessness entangling itself around me. I peered at the others. Craig had taken off his hat and clutched it in his hands, repeatedly clenching and unclenching it. Sora poured over a few of the advertisements near the men's bathroom, moving from one to the other but seeming like he didn't see them at all. I recognized the feeling: a general anxiety invaded the air. We waited for something but what? At first, I thought it was the girls, but the hair along my arms and the growing lump in my throat made me think otherwise.

"What is taking them so long?" Craig asked, his voice lacking its usual nonchalance. As he spoke, his words almost echoed, and it hit me. The heaviness in the air was silence. I strained to listen, but there were no sounds of motion. The rumble of the trains, even quiet as they were compared to others of their ilk, could usually still be heard throughout the station. *Where are the people?* I looked around. The area was deserted. No revelers, no commuters, no police. Even the lights flickered. A cold stab of trepidation lanced down my spine and filled my stomach. It was unheard of.

"Hey, do you..." I started, but my words felt weightless. As I paused, I heard the sound of soft tapping. It came from the walkway that would eventually take us to the street. It reminded me of the noise a cane made when striking the floor, yet the tone seemed different, a hollow echo and much too quick to be a person walking.

Craig knocked on the bathroom door. "You guys all right?"

I heard a muffled reply, but my attention lingered on the tapping sound. Louder and closer, *tap*, *tap*, *tap*. Old memories of pranks gone by resurfaced, and with them the old feelings bubbled up like searing tar, coating my brain. The time Jenny Banks locked me in the old shed at camp; when my sister put a real snake in my bed; and how I fainted when Carlos García and his friends dressed like monsters and chased me through the woods during my fourth grade field trip. Those dreadful feelings saturated my skin, increasing with each tap.

The door to the bathroom opened, and Ayane led a very ill-looking Marcy out, her sandy hair a disheveled mess.

"I'm fine," Marcy said, the slur in her voice barely present. I paid them no mind. I couldn't move. My heart pounded in rhythm to the quickening taps.

"You okay?" Ayane's words brought me out of my panic enough to face her. She started to say more when her eyes looked past me, toward the direction of the tapping. She made a questioning sound, and I followed her gaze. A shadow appeared from around a corner. The tapping was louder now, closer. Ayane jerked. I knew she heard it. She shot me a perplexed look, but I recognized in her eyes what I felt. The sound touched on something primal, a reptilian fear. *We shouldn't be here.* I started to grab Ayane when the shadow crossed the corner and a figure appeared.

I pulled her away as the figure approached. The flickering lights kept them shrouded until they were only ten feet away when they stepped forward beneath bright illumination. I'm not sure what I was expecting, but I was almost happy to see the man from earlier. Ayane relaxed in my grasp as well. When the feeling passed, the realization of who stood before us in a strangely desolate section of the Hamamatsuchō Station reared up, and a new anxiety stole my ligaments.

Sora yelled at the man and moved toward him. Craig remained beside Marcy, who hung upon him like ivy on a wall. The man yelled back, his countenance contorting his attractive features into something grotesque. The change startled me, how quickly it occurred. From what I could discern, Sora told him to get lost while he was berating Sora for going along with the *Gaijin*. They said a number of phrases I wasn't familiar with. I could tell by the expression on Ayane's face what they uttered was quite unbecoming. The situation grew tenser as Sora closed the distance, looming over the man. Craig tried to move closer, but Marcy held him back—whether it was on purpose or not, I couldn't say.

"Just leave us alone, bro. We're tired of your harsh vibes!" Craig said, his tone laced with exasperation. This only served to ramp up the shouting match to a tide of anger between the three of them. Within the waves of shouting, my attention drew to that tapping sound again. It came in the small silences between their words, and with every tap, it grew louder. I looked for its source, and my gaze settled on where the man had come from.

A few things happened very quickly. Craig and Marcy gave a yell of surprise as Sora staggered away from the man, his hands clutching his stomach. I turned to see the attractive man brandishing a knife, its blade slick with Sora's blood. His humorless eyes moved from Sora to the rest of us, settling on me. He looked deranged. I should have been terrified. All night he had been fixated on me for no apparent reason. He threatened me; he just stabbed Sora. Yet that tapping sound still rang in the air and movement behind the man drew my focus.

I stared dumbly. I had to be seeing things. Ten feet behind him crept a woman, her age indeterminate due to her long black hair covering part of her face. She wore a white blouse stained with old blood. She crawled on her hands, a long staff in one, seemingly helping her move. The rest of her was gone. Where her waist ended, a bloody stump remained. Pieces of her torn clothes and flesh dragged behind her along with part of her spine, the source of the tapping sound.

"What the fuck?" I muttered. It had to be a trick, some

extremely detailed Halloween costume. But if that was the case, why did I feel such terror in my chest?

The others didn't see her at first. Sora had backed up to Craig, who put himself between him and the deranged man. Ayane darted toward Sora while Marcy was fumbling in her purse. She finally pulled out her cell and started to dial. I watched her eyes fall to the girl and knew I wasn't seeing things. Marcy froze, her head tilted like a dog's. Sora mumbled something and pointed at her then, his blood dripping from his hand. Ayane was next, and I saw her pale as her brown eyes went wide. The last was Craig and the man. Craig appeared more confused by her presence, still keeping his attention on Sora's assailant while the man peered over his shoulder, then turned to face her.

He shouted at her, his disdain evident. She closed the distance between them quickly. I blinked, and she was only three feet from him. He swung at her with his knife. For a moment I thought he cut her face. His movement ruffled her hair, revealing bloodshot eyes and a young face. She glared up at him, then lifted her staff. Only then did I realize it was actually a scythe. The blade, stained brown, still glinted in the flickering lights. That silence came back, but it only lasted a moment as she swung.

I finally understood how something could be so quick and yet excruciatingly slow. Her scythe tore through the man's torso as though he was no more dense than wheat in a field. Blood splattered outward, peppering Craig, who back-peddled away. The man stood there, unmoving. Then, with a strange sucking sound, he began to slide backward. I had the oddest image of an egg dripping down the side of a wall as I watched his upper body plop on the station floor, his lower half following a few seconds later.

Someone screamed. It might have been me. It broke me out of my horror. I dropped my bag and raced to Ayane. Grabbing her, I shouted at Craig to move. Thankfully, it didn't take much convincing. Between me and Ayane, we dragged Sora and started to run, Craig and Marcy right behind.

We dashed back the way we came, meeting no resistance as there seemed to be no one else in the entire station. Behind us, the tapping resumed, spurring us on. As we headed down toward the nearest platform, Marcy let out a shout and pointed at a waiting train. We veered to it as the tapping grew louder and closer. No one waited before us as we darted toward the nearest car and slipped inside. We set Sora on one of the benches.

"Shit, she's coming!" Marcy cried.

I turned to see and wished I hadn't. She crawled on her hands, the scythe still in her grip as her protruding spine rapped upon the hard ground, the rhythmic approach of death. There would be no escape if she got inside. I had no trouble believing she could swing that scythe in here. We were past the point of rational thought.

Ayane sobbed what sounded like some prayer in Japanese while Craig slapped the doors, yelling for them to close. Someone must have heard him for just as she was almost upon us, the doors snapped shut so quickly they could have taken a person's hand off. Craig jerked back from the force of it. The train started to move, and we watched the girl linger at the platform for a moment before she turned and crawled away.

I wish that was the end of our troubles. It wasn't.

Craig watched from the window for a few moments, then turned to Sora. "We need to get him to a hospital," he said as he took off his cowboy vest and held it to Sora's wound. The man had stabbed him in the abdomen.

Marcy pulled up her cell and started looking for the nearest hospital. "I'm not getting any service. Are you kidding me?!" She let loose a flurry of curses. She glanced at me. "What about yours?" I blinked at her, her words not registering until she gave a guttural growl. I pulled out my phone, but she snatched it from my hand. "Yours isn't getting anything either." She tossed it roughly, and I hurried to pick it up.

"Do you know where the hospital is?" Craig asked Ayane. She still muttered to herself in Japanese until he seized her.

"She was real." Her voice was low, almost a whisper. "Teke Teke. That was her." He shook her, wanting an answer. She peered up, finally seeing him. "Near Tamachi Station."

As Craig began talking to Sora, I finally looked around, taking in the train. Where a normal car was beige with green striping denoting it as part of the Yamanote Line, the walls here were dark with no striping at all. Only four doors lined the car along with another door at the front and rear, a means to move from one car to the other. We were in Car #4, and aside from us, it was empty. To make matters worse, we were going the wrong way.

"This is the inner circle," I said. I had to repeat myself to get their attention.

"What?" both Craig and Marcy exclaimed.

Sora let out a slight laugh that ended in a groan.

Ayane spoke quickly in Japanese, switching to English halfway through. "We can get off at Shimbashi then."

It wouldn't be long. The trains were always so fast. *A few minutes. Not even.* And yet as the train hurdled down the tracks, the wheels screaming, I felt no lurch signaling it would decelerate. I moved toward the window. We should be stopping; instead, we hurried past Shimbashi.

"What is the conductor doing?" Craig shouted.

Marcy moved toward Car #3, perhaps heading to the conductor's car; I wasn't sure as I still stood at the window trying to contemplate what I just saw. In that brief moment we passed the station, dozens of people stood on the platform, with their backs to the train. It didn't make sense. None of this made sense. But the longer I looked out, the more I felt an icy ball of panic form in my gut. The city looked wrong. Even in the late evening as it was, Tokyo would have bright lights, neon glows, and flashing advertisements. I turned to the opposite window. Heavy shadows and flickering firelight painted more traditional Japanese architecture, the kind found more commonly in Kyoto.

Before I could consider what it meant, the train started to slow as we neared Yūrakuchō Station.

"Finally," Craig said. "Come back!" he called at Marcy, who had nearly reached car #1.

We pulled into the station, and I stared at the platform, confusion becoming revulsion. Flame-lit lanterns shed a sickening orange light, spreading deep shadows, though it wasn't enough to hide the horror. Bodies littered the ground outside the train, most a mishmash of bones and limbs. Hanging beside the lanterns were ribcages, the meat long since stripped away. They swung in the breeze, a keening rattle emanating from them. I tried to rationalize this. It had to be a terrible Halloween prank. But some awful instinct laughed at me, laughed as it pleaded with me to run. I started to turn but froze as the doors opened and the smell from the outside flowed in. We gagged, all of us, as it rose up and slid down our throats, the malodourous scent of burned flesh and rotted meat. If I had eaten, I would have vomited right then. Sora moaned while Ayane covered her face with both hands.

Craig began shouting then. He yelled for Marcy to hurry. I stood closer to where car #4 met car #3 and looked up to see her, but more importantly to see what lumbered behind her. The image came in pieces: soot-stained skin, segmented arms, yellow eyes rimmed with red, and a bone-white mask with tusks and horns. It reminded me of an oni from an anime I saw years ago. But those were just stories.

I stood transfixed. Marcy glanced behind her, let out a scream, and ran. It pursued her, keeping pace despite its size. A chortling shriek exuded from it. Marcy threw out her hand for someone to grab, for me to grab. I heard Craig shouting and Marcy screaming, but I couldn't move. The monster gained on her, and I knew it would catch her. Then it would get the rest of us.

I did the only thing I could: I shut the door and locked it.

The monster grabbed her by the waist when she was five feet away, its insect-like arm, its flesh more akin to chitin, gleaming in the low light as it wrapped around her and yanked her back. I stood frozen, watching, when something strong grabbed me and shoved me hard into the wall of the train. I slammed my shoulder and slid to the floor. The pain reverberated through me, mingling with the rumbling of the tracks. Craig pounded on the door, looking through the small window. He was about to open it when Ayane flung her arms around him and tried to pull him away.

She yelled, her words lost in the screams that sprang from the other car. Marcy's cries split my heart. I shut my eyes and covered my ears, hoping that would make a difference. It didn't. They echoed around me, but after what seemed like forever, they began to recede until only quiet weeping remained. I looked up. Craig had his hands on the door, head bowed. Sobs racked his body. Ayane still clung to him, but after a few minutes, she finally released him and stepped away. I got to my feet and moved toward him.

"Craig," I started, but the rest was lost in a flash as he whirled around and smashed his fist into the side of my face. I crumbled into a bench. My head spun. I tasted blood. Between my shoulder and my jaw, my left side ached.

"Why did you do that? She could have made it!" Craig's voice bellowed through the car.

"I...It was coming..." My words were swallowed by Craig's anger. He screamed at me. I had never heard him like this. Ayane backed away from the door and from Craig as I shrank onto the bench. Heat coursed through my cheeks. His words dredged up older nightmares and wretched experiences, and a part of me wished I had just left the door open.

Craig continued his tirade for a few moments more until Sora finally yelled at him to shut up. In the sudden hush, he added, "I'm sorry. But she was not going to make it." Sora's voice came in shallow gasps toward the end. Craig glared at him then at me before walking to the other side of the car. Ayane danced out of his way, then returned to Sora, speaking to him softly.

It took me a bit to recover. When I did, I moved closer to Sora and Ayane. "How is he?" I asked her.

She gave me a grave look.

"We should be passing Tokyo Station soon. Maybe we can get off there."

Sora shook his head. "We just passed it." I had to strain to hear him. I glanced out one of the windows and saw he was right. At least it seemed so. The skyscrapers were in the same places, but the style was completely different than what I was used to. Like looking into the past, the buildings displayed sloping roofs and curved eaves with lanterns hanging from them. I could have easily imagined it was a normal moment if not for the bodies dangling beneath the lanterns. My gaze moved past them onto the silhouette of a figure in the distance. My lips quivered. Some things shouldn't be seen. Some things couldn't be understood. The figure in the distance moved slowly, slipping between the buildings as one would step between dense trees. Despite its humanoid shape, its sheer enormity baffled me.

I turned away from the window.

A choking fit seized Sora, and when he finally settled, crimson stained his teeth. He wouldn't last much longer. But the train didn't show any sign of stopping. I didn't know what to do. I checked my phone again. Sora's laugh startled Ayane and me.

"It...won't...work." He clutched Craig's vest to his wound.

"Why?" Craig asked as he strode over. "Do you know what is going on?"

Sora shook his head, then spoke softly in Japanese. Ayane looked shocked, responding back in kind. She kept saying, "It can't be," over and over until Craig gripped her arm and she peered up at him. She shot a look back at Sora before she spoke. "He thinks we aren't in Tokyo anymore. Not the one we know."

The implications, like an avalanche, careened down the slope of my mind. The Teke Teke, the strangeness of the station, this train, all of it was connected, though when did we stumble away from the world we knew? I didn't know. *Could it have happened as we waited for*

Marcy or when she slipped from the group and we followed? And how? Was it Halloween? The thinning of the veil as the old stories claimed? Too many questions exploded in my brain. Like the snapping of a twig, my objections to what I had been seeing fell away. It was the only thing that made sense. How it happened didn't matter. Only one thing did.

"How do we get back?" The others turned to me, even Sora, who looked as pale as that monster's mask. Both Ayane and Craig started to open their mouths, but Sora spoke first.

"I...don't...know."

His words were more of an effort, and with sickening certainty, it hit me we were watching him die—slow but eventual.

The train lurched. I grabbed on to Craig to steady me. He shook me off, and I nearly fell to my knees. Ayane looked out one of the windows and gave a soft cry. Before I could ask what she saw, a guttural voice filled the air. Disembodied and harsh, the voice spoke in Japanese, the words almost dripping with malice. It took me a moment to realize it was an announcement. It informed us that we were at the Ikebukuro Station, and it kept mentioning the phrase "yakō ressha" or Night Train. I didn't have time to process that meaning. The train slammed to a halt. The side doors opened, and with them another fetid smell oozed inside, more burned flesh but this time mixed with the pungent aroma of death. A black, scaled claw gripped the threshold of one of the side doors, then a bone white face appeared as the monster stepped inside.

Ayane screamed before backing away. Craig grabbed Sora and started for car #5. I hurried to catch up, falling in line with Craig to help him with the injured man. Ayane reached the other door and opened it. In the back of my head, I thought the monster could just slip out and cut us off. It didn't, though. We were nearly to the door when we were dragged back, the sudden momentum sending Craig and me to the ground. The monster lifted Sora away from us.

I looked. I shouldn't have. He screamed and kicked. He seemed so small then. The monster drew him to its face. I thought it was a mask. Then its lips parted. Opening wider and wider, it became a gaping maw. Inside were pieces of torn flesh, chipped bone, and teeth beyond count. Between two incisors, I caught a glimpse of familiar sandy-blond hair. Ayane wailed behind me. I sensed Craig move. I remained on the floor, mesmerized. Sora struggled, his wound raining blood. It cascaded into the monster's open mouth before it arched its neck and swallowed Sora whole.

I heard screams slither out of its closing mouth, then a series of loud crunches. It turned its head toward me and let loose a hacking laugh. My thighs dampened, a distinct smell emanating around me. I didn't care. I turned and crawled toward the door, finally getting to my feet. Craig stood in the threshold. He peered at me, a strange look on his face. I knew then what he would do. I shook my head as I sped toward the door. His hand lingered on the door's edge. I could almost hear his muscles tighten. I screamed, my words gibberish. I shut my eyes. I couldn't bear to see his face any longer.

I rammed into something and once more hit ground. Only then did I open my eyes to find Ayane entangled with me. I got up slowly and turned to see Craig shutting the door behind me and locking it. The train rocked and began moving again. In the door's window, the monster gazed at us with those yellow eyes.

Craig, panting, turned to face us, shame like a shadow crossing his face. He wouldn't meet my eyes. He knew I knew. I didn't say anything. What could I have said?

He took a breath, then spoke. "Now what do we do?"

Ayane shook her head, her arms wrapped around herself. She blinked rapidly, her eyes already puffy from the tears. I wanted to comfort her. I wanted to change my pants. I wanted to be home. And I wished I had never gone out. Halloween and I don't mix. Nothing good has ever come from it.

An ear-piercing sound ripped through the car, and we all flinched as we clasped our heads. I looked for the source and found it quickly. The monster scratched at the glass. It grinned, and a muffled laugh rattled the door.

"He's fucking with us!" Craig said and moved closer to it. "Come on! What are you waiting for?"

"Don't!" Ayane and I said together.

"I'm not stupid," he said back at us but kept his eyes on the monster. It continued to smile at Craig, its too-big eyes filled with mirth.

"What is it?" I asked Ayane. She frowned and backed away from the door, moving closer to the next car. I followed.

"It's not an *onryō* like Teke Teke. I think it's a demon, an oni."

I had the same thought. Craig and the monster continued their staring contest. I suppressed the shivers, both from the situation and the coolness in the car. We passed Ikebukuro. Shinjuku would be soon. *Could we try to get off there? And if we did, could we find our way back to our world?*

"Have you ever heard of something called the Night Train?"

Her face twisted up. I could almost see her thinking. She whispered something in Japanese, then instinctively gripped one of the handles above her as the train swayed a bit. I grabbed onto a nearby bench. "There are *yūrei-kikansha*, ghost trains..." She shook her head. "I don't know if that is this. I don't know all the stories. My brother is into all of that." She glanced up at Craig. "Leave it alone!" she pleaded.

Craig eyed the monster for a few more moments, then turned away, moving over toward us as the train lurched again. I could feel the deceleration. I shot a glance at the monster, the oni. It moved away from the door. *It's getting ready to slip around once the doors open.* The thought chilled me.

"We need to move," I said. They followed my gaze toward where the oni had been, and I could see they came to the same conclusion I did. That disembodied voice filled the air yet again just as the train slammed to a halt. As soon as the doors opened, we fled car #5 for car #6, then skidded to a stop. People funneled into the car, rapidly filling the space. A stink of death circled them, as did flies, the buzz of which grew louder with every addition. They reminded me of the group I saw earlier with their backs turned to the train. I saw them clearly now and nearly dry heaved. For some, the flesh sloughed off in places only to hang like rancid stalactites; for others, they bore eyeless faces and broken bones. They didn't speak, only continued to step into the car, filling it like sand fills an hourglass.

Craig turned to lock the door behind us just as the oni stepped into the car we were just in. It banged against the door angrily, then hurried out one of the side doors.

"Move!" Craig yelled.

The stench assaulted us as we fought our way through. The mangled commuters kept coming, shoving us back and forth. We had only gone a few feet and already we were separated. I reached for the others, but a woman missing a jaw, her tongue lolling up and down as she moved, blocked my way, forcing me to dance around her. They seemed to not notice us at all. I tried to understand what they were doing, but none of this made sense. The farther we went, the stranger the mangled commuters looked. I passed a few that appeared as though they just got off work while those beyond them wore kimonos and armor. A finely dressed woman, her skin heavily burned, brandished a bladed pole. A young man missing half his face carried a sword, unsheathed. When the man turned, the blade sliced into the commuter beside him. Dark red blood seeped onto the floor, making it slick. It was like some twisted mockery of the *Gaijin* Train, a gruesome Halloween party.

I nearly slipped on the wet floor and had to clutch one of the commuters to steady myself. I lost track of the others. I peered around. The doors slammed shut, dismembering a few of the commuters who hadn't quite made it into the car. Blood pooled where their bodies fell, though they were quickly swallowed by the crowd. Movement caught my eye. One of the commuters back the way we came flew into the wall as something large with a bone-white face tried to force its way through.

"It's coming!" I screamed and started shoving my way past the commuters. The train pitched, and I fell into a colorfully robed man holding a dagger. Pain erupted in my side. I didn't have time to dwell on it. Bodies flew behind me as the oni grunted his approach. I felt a hand grab me, and I nearly elbowed Ayane in the face. She bore a slash across her forehead that bled down her nose. Darker blood covered her hands and pants. Wordlessly, we pushed toward the door, ducking past two arrow-ridden samurai before finally reaching car #7.

"Did you see Craig?"

"We got knocked down. I lost him as I crawled." A solemn note clung to her words, a finality she didn't elaborate on but was plain to see. Nevertheless, I peered back, scanning the group for him. The oni still barreled toward us, but I saw no sign of Craig. I shouted his name but got no reply. "He's coming!" Ayane said as the oni crushed a thin commuter in front of it.

I glanced around frantically. The oni drew closer but started to slow as the commuters were now a tangled mass of limbs. It let out a roar that nearly split my head.

"I think it's stuck," I said.

The oni muttered to itself, its words a rumble I couldn't discern, but its eyes blazed with fury. I called for Craig but still heard nothing, saw no indication he lived. My side burned, and I finally stole a glance at it. The cut was small and only a tiny bit of blood eked out, staining my shirt. It could have been far worse, though moving did cause it to hurt.

"What do we do?" I didn't want to close the door. The mangled commuters made no effort to move to this car, and the oni had stopped trying for the time being. But leaving it open was a big risk. The look on Ayane's face told me she had no real answer.

I left the door open but stood beside it, ready to shut it if I had to.

As the train hurdled down the tracks, we passed more ancient buildings and horrid displays. I saw that large figure in the distance again and quickly averted my eyes. We careened by a number of stations without halting, and I had to wonder if there was any rhyme or reason to where the train stopped. *Could such thoughts even apply here? Why didn't the oni cut off our escape? Why didn't the Teke Teke catch us? She was fast enough.* These thoughts occupied me as the train made its way.

"If we can get off at Hamamatsuchō Station, do you think we can get out of here?" Ayane asked when we passed Ebisu Station, her voice low, almost seemingly afraid to speak the words.

I considered for a moment, then sighed. "I think it's our only chance." I peered back at the door and the car beyond. The commuters were so tightly wrapped together, the oni couldn't move. It stood silent, its eyes set on us. It licked its lips, its black tongue on white skin. I shuddered, and it smiled. I shifted my gaze, looking for any sign of Craig and finding none. Thoughts of Marcy and Sora floated in my head, and I wanted to sob. A hand fell upon my shoulder, and I flinched. Ayane looked at me, her face a cemetery. I leaned my head on hers, avoiding her gash. We remained like that for a little bit as the train passed three more stations.

As Shinagawa came and went, I thought we were home free. Only Tamachi was left before Hamamatsuchō Station. Then, as if fate wanted to prove me wrong, the voice of the announcer bellowed around us and the train began to slow. There was no station here, not between Shinagawa and Tamachi, yet the train was heading for a stop. I turned to the still-open door, and the oni grinned at me. Ayane and I shared a look, then she darted over and shut the door. The train stopped, and we watched as some of the mangled commuters began to exit the train, some actually crawling on their hands and knees.

We didn't wait. We dashed to car #8 and shut the door behind us, then continued to #9, wanting to put as much distance between it and us. But as we reached #9, we skidded to a halt. Though set up like all the other cars, this one was occupied by more oni. Some were small, others barely fitting within the compartment. They had their backs to us, their attention centered on the people hanging from the handles in the ceiling. Grotesque and violent, the people in car #9 were being tortured. The oni cackled and sang as they flayed and burned their victims, relishing the atrocities they committed. It was like a game, a twisted Halloween game. Perhaps that explained the Teke Teke and bone-faced oni's actions; they hunted for sport.

Ultimately, their motivations didn't matter as Ayane and I backed away, still unseen by the occupants within car #9 just as the side doors shut and the train resumed its trek. My side still burned as I lowered myself beneath one of the benches; Ayane followed suit. My eyes lingered on the vile oni, but I could only stomach looking at them in bits; their actions repulsed me on a fundamental level.

The screams of the tortured remained with us as the train continued and only drowned out when the announcer's voice tore through the air. We pulled ourselves up and peered out of one of the windows. Hamamatsuchō Station inched closer. Ayane gave a shriek, and I turned in time to see a spidery oni looking right at us. Its segmented jaw opened in a squeal, and it charged. We didn't wait. I trailed Ayane as she sped for the door back to car #7. She flung the door open, and we raced through before we shut it behind us.

A guttural laugh sliced through the air as I was jerked upward by my leg. Upside down, I screamed as the bone-faced oni lifted me up. Its jaw began to open. Endless rows of teeth greeted me. Rotted meat and ash wafted up as his bark-like black tongue licked my face, taking bits of skin with it. The train shifted then, the motion saving me as I swung away from the oni's snapping maw. As the train decelerated to a stop, I swung back toward my imminent death.

A blade punched through the oni's side, splattering me with its brackish blood. It dropped me hard. Ayane grabbed me and helped me up. I spied a familiar face. Craig, wielding that bladed pole and bleeding from numerous wounds, thrust at the oni once more.

"Go!" he shouted.

I wanted to ask how he survived and if he heard us talking about a way out, but there was no time. The side doors were open. We started for the nearest one and were almost there when Ayane yelped. The spidery oni had grabbed her arm. Without thinking, I charged at it, and with every ounce of might I had, I rammed into it. It staggered back and let her go. I pulled her away and headed for the door. Craig still kept the bone-faced oni busy, but I doubted he would last much longer. I shouted for him to get out as I stepped through the door. Ayane was right behind me when the spider oni grabbed her leg. She kicked it hard in the face. She reached out to me, and I grasped her arm and started to pull her toward me.

The doors snapped shut.

I fell back onto the hard station floor. I still held Ayane's hand. I looked up to see her face in the door's window, shock and horror twisting her features before the train pulled away. I shook violently and dropped her hand. I crawled away from it, gasping for breath. I didn't watch where I was going. I only knew I had to get away from it, from that train. I climbed up to my feet and ran blindly until I crashed into something hard. I started to fall when hands grabbed me. A blank white face stared at me. I screamed and thrashed wildly.

"Whoa, easy buddy!" a masculine voice said. The figure quickly lifted their mask to reveal a scruffy tanned face with big brown eyes. "Didn't mean to scare you."

Breathing hard, I looked around. Dozens of people stared at me, some in costume while most were just evening commuters. An outer circuit train roared beside the platform, and the commuters made their way to it. The tanned man offered a grin. "Do you know where the Halloween train is? Did we miss it?" I didn't answer. I sped past him as fast as I could.

An inquiry was eventually made into the disappearances of Sora, Craig, Marcy, and Ayane, but no one ever found anything. What happened to her hand, I couldn't say. Of myself, I don't leave my apartment much anymore. I tried to take a train—not the Yamanote—but I could have sworn I saw Ayane's face in a window's reflection. Now I stay home most nights and always on Halloween.

WITCH HUNT
DAVID ANTHONY

Karla Weston's head flew up at the sound of screeching tires, heart hammering, her hand going immediately to the grip of the pistol on her belt. The black sedan came flying down the long road leading from the entry checkpoint like a demon escaping hell, spun around the corner, and screeched to a halt mere feet from her. Two men got out. They were big men, dressed head-to-toe in black, with pistols dangling from their thick belts. The driver hid behind a black hood with a sinister white skull emblazoned on it, his partner behind a red grinning devil. Red Devil went around and opened the back door of the car, ushering someone out.

The girl couldn't have been more than eighteen or nineteen. She had a rebel air about her with a black leather jacket hanging over her tight shirt and torn jeans, her fair skin contrasting sharply with long, raven-black hair. Her nose was pierced, and she had on far too much makeup. Her hands were cuffed behind her, but Red Devil still pulled out his pistol and shoved it into the small of her back, putting a hand on her shoulder as he guided her over toward Karla.

"Evening, Weston," White Skull said as they approached. "Been busy tonight?"

"Like every Halloween. You'd think people would know how to obey curfew by now."

"What? And take away all our fun?" Red Devil said. "Who'd want that?"

I would, Karla thought but didn't say. She'd love nothing more than for Halloween to be boring again, the worst things on their agenda being to bust drunk drivers or break up high school parties gone too far. Not this. This wasn't what she signed up for the police force to do.

"Ah shit, not another one." Karla's partner, Jimmy Kilpatrick, stepped up beside her, eyeing the girl and shaking his head. Jimmy was a shorter, skinnier version of the other two, but his mask was a green goblin with a drunken grin. Karla's own mask was a mouthless china doll with a cracked skull. "I don't know how much more of this I can take."

White Skull sneered at him. "Stop being such a pussy, Kilpatrick. You'll take as much of it as you have to because it's *your job*, and it's what we have to do to keep people safe."

"That doesn't mean we have to like it," Karla said.

"Nothing wrong with enjoying your job a little," Red Devil countered.

"No, I guess not...if you're a sick, fucking sadist, Kowalski."

"What the fuck ever," White Skull—Edgar Valdez—said to her. "Rules are rules and this bitch fits the profile. Take a look."

Karla crossed her arms as she appraised the girl. "What evidence do you have?"

"Glad you asked." Karla couldn't actually see the smile on Kowalski's face through the grinning devil mask, but she could hear it in his voice. "First, there's the obvious: she's female, she's out on Halloween Night, and she's got the tattoos. Here, let me show you." Kowalski pulled out his survival knife and began cutting away the girl's clothes. She protested and tried to pull away, but Valdez stepped in to hold her.

Karla was suddenly angry. "You don't have to take all her clothes off!"

"It's no problem, really." There was perverse glee in Kowalski's voice.

When the girl was fully naked, they held her still, allowing everyone to see her tattoos. She had quite a few: a green-and-black dragon wrapped around her left arm in a spiral pattern, spewing orange flames up toward her neck; an elaborate black-and-gray skull on her right leg; and a series of small stars over her shaved pubic region. She had Chinese writing on her left thigh and a smattering of other symbols here and there that could have been tribal or some other type of design Karla had no knowledge of. But she knew what the others were thinking: they could be occult symbols.

They could be used in witchcraft.

Karla didn't believe in witchcraft herself, had never seen any evidence of its existence, but after what happened six years ago they no longer took chances, especially on Halloween, a night when dark spirits were said to walk among them and the potential for magic was at its highest.

The night the massacre happened.

"This one was of particular interest to us." Valdez pointed out a tattoo just below and between the girl's modest breasts: a sinister-looking creature with the head of a goat and body of a man, seated cross-legged, with a circle made up of symbols surrounding it. "Looks pretty fucking satanic to me."

"It's not!" the girl protested. "It's from the cover of a heavy metal album. Please, you have to believe me. I'm not a witch!"

"We don't have to do shit," Valdez said. "We're in charge here—not you!"

"Ease up, Valdez," Karla hissed. Her blood was starting to boil. "Stop holding her so tight! Didn't you listen to any hardcore music when you were a kid or get stupid tattoos you later regretted? People are still innocent until proven guilty. This doesn't prove anything."

"No? How about this one?" They spun her around, and Karla sucked in a shocked breath. On the girl's back, etched in eerie crimson ink, was an upside-down star with a circle around it, a symbol known by all to be involved in witchcraft. "Believe us now?"

They turned her back around, and Karla stood there, studying her for a moment. The girl was obviously terrified, her green eyes swimming with tears. She reminded Karla of herself in her teenage years, rebellious and naïve, willing to do anything to piss off her police officer father and gain his attention. Karla still had a few tattoos of her own to that effect, along with foolishly gained scars, regrets, and a barely dodged minor-in-possession charge. But all of that attitude and recklessness had vanished when her father had been shot and killed on a routine traffic stop. That's when her life had turned serious. This girl's was about to.

Karla pulled off her mask. The others let out startled gasps and murmured admonishments, reminding her their spells get much nastier and much more targeted once they'd seen your face, but Karla ignored them. "What's your name?"

The girl sniffed back a tear. "Hannah."

"Hannah, do you understand why this is so serious? Why everyone is so afraid?"

"I think so. It's because of what happened a few years ago. Because of the massacre."

"That's right. Six years ago, a group of self-proclaimed witches announced their presence to the world by murdering six hundred and sixty-six people at very large, very public parties on Halloween Night, all across the country, supposedly using spells. There have been witchcraft-related killings every year since. Now, everyone is afraid of this night, and very suspicious of anyone out on it, especially women with occult tattoos like yours. That's why we have a curfew. What were you doing out tonight?"

The girl shrugged. "I snuck out to meet my friends. We were going—" She stopped, glanced back nervously at the other officers, and then sighed. "We were going to a party. I know there's a curfew, but not everybody's afraid. People still have parties. And there's going to be a big one tonight."

"A party?" Kowalski said. "Where? Who's throwing it?"

The girl shrugged again. "I can't tell you that."

Karla frowned at her. "Why not?"

"My friends wouldn't like it."

Karla's frown deepened. Clearly, she wasn't getting through to this girl. "Hannah, I don't think you understand what's going on here. You're being arrested on suspicion of *witchcraft*. That's a serious crime. The penalty, if you're convicted, is death."

Hannah's eyes became hard and defiant. "So what? What are you gonna do, pig? Burn me at the stake? Go ahead and try! I dare you!" She spat in Karla's face.

Karla reeled back a step, wiping the spit from her cheek. She couldn't believe what had just happened! Here she was trying to help this girl, trying to save her life, and she just spat in her face? What the hell was wrong with her?

"That's it," Kowalski said. "Happy fun time is over. Time for your party to get started." Suddenly, he and Valdez were ushering Hannah off toward the back of the parking lot. The girl thrashed and screamed and shouted curses at them as they hauled her away.

Alarm exploded through Karla, like someone had injected red-hot molten lava into her veins. "What the hell are you guys doing? You need to take her to booking!"

"Not tonight, we don't. Lucky witch gets a free pass straight to the big show."

"You can't do this!" Karla grabbed at Kowalski's shoulder, but he yanked free. "Everyone deserves a fair trial, regardless of their crime! You can't just make an accusation against someone and assume their guilt! That's not how justice in this country is supposed to work!"

"Special circumstances," Valdez replied. "We're talking about national security here."

Karla looked to Jimmy Kilpatrick for help.

"Guys, she's right," he said timidly. "This girl needs to go inside. She deserves a trial."

"Shut the fuck up, pussy," Valdez said.

Jimmy just shrugged at Karla, his green goblin mask looking helpless and stupid.

She turned and dashed back up toward the building where she found Olivia Wang exiting one of the side doors.

"What's with all the shouting?" Olivia asked.

"Olivia! Go inside and grab the chief! Valdez and Kowalski just picked up a teenage girl, and they're taking her straight out to the stakes to burn her as a witch!"

The younger officer seemed confused. "Is she one?"

"That's the point—we don't know! She hasn't even been tried yet!"

Olivia started to turn back toward the building but then stopped, hesitating.

"Go!" Karla said firmly. "Now!"

Olivia spun and disappeared back inside the building.

Karla sprinted across the darkened parking lot to catch up with the others, her ponytail coming loose and stray wisps of long blond hair spilling out across her face and into her eyes. She brushed a strand back as she gazed out at the horrific scene before her.

Where the blacktop of the parking lot ended, the execution grounds began. It was bare earth from there all the way back to the twelve-foot-high chain-link fence that surrounded the property, topped with razor-sharp rolls of barbed wire. Three thick, ten-foot-high metal poles had been erected in the dirt field. They were permanent structures, well-used, charred, and covered with ash. A small fire still blazed at the foot of one of them, the dying flames licking lazily at the blackened skeleton affixed to the pole with iron manacles and ankle clamps. The pole in the center had a fresh pile of wood and debris beneath it. The air around them was clogged with smoke.

To one side of the field, an iron cage had been constructed, and four naked, heavily tattooed women were trapped inside, screaming and pleading for mercy from their captors. The youngest of them was a striking redhead in her late twenties with large breasts and pierced nipples, the oldest a stern-faced, dark-haired woman somewhere in her fifties. The older woman was the only one not crying out. She stood rigid, impassive, staring down anyone who dared lock eyes with her. There was something cruel about her, Karla thought, something dangerous. Karla didn't believe any of them were truly witches, just women who'd had the wrong tattoos and made enemies with the wrong people in the days leading up to Halloween and found themselves accused and quickly convicted of witchcraft by a fearful, superstitious public. She couldn't save any of them, but Hannah hadn't been convicted yet, and Karla was damn well not going to let her burn until she had been.

A large, muscular black man was throwing the last few scraps of wood onto the pile at the base of the center stake. Officer Elijah King was an intimidating sight. Standing nearly seven feet tall, shirtless, and sweating in the heat from the flames, clad in black pants, long black gloves, and a sinister black hood, he took on the appearance of a medieval executioner, exuding the silent menace and soullessness of his role. Karla knew that wasn't who he really was. Most days Elijah was easygoing, a family man and dedicated police officer. But this time of year he became brooding and reserved, no doubt thinking about how his aging parents had been murdered by witches at a Halloween dinner party six years ago today.

He unlocked the iron cage with a key off his belt and swung open the door. There were shrieks of terror from inside. A skinny, light-skinned black girl with long hair and a tattoo of a snarling demon on her right thigh screamed as she tripped and fell in her attempt to get away, then scrambled to the back of the cage on hands and knees. The older woman didn't move. Elijah almost reached for her, but something in her cruel eyes made him hesitate, and instead his massive hands gripped the forearm of the pretty redhead, pulling her out and slamming the door.

"Elijah!" Karla shouted. He turned at the commotion behind him, saw the officers approaching with their new prisoner. "This girl hasn't been tried yet. You can't burn her!"

"The hell you can't," Valdez responded. "You know the new rules just as well as we do, King." He looked at Karla. "We've had some serious threats tonight. There's a lot at risk, and we can't take chances. They all have to burn."

Karla turned back to the big executioner. "Elijah, you can't do this. Not to her, not until she has a fair trial. Everybody deserves that, regardless of the risk. You have to see that."

Elijah looked from Karla to Valdez and then back, and his eyes hardened. "I don't make the rules here. I just enforce them. And in this case, I agree with them. What if this girl is a witch? She looks the part. What if we do nothing and she uses her power to murder innocent people? Then that blood is on us. No, Valdez is right: they all have to burn. And *she* goes next." He turned, dismissing them, and dragged the redhead the rest of the way to her stake.

Karla's heart sank. This wasn't the way it was supposed to work. She had become a police officer to protect people and uphold the law, and that meant accused criminals had to be given a fair trial and convicted by a jury of their peers before sentences were handed down. Maybe Hannah was a witch and maybe she wasn't, but that was for the jury to decide, based on hard evidence—*not them*. She watched as Elijah easily lifted the screaming redhead up onto the stake, strapping her arms and legs into those merciless metal clamps, and then backed away.

Valdez approached the redhead, his eyes roaming up and down her naked body, taking in the patch of red pubic hair and her large breasts with their pink, pierced nipples, and he shook his head. "What a waste." He hooked a pinkie through the ring protruding from her right nipple. "Won't be needing this anymore, will you?" He yanked it out, and she grunted in pain.

"Stop it, you asshole!" Karla yelled at him. "Just leave her alone."

He threw up his hands, feigning innocence. "What's it matter?

She's going to be one barbequed bitch in a couple of minutes anyway. Might as well recycle these."

"Oh, it matters." The voice belonged to the older, dark-haired woman inside the cage. She hadn't moved from her spot and was staring at Valdez with her cruel eyes. "Violence matters, spitefulness matters. How a person dies and the hatred emanating from her killers matters. To us. You are filled with hatred, Officer Valdez. And we will use it to kill you."

He locked eyes with her for several long seconds, challenging her, but then his resolve wavered and he looked away with a nervous laugh. "Whatever, lady. You're gonna be toast in a few minutes too, so keep on running your mouth while you still can."

"The name isn't lady."

"Don't care. Your name means shit to me." He turned to Elijah. "It's getting cold out here. I need some heat on my face! Let's light this redhead bitch up!"

The air was thick with tension as Elijah lit a torch and started applying it to the brush and wood stacked under the redheaded woman. She thrashed wildly and pulled at her restraints as she pleaded for mercy, tears streaming down her face. The flames grew quickly, lapping at her naked feet and legs, and she thrashed harder, jerking furiously against her bonds. But the metal clamps held tight, and her skin began to blister and blacken, her screams turning into high-pitched shrieks of agony. Her pubic patch began to smoke and then caught fire, as did her long red hair, the flames quickly eating their way to her scalp. Her large breasts split open in several places, and the fat steamed and sizzled as it rolled down her body in scalding rivulets. The horrid smell of burning meat permeated the air. It took nearly ten minutes for her to lose consciousness.

And then the chanting began.

All eyes turned to the older woman inside the cage. Her eyes were closed and lips moving, uttering words in another language, repeating them over and over. Karla had a roommate in college who'd taken several Latin classes, and she recognized the sound of the language, though not the meaning of the words. But something about them made her skin crawl. The thin black girl stood up and joined the chorus, as did the other woman in the cage—a blonde with long hair and one side of her head shaved, and sinister symbols tattooed on the shaved patch.

Valdez was visibly disturbed by the chanting. "Shut up!" he yelled, pounding on the bars of the cage with his nightstick. When that failed to achieve results, he turned to Kowalski. "Fuck it. Let's light this one up too. Take her cuffs off. We'll burn 'em all right now!"

To Karla's shock and horror, Hannah took up the chant as they removed her cuffs. Her freed right hand immediately went to her privates, and she appeared to be masturbating, a twisted grin on her face as they ushered her toward the stake that was to be hers.

Karla felt like she was in some kind of nightmare. Fear drove an icy, skeletal fist inside her chest as her heartrate jackhammered, her brow breaking out in cold sweat. The sky above them seemed to darken, the obscene chanting increasing in volume, becoming more forceful, more hateful, and the flames roasting the corpse of the charred witch grew wilder, leaping and dancing with unrestrained hunger. Something was happening, Karla thought.

Something terrible.

Everything seemed to happen at once after that. Karla heard shouts from behind her and turned to see Olivia Wang and Chief Goodwin headed in her direction. The pair stopped mid-stride as the roaring engine of a large vehicle could be heard screaming down the road from the entry checkpoint. A huge black truck came into view, its front end equipped with a savage-looking ram designed to resemble the jagged teeth of a beast. The truck crashed through the gate arm at the checkpoint and kept on coming, rocketing down the road toward the station.

Karla pulled her pistol, preparing for a fight, but suddenly there was a whoosh of flames and she felt intense heat on the nape of her neck. Someone behind her screamed. She turned to find the fire raging out of control, the blackened skeleton of the redhead barely discernable beneath it. Elijah had gotten caught in the blaze, and his clothes and skin were now aflame. He stumbled backward, swatting at the flames. He succeeded at putting them out, but in doing so, his bare back collided with the metal cage, and the older woman seized him from behind. She dug her long fingers into his eyes, driving them deep into his sockets, causing thick streams of blood to come oozing out. His screams grew hysterical.

"Let him go, you bitch!" Karla aimed her pistol at the woman, but she couldn't get a clear shot. She tried to maneuver around, but the crazy witch kept Elijah positioned between them.

Valdez also had his weapon drawn, but he didn't hold back. He fired off three quick shots, but the woman used Elijah as a human shield, and the bullets dug into his burned chest, opening up bloody holes. Elijah jerked twice and then slumped in her grasp.

Out of the corner of her eye, Karla sensed movement. She glanced over just in time to see a flash of metal between Hannah's naked thighs. She had only a fraction of a second to take in the flickering orange firelight reflecting off the metal of the switchblade the young woman had just pulled from inside herself and snapped open before Hannah drove the weapon deep into Valdez's neck, sending out a thick crimson geyser.

This time Karla didn't hesitate. She raised her weapon and put a bullet through the side of Hannah's head, sending gore and chunks of brain matter spraying out the other side as the girl's body spun a graceless pirouette and flopped to the ground. There was a loud clank of metal, and the door of the cage swung open.

The older witch emerged from within, stepping over the corpse of Elijah King, her cruel eyes fixed on Valdez. He lay on the dirt with a hand clamped to his neck, trying in vain to stay the flow of blood. "You should care about names, Officer Valdez. Mine is Carmela Schwartz, and I am the leader of this coven." She nodded, and the blonde with the shaved patch in her hair stepped forward, retrieved Hannah's fallen blade, and began stabbing Valdez repeatedly in the stomach and groin. He let loose a high-pitched scream as he tried to fight her off.

Kowalski shouted and tried to raise his pistol, but Carmela Schwartz uttered a simple command in Latin, and the flames leaped wildly, reaching out and scorching the officer's arms and hands, causing him to scream and drop the weapon.

Shots rang out from behind them. Several cops had emerged from the building and were engaged in a shootout with four black-robed, masked assailants that had exited the truck. Their figures said these assailants were female, and they carried semi-automatic pistols and rifles and were using the truck for cover. Another vehicle—this one a black SUV—screamed through the checkpoint and down the road, passing the stopped truck and heading in Karla's direction.

Jimmy Kilpatrick grabbed Karla roughly by the arm. "We need to get inside. Now!"

She glanced back over her shoulder at Carmela and her two coven sisters. The blonde had a struggling Kowalski in her grasp and was stabbing him over and over in the chest with Hannah's knife. The skinny black girl had somehow opened Valdez's chest and pulled out his heart and was using his blood to draw a circle around Elijah King's corpse. Carmela Schwartz locked eyes with Karla and began walking steadily and defiantly toward her.

Panic ignited inside Karla, and she felt her bladder partially let loose, warm urine running down her legs. Jimmy screamed something in her ear, and the two took off running toward the station. The chief shouted something that Karla couldn't even begin to comprehend in her current state, and then he and Olivia Wang joined them in their retreat.

Before they entered the side door of the building, Karla took one last look at the battlefield the station grounds had become. All of the other officers had been killed, the two vehicles converged on the execution site, and the robed and masked witches had joined the others by the fire. They stood around Elijah King's body, chanting a spell in Latin.

A hand fell onto Karla's shoulder, and someone shouted in her ear, but she couldn't tear her eyes away. The chanting voices reached a fever pitch as the flames leaped high into the darkened sky, and then something happened Karla couldn't believe, couldn't understand.

Elijah King sat up.

The empty sockets beneath that executioner's hood seemed to lock onto hers, smoke rising from his scorched and bloodied chest, as he slowly rose to his feet. Karla spun around in a terrified daze, hurrying inside the building and slamming the door behind her.

Inside the bullpen, confusion reigned. The power had inexplicably gone out, all the lights and computers refusing to work, and their vision was reduced to the illumination they received from several flashlights that produced strangely dim beams, as if all their batteries were going out at the same time. Someone reached for a desk phone, swore, and slammed it down. Someone else tried their cell phone and reported no signal. Someone else reported the same. Karla could barely focus on any of it. She kept seeing Elijah King rising from the ground, like a vampire pushing open its coffin at sunset, hungry for blood.

Hungry for hers.

"The witches did this." Jimmy Kilpatrick yanked off his goblin mask and slammed it down onto a desk. "They cut off the power, our cell phone reception. They're shutting us off from the outside world, making sure we can't call out for help."

"Jimmy, do you actually have to work to figure out the dumbest thing to say in any given situation, or does it come naturally to you?" This came from Betsy Fisher, the smart-ass twenty-one-year-old blonde who worked down in Records. Karla wondered what she was doing here so late but then saw that Kyle Hart was here and remembered he was working graveyard tonight in Dispatch. Karla glanced at the young blonde's smeared lipstick and wondered idly if she'd been keeping Kyle company by sucking his dick while he was supposed to be working again.

"You weren't out there," Jimmy replied defensively. "You didn't see the things they could do. They're...powerful."

Betsy rolled her eyes. "Listen, Limp Dick. All of that spell-casting crap is made-up Halloween bullshit. They can't really cast spells. If the power's out, it's because they cut some wires or blew some fuses or something. They didn't cast an evil blackout spell on us."

"Stop calling me that. It was just that one time, and I was on medication—"

"Whatever."

"—and I *was* out there tonight. I saw them make flames leap out at us. I felt something in the air when they were chanting. And I saw them kill King and Valdez and—"

"Wait, King's dead?" Kyle said. "What the hell?"

"Was dead," Karla corrected. "He's not anymore."

"I don't know if that's true," Olivia chimed in. "I mean, did anybody check his pulse? Do we know he was really dead?"

"I saw him take three to the chest," Jimmy said. "After that bitch gouged his eyes out!"

"That doesn't necessarily mean—"

"I *know* he was dead," Karla said. "I didn't have to check his fucking pulse. And that thing that got up...that wasn't Elijah. Not anymore."

"That's enough," Chief Goodwin called out, reentering the room from his office. "We're in some deep shit here. We can't get ahold of any of the officers in the field, so we're on our own. We need to lock this place down right now and hold out until end of shift."

End of shift. That meant morning. Karla didn't think they'd survive that long. But the chief was right; they couldn't depend on outside assistance. If help did arrive, it would most likely be single cars of officers arriving to bring in prisoners, and the returning officers would immediately be engulfed in this communication black hole with the rest of them and probably killed. No, they couldn't rely on help coming. They needed to find a way to do this on their own.

Glass shattered in the hallway.

Everyone froze. The sound was quickly followed up by a harsh crunching of metal and a metallic banging. It was impossible to see from here, but Karla knew that the door to the east parking lot had just been smashed open. Her heartrate took off, beating at a frantic pace, as she slid her pistol from its holster. She tensed, ready for what she knew was coming. Heavy footfalls thumped slowly down the hallway, and a huge shadow appeared in the bullpen doorway.

Elijah King's massive frame filled up the entire entryway. He stood deathly still, and Karla watched his chest, hoping to see it rising and falling, but he didn't appear to be breathing. She felt his gaze burning on her, although he no longer had eyes. Hatred radiated off him, a cold and merciless energy he'd never possessed until now. His right arm was raised and a long metal pole protruded from it into the room with them. She couldn't see the other end—the one slung over his shoulder. It disappeared into the shadows behind him.

"King! You're alive!" Kyle Hart hopped off the desk he was seated on and approached the big man, a grin pulling at the corners of his mouth. "These dumb shits thought you were dead. I told 'em no way some wannabe witches could ever take you..." His grin faded as he took in the bullet holes in Elijah's bare chest, the blood, the gore-filled eye sockets. "Oh shit."

The blade of the axe was larger than any Karla had ever seen, surely too heavy for any mortal man to wield. But Elijah King was apparently no longer mortal, and when he brought the weapon down on top of Kyle's head, it easily cleaved it in half, continuing on down and splitting his torso in two, stopping at his waist, like a tree struck open by lightning during a violent thunderstorm. Karla's face and chest were sprayed with a tidal wave of hot, sticky blood, which got in her eyes and soaked her shirt. She heard hysterical, terrified screams all around her and after a long, surreal moment realized one of the people screaming was her.

She frantically wiped blood from her eyes using her shirtsleeves and looked up in time to see the Executioner entering the room. Kyle's corpse must be a rubber movie prop covered in cow's blood as King put a huge, booted foot on it and yanked the weapon free. It had to be. This couldn't be real, she kept telling herself. It had to be a terrible dream. Karla heard shots being fired off, saw Olivia Wang standing just a few feet away from the thing that was once Elijah King, rapidly pulling the trigger of her .45. More holes sprouted in the Executioner's chest, but the black sludge that sprayed out could hardly be called blood, and the bullets failed to even slow him down. He swung the gigantic axe in a swift, horizontal motion, and Olivia Wang's head sailed across the bullpen to bounce off the far wall and thud down onto the floor.

People were running from the room now, screaming in terror as they scattered and tried to escape deeper inside the building. But Karla couldn't move. She was frozen in place, her heart pounding like a runaway freight train. The big man swung his axe again, and a male arm came sliding across the tile floor toward her, leaving a slick trail of blood. The chief's arm still clutched his pistol as it came to a stop at Karla's feet. She stared at it, uncomprehending, heart pounding furiously, until she heard heavy footsteps coming in her direction.

Elijah King raised the massive weapon over his head, preparing to bring it down on Karla and cleave her open like he had Kyle. But at the last second, she came to her senses, diving out of the way as the weapon clanged to the floor, dropping and rolling down one of the aisles between cubicles. She popped up and fired off several shots, opening more holes in King's arms and torso. He responded by swinging the axe again, taking off the tops of two cubicles and sending monitors, phones, and office supplies spraying across the floor.

She couldn't stop him this way. Bullets were useless against him. Instead, she dashed up the adjacent aisle and out the bullpen, heading down the hallway toward the briefing room. She needed to find somewhere to hide, to stay safe until morning. But she had a terrible feeling this thing that was once her friend wouldn't stop until she was dead.

Karla spent several long, harrowing hours in hiding, moving from location to location within the empty building, trying to stay quiet and move stealthily whenever she'd heard those heavy footfalls coming near. Once, she'd heard the sound of an approaching vehicle outside the station. She'd quickly found a window overlooking the parking lot, banged on it, and screamed hysterically. The officers couldn't hear her, but the Executioner did. She'd heard his heavy footfalls in the hallway and immediately took off, the screams of the officers as they stepped out of their vehicle and were butchered by the waiting witches chasing her back into hiding. The witches themselves never entered the station. Karla couldn't understand it. The undead Executioner prowled these darkened hallways, searching for her, but his creators never entered the building, never attacked her.

At least, not yet.

Now, she crept from her hiding spot in one of the upstairs offices and peered out the window. She could see them down there in the parking lot, all clad now in black robes and hoods. Several of them stood in a circle near the iron cage their sisters had been held captive in, still chanting. Karla wondered if that chanting was the cause of the ongoing communications blackout...or what kept the dead man walking through her station hallways.

A loud screech of static made Karla nearly jump right out of her work pants. She gazed up at the public announcement speakers as Carmela Schwartz's voice drifted down to her.

"Are you still alive in there? I know you are. I can feel your presence, your life force. Would you like to stay that way? You have something I want. Our sister that you burned earlier this evening, the one with the pretty red hair, her name was Taylor O'Shea. Taylor had some personal artifacts that you confiscated upon her arrest. I want them. Bring them to the door at the east parking lot and your lives will be spared. Fail to do so, and my pet will end his cat-and-mouse game and simply tear you to pieces. You have one hour. I suggest you hurry."

Static echoed from the speakers again, and then silence fell.

Taylor O'Shea. The redhead. Karla recalled Valdez and Kowalski bringing her in earlier this week. Her things should still be here. She needed to find them. Fast.

Karla crept silently through the darkened hallways to the property room, down near the holding cells. She paused outside the doorway and clicked the safety off her pistol. Someone was already inside, the door unlocked and standing ajar. She heard rustling around and boxes being moved. She peeked inside but couldn't see past the tall metal racks and the boxes stacked on them. She moved inside, maneuvering around until she had a clear line of sight.

"Freeze!"

Jimmy Kilpatrick let out a startled gasp, dropped his knife, and stumbled back from his crouch to land hard on his butt. "Oww... damn it, Karla. What'd you do that for? You know there's a maniac out there, right? You can't just go sneaking up on people."

She lowered her weapon. "Maybe you should be more aware of your surroundings and you wouldn't get snuck up—"

"*Hey!*"

This time they both let out little shrieks of surprise. Karla raised her pistol, and Jimmy fumbled in his holster for his, pulling and dropping it, but their efforts were wasted.

Betsy glared at them, arms crossed. Her eyes were red and her face stained with tear-streaked mascara. "You guys going to shoot me now? Not enough people already dead tonight?"

Jimmy took a deep breath. "Holy shit. You people have got to stop doing that. I'm going to have a heart attack."

"Good for you, Limp Dick. So are we gonna get Tiffany O'Twat's stuff and give it to Psycho Queen so they can get the hell out of here already or what?"

Karla holstered her weapon. "Maybe. Let's see what it is first."

Jimmy picked up his knife and finished slicing open the box. Inside were the clothes Taylor had been picked up in: a crimson, low-cut blouse, a pair of jeans, a black bra, and panties so small they were hardly more than a thin strip of fabric. There was a black bag that Jimmy immediately dumped out. They took stock of its contents: a driver's license, lipstick, cell phone, condoms, chalk, a knife with a strange, curved blade, a cloth doll...

"Let me see that." Jimmy handed her the doll. At first, Karla thought it was something used in spellcasting, a voodoo doll of some kind. It was small, with blond hair and a friendly smile, and Karla felt her initial analysis was incorrect, that it had been created for an entirely different purpose. She squeezed it and felt something hard inside. "Give me your knife."

Jimmy offered it to her, handle first. "Better be careful. That thing might turn you into a frog or something."

She shook her head. "There's something inside." She sliced off the head and reached inside. Her probing fingers were rewarded with a thin, metallic device.

"That's a zip drive," Betsy said. "What do you think's on it?"

"Something they don't want us to see." Karla made up her mind. She looked around the room and then ran out into the hallway. The others followed. There was a fire extinguisher behind a glass panel on the wall, and Karla used her elbow to knock out the breakable glass.

"What are you doing?" Jimmy asked.

"This zip drive is what they're here for," she said. "I'm sure of it. Whatever's on it has to be pretty important, and we're not giving it back."

"Then what are we going to do?" Betsy asked.

"We're going to use it to draw her in," Karla said. "And then we're going to kill her."

The blonde with the shaved patch was waiting for Karla outside the door to the east parking lot, clothed now in one of the long black robes, a hood pulled down over her head. She was flanked by two of the masked witches, both wielding semi-automatic weapons. They said nothing as Karla stepped over the broken glass that littered the hallway and up to the twisted hunk of metal that was once a door.

"I found the zip drive," Karla said. "I know what's on it. I'll return it, but only to Carmela herself. She has to come inside and get it."

The blond witch narrowed her eyes. "What's stopping me from just killing you and taking it right now?"

"Think I'm stupid? I don't have it on me. It's hidden inside the station. Anything happens to me, you'll never find it—but the police will. They'll use what's on it to destroy all of you."

The other woman thought it over. "I doubt she'll agree to this, but I'll relay your message. Where should she meet you?"

"The place where her Executioner takes his victims. Tell her to come alone. Bring anyone else and I go back into hiding until morning, and she'll never find it."

The witch left to deliver her demands, and Karla disappeared back inside the building.

The conference room overlooked the east parking lot, so Karla knew immediately when Carmela entered the station and was able to confirm she came alone. She forced herself to stop pacing. She hated waiting in here. Karla hadn't seen or heard from the Executioner in a while, but clearly he'd been busy, and the bodies of her fallen comrades were piled on either side of the long wooden table that took up the center of the room. Before she'd averted her eyes, she'd caught glimpses of Chief Goodwin, Olivia Wang, Kyle Hart, as well as several prisoners and staff members who'd been inside tonight and met up with the Executioner's axe. They were in piles and pieces, and a thick, coppery stench hung in the air, making Karla's stomach churn. She felt like she was on the battlefield of some terrible war and had the urge to flee, but she couldn't. This was where it had to happen. She had to be brave and face what was coming.

A cloaked silhouette appeared in the doorway, her presence a powerful, brooding terror. She stepped inside, and the hair on the back of Karla's neck stood on end. Carmela hadn't come alone. Another shape moved into the room behind her, his heavy footfalls preceding his arrival. He stepped up beside his master at the far end of the conference table.

"I said to come alone."

Carmela's cruel eyes burned into hers. "I brought no one inside with me."

"That's a bullshit technicality."

"And yet...here we are. Where is my zip drive, officer?"

"You'll get it. But I want him decommissioned first. He was my friend. It's not right, what you've done to him. Make it stop. Now."

"I cannot do that. The curse on your friend will be broken at sunrise, when the thing dwelling inside his corpse is forced to go back to Hell. Until then, be assured that I can keep you protected from his wrath using this..." She opened her cloak and pulled a long silver chain from around her neck. At its end dangled a doll not unlike the one they'd found in Taylor O'Shea's bag, only this one had been made to resemble Elijah King and covered in dried blood. There was something unnatural about the doll, and after a few seconds, Karla realized it was moving, its eyes fixed on her. She thought she was going to shit her pants when it called out her name.

"What the fuck?" Karla said. "*What the fuck!*"

The older witch grinned. "As long as your friend's soul is contained inside this doll, he is safe from harm. And my pet is kept under control. Now, let's have my zip drive."

Hand shaking, Karla produced the item and laid it on the table. "What's on it?"

"You don't know? I thought as much. With the power off, you wouldn't be able to connect it to any of the computers. How could you access it? That's too bad for you. On that drive, among other things, are the identities of every witch in our coven, all across the country. It's heavily encrypted, of course. But now you'll never have a chance to try and crack it."

"You're right; I didn't know. Just like you didn't know how many officers were inside the station tonight or what kind of arsenal we had. It's a small precinct, and even on the busiest of nights we don't have a large staff, but tonight most everyone is out on the streets. You didn't know that, and that's why you sent him. He could terrorize and control us and make us recover the drive for you. That way you wouldn't have to risk any of your own people."

"You're smarter than you look, officer. Now...slide it over."

Karla put two fingers on the device. "First you slide over the doll."

"That wasn't part of the deal. You wouldn't be able to control him, anyway."

"Doesn't matter. As long as you can't."

Carmela glared across the table at her, anger lighting her eyes. "I've had enough of this nonsense. Kill her, my pet. Rip her heart out and bring me my prize!"

The Executioner started in Karla's direction.

She held her breath and waited until he was halfway across the room, dangerously close, and then gave the word. "*Now!*" She hauled the fire extinguisher up from underneath the table and blasted the Executioner with it, a thick chemical cloud billowing out into his face and driving him back. At the same time, Jimmy Kilpatrick sprung up from his hiding spot under the pile of corpses on Carmela's right, knife in hand, and lunged for her throat.

The plan fell apart almost immediately. Carmela was much faster than they had anticipated. It was as if she had sensed Jimmy's presence, expected his attack. She dropped the evil doll and caught his knife hand, stopping the vicious downward stroke and thrusting the weapon away from her. From somewhere inside her cloak, she produced a knife of her own. She drove it into Jimmy's side, and he howled in pain, dropping to his knees.

At the same time, the Executioner recovered from the chemical assault and swatted the fire extinguisher from Karla's hands. The metal canister banged against the wall and rolled across the floor, and the giant raised his axe overhead. He swung it down, and Karla dove out of the way just in time. The blade cleaved an office chair in half, sending metal and plastic spraying in either direction. Karla hit the ground and crawled under the table just as he swung the weapon again. This time it bit into the wood a mere two feet from her head, the curved blade protruding from the underside of the table and grinning at her with malicious glee.

On the other side of the room, the pile of dead officers to Carmela's left begin to move and undulate, and Betsy sprung up from beneath it, covered in gore. She leaped forward and dug a curved blade deep into Carmela's shoulder. The witch roared with fury and threw an elbow back, connecting with Betsy's mouth and sending her sprawling back into the pile of corpses. Carmela dropped the injured Jimmy Kilpatrick to grab a fistful of Betsy's blond hair and yanked her roughly to her feet. She pulled the curved blade from her shoulder and put it to Betsy's throat.

The Executioner advanced steadily on Karla, chopping away at the table, leaving long, jagged gashes in the wood and sending splinters raining down on her. She crawled backward on her hands and feet, each strike coming closer and closer. Her right hand landed on something small and fleshy. The thing let out a high-pitched squeal, and she turned to look at it. A miniature Elijah King stared up at her on its chain. She snatched it up and rolled out from under the table.

"That's enough!"

Everyone turned toward Karla. She brandished the King doll toward him like a wooden cross. The Executioner stopped his attack and stood ready, brimming with violence but immobile. Carmela released Betsy, and she moved quickly away from the witch.

"Give that to me," Carmela hissed. "You'll never be able to control him. He'll kill us all."

"She seems to be doing a pretty good job to me," Jimmy said.

"I am, aren't I?" Karla said. "Think I'm getting the hang of this."

"You have no idea what you're doing. Give it back, and we'll leave. You can keep the zip drive. We can all just walk away from this."

"I've got a better idea," Karla said. "King..." She pointed at Carmela. "Kill her."

The Executioner stalked slowly and menacingly toward Carmela. She begged and pleaded and tried to make demands, but still he raised his axe high above his head and brought it down on her, slicing through her upraised arms and head and spraying them all with gore.

After that, they stood silently, staring at each other and the giant killer that was now under their control. Finally, Betsy asked, "What now?"

Karla shrugged. "We're alive. We've still got the zip drive, we've got him, and there are still a few hours left until sunrise. I think those witches out in the parking lot could use some company, don't you?"

"Fuck yeah," Betsy replied.

Then Karla gave an order so horrific that it sent a chill rippling down her own spine, and the enormous Executioner exited the room, axe resting on his shoulder, heading down the darkened hallway and out the building to continue his bloody Halloween celebration.

FUN-SIZE TRACI
DAVID RIDER

Traci passed away on Halloween and the Parkers' love for the holiday died with her.

Mr. Parker found her body near the stairs. He choked off a shriek and pressed two fingers to her throat, hoping against hope that her skin wasn't as cold as it felt. When he failed to find a pulse, his anguished scream woke his wife.

Mrs. Parker dashed out of their bedroom, pulling on a robe as she raced to the basement door. She saw him crouched over Traci, unmoving in her Care Bears pajamas. She almost took a header in her hasty stumble down the stairs but recovered her footing just long enough to drop to her knees on the floor between them.

He stammered, "Sh-She must've wanted t-to try on her costume again," spotting the black-and-white skeleton costume in her stiff grip.

With tears streaming down her cheeks, Mrs. Parker stroked the girl's pink champagne–colored hair. She wailed, "My precious girl!"

The Parkers cradled Traci's body until the shadows grew long.

They didn't answer the doorbell when the neighborhood kids began their rounds at four o'clock.

They didn't leave the basement until well after seven, when the last trick-or-treater of the 2013 season gave up on getting candy from the dark household.

The Parkers knew Halloween would never be the same.

Their little Traci was dead.

Mrs. Parker called, "Another Rick and Morty," from the front window.

Mr. Parker didn't care. He laid on the couch under a fleece blanket, tired eyes fixed on the ceiling. He listened to her open the door for two teen boys who couldn't muster a shred of enthusiasm with their chorused, "Trick or treat."

"Take two," Mrs. Parker said.

They took three without thanking her.

Mr. and Mrs. Parker's thoughts had revolved around Traci for the past twelve months. After they'd buried her, they were left with feelings of aching, persistent numbness and couldn't move past the soul-crushing vacancy in their lives. The missing girl had been their everything.

"Here comes a Winter Soldier," Mrs. Parker said in her monotone voice.

He shook his head at her attempt to feign normality. He knew she still wept on random mornings, triggered by the realization there was one less breakfast to prepare. Hell, today was the anniversary, and he'd found her curled on the shower floor, bawling her eyes out. "Our little girl came to us, and left us, on a Halloween afternoon! Think about the cruelty of that! Halloween was her special day! *Our* special day! It's just not fair!"

The last time he'd wept was the previous month, the day his wife wondered aloud if they should pack up Traci's things.

"We're never doing that," he said.

"But it's all just...sitting out. How would that look? Besides, she's not going to come back and pick up where she left off."

He pinched away tears summoned by the mere suggestion of letting her memory go. "I said no! We're never doing that!"

So Traci's things stayed where they were, including the skeleton costume she'd been holding in her final moments. It sat draped over the chair by her bed.

Mrs. Parker checked the microwave clock in the dining room.

It was 6:59.

She stepped out onto the porch and scanned the dark court. No colorful costumes darted across lawns or driveways. No lazy parents cruised along in their vehicles to keep tabs on their children, because walking, apparently, was so goddamned hard. Their asshole neighbor across the street, who always waited until Halloween hours were over to speed home from the bars in his Mustang, hadn't arrived home yet. Another season had ended. She went back inside, latched the screen door, and turned toward the hallway. Before she had a chance to say, "I'm calling it," there came a knock.

She jerked, startled, and swung her gaze through the screen.

A skeleton stood on the porch.

"Jesus!" she said.

The skeleton didn't reply. It held out a pillowcase in two gloved hands.

Mrs. Parker didn't move. Her throat constricted.

The skeleton cocked its head a few degrees, waiting.

Mr. Parker sensed something from the couch. "What is it?"

In the orange porch light, she couldn't see eyes through the holes of the rubber mask. The sockets were inky voids.

The skeleton raised its sack higher. It had a Care Bears pattern exactly like the pillowcase on Traci's bed.

Mrs. Parker said, "H-Honey...?"

He ignored her.

Realizing her husband wasn't coming, she fumbled with the

hook latch. It took three tries to free it before she pushed open the door. She wanted to say hello, wanted to say *something*, but couldn't find her voice.

The skeleton didn't speak either.

Mrs. Parker held the bowl out, waiting for the skeleton to choose its candy.

It waited for her to do it.

She grabbed a fistful of fun-size Kit-Kats.

"Fun-Size." That was their nickname for Traci. She'd stood four-eleven and hadn't grown in the last year before her death. "You're not short," Mrs. Parker had told her. "You're fun-sized, sweetie." And, good lord, how Traci had *hated* that nickname.

The skeleton on their porch stood exactly four-eleven.

Mrs. Parker knew this because the riser into the house was six inches high, her husband's old grease pencil tally where he installed the hook on the inner door was at the five-foot mark, and the top of the skeleton's skull came a good seven inches below that.

Her fingers trembled as she deposited the candy into the sack.

The skeleton nodded once, then turned away.

Sticking out of the back of its mask was a pink champagne-colored ponytail.

Mrs. Parker dropped the bowl.

Mr. Parker came dashing around the corner.

She pointed to the black costume melting into the night.

He saw it but didn't believe her explanation.

The notable Halloween costumes the following year consisted of half a dozen inflatable T-Rexes, a walking Starbucks cup with

"Lucas" written on the side, three Ant-Men, and a pair of Babadooks.

That was also the year Mr. Parker tried to bend his wife over the kitchen island without having a condom ready to go.

"Stop," she said, rebuffing him.

"Come on," he said, still trying to lift her skirt. "They won't start ringing the bell for another hour."

"I said *stop*." She disengaged herself from his groping embrace.

"Don't you want—"

She blurted, "No!" more harshly than she'd intended.

"For fuck's sake," he said, pouting the way he tended to do.

"I can't. I just…I can't. Maybe later."

He re-zipped his khakis, not replying.

She waited until he finished buckling his belt, then stepped into his arms, letting him hold her.

They stood in silence a while before addressing the real issue.

He whispered, "Do you ever want to…"

She shook her head against his chest. "I'm not ready to go through all that again. It's a lot. I can't—"

"Shh, I know. But I want another girl."

"I do, too. They're just so much work. And so much heartache."

They had pizza delivered and sat in the living room together once the kids started coming. They killed a bottle of Apothic Red.

At 6:59, there came a knock.

This time Mr. Parker saw the little skeleton.

He took longer than his wife had the year before to open the door.

She'd been right: you couldn't see its eyes.

Tears flowed when he saw the pillowcase. More came when he dispensed candy into it and its head turned and the pink ponytail bounced away.

They opened another bottle of red and got too wasted to screw.

The Parkers lost their patience with every Harley Quinn and Eleven from *Stranger Things* that came to their door during the last hour.

"Now who the fuck's this one?" Mr. Parker said, checking his watch and seeing it was six-fifty.

"I don't know," she said. "Kate McKinnon Ghostbuster, I guess."

As the minutes crept by, she got too antsy to wait inside any longer. She carried kitchen chairs out to the porch.

"You think she'll..."

"Dunno," he said.

"But I'm sure she'll..."

"I said *I don't fucking know!*"

At five minutes till, a Demon Nun stalked up the driveway. Given her height, it had to be a teenage boy.

"They don't bother saying trick-or-treat anymore, do they?" he said, even as the Nun selected Snickers bars.

"That stopped awhile back," she said.

They didn't speak for several minutes.

When his watch showed one minute to seven, they looked at each other. She stood and went down the driveway to survey the entirety of Mason Court from the curb. Not a soul stirred in either direction.

He came down to join her.

She took his hand, interlacing their fingers.

He rested his stubble-covered chin on her head.

After a few minutes, they sighed and turned.

The skeleton stood waiting for them.

It looked exactly the same.

It hadn't gotten taller.

The white rubber of its skull mask still had no wear and tear.

The glow-in-the-dark bones on the front of its costume appeared brand new. The Care Bears pillowcase looked freshly laundered.

It cocked its head and held up the sack.

Mrs. Parker whispered, "T-Traci?"

The skeleton didn't acknowledge the name.

"Sweetie," Mrs. Parker said, leaning down. "Is that you?"

It didn't move.

Her husband's face contorted, morphing into one she knew well and tried never to provoke. Even as he reached out to grab it by the arms, she stepped forward to intervene.

"No!" she said, deflecting his hands.

"Who the fuck do you think you are?!" he yelled at it.

Mrs. Parker turned sideways between them, holding her husband at bay while dipping a hand into the pocket of her hoodie. She retrieved a pack of Skittles and dropped it into the sack.

The skeleton nodded and circled around them, its ponytail the same length as always.

"This is a cruel fucking game you're playing," Mr. Parker yelled after the little figure.

Twelve months later, Mr. Parker's mood had shifted to a deeper, angry skepticism, while Mrs. Parker's was more akin to that of a child creeping downstairs to catch Santa eating cookies by the hearth.

She'd set aside a variety of treats just for the skeleton: a Whatchamacallit, which had been Traci's favorite candy bar; three sour apple Blow Pops; and a bag of Trolli gummies, her favorite sweet candy. They'd been wrapped in red-tinted cellophane with a note written in cursive that said, "We miss you."

After the fourth Spider-Man and umpteenth Pennywise accepted their treats, Mrs. Parker announced, "It's practice time." She pulled her lawn chair closer to the porch's edge.

He kept his by the door, arms crossed, glowering at her.

"She only appears when we're not looking," she explained. "So at 6:59 we'll both close our eyes and—"

"You're acting like she's the Great Fucking Pumpkin! It's just a kid screwing with us! A disturbed kid, at that! Toying with our grief!"

"It can't be! She has the same hair col—"

"Give me a break!" he said, leaning forward. "I see that one girl with pink hair pedaling past on a ten-speed every time I cut the lawn! It's not uncommon!"

"But she stays the same size! Teenage girls grow! And the Care Bears pillowcase! Just like the one Traci—"

"You need to get a goddamned grip!"

Mrs. Parker folded her arms across her chest. "You'll see."

"Yeah, I *will* see," he said. "And when I rip the mask off her stupid head, you'll see, too!"

The skeleton didn't show up that Halloween.

Mrs. Parker felt it was because her husband didn't believe hard enough.

The skeleton didn't appear the next year, either.

A group of rowdy high-schoolers were the only ones to arrive after trick-or-treat hours had ended. Michael Myers, who'd become popular again, led the mob. Lined up behind him were a Slender Man and a Black Panther with white skin showing between his sleeves and clawed gloves. Then there were villains like Hela, a terrifying clown named Art, and a pint-sized Thanos, who phoned in his ensemble with a mask, cargo shorts, and Converse.

Mrs. Parker had to ask the last two girls—an Asian and a pretty blonde—who they were. "Eve Polastri and Villanelle," they explained in bored tones, clearly tired of the question.

Mr. Parker remarked, "You're not even wearing costumes," and they rolled their eyes in the way teenage girls have mastered before they can drive.

The Parkers sat in their dark living room until well past nine, positive the long-expected visitation would come at any moment. When it didn't, they turned off the porch light at ten and retreated to their bedroom. She didn't ask why he turned on the TV and kept the sound muted, because she also wanted to listen for the knock.

October ended without it.

The following year's season kicked off with a Captain Marvel and three of the vampires from *What We Do in the Shadows*.

A few children did show up wearing skeleton costumes throughout the evening. They all had cheap masks and visible eyes behind them, rather than the disconcerting blackness that they'd witnessed from their mystery skeleton. None of the kids were the right height.

The only Traci-aged girl who stood around five feet tall was one who wore the flowery costume of the doomed protagonist from *Midsommar*, but she didn't look like Florence Pugh...she looked more like Flo from the insurance commercials.

After a Miles Morales Spider-Man left their porch, ending the official hours for another year, Mrs. Parker began to weep.

Mr. Parker held her and tried to offer comfort.

It felt like their little Traci was gone all over again.

A virus overwhelmed the planet, and a great many people died.

Executive orders were announced, states went into lockdown, and society adapted to a new way of life. Summer came, but the usual outdoor activities remained paused. When the fall semester rolled around, children stayed home. Grade schools and universities switched to remote learning. Everyone grew tired of having to wear personal protective equipment—and some people outright refused—but once Halloween arrived, the kids were only too happy to swap one mask for another.

While the Parkers knew Halloween had changed for the worse years ago, they now saw a similar flavor of disappointment on the faces of their neighbors.

As much as everyone tried to pretend otherwise, nothing felt the same that season. The streets were fuller than they'd been for the past seven months of the pandemic, but there weren't as many trick-or-treaters. The kids, for their part, were thrilled to run around together, while a greater number of parents than usual supervised from their vehicles. If a collective of grown-ups did walk the sidewalks, they carried beer cans or pulled wagons with pony kegs.

Few people wanted to open their door for possibly infected children. The ones who did wore blue masks hiding cautious smiles that couldn't be seen by the Witcher characters or the Mandalorians. Despite Halloween being the one time of the year they didn't mind unexpected visitors on their porch, the Parkers chose a different option. Like many other folks, they set their candy bowl on a footstool at the end of their driveway and waved from the open garage.

The sun set.

The roads cleared within half an hour of the nearest streetlight activating farther down Mason Lane.

Darkness descended on the cul-de-sac.

The skeleton came back.

It appeared before the candy bowl.

At first, the Parkers didn't see it. They'd been shaking out a large blanket to spread between their chairs and across their laps. Then Mrs. Parker let out a whimper. Mr. Parker gasped. They stayed seated, frozen in place.

The skeleton cocked its head.

They glanced in disbelief at each other.

Mr. Parker whispered, "Does she...look different?"

Mrs. Parker replied, "No. Exactly the same."

"Why isn't she raising her pillowcase?"

"Because the candy is right there and we're here."

"Why aren't we approaching her?"

She paused and said, "Because COVID?"

He scoffed. "You actually think, even if that is Traci—which it's *not*—that she'd bring COVID from beyond the grave?"

They sat in silence, hearts thumping, too afraid to move.

The skeleton waited a few moments, then reached up and stuck a bone-covered glove into the bowl. It took a candy, put it in the sack, and moved across the road without looking away.

The Parkers watched it cut between houses and vanish.

Everything had changed that year, for sure, but at least one thing felt like it was returning to normal.

The Parkers gave each other the virus—for a second time—the week before Halloween.

They didn't know who caught it first but narrowed it down to two possible days. It was either the Monday Mrs. Parker went to Home Depot to restock their duct tape or the Tuesday Mr. Parker drove to the Amazon hub locker at the liquor store to pick up his electronics delivery. They hadn't worn masks all year and had both spoken with maskless cashiers.

The couple had refused the vaccines their age group had qualified for since April. "No one injects *me*!" Mrs. Parker had declared, ending the discussion about whether they should take preventative measures to lessen the effects if they ever got sick.

Now those effects were wreaking havoc with their immune systems. By Friday, neither could smell or taste. By Saturday, they felt lethargic. By Halloween on Sunday, it was all they could do to carry the footstool to the end of the driveway, set the candy bowl atop it, and assume their positions in the garage like last year. They huddled under their blanket, annoying the shit out of each other with their non-stop coughing and throat clearing.

They had questions about the costumes they were seeing. Since first catching the virus over the summer, they'd missed a few movies and shows. Why was Black Widow back? Or Loki? Hadn't they died? And why were young kids dressing like *Squid Game* contestants? When Traci was alive, they never allowed her to watch anything like that.

The Parkers also couldn't understand why so many girls wore skeleton costumes. Neither had heard of musician Phoebe Bridgers or known that she and her band had been touring in black suits with white skeleton bones since her last album's release. All they knew was more teenagers than ever before hit the streets wearing the same type of costume that Traci had worn the year before her death.

It unnerved them to the point where, at first, they weren't sure it was *their* skeleton that appeared in the driveway.

They sat forward, hacking, and squinted at it.

The glowing bones seemed brighter than other costumes, and the mask had the right eyes—with the brows angled downward toward the nose, as if a skull could display anger. It also carried the prerequisite pillowcase.

The skeleton cocked its head.

"Traci," wheezed Mrs. Parker. "We love you."

It took a candy and stepped back into the road, preparing for its vanishing act.

That's when the skeleton became illuminated by headlights coming from its left before being bathed in brighter high beams as a speeding car zoomed into view. Their drunk neighbor was home early, driving faster than anyone should on Halloween night. The skeleton's ponytail whipped when it turned its head in surprise toward the approaching Mustang. Its reflexes were quick, and it managed to leap into the air. The car's windshield clipped one of its feet when the skeleton tried to vault off the hood. Its body flipped head over heels. Through some miracle, the skeleton landed on its feet like an acrobat. It sprinted into the darkness before their asshole neighbor brought his car to a screeching halt.

"*What the fuck!*" Mr. Parker shouted, causing a fresh round of coughing.

"*It* is *Traci!*" Mrs. Parker cried, getting out of her chair. "*This proves it!*"

Mr. Parker said, "What are you talking about?"

"*You know as well as I do she was a gymnast!*"

But aside from the fact that a dead girl's supposed ghost had been physically struck by a vehicle, her husband suspected something else based on what he'd seen.

Mr. Parker seemed to prove his suspicions about the skeleton's true nature when he chased it a year later.

He'd caught the virus a third time some months earlier. By that stage, one doesn't fully recover from the symptoms. However, Mr. Parker felt well enough to follow through with his scheme...unbeknownst to his wife. He thought, *Time to get some fucking answers.*

When the skeleton appeared at its expected time, he yanked the blanket off and full-on sprinted toward it.

"*Honey, no!*" Mrs. Parker called.

Mason Lane still had a few trick-or-treaters on their way home, and it was toward them that the startled skeleton ran.

Mr. Parker stayed right on its heels.

The skeleton juked to the left when he'd come within grabbing distance. It bolted between two houses—ones with chain-link fences around their backyards.

"I've got you now, you bony bitch!" He saw the fence ahead wasn't that high, but it should slow the skeleton long enough to grab its goddamned ponytail. He grunted. Fire seared his damaged lungs. Even so, he was going to catch his prey. The streetlight on the next block silhouetted its lithe shape as it neared the dead end.

The skeleton leaped toward a fence as tall as it was, slapped both palms on top, and swung its legs over with skilled ease, not slowing down in the slightest. It landed and kept sprinting.

Mr. Parker cursed yet somehow managed to pull off the same maneuver. He stumbled on the other side, regained his footing, and tore even faster after it. The sounds of his tortured breathing became louder as the longtime COVID effects presented themselves. He couldn't maintain this pace. But his legs were longer than the skeleton's, and he closed the distance.

Upon reaching the other side of the yard, the skeleton prepared to execute another move. Legs pumping, arms moving like pistons, the pillowcase fluttering behind, it jumped.

Mr. Parker grabbed for the skeleton while it was airborne. His fingers found the pillowcase instead and tore it from its grip.

The skeleton kicked its legs into the air, keeping its hands on the fence top to prepare for a flip.

In the moment the skeleton was upside-down, as if in slow motion, Mr. Parker watched the fabric of its costume pull tight against its torso in the streetlight beyond.

Then it somersaulted in mid-air and landed on its feet and kept running.

But he'd seen what he suspected all along.

"You've got tits!" He managed to clear the fence, tumbled and rolled to his feet, and dashed from between the houses with the pillowcase in his hand.

Three trick-or-treaters who happened to be passing by witnessed a wheezing, grown-ass man with a stolen bag of candy, hollering and chasing a short kid.

One of the teens, wearing a Doctor Strange costume, said, "Who the hell's that?"

His companion, dressed like Pearl and holding an axe, replied, "That's Mister goddamn Parker."

The third teen, in a Ghostface costume, said, "What's his deal?"

Mr. Parker couldn't keep up with the skeleton, who dashed between two more houses and got away clean. He kept gasping and screaming, *"That skeleton's got tits!"*

"He and his wife are the neighborhood psychos," said Pearl.

The mystery of the Traci skeleton ended ten years to the day after the girl died.

Neighborhood boys trick-or-treated as The Flash and Rocket Raccoon. Girls dressed as Wednesday Addams, Ellie from *The Last of Us*, and M3GAN.

For the first time in a decade, Mr. Parker also got into the Halloween spirit by constructing a dummy that looked exactly like him. He'd paid an Etsy merchant a few hundred bucks to create a lifelike rubber mask of his own tired, beard-stubbled face. He put it on a mannequin, dressed it in his flannel and khakis, and propped it on a lawn chair in the garage.

Based on what her husband had witnessed the year before, Mrs. Parker had finally decided it was time again—and agreed to be his accomplice. The operation started with her sitting next to Mr. Parker's doppelgänger and speaking to it for the designated three hours until the kids went home with their candy…or until that damned imposter skeleton made its appearance.

And there it was, right at 6:59.

Except it had no pillowcase.

That was in Mr. Parker's hands as he crept from his hiding place in the neighbor's bushes across the street. He snuck up behind the skeleton, who stood facing Mrs. Parker and the Mr. Parker dummy.

The skeleton realized the man was fake a second too late.

He pulled the Care Bears pillowcase over the skeleton's head and seized it in a bear hug from behind. Before it could scream, he covered its mouth and carried it into the garage while it kicked. Mrs. Parker punched the garage door button, and it rolled shut behind them. She took a syringe from her hoodie and stabbed the squirming skeleton in its ass cheek. Within moments, the struggling stopped.

It laid motionless at their feet.

The Parkers waited until the girl in the costume regained consciousness to unmask her.

She wore two of them: one was the angry skull mask, the one beneath was part of a sheer black body stocking that covered her head. It had been unzipped in back to allow her pink champagne hair to hang over the costume's back collar.

They yanked the stocking forward to reveal her face.

Mrs. Parker's eyes narrowed. "That's not our Traci."

"No, that's the girl who used to bike past the house," Mr. Parker said. "Just some short college girl."

The girl's head lolled, still affected by the injected sedative. Drool dribbled from her lips as she mumbled, "You...you psychos."

"Oh, *college*," Mrs. Parker said, grabbing the girl's ponytail to yank her head back and study her face. "Guess that explains why she was gone for three years."

"Until the shutdown," Mr. Parker said.

"*Until the shutdown!*" Mrs. Parker repeated. "Then she came home for remote learning!"

"Right."

"So she's not our little Traci at all."

"Nope."

"Use her real name, you sick fucks," the girl said. "Why can't you *ever* say her real name?! This wasn't supposed to take ten fucking years."

They glanced at each other, awareness dawning on their faces.

"She was my best friend," the girl said, tears welling in her eyes. "We were supposed to go trick-or-treating together that year. We had matching costumes and everything. Then I got strep days before Halloween. So she went alone, promising she would text me her location block by block. The texts stopped after Mason Lane. And she never came home."

"That's when our Traci came into our lives," Mrs. Parker said.

"*That's not her name!*" the girl yelled. "And the cops wouldn't listen or do anything to find her! Her folks split up and moved away. I was the only one still here who cared." She looked around the basement. One corner of the room was furnished with a toilet, out in the open, and a twin bed. A thick chain ran from its metal frame to a shackle clamped around her own ankle. She struggled against the duct tape holding her wrists to the chair's arms. "Where is she, you psychos? Did—did you murder her?"

"We didn't murder anyone," Mrs. Parker said, stroking the bangs from the girl's eyes. "We're not monsters."

"We think she died of a heart attack," Mr. Parker said.

The girl's chest heaved at this news. "No shit! She had to quit gymnastics because of a congenital defect!"

Mrs. Parker nodded with a *that explains it* look. She put a comforting hand on the girl's shoulder. "And what about you, dear?"

The girl stared up at her.

"Do *you* have any heart problems?"

The girl didn't answer, fear creeping across her features.

Mrs. Parker smiled at her husband. "She's healthy."

Mr. Parker smiled back. "And perfect."

Mrs. Parker bent to dry the girl's eyes with her sleeve. "Would you like to be our new girl?"

Mr. Parker added, "And live with us forever and ever?"

The girl didn't answer.

"Will you be our new Fun-Size Traci?" Mrs. Parker said.

They held hands, waiting for her answer.

She nodded once.

Mrs. Parker kissed the top of her head.

Mr. Parker did the same.

The girl whispered, "There's just one problem."

"What's that, dear?"

She grinned maniacally up at them. "I've been live-streaming you motherfuckers since before you grabbed me. And I have twenty thousand followers."

Their smiles vanished when they saw a camera lens poking from a hole in the costume's breastbone.

Mr. Parker yanked the outer costume over her shoulders. An iPhone hung from a lanyard around her neck. He flipped it around. It was recording a video.

The girl laughed in his face. "You stupid, psycho fuckheads!"

Mr. Parker didn't seem concerned. "How are we stupid?"

Mrs. Parker frowned. "And, by the way, how are we psychos? That word's not nice at all, Traci."

"*You're being broadcast*," the girl shouted. "What don't you get?!"

"I don't think so," Mr. Parker said. "I upgraded my cell signal jammer's firmware yesterday. Nothing *can* be broadcast from anywhere inside this house."

The girl's smile fizzled. "Well...it doesn't matter, dipshit! I activated the stream before I ever got close to this house of horrors!"

"Maybe you did," Mrs. Parker said, "and maybe you didn't."

"I fucking *know* I did. At the very least, my followers will see me being abducted outside. Police will be called and could be on their way right now."

Mr. Parker said, "If they do anything at all."

Mrs. Parker pulled the girl's head to her bosom. "Our little girl is so smart, isn't she?"

"She really is," Mr. Parker said, embracing them both. "Nothing to do now but wait and see what happens."

Mrs. Parker agreed. "In the meantime, we're all together again. A normal, happy family on the best day of the year."

They held their new Traci and listened for sirens.

BLIND DATE

SARAH CANNAVO

"I really wish you weren't going out tonight," his grandmother said again as he finished putting away the groceries he'd brought, her withered fingers worrying her rosary beads, their wood worn smooth through years of being handled.

Dustin grinned, closing the kitchen cabinet. "Don't worry, I'll check my candy for razor blades before I eat any."

"Smart aleck," she muttered without malice, adding as he pulled her prescriptions from the paper pharmacy bag and started sorting pills into her plastic container, setting up her doses for the week. "I can do that, sweetheart. You don't have to."

"I know you can, Gran," he assured her. "I just like to help."

Her anxious expression softened, and she let the rosary beads fall away, reaching up to brush an errant lock of dark hair back from his forehead before placing her hand on his cheek. Her touch was cool and dry, and though age had wrinkled her hands, they were still strong, capable. "Such a good boy," she said, her shining blue-green eyes meeting his brown ones. "Just like your father."

"Thanks, Gran," Dustin said, and she patted his cheek before letting him go. "Seriously, though, why do you have such a problem with me going out tonight? Is it because it's a blind date? Madeline set it up, and I trust her judgment. I thought you liked Maddie, too." Madeline Harker was a witch—not a Wiccan but an honest-to-God witch, black cat, flying broom, and everything—from a family with deep roots in their small town of Shady Grove, New Jersey. Though she and Dustin were around the same age, they hadn't really interacted much before he'd started volunteering at the local historical society, where Madeline worked, and they'd struck up a friendship. They didn't often get involved in each other's romantic lives beyond advice or offering sympathetic ears and shoulders, but she had a friend named Kira she was sure he'd hit it off with. After listening to Maddie talk her up, he thought he might, too, and he'd let her set them up. The fact that the first night that worked for both of them was Halloween had seemed like a fun fluke of the universe's part.

His grandmother waved him off as the tea kettle started whistling, her slippers whispering across the linoleum as she moved through the late-afternoon sunlight slanting into the kitchen and took the kettle from the stove, cutting it off mid-scream. "I *do* like Madeline. She's a nice girl, and that salve of hers makes my joints feel better than anything the doctors ever gave me. And if she's vouching for this Kira girl, I'm sure she's all right, too." The scent of cinnamon, warm and spicy, wafted through the kitchen as she poured the tea into two china cups she'd had since she'd married Dustin's grandfather sixty-five years ago. She passed one to Dustin. "But Dustin, honey, it's Halloween."

A fun fluke on the universe's part to everyone but Gran, apparently. He should've known that was it; Agnes Campbell Rourke was old school in her beliefs, always had been. A baby born with a caul over their face would grow up to have the Sight; carrying a rowan cross tied with red thread would bring you good luck; covering the mirrors in a house where somebody had just died would keep their soul from getting trapped on the earthly plane instead of moving on to Heaven or Hell, wherever they were meant to go.

And...

"The veil is thin tonight," his grandmother said, taking her tea into the living room. Dustin followed, stooping almost by instinct to avoid cracking his skull on the entryway; her house, like many in town, had been built during Colonial days, with doorways and entryways never meant for his six foot two frame.

"The veil between the worlds of the living and the dead," he said, remembering the stories she'd told while he was growing up. His father hadn't taken them as seriously as Agnes had; neither of his parents had. But they'd never disparaged them, either, which Dustin always figured had more to do with the respect they'd had for his grandparents than any actual belief in worlds beyond this one.

Gran nodded, a few wisps of white-gray hair curling against her cheek. "It's the thinnest it is all year. And that means spirits can cross over from their world to ours as they wish." She bypassed the soft brown sofa, the worn armchair that had sat empty for the last four years, and stopped at the brick fireplace, setting her teacup down on the mantle. She picked up a framed photograph that rested there, a sepia-toned shot of Agnes and his grandfather Donald back when they'd first bought this house. "And not just good spirits, like my Donnie or your parents, if they ever decide to come back; no." She put the photo back in its place, broad-shouldered, dark-haired Donald looking at them with his arm around his beaming, curly-haired slip of a wife, and took her tea up again, turning to face Dustin with deep creases of worry in her face. "All kinds of spirits—tricksters, mischief-makers, malevolent souls, and things that've never been human, all loose in the world looking to cause chaos and harm. On Halloween night you never know what's what and who's who, so you have to be careful, Dustin, in case one of the dark spirits decides to interfere with you."

Dustin took a drink of his tea to hide his smile. He loved his grandmother, he really did, and knew she meant well. But he'd spent his whole life in Shady Grove, and in twenty-four years he'd never encountered any spirits—which, if the stories were true, was something of a record for this town—good or bad, on Halloween or any other day of the year.

"I've been out on Halloween before, Gran," he reminded her patiently, not wanting to appear patronizing. "I trick-or-treated every year when I was a kid, and I went to all kinds of parties when I was a teenager and in college, and nothing bad ever happened. Well, nothing involving ghosts, anyway," he amended, remembering a few incidents from those parties whose particulars he was in no hurry to impart to his grandmother.

"Costumes," she said, almost to herself. "Costumes help; they disguise you, the spirits aren't sure..."

"So you want me to dress up as Zorro for my date tonight?" he said, flourishing an imaginary rapier. "That'll keep me safe from the ghosts?" He relented when he saw the look on her face. "Aw, Gran, I'm only kidding. But really, I'll be fine. We're just meeting up at the Harvest Moon for some drinks and dinner, nothing fancy. I'll probably be back at my place by eleven." Whether or not he'd be alone would depend on how the night went, but again, there were some things he didn't need to share with her.

She shook her head, shivering and rubbing her arms as though some of the autumn chill had crept into the house. "I just don't like it. My old bones are telling me something's going to happen tonight."

"Sounds like you need some more of that salve." Dustin gently took her arm and guided her down onto the couch, setting his cup beside hers on the doily-covered coffee table. He glanced across the room at the little clock perched on the tall walnut bookcase, its gilt hands ticking across a white face: just after three. "Look, why don't you try to enjoy the holiday a little bit? Find yourself a nice monster movie marathon, watch some of those creature features you and Pop used to see at the drive-in over in Gold Oaks? Or *The Great Pumpkin*, maybe; that's always good. And don't forget, Smoky's show starts at seven." Smoky Pollack was the night-shift DJ on the local community radio station, broadcasting an eclectic mix of rock 'n roll, wild stories, and call-in segments until midnight. On Halloween he turned the weirdness up to eleven, interspersing his spooky playlist with callers telling what they swore were true stories about encountering ghosts, strange beings, and all manner of monsters right here in the good old Grove. He capped the whole thing off with a reading of "The Legend of Sleepy Hollow" in his low, gravelly voice, the recitation and the Halloween show itself a tradition in town for years.

His grandmother sniffed. "He's a hooligan," she said, but with as much malice as when she'd called Dustin a smart aleck earlier. She was softening, he thought, catching the faint smile that twitched the corners of her lips.

"You got everything? Your medicine's on the counter, and remember, call any time if you need something." He bent and kissed the top of her head, but as he straightened, she gripped his lean arm tight, and he paused, startled. "Gran?"

"If you're going to go, take this, at least." With her free hand, she reached into the pocket of her sweater and pulled free something she placed in his palm: a Saint Michael medal, its thin chain coiled like a snake. "It was your grandfather's," she said, folding his fingers over it. "The dark things out there can't stand the touch of anything holy. Promise me you'll wear it, Dustin."

"Okay, Gran, sure," he said, to put her at ease more than anything, looping the chain around his neck and tucking the medal beneath his black T-shirt. The image of Saint Michael the Archangel was cool against his collarbone but warming at the touch of his skin. "Thanks."

"You're welcome, sweetheart." She squeezed his arm, more gently this time, and released him, smiling now that she knew he'd be protected. "I hope you have fun."

"So do I."

"Not *too* much fun, though." She shook her finger at him, though she was still smiling, a mischievous gleam in her eyes.

"Gran!"

She laughed at the pained look on his face. "I was young once too, you know," she reminded him. "Granted, it was a long, long time ago, but I suspect some things are still the same."

He laughed, too, hugging her goodbye, catching a whiff of perfume, the powdery floral scent inexorably tied to her in his mind. "Happy Halloween, Gran."

"Happy Halloween, Dustin. Be careful out there."

"I will, don't worry."

She would, though, he knew, probably until the clock hit 12:01 a.m., November first, and the veil returned to whatever its usual thickness was. *Roaming ghosts.* He shook his head as he locked the front door behind him and jogged down the steps, the Saint Michael medal bumping against his chest as he headed home to get ready for his date. He had plenty of time, but he didn't want to put it off too long and keep Kira waiting.

Dustin wondered how long he should wait before he texted Madeline, at least, to see if she knew where Kira was. He couldn't call or text Kira himself; he didn't have her number, Madeline having played intermediary for them the whole way. The system had worked, up til now.

He'd been at the bar of the Harvest Moon for about an hour before he caved and texted Madeline; he didn't get an answer, neither the first time nor the two more he sent over the next half hour, and it was only when he called and got her voice mail that he remembered. *Witch. Halloween.* Tonight was a Sabbath, and at the historical society the other day, she'd mentioned she'd be spending it with her family. No doubt the festivities were keeping her too busy to check her phone regularly.

Great.

His first date in an unpleasantly long time, and it looked like he'd been stood up. Next time he was supposed to go out, he was going to have Maddie check her scrying mirror first make sure the girl would actually show.

He waved the bartender, Michelle, down to close out his tab, doing his best to return the smile she flashed him and accepting the fun-size Snickers bar she slid him with his bill with a nod of thanks. "Do me a favor," Dustin said, unfolding himself from his stool and standing. "If a chick named Kira calls or comes by looking for me, tell her I went home."

"Sure thing, Dustin," Michelle said, pocketing the tip he'd left on the bar. "Happy Halloween."

He fought back a snort of disgust. "Yeah. Happy Halloween."

Instead of their usual mood music, the Harvest Moon was piping Smoky Pollack's show through their speakers, and Dustin left the restaurant with the sound of the Swing Rays singing about Hell-O-Ween Night fading behind him. The crisp night air washed over him, cooling his flushed skin and carrying with it the bittersweet scent of decaying leaves and a hint of something burning—a fire pit somewhere, maybe—a combination that sang unmistakably of autumn.

The restaurant was only a twenty-minute or so walk from his apartment on Pine Street, which was helpful with his Charger currently lodging at Francis's Garage courtesy of a busted radiator. He briefly considered calling for a ride now but decided, *Screw it,* and set off on foot, leaving the Lyfts for whatever drunken werewolves and sexy Raggedy Annes might need them. As he walked, he tried to console himself—maybe Kira hadn't deliberately blown him off; maybe she'd had car trouble too, or a family emergency, and was having the same communication problems he was.

No matter the reason, what was done was done. All he wanted to do now was crash on the couch, order a pizza; maybe he'd take some of his own advice and catch a few monster movies, or tune in to whatever was left of the WHTX Halloween Spook-Tacular, end the night with Ichabod Crane and old pumpkin-head instead of a pretty blonde.

It was late and truly dark; most of the trick-or-treaters had headed home, though Dustin glimpsed a few stragglers scurrying down the sidewalks here and there. They laughed and traded treats, bartering for better candy, their small, quick feet sending fallen leaves skirling through the puddles of amber light under the streetlights. He smiled at that, remembering being eight, nine, ten years old, a Transformer, a ninja, a cowboy, making his way from house to house with Tommy Minetola and Robbie Osterman, arguing about how many Tootsie Rolls equaled a Reese's Cup and jealously guarding their Hershey bars above all else. It was nice to see, like his grandmother had said, that some things stayed the same through the years.

After a block or two, the streetlights were spaced farther apart, leaving larger gaps for the night to slip through. The moon above was full, or near enough, but the rustling canopies of the many oak and maple trees along his route caught much of its cold white light, leaving only scraps to filter through and dapple the darkness around him. He walked with his hands in the pockets of his gray jacket, the scuff of his shoes on the pavement echoing in the absence of any other footsteps.

Gran'll be happy, at least, Dustin thought. Not about Kira's no-show, but about the distinct lack of spooks seeking another snatch of human life, even if just for a night. *I guess her bones were just warning her about my date. Or lack thereof.*

"Excuse me."

He started, turning. A few feet behind him on the sidewalk stood a girl, shorter than him—but that was nothing new—and well-built, her body shown off by her black corset top and tight tiny skirt, a few tears in her dark tights. He appreciated the outfit, but how in the hell wasn't she cold? It wasn't freezing out, but it also wasn't really corset-no-jacket weather, either. And how hadn't he heard her approach? They were alone, the street quiet enough for his own steps to resound—had he been *that* deep in thought that he'd missed hers coming up behind him?

"Yeah?" he asked, trying to cover how she'd startled him.

She brightened when she saw his face. "It *is* you! Oh, I'm so glad; I thought I'd missed you."

"I'm sorry, do I—" He paused, peered closer at her, trying to get a fix on her features in the dim light. Her blond hair was shorter than it was in Maddie's photos, pulled back in two pigtails by black ribbons that matched the straps of her corset, and her eyes looked more blue than green, the shape of her pale face a bit sharper than he remembered, though softened by the curves of her cheeks, the upturn of her nose. She looked to be in her early twenties, so around the right age, and allowing for the tricky lighting and what makeup could do... "Wait a minute. Kira? Are you Kira?"

She was smiling, and something inside him lightened. So he *hadn't* been blown off after all. "I'm so sorry," she said, twisting one of the black leather bracelets she wore around her slim left wrist; its edges were frayed, as if this was a habit of hers. "Really, I am. You must've been waiting—*gah,* how long? I didn't think I'd be able to find you—not that I blame you for leaving. I would've done the same thing."

"I tried to call Madeline and see where you were, but she didn't answer. I think her Sabbath is keeping her busy," Dustin said.

Kira's grin grew. "Everybody's busy tonight," she said with a subtle shift of her hips, eyes shining, "or at least they ought to be," and Dustin made a mental note to give Michelle an extra-large tip next time for passing his message along.

"Well, I wasn't all that busy, but I think that's changing. I'm Dustin, by the way, Dustin Rourke." He added sheepishly, raking a hand through his hair, "But I guess you already knew that."

He liked her laugh, warm and rich in the October air. "I'm very glad I caught you, Dustin Rourke." He also liked the way his name sounded on her lips; there was a lot about her that he liked, despite the night's rocky start.

"I'm very glad you caught me, too," he admitted. "So you're hoofing it too, huh?" He glanced down at her black high-tops, flowers drawn on the white rubber toes in black-and-purple marker.

She made a wry face. "Cars suck, don't they? At least everything in this town's within walking distance."

"There's definitely something to be said for that." He stuffed his hands back in his pockets and rocked a bit on the balls of his feet. "So, uh, did you still feel like doing something? I know it's a little late, but I'm up for it if you are."

"We've got the night. We might as well use it," Kira said, smile returning.

"I was sorta hoping you'd want to stick around." He gestured back the way he'd come. "So did you want to go back to the Harvest Moon, or...?"

"Why don't we keep walking a little while longer?" she suggested. "As long as you're not too tired of it, anyway. All the kiddies have gone home, so we'll have the streets to ourselves—except for all the ghoulies and ghosties and long-legged beasties and things that go bump in the night, of course."

Dustin chuckled. "Sure, we can walk," he said, and she slipped her arm through his, like they were a pair of old-time lovers strolling through a park in a painting. "Aren't you cold, though? Don't get me wrong, I love the outfit; it's making me feel kinda underdressed, actually. But you can have my jacket if you want, here—" He started shrugging out of it.

She tightened her hold on his arm before he could finish, though, and stretched up on her toes, gifting him a quick kiss on the cheek. He started at the spike of ice he felt at the touch of her lips on his skin, but it was quickly chased away by the warmth with which she looked at him as she murmured, "A gentleman. Lucky me." Voice returning to normal, she added, "Keep your jacket, Sir Dustin. I don't mind the cold."

Before he could insist, she started walking, and he moved with her, almost unconsciously. He had no particular destination in mind and neither, it seemed, did Kira. The pair wandering through streets that proved, as she'd predicted, empty, aside from some plastic skeletons clacking in the occasional tree and jack-o'-lanterns glowing on porches. Some houses had herds of cars parked in their drives or at the curb, "Monster Mash" or "Thriller" issuing from living rooms where shadows danced in lit front windows. He knew a few people who were throwing parties tonight but felt no urge to seek them out, content to walk and talk with Kira. He got to hear her laugh a few more times as he told stories about his job at the local bookstore (where, he was half convinced, one of the reasons he'd been hired was his height) and his volunteer work at the historical society.

"Why there?" Kira asked.

"What do you mean?"

"Most guys your age spend their free time playing video games or fixing up their cars, not going over old journals and playing tour guide. So why do you do it?"

"I don't know," Dustin said, then amended, "I mean, I do it because I like it, but I don't really know why I like it. Maddie, yeah, it makes sense, what with her family and all, but me...I dunno. From the time I was a kid, we'd go on field trips to all the historical spots in town, and the other kids in the class would be off giggling over Josiah Greenwood's chamber pot and I'd be reading all the little plaques talking about who did what when. It's fascinating stuff, some of it, and I guess...I guess I just have a thing for history. It's important to remember what came before." It was his turn to laugh, self-deprecatingly. "Bet Madeline didn't warn you she was setting you up with a nerd, huh?"

"No, I totally get what you mean," Kira assured him. "I'm actually a bit into history myself. It's like with people—they may die, but they aren't truly gone until they're forgotten."

Dustin felt a pang, but he wasn't about to dig into those wounds now, so he said only, "Exactly," then changed the subject. "What about your job? Madeline said you just started at the bakery."

"Oh, a bakery's not a good place for history," she said, grinning. "All the old stuff gets taken out of display cases, not put into them."

He was laughing when she stopped dead, squeezing his arm with surprising strength. "Ooh, look!" she said, excited as a child at a carnival. "We should go in and explore—it's perfect for Halloween."

Dustin's first impression was of the grassy expanse, and he thought for a moment they'd meandered their way to the town park. Then he saw the stone slabs and marble angels rising from the grass, gleaming in the moonlight, and realized where they actually were. "You want to explore the cemetery?"

"Yeah, why not?" She wiggled her fingers at him, like a cartoon witch casting a curse. "What's the matter, too scared of ghosts to try it?"

"All kinds of spirits—tricksters, mischief-makers, malevolent souls, and things that've never been human, all loose in the world looking to cause chaos and harm." But he banished Gran's voice to the back of his mind and said, "Actually, I'm not sure if I believe in ghosts or not."

Kira's laugh was incredulous this time. "Seriously? You're friends with a witch but you don't know about *ghosts?*"

He held up his hands, grinning. "I've *seen* Madeline do magic. I've never seen a ghost. Granted, the whole magic thing makes spirits seem a bit more likely, but still."

She slipped her arm from his, facing him, and tapped the tip of his nose. "Sure, but I think the real question is, do ghosts believe in *you,* Sir Dustin?" She moved closer to the cemetery, almost skipping, and propped one high-top-shod foot on the low stone wall that wreathed it. The black wrought-iron gate at the front was locked at night, but it was almost a symbolic gesture considering how easily the wall could be scaled, although the horror stories that went around about what had happened to various trespassers within it over the centuries probably deterred some would-be legend-trippers —while attracting others, no doubt. Not to mention that the SGPD would probably be checking the place out at some point tonight to chase out any vandals, Goth kids making out on graves, or whoever else might be lurking there.

"Just think about it as another field trip." Kira held her hand out to him, beckoning, eyes bright. "Come on, it'll be fun."

It was Halloween. She was hot. It was as simple as that.

He followed her over the wall.

Shadow Grove Cemetery was the only local spot that retained the town's original name, although several others, such as Shadow Lake, which was deep in the woods, still bore their original names as well. The town's name had been changed in the 1800s, with inhabitants hoping the switch would help their home shed the dark associations of its past and project a more cheerful, welcoming image. How the cemetery had escaped this rebranding, Dustin didn't know, but it seemed appropriate; what better place to hold onto a town's history than the one where those who'd made that history were laid to rest?

His parents were buried here, as was his grandfather, under a stone that already had Gran's name and birth date carved beside his. He and Kira didn't pass them, though, as they moved among the graves, past the more recent ones at the front of the cemetery and deeper into its heart, where the older stones and tombs were located. Half of Dustin's attention was on Kira, half on where he was stepping so he wouldn't trip over any tree roots or gravestones, but Kira didn't seem to share this concern, her movements easy and graceful as if she could find her way through blindfolded if she had to.

"Have you done this before?" he asked, half laughing, as he narrowly avoided Albert Frohicky, 1880-1936, Beloved Husband and Father, whose low headstone was half hidden by the grass.

"A few times," she said, flashing a smile at him over her shoulder. "It's better with you here, though."

"Thanks."

She stopped, so he did too, his skin prickling as Kira turned and leaned in so her body almost but not quite touched his. "It's boring here by myself," she said, her voice lower, throatier now, her gaze roaming up him until her eyes met his, clear bright blue beneath long, soft lashes. "How's the line go? 'The grave's a fine and private place/but none, I think, do there embrace.'"

"You want to embrace?" Dustin asked, somewhat hoarsely, eyebrow arching.

He caught the mischievous gleam in her eyes before she stretched up, bringing her lips within an inch of his and murmuring, "If you can catch me," before she darted away, quick and sleek as a fox streaking through the grass.

"Wait, what?" Dustin blinked, thrown, his brain taking a moment to catch up, as it had when they'd first arrived at the cemetery. He'd be spending the whole night a step behind her, apparently. "Are you serious?" he called after her.

She didn't stop, a laugh drifting back to him her only response. *Jesus, she* is *serious.* He considered his options a moment, an amazed laugh of his own bubbling up, and then took off after her.

There were some trees in the graveyard—an owl hooted from the upper branches of one as Dustin ran by—but they were scattered, letting the moonlight spill down unfiltered. Her pale skin made Kira seem a beam of it that had broken free, a wisp of whiteness leading Dustin deeper into the maze of graves, but even though this made her easier to keep track of, he couldn't catch her; a few times he came close, long arm reaching out and a triumphant, *"Gotcha!"* on the tip of his tongue, but she would slip away before his fingers could brush her shoulder, before he could get any hold. Again and again she eluded him, with the same easiness with which she'd walked among the dead earlier, and the few glimpses he got of her face showed an amused smile, the same wicked gleam in her eyes.

"Come on, Sir Dustin, you can do better than that!" she said, deftly avoiding another swipe and darting sprite-like around the stone angel weeping over Annabel Usher, 1745-1768, *She sleepeth in peace forevermore.* "Oh, so close!"

Another few steps, just another few steps and he'd have her this time, each stride eating up the distance between them...

And then she was gone.

He skidded to a stop, panting, and looked around once, twice, to make sure he hadn't just missed her, but Kira was nowhere to be seen. In the stillness he heard only the rasp of his own breath, the rustle of leaves, the soft, chill sigh of the breeze—but maybe it wasn't so strange he couldn't pick up any footsteps from her, he thought, remembering how she'd snuck up on him on the street.

"Kira? Where'd you go?" he called, suddenly more mindful of where he was standing and what he was surrounded by. Carven skulls leered up at him from headstones, marble maidens gazed mournfully down from their plinths, stern-faced angels atop tombs glared as if demanding why he was disturbing their charges. Goosebumps sprang up on his skin, and he shivered. You didn't have to believe in ghosts to feel creeped out in a graveyard, especially at night, and without someone else's company and conversation to keep it at bay. "Give me a hint."

"Aw, where's the fun in that?" floated back to him, and he turned in the direction he thought her voice had come from, figuring she'd ducked behind one of the monuments or crypts nearby. The markers around him were older, many cracked and chipped, some beginning to crumble, the names and inscriptions worn faint by weather and time or obscured by clots of moss; these were the earliest graves in the place, the farthest, most isolated part before the wall that marked the boundary between hallowed ground and the unconsecrated field where Shadow Grove's unshriven dead had been buried.

"The veil is thin tonight...the thinnest it is all year."

He was about to call out to Kira again when he saw her—a pale female form, anyway, slipping into a small stone crypt several feet ahead of him.

How the hell did she get it open?

He slowed to a jog as he neared, knowing there was no way he could lose her now, and stood just outside the creaking door, reluctant to follow her in. "Got you," he said, though the cold air emanating from within dulled the enthusiasm he might've once announced this with.

"Not yet you don't," she said, tone light and teasing, words bouncing off the walls.

"Look, maybe we shouldn't do this." The crypt's interior was pitch-black, the moonlight not reaching far past the threshold, but Dustin thought he could pick out a slight bit of movement, a shadow among shadows. "Being in the cemetery's one thing, but this —" He gestured at the crypt, the cross on the roof stark against the black-blue sky, BROCKDEN carved in Latinate letters above the entrance and flanked on either side by ravens clutching rolled-up scrolls in their talons. "This is something else entirely."

"I really don't think the Brockdens will mind," Kira said. "Besides, we're not going to trash the place, just explore a little. Come on, Dustin, *please?*"

This was weird. This was weird, and he should probably leave. But even as he opened his mouth, refusal ready to go, he paused. Who knew what shape the place was in? She may have chosen to go in, but he didn't want to leave her there to get hurt.

"Just a few minutes?" he asked.

Her laughter issued from the darkness. "If that's what you want."

Are you *serious?* a voice in his mind asked disbelievingly. Ignoring it, exhaling heavily, Dustin stepped into the crypt, and the door slammed shut behind him.

"What the *hell?*" He spun, sunk in darkness, his heart pounding against his ribs, and pushed on the door, leaning into it with his shoulder when it wouldn't budge. The breeze had to have closed it. But if so, what was holding it shut now? It wasn't locked, obviously, or Kira wouldn't have been able to get in. *So why...can't I...open it?*

"Kira, I think it's stuck," he said, pausing his efforts, adding as something occurred to him, "Is there someone else out there? Is this a joke?" Was *that* really why she'd been so late? Not car trouble, but setting up some Halloween prank for him, with or without an accomplice's help? *"I'll get him to the cemetery and lead him to the crypt, and then once we're inside you shut us in. It'll be great!"* Suddenly the date he'd been on with a chick who'd had a pet lizard and insisted on bringing him along didn't seem so bad. *"Kira?"*

No answer. Fishing his phone from his pocket, Dustin turned the light on and swept the crypt, wall to wall, floor to the ceiling he had to hunch beneath.

Kira was gone.

His heartbeat sped up, his blood roaring in his ears, sweat breaking out on his skin despite the coolness of the night. It wasn't possible; it was cramped quarters inside the crypt, no places to hide unless she, for some reason, had decided to curl up in a vault with one of the Brockdens. But he would've heard her moving, would've heard the heavy stone slab scraping and shifting—if she even had the strength to lift it. Not to mention he would've felt her passing him if she'd squeezed by and shot outside; she was fast, but she wasn't microscopic.

So then where the hell *was* she?

"I love epitaphs, don't you?"

It was her voice, but it was coming from outside. There were decorative bars of black wrought iron set in the door, and Dustin brought his face to the gap between them, gripping the rusted scrollwork so tightly the cold metal dug into his skin. "Kira?" He shook the door; it rattled but wouldn't give, and his gaze went back to the graveyard, darting frantically about in search of her. "Kira!"

She strolled into view as if she had all the time in the world, her tone as conversational as it'd been when they'd been talking about his job. "They're so short, but they can say so much. A good funny one is hard to beat, but I always preferred ones like these." She crouched in front of a nearby stone, sweeping away a swath of moss almost reverently, and read, "Augustus Glenn. 'As I am, so shall you be,/prepare yourself to follow me.' That's a *real* golden oldie right there," she said, standing. "Our forefathers, they got it. Epitaphs help us remember the dead, sure, but they also remind the living that they'll be dead and buried someday, too."

"That's fascinating, Kira," Dustin said, fighting to keep his voice even while sweat trickled down his temple, his neck and shoulders starting to scream from being hunched this long. "Could you let me outta here, please?"

"What's your hurry?" she asked, an undercurrent of laughter bleeding into her voice. "You'll be back here soon enough."

"Kira, let me the hell outta here!" he said, somewhere between a snarl and a shout, shaking the crypt door so hard small crumbs of mortar fell from the stones it was set in.

She sighed, as if disappointed. "You're no fun," she said and vanished again.

He had no time to absorb this, though, because in the same instant the crypt door swung open and he spilled out, scrambling to keep on his feet. His only thoughts now were of escape, and he ran as he'd never run before, charging blindly through the graves back the way he'd come, almost falling over a few headstones and clipping himself on a crumbling stone slab, barely feeling the burst of pain in his leg through his panic. He couldn't see Kira, but he could hear her, her laughter floating through the air ahead of him, behind, off to the side, everywhere and nowhere at once; at one point it sounded right in his ear and he flinched away, but the laughter only grew louder, as if she was enjoying his fear.

"My old bones are telling me something's going to happen tonight."

If he got out of this, he was going to listen to Gran's old bones from now on; he'd stay put every time they ached and never complain about it—he'd whistle like a bluebird the whole time, because at least he'd be at home and safe and not running through a cemetery in the dead of night. And he'd have some questions for Madeline, too, whenever she decided to answer her goddamn phone. *So, Maddie, you decided to mention Kira's a Taurus but not that she's a—well, what the hell is she?!*

"Boo!"

She leaped on him from behind, dark earth and star-speckled sky whirling around him as the impact threw him to the ground and sent him rolling. When the pair came to a stop, Kira was atop him, disturbingly cheerful—and strong, Dustin found when he tried to free himself and couldn't budge her.

Oh God oh God oh God—

She placed her pale hand on his chest, the ice of her touch seeping through the shirt his open jacket had exposed, bleeding into his skin so sharply it almost burned. "Your heart's beating so *fast*," she marveled, eyes shining with unnerving delight. "You have no idea how much I miss having a heartbeat." Ignoring the stricken way he gaped at her, she went on, in the sultry tone that had so attracted him before, "And you're so *warm*—oh, I *love* it. See, I told a little lie earlier, and I know it's not right to start things off with a lie, so I'm going to come clean before this goes any further. I *do* mind the cold, Dustin. In fact, I hate it." Something flickered across her face then, black and bitter, turning her features gray and gaunt, as if she'd just crawled out of one of the graves around them.

But it was gone before he could be sure he'd seen it, her beautiful mask back in place. He wasn't swayed by it anymore, though, redoubling his efforts to break free but failing just the same. "Get *off* me!" he said, forcing the words out through his terror. In his struggles he felt a feather-light touch on his chest, something sliding across his collarbone, only dimly registering it and quickly forgetting it as she refused to move. "Kira, I swear to God if you don't let me go—"

"But you're so warm," she repeated, blue eyes going black. "And I am so, so tired of being cold." Her hand crept up his chest, spreading her chill like a poison, leaving him wide-eyed and gasping for breath beneath her. "Who will remember you, Sir Dustin? What will they carve on your stone?"

She leaned down, and he realized she was about to kiss him with as much horror as he would've once felt desire, incapacitated by her touch and helpless to resist. "Prepare yourself to follow me," she breathed, her lips brushing his, before their mouths met.

The cold flowed through him, filling him from head to toe. His lungs felt shriveled, screaming for the air Kira was stealing, his arms and legs useless as limbs carved from marble. His vision wavered, blackness eating away the edges, moving inexorably toward the middle.

Gran, I'm sorry, he thought as a choked gasp wracked his chest, piercing him with an arrow of pain. *I'm sorry I'm sorry I'm sorry—*

Kira broke her mouth from his with a howl of outrage and pain, the ashen shadows returning to her face as it contorted. She glared down at him, eyes blazing, before she disappeared, leaving Dustin sprawled there bewildered and panting, sucking the cool night air into his burning lungs, his mind whirling, working to catch up. Where had she gone, and why had she let him go when he was so totally in her power?

As he pushed up to a sitting position, something slid across his chest: *the Saint Michael medal*, he realized, catching it in his shaking hand. It must've shifted out from beneath his shirt while he was trying to escape Kira's grip. He remembered the brief touch he'd felt on his collarbone while her hand was roving upward, farther, farther...

"Promise me you'll wear it, Dustin."

He had to get the hell out of here, medal or no. Grabbing hold of a nearby headstone, he levered himself up, unsteady as a newborn lamb, and kept a wild eye out for Kira as he hurried toward the cemetery gate, not knowing if she'd been chased off for good or merely repelled for the moment. He wasn't sure if he was actually being watched or if his panic was making him paranoid, but either way he couldn't shake the sensation and pushed himself harder despite his weakness, the lingering ache in his chest.

He made it to the wall unmolested, scrambling up and falling over it more than climbing, and once he was back on the sidewalk he stood there breathing heavily and looking around at his quiet suburban surroundings, as still and forlornly serene as if nothing whatsoever out of the ordinary had occurred.

The ringing of his phone almost sent his skeleton bursting from his skin and clattering down the street. Fumbling the phone from his pocket, he found Madeline's face smiling up at him from the display. Something coalesced inside him at the sight, hot and cold at once, and he answered with a snapped, "What the hell?" even as a small, rational voice in the back of his mind pointed out that Maddie was his friend, and not psychotic; she never would've set him up with Kira if she'd known her true nature. "What the *hell,* Maddie?"

"I know, I know, I'm sorry," she said. "I just saw your texts from earlier; Kira's, too. She feels horrible about what happened, and she wants me to apologize for her."

"Apologize?" His voice cracked in disbelief—could he have actually heard that right? "Are you—are you screwing with me? She wants to *apologize?* Maddie, do you know what she *did?"*

"Who will remember you, Sir Dustin? What will they carve on your stone?"

"Yeah, she told me," Madeline said, alarmingly casual. "She feels really bad about it, trust me, but it's kinda on me, too. If I was gonna play Cupid, the least I could do would be to keep my phone on. She really wants to make it up to you, though, and she asked if Saturday works for you."

"Sa..." He couldn't even choke the word out.

"Are you all right, Dustin?" Madeline asked, concern finally tingeing her voice. "I know it sucks to be stood up, but she really does want to go out with you. Hopefully next time she won't have to take her sister to the hospital."

Dustin blinked. "Wait, what?" Maybe he'd cracked his head on a gravestone, scrambled his brains a bit, because this was making less and less sense by the moment.

"Uh-huh, she was visiting her sister in Gold Oaks this afternoon, and her sister fell down the stairs; they thought her leg might be broken, so Kira had to drive her to the ER. It turned out to just be a sprain, but they were stuck there for hours, and that's why she didn't show."

"Didn't...show?"

"Yeah. Isn't that what you're mad about? Dustin? Are you okay?"

He didn't answer her, couldn't, her repeats of, "Dustin? *Dustin?*" growing fainter as he let his hand fall to his side. Brown leaves and candy wrappers, the detritus of another October thirty-first, eddied around his feet, tree branches rustling softly as he turned to face the cemetery. And from its depths came a snatch of laughter, rich and warm, drifting into the night.

SLAUGHTERHOUSE X

DW MILTON

Alex applied pressure to the kid's mangled arm, noting, "You're lucky, it missed the artery."

Stopping the bleeding and dressing the wounds were easier than calming the terrified boys, so she didn't even try. However, the irony did not escape her. She and Dee had listened to these three braggarts while standing in line for thirty-five minutes waiting to enter Slaughterhouse X. The three claimed that they were not scared of anything and that this place was *for punks*. However, the attack had reduced them to three blubbering puddles, one having peed himself. Alex couldn't blame him.

Now a den mother, she wished that she and Dee had opted to go to Billy's instead for Halloween.

"What are we gonna do?" one of the kids sobbed.

Alex looked around; if there was some place she could hide them, they might have a chance. Whoever these murdering fucks were, they were serious. The current scene was straight out of *Children of the Corn*. The set consisted of a weather-beaten plywood house located somewhere in the middle-of-nowhere Nebraska and included a ridiculous cornfield. It even had a stripped-down car up on cinderblocks for effect.

The trunk, Alex thought.

Before she could direct the boys to the junker, a chorus of screams echoed from the other room. The room they had just escaped. The one with the swinging circular saws.

Alex slid her belt out of her jeans's loops and secured it over the boy's wounded arm. The other two crowded in tighter, hiding their heads. She bent low and whispered, "Okay, see that old car over there? We are going to run for it, open the trunk, and get in."

The injured kid moaned, "Nooo. Don't leave us!" The other boys sobbed in agreement.

"I am not leaving you," she reassured. "I need to hide you so I can find a way out of here. If someone comes in here like in those other rooms, I can't protect all three of you. You need to be somewhere safe so they can't get you."

"Why? Why are they doing this?" another cried. "Why did they hurt my brother Jack?" Jack, the oldest looking of the three, wrapped his good arm around his sibling.

"I know," Alex concurred. "Can you be brave for me just a little while longer?" Tearful, they nodded.

Alex led them, keeping low and constantly watching the door to the farmhouse, as they maneuvered to the heap. It was an older model from the fifties or sixties with a large backseat. She hoped it also meant a large trunk. At the rear of the vehicle, Alex felt around for the button, figuring a vintage like this one didn't have a remote. She found it and popped the lid. Peering into the dark space, she hoped it wasn't full of rattlesnakes, dirty syringe needles, or some sick shit; that would be the kind of prank these homicidal jerks would pull. Hearing and seeing nothing within, she lifted the lid higher.

"Get in," she told the boys. They hesitated, so she stood and opened the trunk completely. It was empty except for an old tire, which she hefted out. Jack managed, with his bandaged arm, to first help the other two inside and then climbed in with her assistance.

Before she shut the lid, she ripped out a taillight from inside, creating an opening.

"There," she said, "can you feel air moving?" All three nodded. "No matter what you hear," she commanded, "you stay in here. Do not come out. I'll knock three times, two short, one long. Got it?" She mimicked the knocks on the hood of the trunk.

With wide eyes, the boys nodded again, the brother hanging on to Jack, the other cradling himself.

"It will be okay, I promise."

Movement by the front door of the fake house caught her eye. Alex quickly shut the boys in and crouched down. The movement brought voices.

A man hollered over his shoulder, "Shut up, Eli! Those kids came in here. They are worth a couple grand each, at least. So start looking!"

Alex crept out into the makeshift cornfield, attempting not to rustle the paper mâché corn. She wanted to get to the scarecrow poised two rows over. The dark flannel shirt and jeans would camouflage her better in the dark light and fluorescent day glow painted all around the room. In her white t-shirt and white jeans (she came costumed as a tooth at Dee's request), she stuck out like a sore thumb. Beneath the scarecrow, she managed to slide down the jeans and free up the shirt, leaving the straw man naked.

She put on the jeans over her own, but before she could button up the flannel, she heard, "Hey, someone's glowing out in the cornfield. Get 'em!"

Two men thundered down the makeshift front porch, their boots stomping on the plywood. Alex turned her back and slid the flannel over her head. Crawling on her stomach, like she was taught back in basic training, she hightailed it to what she thought was a back corner of the set, only to realize there was nothing to hide behind. A black curtain hung from the rafters of the former K-mart ceiling, serving as sort of a partition between each scene. She peeled back the duct tape holding the fabric taut, lifted the fabric, and peered into the next room.

Crashing noises in the cornfield notified her that the two men were close. The adjacent space was dark except for hanging lowly lit lights hovering over an operating table. The room looked like a back alley surgical theater. Printed on a set of yellow barrels was the biohazard symbol. One barrel even had the word *Chernobyl* stenciled on it. What she did not see was an obvious exit. So far, all the other corridors or rooms she had been through had a door or some way to move forward. In this space, there was no apparent way out.

Alex left the curtain hanging askew, hoping the two thugs would take the bait; she split the difference and headed back down the row of paper mâché stalks, holding her breath as she passed the brutes.

"Look there!" one exclaimed. "The curtain!"

The two pushed on as Alex slithered back to the house. If this room was like the others, the front door led to the next room and, hopefully, to an exit.

She made it to the porch and scampered through the doorway, which revealed a poorly lit, long, skinny hallway, much like the one she and the boys had just escaped. She paused. Alex expected anything and nothing at the same time.

The chamber where she left Dee with the other injured and dead was a Medieval hall that appeared innocuous at first. A large table displayed a massive feast. Tapestries and banners hung from the walls and ceiling. Two fully decked suits of armor flanked the far wall with a large, oak-paneled door. One knight raised a naked sword. The other wielded a hanging mace. Flickering light from suspended torches and candles danced on the mannequins sitting at the tables, posed as guests enjoying the food.

A king and queen sat at the place of honor. Dee had stepped closer to the queen. Already freaked out and wanting to leave because of the man at the entryway, Dee was not prepared for the fright. The wavering light reflected off the actor's gold crown encrusted with jewels but did not reveal the dagger concealed under her gown. As Dee bent close to examine the prop, the actor stabbed at Dee's chest. Only because Alex had caught a glimpse of the shiny metal and was already holding Dee's hand in moral support was Alex able to snatch Dee away in time.

"What the hell!" Alex exhaled as Dee slammed into her.

The woman did not stop. She came at Dee, dagger raised. Dee screamed. The dagger came down and slashed at Dee's costume, a large cardboard box that mimicked a container of dental floss. The box shoved forward under Dee's weight, creating a space between Dee and the dagger. The thick, corrugated paper held fast against the slashing cuts, protecting Dee from the blade.

Alex grabbed a standing candelabrum and slammed it down on the hand brandishing the knife, hollering, "Get away from her!"

The king and his guests sat motionless and mute.

The woman retrieved the dagger, laughing, "We got a live one! How much extra for you?"

Simultaneously, there was movement everywhere as faceless figures clad in black body suits emerged from the walls, under the table, and behind tapestries. Dee lost her shit and shrieked in Alex's ear. The dark things grabbed at the couple, pulling them apart. Dee grasped at Alex. Alex slugged the first one she saw.

"Get away from us!"

Making contact, Alex spun and gut punched a second, the one wrestling with Dee.

"Let her go!" Alex commanded.

He let out an audible, "Umph!" and released Dee to grasp his stomach.

As the ruckus ensued, the door from where Alex and Dee entered the room opened, and the two friendly couples who were waiting in line behind Alex and Dee joined the party. Initially giggling and holding on to one another in mild hysterics, they all froze when Alex kicked the third black cat suit and hollered, "Get out of here! They are trying to kill us!"

Unfortunately, the newcomers believed Alex's emission to be part of the act and let the door shut behind them, sealing their fate. As if on cue, the knight bearing the mace came alive. Swinging the spiked metal ball with a practiced hand, it made contact with the nearest woman, smashing her head in like a deflated basketball, spraying blood and brain matter on the guy standing next to her.

Fresh blood having arrived, the queen struck out with the dagger at the woman's dumbfounded date, slicing him up the middle, skillfully eviscerating him where he stood, insides falling out. She withdrew the dripping metal only to send the blade into an unblinking eye. Both ruined forms crumpled while their friends screeched in horror. One of the men from the other couple deftly avoided the next swing of the mace and slammed his large, well-built physique into the knight, knocking the metal-clad character off balance.

Taking advantage of the distraction, Alex grabbed a large serving fork off the table and stabbed the crowned witch in the lower back. The crone screamed. Alex then grabbed Dee, shoving Dee behind her while still wielding the bloodied fork.

"Take the other," the murderous woman ordered before disappearing behind a tapestry. Three cat suits obeyed, surrounding the fourth member of the new group, a plump but handsome man who ineffectively fought off his aggressors. He struggled as the creatures in black dragged him through the slit in a curtain. Before making his own exit, the knight, recovered from the body slam, brought the mace ball down on top of the muscular man's leg, smashing it to the bone.

The man cried out in agony.

The knight took his leave.

Dee and Alex rushed over to the wounded man. He writhed in agony, repeating, "Anthony, Anthony, where did they take Anthony?"

The woman with the collapsed head moaned.

"Oh dear God," Dee gasped. "Is she still alive?"

Back in the corridor, Alex waited, watched, and listened. The screaming had stopped, which frightened her even more. She had barely registered the horrific sounds but subconsciously knew it was there. It was a gruesome soundtrack when they were battling the queen and cronies as well as when she and the boys sliced their way through the rusty hanging saws. She remembered something when she hid the boys. It drove her adrenaline in the cornfield. Now it seemed both the rush and the terror had paused.

What the fuck was this place, Slaughterhouse X? As far as she knew, it was the old K-mart, which some group rented and advertised as a sort of funhouse. The flyer Dee showed her was hand drawn and photocopied. A severed head sat atop what looked like an old grain silo doctored up to look like a Cold War missile. A cartoon bubble strategically placed next to a poorly drawn figure wearing a gas mask and holding a chainsaw read:

Looking for some flesh Halloween entertainment?
Find it at Slaughterhouse X
Only $5 Admission
Costumes welcome

Alex laughed when she read the flyer; the idiot who made it had misspelled *"fresh."*

All of them started their Halloween evening standing in line together, the three boys in front, the two couples behind them. It was a lot of waiting. Dee left work early yesterday to pre-purchase the tickets at the storefront box office, hoping they would be whisked on through, but it turned out that it didn't matter. Everyone had bought tickets early and everyone was waiting. If Dee had not already spent the thirty bucks, Alex would have conned her into ditching.

"Did you fill out the consent forms and waivers?" Alex heard the girl ask from the mixed doubles.

Although she didn't know his name at the time, it was Anthony who answered for himself and his boyfriend, the stocky guy who nailed the armor-clad Sir Homicide before the knight viciously retaliated. "Yes, and wasn't it so weird that they asked all those questions?"

Alex turned to Dee. "What questions?"

"Oh, I don't know," Dee said evasively. "They asked age, gender, race, and religion. You know, just demographic kind of stuff."

"I don't like it. Why would they be asking that? Isn't this supposed to be some sort of entertainment? Why the hell do they need to know about our religion?"

Dee rolled her eyes. "Come on, you old stick in the mud, it will be fun." She squeezed Alex's arm.

It was the guy at the door who changed Dee's mood. He scared the crap out of her. The Ringmaster, or at least he was dressed like an announcer from an old-fashioned circus, was taking tickets, then segregating the attendees off into lines, each leading to a separate chute: Chute #1, Chute #2, all the way up to Chute #10. All of them, Dee, Alex, the three boys, and two couples, had been prodded off to Chute #3.

Dee wanted to enter through Chute #1 (her lucky number) and foolishly paid an extra five bucks for the choice, but when he took their tickets, the Ringmaster denied her.

Leaning in, fetid breath on her face, he hissed, "Filth like you only deserves to be chattel."

Dee sucked in her breath as her eyes widened. She shuddered, painfully squeezing Alex's arm. She would not let go until the murdering stopped.

Now alone, Alex considered her next move. She had already decided that Slaughterhouse X must be a maze. Whatever psychopath designed this madhouse knew exactly what he was doing. Using the taped-down curtains as dividers or partitions was smart. It gave the illusion of a solid and sturdy wall in the faint light but allowed for a Houdini's escape. Alex deliberated. The fastest way through anything was a straight line. If she cut under each partition in a single direction, essentially moving in a straight line, she should hit a wall. Walls have real doors, such as exit doors. A former large retail store like this had to have fire doors. Hit a wall, find a fire door, and BINGO, outside!

Alex began walking forward, feeling along the edge of the fabric for tape or a tear or some sort of weakness. She got about halfway down the passageway when she felt cold air rushing past her hand.

Sliding her fingertips along, she found a slit in the fabric. She widened the seam to see what mess she was in now. It appeared to be a locker room. A lone sneaker sat under a bench. Never having worked in retail, she wasn't sure if this was part of the set up or really left over from the department store.

She needed a weapon. The corridor of saws and the farmhouse contained nothing useful. She scolded herself for not keeping the fork she jabbed into the queen's side, which reminded her of Dee. She took a moment to worry. Alex knew Dee could handle herself if she was so inclined. Perhaps, Alex hoped, the Ringmaster, the queen, and the ninjas had sufficiently pissed her off. Yet what Alex really wanted was for Dee to stay hidden, like Dee promised she would, until help arrived.

Recovered and resigned, Alex rummaged through the lockers; besides the sneaker, there was not much. A dead ballpoint pen, a discarded K-Mart nametag that read *"Bob,"* and a dried-out Speedstick deodorant. Alex pocketed the pen and nametag—both had points that might be useful—but left the deodorant. Disappointed that there were no cleaning chemicals or a broomstick to pilfer, she instead removed the shoelace from the lone sneaker and tied the strawman's jean loops to her jeans. She had used her belt as a tourniquet on Jack's arm and the scarecrow's pair of denims were at least an extra-large; both pairs of pants threatened to slip to her ankles. The real win, however, was the rusty crowbar she found tucked behind a garbage can.

She stepped into the tiled washroom where she saw her reflection in the mirror. She fit in well with the horror. Blood from the earlier carnage caked her hair, face, and neck. Her too big scarecrow garb gave her body a lumpy disfigurement.

A toilet flushed. Alex slid back into the shadows and crouched down, scanning for feet. She identified a boat-size pair of Doc Martens planted in the third stall from the door. Alex had no time to hide, but if she could rush whomever it was at the sink, she might have a surprise advantage. Even a homicidal maniac should still have some semblance of personal hygiene.

A giant stepped out of the stall. One of the cretins from the cornfield. Alex hesitated. The bully opened the locker room door and left. She waited a beat before she opened the door to peek out. She looked both ways down the corridor. Hovering over a large door at one end of the passage, she saw exactly what she was looking for: a glowing red EXIT sign. Glancing one more time behind her, Alex took off for the fire door. About ten yards from the exit, she dipped her shoulder and mentally prepared herself for contact. If she had waited five more seconds, she would have seen Eli, the larger of the two fellows from the cornfield, step out behind her. Before she hit the door, Eli called out to Samuel, the other monster, who was in the far office adjacent to the EXIT door.

Samuel strode out in time to see Alex coming straight for him and held out a burly arm. The effect was what World Wresting fans affectionately called a clothesline. Alex's chest smacked into Samuel's arm at ramming speed, flipping her legs out from under her. Legs in the air, she whipped around and onto her back and shoulder. Already turned in preparation for collision, she spared her head full force when she hit the floor, but the crowbar tucked in her back pant leg dug deeply into her side.

Samuel laughed. "Where do you think you're going?"

Eli joined them. He reached down with a gigantic hand, lifting her to his eye level.

"She looks like Scary Tom in those old clothes," was the last thing she heard before Eli backhanded her into darkness.

Alex came to bound, gagged, and shoved in a defunct dressing room. She heard moaning coming from somewhere. Maybe next door. *Dee!* Her heart leaped. Then her brain took over and hoped not. Whoever it was sounded half dead.

Alex looked around the stall. Stripped. Even the mirror and hooks were ripped off the walls. She rolled around on the floor, feeling the filthy carpet for something, anything, to work the duct tape that held her hostage. If only she could find...Bob! The nametag! It had a pin. If she could just...get...to... Alex contorted and wiggled. Her captors had done her a favor by snatching away the crowbar. She could maneuver better without that solid shaft of metal jacking her in the side, which ached relentlessly.

Alex squealed behind the sticky gag; the psycho brothers weren't that thorough, and she still had the pin in her own pocket. Rising on her knees, face on the floor, she raised her elbows to slide her hands into Scary Tom's pants. Both the nametag and ballpoint pen were there, tucked in her left hip pocket.

The tip of the pin had a point that wouldn't draw blood but was enough to puncture the haphazard layer of duct tape connecting her hands. Once freed, she ripped off the gag along with three layers of skin and what felt like her bottom lip. The pinpoint was almost useless for the tape at her feet, but once she created enough of a hole with it, she wedged her fingers through, tearing and pulling until her legs separated.

The moaning withered to an occasional groan.

Similar to the bathroom stall, she peered out from under the door, looking for feet. Nothing in the stall across from her nor in the space in between. She crawled out under the dressing room door, staying low. A single flickering fluorescent light cast seizure-inducing shadows in the other booths; however, it was enough light for Alex to determine they were empty. As she reached the final dressing room, the moaning stopped.

Alex almost panicked.

Dee, she thought, *what if it's Dee?*

She had no idea how long it had been since they decided to separate when Alex went looking for the source of the screams and found the three kids.

She forced herself to breathe and prepared for the worst.

She rolled to the final booth and glanced under the door.

Oh, thank God! she thought.

It wasn't Dee; it was Anthony, part of the two couples that the queen and her minions dragged away. Alex let out a guilty sigh of relief. He was in bad shape. She crawled into the booth and touched his shoulder.

Startled, he opened his remaining but useless eye. All she saw was his terror. All he saw was darkness.

She whispered, "Anthony, it's Alex. I was with the other woman in line before you." His shoulders sagged. Fresh tears dripped from his destroyed eyes. He tried to speak, but a thick wad of coagulated blood slithered from his mouth. Someone had cut out his tongue.

Alex cried with him. Of everything she had seen during her time as an army medic, the sheer savageness raged upon this helpless man far exceeded her worst waking nightmare. His hands had also been duct taped, along with his feet, probably before the horrors rained down upon him. He was no fight or flight risk now, rendered blind and dumb.

She needed to hide him. Stash him some place where, if those bastards came back, they wouldn't easily find him. She *hoped* they wouldn't find him. She could not take him with her. Her plan to find a way out stood.

Alex whispered her plan to Anthony. He pleaded silently for her not to leave him, but in the end, he had to acquiesce.

The question was where she could hide him. Unlike the farmhouse scene with the car, this was an unused fitting room. Maybe there was a closet or... Alex looked back at the entrance—a counter. She booked it to the counter. Underneath were a set of cabinets. She opened one to reveal that not only were the cabinets empty, but also not partitioned and quite large.

She returned to Anthony.

With him safely tucked away, she figured out her next step. Before the store permanently closed, Alex remembered trying on a dress in one of those fitting rooms. It was strange because a doosey of a summer rainstorm began while she shopped. Typically, in such a large store, one may be able to hear claps of thunder but not the patter of the rain drops beating against the walls, but for this one, she could. The rooms must have backed up against an outside wall. If she kept along the wall, she should hit another exit, and this time she was not going to let those motherfuckers stop her.

Alex passed around the counter to where it met a wall. A leftover clothes rack stood about three feet away. A metal arm hung crooked and loose. Not as good as the crowbar, but it would do. She wrenched it free. A stripped bolt stuck out on one end. She indulged for a moment, envisioning it driving deep into one of the queen's eyes.

For Anthony, she thought and moved on.

Makeshift weapon in hand, Alex moved along the wall.

As she followed it, the farther she got from the fitting room and that spastic fluorescent bulb, the darker the space got. In the near black, she continued to creep along, feeling with her hands more than seeing with her eyes.

About thirty steps into the blackness, she hit something solid. It felt like another wall, which didn't make sense. It should have been open all the way to the corner, and Alex didn't recall the changing rooms being so close to another structural partition. It must have been something added by the designer of this freak show. Opposite to that barrier hung another black curtain, which didn't help. The curtain veered away at a kind of diagonal. As far as Alex could tell, if she stuck to the wall, she would have to crawl under the curtain, which could have God knew what behind it; or she could go back and try to go the other way around the other side of the fitting rooms. Neither choice enthralled her.

Ready to turn back and start over going the other way, she reached up and hit something metal. A rung. Still feeling more than seeing, she realized it was a ladder bolted to the concrete blocks. Looking up, she saw a catwalk in the shadows of the rafters.

Now why didn't I think of that before? she reproached herself. She didn't have to go back. She could go up. Tucking her weapon—or whatever you would call it—in her Scary Tom pants again, she grasped the rungs with both hands and shook. The ladder remained steady.

Here goes nothing.

Hand over hand, she ascended into the rafters. Every once in a while, she glanced back in case someone down there looked up. Never before having a fear of heights, Alex wobbled a little when she reached the catwalk, which must have been at least thirty feet off the ground, but it gave her a clear view of the entire top of the building. She squatted watching for movement. Who knew if any of the cat suits patrolled up here?

She took out her metal club and moved forward. As far as she could tell, she was alone. The catwalk ran in three parallel sections down the length of the store. Unfortunately, all the crosswalks uniting the catwalks were at the other end. She would have to traverse the distance of the department store before she could turn.

She looked down into the spaces and stopped. She was right about Slaughterhouse X being a maze. Black partitions separated artificial rooms of all shapes and sizes. As she forced herself to continue walking, she noted what she saw, but it never really registered. It seemed that every single Slaughterhouse X attendee was dead, dismembered, and/or dissected. There was a bloodbath in every room, in every scene.

An Aztec priest stood on a staggered pyramid with his blood-stained hands raised to an angry god while a pile of heartless corpses lay strewn below. A summer camp massacre villain rip-off sat encircled by eviscerated Slaughterhouse X patrons. In the back alley operating room, body parts dripped from the three barrels marked biohazard. From above, the swinging circular saws, now stained and dripping, reminded her of *The Pit and the Pendulum*. Even the cornfield scene now nauseated her.

Was the trunk of the junker still closed?

Alex couldn't look.

The rooms and the bloodshed went on and on and on.

How? Alex sank onto the metal grate. Then she realized how easy it probably was. When she and Dee were attacked, the couples who entered moments later thought it was part of the act. In fact, Alex had upset the queen by striking back. The queen was not expecting it. No one was expecting it.

Corralling the patrons off through separate chutes led the lambs to the slaughter. Lure folks in and then attack from behind. That's why the boys had made it to the Edgar Allen Poe suite before they were attacked. It made sense why she and Dee were at least two rooms in before something happened.

Alex imagined that there must be a whole army of them.

What a bunch of sick fucks! It was all Alex could muster.

She didn't know how long she sat there; but when she was finished, she wiped her nose and dried her eyes. She had to get out. She had to get help. Alex could not bear to look down anymore, so she glanced up. AC ducts. Pipes. Sprinkler system. Fire Department.

Holy shit! Oh please, please, please, still work.

Alex didn't smoke or carry a lighter; but last Christmas, Dee accidentally set off the sprinkler system in their apartment by hanging garland off one of the sprinkler heads. The water damage was limited, but the two hundred dollar fine and a soaked Christmas tree definitely dampened the holiday cheer. If Alex could hit one or could bump it, she might be able to activate it, triggering an alarm and help.

Alex got up and scanned the ceiling for sprinklers. It was not easy. There was such little light from the catwalk into the rafters. She would need to follow the pipes. Alex found a sprinkler head about halfway down the catwalk, suspended about thirty feet over the department store floor. Two sets of pipes about the size of Alex's forearm passed by the head just enough that if she could climb out to it, she could take a swing with her broken clothes hanger.

Easy peasy, right? She sighed.

Alex tucked the metal stick back in her pants and climbed up on the railing. She was able to grab hold of the pipes and hung there for a second.

Man, I am out of shape, she reflected as she attempted a pull-up. Too many nights on the couch enjoying a pizza and a movie with

Dee. She and Dee met after Alex left the army, and even though Dee hated the gym, Alex made herself and Dee a promise right there, if they got out of this shit, they were both going to get fit.

Alex swung out and over the floor. Concentrating on her task, she refused to look down, not because of the height, but because of everything else. Hand to hand, she slipped sideways, closer and closer to the flowered spicket. Arms shaking, she reached it. She rested. Knowing her right arm was stronger and could hold her weight on its own, she reached into her and Scary Tom's pants to take out the metal arm. She hung again, resting a moment to get her bearings. Then with all her might, she slammed the metal tip with the bolt into the sprinkler head.

Nothing. No water, no alarm, no help. Just a loud clank as the metal head spun off into the darkness, leaving her in disbelief.

God fucking damn it!

And she was sure every motherfucker in this Army of Maniacs heard the decapitated sprinkler head separate from its sad little pipe. Not to mention she was dangling thirty feet above a killing floor.

Alex laughed. Out loud. The sound startled her as it echoed through the space.

Now what?

She could shimmy back the way she came, hand over hand, back along the pipe, but Alex recognized she didn't have the strength or the heart. Dee was most likely dead. Piled in one of those corpse mounds. Same with the boys. Maybe poor Anthony with his boyfriend. She wanted to join them. Never in all her life had she felt so wretched and so hopeless.

Alex gave up and let go. Having avoided the view below, she did not see the heap of disfigured patrons beneath her. At least half as tall as she was up high, it easily broke her fall when she hit and then squashed, squished, and rolled down the side of the hill. At the bottom, she laid there, waiting.

Surprisingly, no one came. Not the Ringmaster, the queen, the knight, the cat suits, or the cornfield brothers. Not a single murderous figure appeared. Dazed, Alex opened her eyes.

Was it over? Was the murder spree finished?

It didn't matter. What did matter was finding Dee, the boys, and Anthony. Dead or alive. She hid them. She was responsible for them. She climbed off the unfortunate attendees and said a prayer for them. All of them. God was definitely not here tonight, but it gave her the strength and mental fortitude she currently lacked.

A machete had been casually tossed aside. She grabbed it. Slicing through the black fabric, she headed in what she thought was the direction of the banquet hall. Instead, she found herself in the cornfield.

She walked over to the junker. She knocked three times. Two short, one long. She took a deep breath and popped the trunk. Three pale faces with terrified eyes stared up at her. She sobbed and dropped the machete.

"Where are we going?" Jack asked. He was weak from blood loss.

"To find Dee."

She adjusted and then tightened the belt on his arm. Before allowing them out of the trunk, she made them swear not to look around. She made them promise to keep their eyes on the ground.

Alex used the machete to bypass the saw room; she could still hear the swipe of the blades slicing through the air.

Once in the medieval hall, she whispered, "Dee. It's Alex. Come out. I think it's over."

There was no response. Alex hissed louder, "Dee! Dee!"

"She's not here," one of the boys whined.

Impatient, another said, "Let's get out of here! Come on, let's go!"

The frightened eyes and anxious pulls at Scary Tom's flannel coaxed her to move on. Before she did, she slid back the tapestry that had been spread over the table to serve as a tablecloth. She peered underneath where she had left Dee with the injured man.

Both were gone. Her heart sank. She decided to get the boys out, then come back and look for Anthony.

Alex led the boys back through the doors that they had used to enter the banquet hall and back through Chute #3, unmolested. Outside the glass storefront, lights bounced off the buildings, giving the scene a pulsating effect. First reds then blues, skipping and leaping as their source revolved. Around and around and around. Alex stood watching, almost dizzy from the effect.

LITTLE MISS 666

SCOTTY MILDER

Excerpt from the article "Surviving Tot Honors Mystery Victim of Halloween Blaze" by Raleigh Corbett. Originally printed in the **The Rocky Mountain Dispatch,** *November 18, 1947:*

PUEBLO — Eight-year-old Samantha Louise Morton, of Blende, went to Pueblo's Roselawn Cemetery Sunday afternoon with her father, George Morton, 41, also of Blende. The sorrowful duo were there to pay respects to the child citizens of Colorado have come to know as "Little Miss 616."

Samantha was one of the many survivors of the hellish blaze that consumed the Caldwell & Fletcher Traveling Circus Act's big-top tent on Oct. 31 at the State Fairgrounds in Pueblo. Samantha was pulled from the inferno with severe burns to her back and legs and has spent the last eighteen days under care at Mercy Hospital in Denver.

While more than two thousand circusgoers and performers escaped the blaze, one hundred and eighty-seven people gave their lives to the flames. That sad number includes Samantha's mother Harriet Marian Morton, 37, her cousins David "Davey" Knox and Rebecca Knox, 12 and 10 respectively, and her younger brother Charles Emory Morton, 6, all of Blende.

Wearing a plain white dress, and with her auburn curls glittering like jewels in the afternoon light, young Samantha weakly clutched a bouquet of red roses as her father pushed her wheelchair up the path to the grave where Little Miss 616 has been laid to rest.

Little Miss 616 was an unknown girl just a bit younger than Samantha. She is included among the twenty-seven unidentified dead discovered within the smoldering tent after the conflagration was finally extinguished. All twenty-seven victims have been interred at Roselawn.

Little Miss 616 was found beneath a crush of victims toward one of the tent's rear entrances. Officials believe her placement beneath several bodies is responsible for her remarkably unburnt appearance. In an attempt to ascertain the saintly cherub's identity, a Colorado State Police photograph taken at the morgue, depicting the girl in her peaceful final repose, was printed on the front page of the Dispatch *two days after the fire. Her visage has since become the angelic public face of this detestable tragedy.*

No family members have, as of yet, stepped forward to claim her remains.

The CSP and the Colorado Division of Fire Prevention continue to probe the cause of the blaze. As our readers well know, the investigation has been deluged by rumors and accusations of arson...

October 31, 2017:

The witch was actually pretty scary, what with her green skin, her puke-yellow snaggle teeth, and all those black warts across her cheeks and forehead. The plastic, pumpkin-shaped bucket clutched in her hand kind of spoiled the effect, though—not that Jordan would have said anything about that.

The witch grinned her repugnant grin and thrust the bucket out in front of her. It ticked back and forth like a hypnotist's pocket watch.

"*Trick or treat!*"

"*Twick tweat!*" repeated Iron Man, who shuffled his feet behind the witch and swung his own pumpkin bucket lazily from side-to-side. Jordan pegged the witch at maybe seven, Iron Man at no more than four: big sis and little bro, with their parents lurking inconspicuously in the shadows. Dad caught Jordan's gaze and ticked off a little two-fingered salute. She recognized him as the sad-looking guy who ran the Kum & Go at 19th and Uintah.

"Ooooooh, no!" Jordan cried, dramatically throwing up her hands to shield her eyes. "Not the Wicked Witch! Iron Man, can you protect me?"

The witch giggled. "I'm not the Wicked Witch!" she said. "I'm just a regular witch!"

"Still," Jordan said. "You gonna step up, Iron Man, or what?"

Iron Man turned to his sister and thrust out his red-gold finger. Jordan figured it was probably supposed to be a gun; she'd only seen the first movie (not by choice) and didn't quite remember how it worked.

"Pow pow pow!" Iron Man said.

"You can't shoot a witch!" his sister scolded. "I'll just magic you to death!"

"Pow pow pow!" Iron Man said again, more emphatically this time. The witch huffed and rolled her eyes.

"Thanks, Iron Man," Jordan said and reached into the wooden salad bowl that she'd filled with candy bars only a half hour ago. "You get two for sticking up for me. Whaddaya want?"

"Snickers!" Iron Man yelled.

"You got it," Jordan said, dropping the candy into his bucket. She turned to the witch. "And you get two for scaring the gollygeewillickers out of me. What's your damage?"

The witch giggled again. "I'll have a Butterfinger and...do you have Rolo?"

"Sure do," Jordan said. She let the witch pick them out of the salad bowl.

"What do you say?" Mom asked from the shadows.

"Thank you!" the witch and Iron Man sing-songed in unison and scampered off the porch.

"You're beautiful! I like your hair!" the witch yelled as the four of them faded off into the night.

Awwww, Jordan thought and looked toward the intersection. The sun had set maybe twenty minutes ago, and the tree-lined street was a mass of shadows punctured here and there by pools of cool, bluish light cast down from the LED streetlamps. Four kids—it looked like a couple zombies, a princess, and Wonder Woman—rounded the corner from Columbia onto Franklin. Two more sets of parents ambled good-naturedly after them. The zombies saw her beneath the porch light and started sprinting. Wonder Woman and the princess took their time—proving once again, Jordan thought, that girls matured more quickly than boys.

Jordan noticed another little girl lurking by the stop sign behind them. She thought the girl was probably supposed to be Elsa from *Frozen*, but her dress was a couple shades too light.

"Trick or treat!" the zombies yelled as they pounded up the driveway.

Led Zeppelin's "Immigrant Song" exploded from the house behind her. Connor's voice rose along with it, blending charmingly—if imperfectly—with Robert Plant's wail.

"Uh oh," Jordan said, smothering her grin and pushing out the biggest, campiest scared-lady-face she could muster. She raised the salad bowl over her head. "Please don't eat me!"

The zombies movie-growled in unison. *"Give us candy and we wooooooooon't!"* the older one moaned in his best *"braaaaaaaains"*-pastiche.

"Dylan," one of the moms scolded half-heartedly.

"Deal," Jordan said to the zombie she assumed to be Dylan and lowered the bowl as they clomped up the steps. The princess and

Wonder Woman came after them, hurrying now at the very real promise of candy.

The kids dug through the salad bowl, bumping into each other and chattering incomprehensibly. They reminded Jordan of the West Coast trip she and Connor took over the summer, when they fed ostriches at this little farm in the hills above Santa Barbara.

Without thinking about it, her eyes flicked to the end of the street.

Elsa or whatever was gone.

By the time Jordan got back to Connor's office, "Immigrant Song" had given way to Thin Lizzy's "The Boys Are Back in Town." Phil Lynott rasped about wild-eyed boys and how them cats are crazy, and Connor—hunched over his laptop, bashing madly at the keys—mumbled along with him. Connor was almost forty-five, born at the very ass end of 1972, and he insisted that this was the music of his babyhood. That it had pushed into him when he was but a zygote and mixed with his DNA. Jordan herself was born just before Limp Bizket and Papa Roach started competing with NSync and Britney Spears for three-minute slots on *Total Request Live*, and she'd long ago rejected all that like cancer. She'd eased out of her Marilyn Manson phase early, grew partial to Clans of Xymox, Bauhaus, old-school Ministry, Fields of the Nephilim, Siouxsie Sioux and Robert Smith and Peter Curtis and all the '80s goth gods. But she could tolerate the '70s shit, at least when Connor was playing it. More than tolerate it, in fact. It reminded her of her dad. She supposed if she ever brought that up in a session, her therapist would have a whole lot to say about that.

Jordan stood in the doorway, watching him—her man, her

boyfriend—and even after a year and a half of their worst-kept-secret affair, the thought still made her heart flutter and turned her knees to water.

Thin Lizzy faded into Fleetwood Mac. "Rhiannon." Connor told her the song was about some ancient Welsh goddess, and then he'd said, *That's you, you know*. And even though Jordan thought of herself as the Jewiest half-Jew who'd ever managed to crawl out of the bowels of central Texas, she added the song to her morning playlist. As she jogged up East Yampa past the CanAm Highway, always fleeing the rising sun that pressed steadily into her sweaty back like an open palm, she absorbed it—committed every slithering lilt of Stevie Nicks's voice to memory, along with every note of Lindsey Buckingham's guitar, every tinkle of Christine McVie's keyboards, and every throb of John McVie's bass. She finally busted it out at karaoke one night back in March. She and Connor were at some hipster bar in New York—Connor in the city for a poetry conference, Jordan (as she so often was) discreetly along for the ride. He sipped his Scotch and watched her, rapt, then summoned the tattooed waitress to their table and paid the check before Jordan finished. Then he'd taken her back to their hotel room and fucked her until she bled, until she thought the fusion-reaction chain of orgasms blasting flare sprays out of her quaking body would make her collapse in on herself like a supernova.

The memory made Jordan feel flushed, smearily hot, as if her internal boiler had notched up a couple degrees. On cue, Connor swiveled in his desk chair and saw her. He was thin and not altogether tall, with pale, hawk-like features and a receding flop of black hair slashed with bands of gray. Objectively, his chin was too narrow and his nose was a little too big. His salt-and-pepper scruff came in bristled and patchy.

Nobody's idea of a heartthrob, in other words. And yet—from the moment she'd first sat in on one of his lectures—the sight of him made her knees weak, caused her stomach to flop and roll and wriggle like an overexcited puppy. It was his eyes, she thought: so brown they were nearly black, intense and intelligent and kind in equal measure, but with something fundamentally unknowable—maybe dangerous—hiding way in the back. Connor was the quintessential "nice man," as her mother would say: safe and supportive and as sturdy as a concrete pylon. And yet...there was always the lurking suggestion that none of that was true, that maybe if you cracked him open lava would come pouring out, and if you stood too close you'd be incinerated. It was that hot breath of the perilous she craved and chased and goaded out of him whenever he took her to bed...but when she woke up next to him, the sturdiness—the *kindness*—was what kept her there.

"Who was it?" he asked, turning the music down.

"First it was a witch who was there with Iron Man, then a couple zombies, a princess, and Wonder Woman."

Connor grimaced theatrically.

"What is it all you Zoomers say?" he asked. "'*So basic.*'"

"Come on." She grinned. "They're kids. Be nice."

"They're kids, so what? You know the first Halloween costume I remember? I went as 'a knight in *The Shining* armor.' My dad cut me a wooden sword and shield on his band saw. My mom made the armor out of paper maché, and my sister Kelly put bloody handprints all over the chest piece and scrawled 'REDRUM' across the helmet with a red magic marker."

Jordan made a retching sound. "That's *insufferable.*"

"I mean, yeah," Connor agreed. "It was my mom's idea. I wanted to go as Ernie from *Sesame Street*. Still, in retrospect I give them props for creativity. No one was gonna let me embarrass the family by going out as something as..." He wrinkled his nose. "As...*BASIC* as...a *ZOMBIE.*"

"Jesus," Jordan said, and giggled into her hand. "You must've gotten beaten up *all the time.*"

Connor shrugged, glancing at his laptop. "Sure did. But look at me now: chasing tenure at a tiny college, publishing the occasional poem in lit journals with fully *dozens* of readers, banging away at a novel I've been working on for fifteen years. Maybe in a couple years I'll be able to ditch my decade-old Prius for a half-decade-old Prius. If Dougie Burns isn't out there somewhere positively *boiling* with envy, I might as well just give up and cut my wrists right now."

"Don't forget," Jordan said, "you're also banging the hot TA."

Connor thought about that for a moment, then nodded.

"Yes," he said. "I am doing that."

"*Secretly* banging, no less." Jordan idly-not-idly fiddled with the top button of her Dickies work shirt. It was black and baggy, but she'd been sure to put on the nearly sheer red bra he liked so much. "I don't know who Dougie Burns is, but isn't that every man's fantasy?"

Connor sighed, resigned to what was about to happen, and pushed himself out of his chair.

"It sure as hell is *mine*." He glided toward her, preceded by his scent. He smelled like tobacco and coffee, just a little bit of sweat, all underlaid with a smoldering musk that was all him.

The doorbell *bing-BONGED* as the fingers of his left hand undid the fourth button of her shirt and his right slid inside to cup her breast.

"You better go get that." The words were hot and low and drizzled right into her ear. She nuzzled his neck, nipping at his throat. *GOD, his SMELL...I love his SMELL...*

"Do I have to?"

BING-BONG...

His fingers found her nipple. Clamped down. She yelped.

"Do you have to...*what?*"

He twisted. She gasped.

"Do I have to...*Daddy?*"

He twisted again, a little harder this time. She felt her body melting into his like wax.

BING-BONG...

"No," he breathed. "You don't."

It didn't take long. It rarely did with them. There was something in their chemistry that was like water and magnesium—had been ever since their first time, when a thesis-advisory meeting unexpectedly devolved into the pair of them panting into each others' mouths and fumbling at each others' belt buckles. Jordan was pleased that, after three-and-a-half semesters and an entire summer, the explosivity between them hadn't much abated.

They did it right there, on his office floor. That was a new one. She guessed it took about fifteen minutes from dropped pants to her orgasm, maybe another thirty seconds for his. Not a personal best, but close. They only missed two rounds of trick-or-treaters.

She rolled off of him and craned up to grab his cigarettes from the desk.

"You okay?" he asked.

"Huh?"

"I didn't...I didn't hurt you?"

Jordan popped a cigarette between her sweat-slickened lips and lit it. Her shoulder throbbed where he'd bitten her. He didn't draw blood—he rarely did anymore, he was getting better at it—but she'd have a hell of a bruise tomorrow.

She sucked in a lungful of smoke and looked down. The naked worry on his face made her want to both laugh and cry—laugh at the absurdity of it, cry with gratitude that it was there at all. Connor was new to the rough sex, the kink, the dom/sub power play, and—hot lava core or no—he was still unsure of himself, no matter how much she buoyed him up.

She knew why. Mental illness ran in his family. His dad had been an occasionally violent drunk. He had a great uncle or something who had, way back when, snapped and carved up his wife in an incomprehensible fit of psychosis before burning her body. Connor had spent his entire life and formed his entire identity around *not* being that person. He was still wrapping his head around the notion that he could want what he wanted—and give her what *she* wanted—*without* being that person.

Sometimes his tentative nature got him all up in his head and in his own way, but mostly she was glad he wasn't like some of the more experienced doms she'd met in the various scenes she'd flitted through over the years—toxic, boundary-pushing predators to whom gaslighting and cruelty came as natural as breathing. A little extra hand-holding on her part was a small price to pay.

"Connor," she said and ran her finger up his slick, almost hairless thigh. "I'm *more* than okay."

BING-BONG...

She wanted to ignore the doorbell—just curl up next to him in his sweat and his awkward silence and go to sleep. But she'd also been looking forward to this night for months; it had been years since she'd not been at some stupid party on Halloween, trying to be as garishly sexy as possible and convince herself she was having fun. The idea of simply hanging around in blue jeans and her Dickies shirt, passing out chocolate and Jolly Ranchers to a bunch of kids, was revivifying. She couldn't yet admit out loud that it was something she actually wanted, but every time she dropped a candy into some kid's bucket she could pretend *I LIVE here, this is MY house, I'm MRS. JORDAN LOOKSTEIN-BRACKENRIDGE.*

"You better get dressed," Connor said. He smiled knowingly, as if he'd read her thoughts.

"I guess I better." She leaned over, kissed him deeply, relished the warm swell of her breast against his bony chest, then slipped the cigarette into his mouth and stood.

LITTLE MISS 666

BING-BONG...

Jordan hurried into the foyer, shoving the tail of her shirt into the back of her jeans as she went. She caught a glimpse of herself in the hallway mirror as she passed. The curly explosion of black hair she'd gotten from her Jewish dad—the hair the little witch had deemed beautiful—was spiking out every which way now. The ocean-blue eyes she'd inherited from her Swedish/Irish mother were damp and rimmed red, as if she'd been crying. She *had* been crying, of course—not in sadness, but pain. Delicious, delicious pain.

Oh well, she thought. Music erupted from Connor's office—Dire Straights this time, "Romeo and Juliet"—as she grabbed the candy bowl and threw open the door.

The sun had fallen, cloaking the street in black. The overhead lamps punctured the darkness somewhat, but their blue-white glow seemed too dim, as if someone had smeared the light in an inky miasma. An ever-so-slight breeze made the pine trees creak way up in their crowns. It stippled Jordan's arms and neck in gooseflesh.

The little girl was all alone—no siblings, parents, or friends anywhere in sight—and it took Jordan less than half a second to recognize Elsa-by-the-stop-sign. Except, up close, she didn't look like Elsa at all. The dress—which Jordan had initially taken for light-blue—was actually a flat white that had filmed down to a sooty gray. It was old-fashioned, high-collared and high-waisted, with poofy sleeves and a lacey frill around the hem that looked oddly chewed. Her long, honey-colored hair hung in two lank braids across her shoulders, looped up to her ears and tied with a pair of equally ragged pink ribbons. Care had obviously been put into the hairstyle, but it was all coming loose. Frizzy blond strands corkscrewed out in a chaotic fringe.

If it was a costume, Jordan had no idea what the girl was supposed to be. A vintage porcelain doll, maybe? Was there some cartoon or kid's book character that Jordan didn't know about?

But then three things happened all at once, and Jordan's mild curiosity—leavened by an anxious desire to get back to Connor and maybe have another tumble—was slurped down, whale-like, by a lunging upswell of terror.

The first thing was the smell. It rolled off the girl in a dry, noxious wave, stinging Jordan's already raw eyes and salting them with tears. It was *smoke*—as bitter and amaroidal as what remained after a house fire but made extra pungent by a sweet/sour underodor that made Jordan recoil, understanding in an instinctual if not-quite-conscious way that it was the stink of burned and rapidly spoiling flesh.

The next thing was that Jordan noticed the black-red splotch broadening up from beneath the dress's collar. It blistered the girl's neck and left cheek. The seared skin glistened—wet and sticky—in the porch light. An obvious burn. A *deep* burn.

The third thing that happened was the girl's gaze. It daggered into Jordan like twin blades, and when she looked into those hazel eyes, she found herself sliding into a long-throated tunnel and tumbling toward a crepuscular absence—a primordial, colorless *lack* —that sank down, forever and ever and ever.

The girl opened her mouth—a moist, red cavern gone soupy with spit and half-congealed blood—and spoke. It was a little girl's voice, high and nasal, but at the same time it wasn't like anything Jordan had heard before. Nothing remotely human.

"It wasn't you," the girl said.

I know her, Jordan thought. Wonder and horror spun around each other, orbited about a central black point in her mind like binary neutron stars.

"It was *him*," the girl said.

Jordan tried to speak. Words stuck in her throat like glair.

How do I know her?

"You shouldn't be here," the girl said.

Music came from somewhere, rolling out of the sky like a distant rataplan and burying the Dire Straits like silt across the mouth of a stream. At first it was just a formless throb, but then it began to coalesce into notes. To structure itself into melody.

Beneath the crash and rattle of drums, she heard high voices and what sounded like an orchestra—horns and strings and trilling flutes, all of it brightly, maniacally exuberant—and for some reason it made Jordan think of the circus.

Again, she thought: *HOW DO I KNOW HER?*

"You shouldn't be here," the girl repeated.

Jordan recognized the song. It was, incongruously, "The Stars and Stripes Forever." And, for some reason, the realization shoved a blaring thought into her head. A single, insistent statement:

You have to run.

You have to run NOW.

Excerpt from the article "Police Insist Rabbi's Nephew Responsible for Circus Inferno," by Frederick C. Bennington. Originally printed in the *The Rocky Mountain Dispatch*, January 7, 1948:

DENVER — Police took Haskel Jacob Kantor, 23, into custody yesterday for the catastrophic Halloween fire that claimed the lives of one hundred eighty-seven people in Pueblo this past Halloween.

Kantor, of Denver, had attended the circus with his fiancé, Devorah Lobel, 17, of Centennial, and two unnamed friends. According to State Police Detectives Ralph Estermont and Carlos Ruiz, Kantor had snuck off behind the bleachers and set the blaze at some point during the first act—a lion-taming performance by renowned big-cat trainers David and Flora Jackson.

"We have several witnesses who saw him go down there," Estermont told this reporter. "Several witnesses. They all said the same thing: he was under the bleachers for at least five minutes, and he came out smirking. Can you believe it?"

According to Estermont, Kantor then collected his two friends and exited the tent, leaving his fiancé behind. Lobel was among the one hundred eighty-seven who died in the inferno.

Kantor claimed he and his friends were simply going out for a smoke, but Estermont quickly dismissed that explanation.

"God knows what his motive could have been," Estermont said. "It's impossible to tell with those people. You can't trust much of what they say."

The fire was spotted by Ringmaster Bufort Higgins shortly into the second performance, which was a high-wire and trapeze act by the Soaring Satrianis. Higgins then cued the orchestra to play the song "The Stars and Stripes Forever," which is a commonly understood distress signal amongst circus workers and roustabouts. Higgins managed to usher most of the 2,000 attendees out before the tent collapsed.

"It was all over in just about ten minutes," Estermont said. "Nearly 200 people died because of, what, some foreigner's prank? Trust me, we're throwing the book at him."

Haskel Kantor immigrated to the United States from Belgium in 1938. According to an unnamed family friend, his parents and siblings all perished at Auschwitz II-Birkenau. Haskel and a single cousin were the family's only survivors. Once in America, both youths were adopted by their uncle, Rabbi Moshe Lemuel Kantor of the Robinson Park Temple in Denver.

However, according to Estermont, the younger Kantor found trouble with the law soon after his arrival.

"He's got a record as long as my arm," Estermont said. "Burglary, auto theft, reefer, selling cigarettes without a tax stamp...you name it, the punk's probably done it."

Muriel Bowers, 63, a neighbor of Rabbi Kantor and his nephews, concurs with Estermont's assessment. "That (expletive) is nothing but trouble," she said. "I reckon he fancies himself the Rocky Mountain region's very own Dutch Schultz. But we'll see about that, now, won't we? We'll see how the punk likes sucking down a barrel of hydrogen cyanide."

Her husband, Frank Bowers, 65, added grimly: "It's just a shame they won't let us stretch his neck out anymore. I personally wouldn't mind watching the little (expletive) flopping around like a fish at the end of a hangman's rope. I'd say, might as well do all them (expletive) Kantors while they're at it."

Estermont and Ruíz insist that there is no evidence that Rabbi Kantor or the unnamed cousin were aware of what Haskel Kantor had planned...

Water running.

Music, distant and booming. Z.Z. Top, "Tush."

When Jordan came back into herself, she was standing at the sink, gazing dully into a casserole dish crusted over with cheese and coagulated globs of marinara sauce like splotches of dried blood. She vaguely remembered that Connor made a vegetarian lasagna last night, that they ate it on his back patio, that afterward they smoked hand-rolled cigarettes and sipped Chianti out of plastic cups and talked about everything—the Halloween horror movie marathon on AMC, standard English-department gossip, Connor's stalkery ex-wife, Jordan's stalkery ex-boyfriend, her pain-in-the-ass parents. They talked about how when/if they ever got married, he had the notion that they should pick up and move to Nags Head and open a little curio shop on the beach or something, spend their nights fucking like bonobos and their days selling seashells to tourists. The important thing would be that they'd be together and nobody would say shit about how he was two decades older and had been her thesis advisor; nobody would fire him if they found out. She said, *But if we fucked like bonobos, I'd have to be the dom,* and he said, *Hey, I don't think I'd mind being a switch every so often,* and she said, *Yeah, but I would.* They talked and smoked and drank and watched the sky go from indigo to gold to purple to a velvet, star-studded black. All this talk of who was the dom and who was the switch got them revved up, so they went inside and their clothes were off before they got to the bedroom, strewn all over the stairs like someone had put an M-80 in their laundry hamper. Connor shoved her onto the bed and uncoiled the rope from its customary place on the bedpost. He told her he wanted to try a new kind of knot he'd been practicing, and when they were done, they lay in each other's arms, satisfied and sore, their sweat cooling on their skin, and Jordan stared at the cracks in the ceiling and thought, *Nags Head sounds nice, is that North or South Carolina?* and finally she drifted off to sleep on the now-familiar, buzzsaw cut of his snores.

She gazed down at the casserole dish and remembered all that, and the only emotion she felt was a sort of anxious, fluttering bafflement. She felt like an invisible hand had come up behind her and shoved, and now her soul was lurching around completely outside herself, watching this black-haired, blue-eyed stranger do all these alien, incomprehensible things. Things that felt disconnected from any sense of agency or choice. It was like watching a character in a slasher movie: you want to shout at her not to go up the stairs because you know the killer is waiting in that dark throat of hallway, but she can't hear you and, anyway, she's a character in a slasher movie, this is what she's meant to do—this is her destiny—so she goes and she does it anyway.

What the hell happened?

She'd been at the front door, and there'd been a little girl. Jordan thought she recognized her. Then the little girl said something. And...

...And the rest of it was gone.

Just what the hell HAPPENED?

She didn't hear Connor shut off the music in his office. She didn't hear him come up behind her. When his arms snaked around her waist and his lips pressed to the back of her neck, she screamed. The knife flew out of her hands and clattered to the bottom of the sink.

"Jesus." Connor stepped back quickly. "Sorry. Didn't mean to scare you."

She looked back into the sink and at the long, wood-handled carving knife. She'd never seen it before. Her stomach did a wet, nauseous flop.

But I wasn't holding a knife. I was holding the casserole dish.

"You okay?" he asked. He put a hand to her back. The Dickies shirt was thick and the press of his palm was light, but for some reason every cell in her skin rioted and tried to scatter away from his touch.

"Yeah," she heard herself say, but that was a lie. The back of her head was pounding: a dull, mindless throb like someone was bouncing a basketball against the rubbery folds of her parietal lobe. Her elbows and knees ached, and her stomach was doing alarming and unpleasant things. Sweat sprang from her pores and slicked her forehead in a mucosal glaze. She forced herself to take a deep breath. "Yeah, I'm okay."

His arms crept around her waist again, the hands clasping together like handcuffs. He kissed her neck again.

"You want to go upstairs?" he whispered. "Get into bed? Watch a movie or something?"

And now it was his smell—his stench, his *stink*—that was making her sick. It shoved itself into her sinuses and curdled like rotten milk, stuck to her nasal passages like diseased phlegm. It was a hot stink, a *living* stink, bitter and sour and astringent with the adrenal reek of his desire. The tickle of his breath against her cheek, the reptilian slither of it in her ear canal, was wet with slime.

"Manhattan," she said without thinking. It was their rarely used safe word, deployed only in the direst of circumstances. And—give him credit—the arms immediately disappeared from her waist. He retreated.

"What's wrong, Jordan?" His voice was filled—overfilled, *dripping* even—with concern, but she heard a discordant note beneath that. Annoyance? Petulance?

She turned to face him, pressing her butt up against the sink to steady herself. She looked at him, and abruptly the angles of his face seemed all wrong. He was like a haphazardly constructed erector set, lopsided and out-of-true in ways that weren't obvious until you really looked. And his eyes—shit-brown and narrowed—seemed dull and piggish, the sockets surrounding them swollen like half-cooked dough.

Rage—connected to nothing she could interpret, tethered to no context she could unravel—bubbled into her throat and stuck there. An impulse seized her—all of a sudden, she wanted to take a fork from the dish drainer and jam it into one of those piggy eyes until it popped. She wanted to hear him shriek: first startled, then in bewildered agony. She wanted to watch the white jelly ooze down his sandpaper cheek, gum itself in his stubble. She wanted to watch the spurt of blood that came after.

What the hell HAPPENED? Jordan couldn't remember the last time her mood had soured so quickly and so completely. She flashed to the little girl's face—that impassive, decidedly unchildlike facade, those all-consuming hazel eyes. Trombones and trumpets and clanging cymbals smashed together in her mind.

"I just..." She swallowed. Some part of her—the part that was still inside herself, that *didn't* feel alien—thought *don't ruin everything.* "I just...I don't know. I'm sort of feeling gross. I don't..."

"Are you sick?" he asked, and then—absurdly—put his hand to her forehead. "Oh Christ, Jordan. You're burning up."

Just like that, all the anger and all the revulsion drained away. She thunked back into her body, and now she was just Jordan Sarah Lookstein again, here in this kitchen on this particular Halloween night. With Connor Michael Brackenridge, the man she loved. The man who, right this minute, was trying his damndest to take care of her.

That alien thing—that new and *hateful* thing—was gone.

"I..."

Something crumbled inside her like an earthen dam. The tears startled her and—she could see with some distant half-emotion that was almost like amusement—scared Connor badly.

"Jordan, honey." He pulled her in a tight embrace, and she let him. "Jordan, it's okay, it's all okay…"

He stroked her hair, and she clung to him and closed her eyes, and somewhere in the darkness behind those shut lids was an unblinking, hazel gaze and the distant, siren shriek of song.

Excerpt from the article "Delivery Truck Driver Sought After Wife's Body Discovered," by David Dufresne. Originally printed in The Rocky Mountain Dispatch, Nov. 1, 1967:

WOODMOOR — *The El Paso County Sheriff's Department, along with Colorado State Police, are looking for Jeffrey Donald Creel, 42, of Woodmoor, after El Paso County firefighters discovered the body of his wife, Josephine Margaret Creel, 35, in the burned-out remains of their house on Misty Morning Drive early this morning.*

"It's clear Mrs. Creel did not die in the fire, but that's all we're going to say on the subject," El Paso County Sheriff Thomas Robicheaux told reporters.

However, sources inside the Colorado State Police have revealed to the Dispatch *that Mrs. Creel suffered a number of grievous, "puncturing" injuries before the fire, indicating that she had been stabbed.*

"It's a blessing, maybe," said one of the sources. "She was most likely already deceased before she was burned."

Jeffrey Creel, who drives a delivery truck for a local bread company, has not been seen since early yesterday afternoon, before the fire that consumed the couple's house at just before the 8 p.m. hour. Neighbors, all of whom who prefer to remain nameless until Creel has been apprehended, described him to this reporter as "friendly enough, but quiet" and "a bit of an oddball."

"You'd see him out there every so often mowing his lawn," said one. "He'd always wave if you passed by, but I don't think I ever saw him smile. Real

serious. Almost, what's the word, dour. And I just about never saw the wife..."

Jordan lay in bed next to Connor, her mind racing as she listened to him snore, and tried to remember the little girl's face.

What she saw instead was an old scrapbook that her Zayde had kept in a box at the back of his closet. She didn't remember how old she was when she found it. She'd been playing in her grandparents' bedroom—putting her tiny feet into Zayde's boots and then *clomp-clomp-clomping* around the hardwood floor and giggling at the heavy sound they made. Then she saw the box, and ever curious, she opened it to find a couple old blankets—moth-eaten and musty—and, beneath them, the scrapbook. All these newspaper clippings were taped to the stiff, construction-paper pages inside. Something about a circus. A fire. A black-and-white photo of a skinny young man with dark, curly hair strapped to some sort of big metal chair. The young man looked terrified. The headline read "CIRCUS KILLER PUT TO DEATH," and she thought, *How do you kill a circus?*

She put the scrapbook back, then went to go find her Bubbe. Bubbe was at the kitchen counter, humming some old Yiddish folk song and rolling out a big oval of dough to make sugar cookies. Jordan tugged on her dress and asked her how you killed a circus.

Bubbe stopped what she was doing, cocked her head, and asked, *What're you on about?* So Jordan told her about the scrapbook and asked again: *How do you kill a circus?*

Bubbe turned white all the way down into the narrow folds of her skin. She looked quickly over her shoulder—later, Jordan realized she'd been making sure Zayde wasn't around. Then she crouched and seized Jordan's chin, digging her fingers in when Jordan squawked and tried to pull away.

You need to learn to stay out of other people's business, Jordan, Bubbe said. *That closet is off-limits now. No more playing up there.*

Bubbe only called Jordan by her name when Jordan was in trouble. Normally, she was "bubbale." Jordan didn't cry, but she wanted to. Instead, she nodded, solemn. Bubbe let go of her chin, patted her head, and said, *I'm sorry, bubbale, I didn't mean to lose my temper. Go watch TV, and when I'm done you can have a couple cookies. But don't you go saying anything to your Zayde about that nasty old scrapbook.*

Jordan went into Bubbe and Zayde's den and watched *Kim Possible* for a while. She didn't really like *Kim Possible* all that much—even young she thought the premise was stupid and Rufus the mole rat was *WAY CREEPY*—but that and *Judge Judy* were the only things on, and Judge Judy reminded Jordan too much of Bubbe, especially when she got all mad and yelly like that. Jordan could still feel the tips of Bubbe's fingers digging into her jaw, and—as she sat there watching Kim and Rufus and Ron Stoppable go up against Dr. Drakken and his minions—she wondered if she'd bruise up later.

Her mind kept turning to the scrapbook, and especially that black-and-white photo of the scared young man in the big chair.

How do you kill a circus?

Eventually, Bubbe gave her a cookie—still warm and gooey the way she liked them—but Bubbe wouldn't talk to her. She just disappeared back into the kitchen. *Kim Possible* ended, and *Higglytown Heroes* came on after that, so Jordan shut off the TV and sat there, thinking about the scrapbook and the scared young man, and that question kept rattling around in her head: *How do you kill a circus?*

It began to take on the rhythm and cadence of music after a while—oddly jaunty and gleeful—and she hummed it to herself: *How do you kill a circus...how do you kill a circus...?*

When her dad got off work and came to pick her up, he and Bubbe had a hushed conversation in the kitchen. Bubbe sounded agitated. Dad sounded annoyed. He often sounded annoyed when he was talking to Bubbe.

Jordan figured they were talking about her and what she'd found in the closet. Dad confirmed it once they got into the car:

Don't worry about it, Jordan. It's not your fault. It's...it's just a sore subject for your grampa. And Grandma doesn't like sore subjects.

Dad never called them "Bubbe" and "Zayde," only "Grandma" and "Grampa." He was the youngest of five brothers—the "black sheep," as he proudly described himself—and he didn't have much use for all the Old World traditions he'd been brought up with. Years later, he and Bubbe would have another one of those whispered conversations after Bubbe started insisting that Jordan have a Bat Mitzvah. Bubbe never brought it up again.

Jordan asked why it was a sore subject. Dad sighed.

Something happened with your grampa's cousin Haskel, he said. *It's why Grampa had to leave Colorado and move to Texas when he was a kid.*

Jordan thought about the young man in the big metal chair. The circus killer. She still didn't know how you killed a circus, but when she thought of the young man's eyes—wide and filled with a despair she couldn't begin to comprehend—she decided maybe she didn't want to.

Dad chuckled. *What, we expecting the president or something?*

Huh?

That song you're humming, Dad said. *It's what they play for the president.*

Oh, Jordan said and stopped. *Okay.*

But why was she thinking about that scrapbook now? Why was she remembering the flat, newsprint image of that terrified young man when she was instead trying to picture the little girl on Connor's porch?

And why was that goddamn *SONG* still blaring in her head?

Connor snorted, rolled over, and plopped his arm across her abdomen. The revulsion—the *anger*—hadn't come back, but she could feel it lurking there, crouching way back inside her like a rapist hiding in the bushes and waiting for someone to come strolling past. She shoved Connor's arm off of her, as gently as she could.

She closed her eyes, saw the terrified young man, then shoved him away and—as she finally began to tumble into the dark circumvolutions of sleep—forced herself to picture the girl.

But instead of seeing her as she'd been—standing there pinned in the porch light, gazing up at Jordan with that strange, stoic ferocity—another black-and-white photo surfaced. Jordan had breezed past it while thumbing through the scrapbook because it was boring and she didn't understand it.

It was a three-quarter-profile close-up of a sleeping child's face. A girl. She lay against a virginal white background, and her twin braids coiled haphazardly around her head.

In the half-second before sleep took her, Jordan realized two things:

She'd been thinking about the scrapbook because the girl had been *in* the scrapbook.

And the girl wasn't sleeping at all.

Excerpt from the article "The Devil Made Him Do It!" by David Dufresne. Originally printed in The Rocky Mountain Dispatch, Dec. 4, 1967:

DENVER — *A source inside the Colorado State Police has revealed that Jeffrey Donald Creel, 42, of Woodmoor, is now blaming "the Devil" for his decision to murder his wife.*

As Dispatch *readers know, Creel was apprehended a few weeks ago at a house in Castle Rock. Detectives have so far remained tight-lipped about the circumstances that precipitated the heinous crime, which saw Josephine Margaret Creel, 37, stabbed repeatedly by her husband before being burned beyond recognition inside the couple's Woodmoor home.*

Our source, however, has finally revealed Creel's diabolical motivation:

"He says the Devil has been coming to him for years and telling him that he had to kill, that he had no choice, that if he didn't do it he would be tortured for eternity, that his lungs would be cut open by demons and made to fill with blood until he choked on it, over and over and over again, forever," the source said. "It's very vivid and very specific."

"[Creel] says the Devil comes to him at night and that he looks like a little boy with blond hair and black eyes," the source continued, "and that he stinks like a chimney, which is how [Creel] knows that it's not a little boy at all, but rather Satan himself."

The source explained that Creel claims to recognize the boy as a child murdered and similarly burned by his own uncle, Mervin Creel, in the tiny village of Friendship, Oklahoma. This reporter contacted officials in Friendship and wider Jackson County and has confirmed the broad details of that earlier crime, which occurred in October of 1917. Mervin Creel was executed by electric chair in 1918.

"He thinks it's a family curse, and he's just the most recent one afflicted by it," the source said. "He doesn't believe that any of this is his own fault. It's really quite astounding."

According to the source, Creel confessed to a number of other crimes, including at least three murders while serving in the army overseas, along with a number of arsons—including the infamous 1947 Caldwell & Fletcher Traveling Circus fire that claimed nearly two hundred lives in Pueblo. Police are investigating Creel's claims, but the source said that they believe most—if not all—of them to be nothing but fantasy and the product of a diseased mind.

The true culprit behind the circus fire, Haskel Jacob Kantor, was convicted and put to death in 1951.

Readers of the Dispatch *will remember that Creel was taken into custody without incident on Nov. 8, while hiding in a closet at the Castle Rock home of his sister and brother-in-law, Dorothea and Michael Brackenridge, both 45. The couple has also been arrested, and among the charges being leveled against them are accessory to murder after the fact and harboring a fugitive...*

From "Humiliation Stanzas" by Connor M. Brackenridge, originally published in *The Flatirons Journal of Night-Black Poetry*, Vol. 6, Issue 4, December 2016:

sometimes i feel him boiling way deep inside
youknowyouknowyouknow
this phantom uncle this apparition
this distant bit of my blood i claimed i never knew
iknowiknowiknowiknow
when i hurt her the way she wants me to
when i put the screws to her
the ropes the ribbons the strings
the bites
the bruises
iknowiknowiknowiknow
he's coming back up
out of the deepest me and
all teeth
into the brightest light
nononononononono

know
he never left

Flying. *Soaring.* Like Wonder Woman in her invisible airplane.

And the ground—so far down there—is near flat but oddly rippled, rolling beneath undulating stalks of yellowing grass and green-black clusters of trees. The sky is lighted like a beacon, like a *way*, and all the roads spiderweb out of it and twist and loop around each other in a ropey tangle of asphalt and tar. She recognizes I-25, slicing like a razor across the plains, shooting up from New Mexico and disappearing into the vast, dead-battery emptiness of Wyoming. She recognizes it, but it makes no sense, because the I-25 she knows is a straight line, and this is layers and layers, folds upon folds upon folds, a spirograph geometry she can't understand.

The roads converge in a city, old and oil-stained, all cracked bridges and black, belching smokestacks. A sooty mural etched along the length of an endless concrete canal. She knows that this is Pueblo—*the Detroit of the Rockies,* Connor always calls it, with a sneer—but even in her dream she understands this isn't the *real* Pueblo. Or maybe it is, and only her dream-mind can see it in its truth. It's a city of the damned.

Of the burned.

Music shrieks out of the sky, and behind it she hears the booming voice of her father: *What, we expecting the president or something?* But this isn't "The Stars and Stripes Forever," no matter how much it wants her to *think* that's what it is. This song is a fleshy, squealing chaos. The trombones are alive and screaming. The drums clatter like bones pounding against dried skin pulled taut over hollow skulls. And the smoke isn't just boiling out of the smokestacks now; it's coming from a vast field beneath her, a canvas city within a city, and this canvas city is on fire, red-and-white pavilions curling and collapsing under the red weight of flames that lick against a sky that has gone from bright-beacon white to a depthless, starless black. People run from the flames—shrieking, crying, some of them burning, more of them dying—and to her they look like ants shriveling under the heat of a magnifying glass.

It wasn't you.

She can't see the face, not quite, but she senses it behind all the smoke and flames. Hazel eyes blasting like spotlights. A little girl. A little boy. A witch. A zombie. A sad-faced clown carrying a single bucket of water. Something red and gold that might be Iron Man or might be a suppurating mass, bulbous and raw, a tumor, a boil, a *wound*.

It was him.

A demon.

A *devil*.

It was HIM.

And Jordan wants to scream—*needs* to scream—but when she opens her mouth, the inferno's heat pushes in and sears her lungs, turns whatever it was she wanted to say into gasping black exhalations of char.

Hazel eyes roll across her like swirling tornadoes. Blond hair flows around them like fire.

A girl, a boy, a tumor, a wound, a demon.

You shouldn't be here.

He wasn't supposed to get away with it.

"Hey."

Jordan poked Connor, in the ticklish spot between his pelvis and ribs. He snorted and tried to roll over, but the handcuffs held him fast.

He opened his eyes.

"Jordan?" Sleepily. "What—?"

"You weren't supposed to get away with it."

He rattled his left wrist against the cuff, blinking. It wasn't very strong—the handcuffs they used weren't, like, police grade or anything—and he probably could have broken it if he wanted to. It didn't seem to occur to him to try.

"Do you understand?"

"*What?*"

Jordan didn't know why she was whispering. She tried again.

"*Do you understand?*"

Connor looked at her, confused and maybe a little annoyed to be woken this way, but not yet frightened. That would come momentarily.

"Jordan, what the hell?"

She imagined what she must look like to him right now: naked, sitting cross-legged across his thighs, silhouetted against the silver-white light of the moon. It must be sexy as hell. She felt something begin to heat up, pleasant and promising, way down in her guts. The rage and revulsion brought on by the girl had entered the chrysalis of the dream, and both she and it had emerged as this brand new thing. This *wanting* thing.

"You." She punctuated each word with a sharp knuckle, thumping his breastbone. "Weren't. Supposed. *To get away with it.*"

Now he looked scared, and the warmth inside her turned white hot and dripping, and her desire for him opened like a carnivorous flower.

"Jordan, I don't know—"

—*what you thought I got away with* was probably the rest of that sentence. She didn't know for sure, because before he could get there, she slid the carving knife between the fifth and sixth rib on his left side, deftly puncturing his lung. He gasped, tried to suck in air as the lung deflated inside him like a balloon.

"Jordan..." It was his final word, drowned in a wellspring of blood. He might have managed something else, but by then she'd stuck the knife between the ribs on his right side. The air left him in a sibilant hiss, which was quickly subsumed by the wet gargle of all that flooded in to replace it.

His eyes whipped wildly around the room as she set the knife aside and curled up beside him, nestling into the warmth of his shivering armpit. She stroked his belly and sternum, relishing the sudden hot wetness of him. The vital fluidity of him.

He coughed, ejecting ropes of blood that looked black in the moonlight. He rattled the handcuffs. He kicked at the ropes. He tried to say something. All that came out of him was more and more of that *wet*.

Jordan closed her eyes, listening to the unsteady flutter of his heartbeat, and hummed to herself. By now the song was familiar. Comforting even. She didn't have much time before the next step. The red plastic gas can that Connor kept in the garage for his lawnmower was now resting, expectant, at the bottom of the stairs. But she was going to lay here and enjoy this sense of intimacy with him for as long as she could.

With her boyfriend.

With her *man*...

Excerpt from the article "New Mystery Surrounds Unidentified Fire Victim" by Rachel Naranjo. Originally printed in The Rocky Mountain Dispatch, Nov. 2, 2007:

PUEBLO—*Pueblo County officials were dealt the shock of their lives Wednesday when they tried to exhume the body of the unidentified circus-fire victim long known to the public as "Little Miss 616."*

The coffin was there, right were it was supposed to be.

But Little Miss 616 was not.

"Someone cocked up somewhere," said Pueblo County Sheriff's Deputy Francis Duran. "It doesn't look like a grave robbery to us. My guess is someone put the wrong body in the wrong casket before the burial. You can imagine the whole scene had to have been chaos. How they managed to put an empty casket into the ground, though...well, I've gotta say that eludes me."

Little Miss 616 is so known because of her mortuary designation. Officials at the time were forced to set up a makeshift morgue in the gymnasium of a local high school. One can almost understand how, in the aftermath of that event, a mistake could have been made.

Almost.

According to Duran, there is no evidence that the grave has been disturbed, and the coffin had not apparently been opened before Wednesday's exhumation. "We don't think there's a crime here, but it's creepy as hell," said County Medical Examiner Lewis McArdle. "I mean, we dug it up on Halloween, for God's sake. No body. It's almost too good to be true."

Like Duran, McArdle suspects that the mis-burial was the result of a bureaucratic mistake. "I don't think we'll ever find her now," he said.

Wednesday's revelation is a bitter disappointment to the Cartwright family of Colorado Springs. Three weeks ago, Melinda Cartwright, 42, found an old photo album while cleaning out her recently deceased mother's home and, within the album, found the smiling photo of a little girl who bears a striking resemblance to the image of Little Miss 616 that has been immortalized in newspapers, magazines, and across the internet for the last seventy years. The girl's photo was inscribed with a single handwritten name—"Sissy"—but no one in the family today seems to know who the girl might have been.

Still, Pueblo officials were intrigued enough by the resemblance to agree to the exhumation. The plan was to conduct a DNA test and see if Little Miss 616 had any genetic tie to the Cartwright family.

But now the mystery is unlikely ever to be solved.

"It sucks," Melinda Cartwright said. "Not to sound too gleeful about it, but that fire is a major part of Colorado history. It would've been kind of neat to be part of that..."

Grafitti found scrawled on the tombstone of Haskel Jacob Kantor, Oct. 31, 1957:

"BURN N HELL U MURDERING CHRIST KILLING YID!!"

Jordan sat in the back of the police cruiser, her hands rudely cuffed behind her (these *were* police grade, no doubt about it), and watched as flames shot from the roof and oscillated across the moon-splashed sky. She could smell it—a dry, chimney reek with some sort of chemical under-stench. The firefighters sprayed jets of water onto the blaze, and that just added a swampy fetor to everything that made her want to gag.

She couldn't smell Connor at all. For that she was sorry.

She was sorry for a lot of things.

It all made so much sense half an hour ago. She'd woken, and she knew—just *knew*—what she had to do. And it had seemed so beautiful. So perfect. So *right*.

Now Connor was dead and she was here and she was going to go away for a very long time. And she couldn't, for the life of her, understand why.

She searched inside herself, trying to excavate a stone of grief for the man she'd thought she loved. The man who took care of her. Who always hurt her in exactly the way she wanted him to. She couldn't find it. If it was there, it was buried beneath volcanic layers of shock and denial.

But the layers would wear away and the grief would reveal itself eventually. Beneath that would be the shame. And when it did, she hoped she could find a way to kill herself. She didn't think she could sit in a cell for the next fifty years and just soak in it.

You weren't supposed to get away with it.

Was that for Connor? For someone else?

For her?

Two young police officers sat in the front seat, murmuring amongst themselves. She knew they were talking about her. She didn't care. The radio crackled and belched.

A boom rolled across the street as the roof collapsed. She wondered what Connor looked like now. If any part of him was recognizable.

She watched the flames and tried to peer into the darkness beyond them. Eventually she gave up and looked down.

On the corner, by the stop sign at the intersection of Columbia and Franklin—and beyond the haze of sprayed water and all the flashing lights—Jordan saw a little girl with honey-blond braids, looped up and tied by her ears. The girl stood beneath the streetlight. Her white dress swayed around her knees.

She watched Jordan.

And, even though she was too far away for her to see for sure, Jordan knew the girl's eyes weren't hazel at all.

They were black.

NIGHT IN THE LONESOME
RICHARD CHIZMAR & W.H. CHIZMAR

"I'm just saying we deserve better."

Frank was slouched down in the passenger seat, his bald head bouncing up and down like a discount-store bobblehead as we made our way down the unpaved road in our unmarked sedan. There was a dime-size tomato sauce stain on his tie. He hadn't noticed it yet.

"Better than what?" I asked and immediately regretted it.

He sat up and gestured out the window. "This kinda bush-league bullshit."

Outside the window was woods on both sides of us. It was October, and most of the branches were bare and brittle. When they scraped against the sides of the car, it sounded like skeletal fingers clawing at a frightened child's bedroom window.

"It's practically midnight," he said, "and they call us all the way out here to east bumfuck."

"I wouldn't exactly call Jarrettsville east bumfuck."

He looked at me, and I knew what was coming.

"What would you call it?"

I shrugged. "Northern Harford County."

"Which is pretty much the middle of fuckin' nowhere. You

remember what we used to call the kids who went to North Harford High?"

I shook my head.

"Duck farmers."

"That's right," I said, smiling. Growing up, we were the poor kids from Edgewood, and even that was better than being a duck farmer. Straw in your hair and smelling like cow shit twenty-four-seven.

The car's right front tire bounced in and out of a deep rut, our seatbelts saving us from kissing the dashboard. I swung the wheel to the left but was too late. The right rear tire found the same hole. The sedan's frame shuddered beneath us, and there was a brief shriek of grinding metal. It sounded like an angry owl.

"And tomorrow we'll have to take the car into the shop," Frank went on. "And fill out a stack of paperwork. And the captain'll chew my ass even though you're the one in the driver's seat."

I knew I shouldn't poke the bear, but I couldn't help it. "Just say it and get it over with. It'll make you feel better."

"Say what?"

"You know what." I was grinning now. "Go ahead and say it."

Scowling. "I don't know what the hell you're talking about."

"C'mon, Frank, just say it."

"I'm not in the mood, Ben. My back hurts, I gotta take a piss, and—aw shit." He was looking down at the stain on his tie.

I laughed and switched off the high beams. Up ahead, maybe fifty or sixty yards, the dirt road opened up into what looked like a clearing. A cluster of police cars and emergency vehicles were parked there, their light bars painting the trees and roadway in flickering shades of red and blue.

"Just say it, Frank."

"Fine." He turned away, stared out the passenger window, and started rubbing the tomato stain with his thumb. He sighed and mumbled, "I fuckin' hate Halloween."

"What have you got for us?"

The pair of uniformed officers that met us at the car were familiar faces. Ken Hopkins was a longtime Maryland State Trooper, just as his father had been before him. In his late thirties, he was a solid cop and still one hell of a softball centerfielder. No one tried to stretch an extra base on Kenny Hopkins. Todd Mackleson worked out of the Harford County Sheriff's Department. Young and ambitious, he looked more like an accountant than a second-year deputy. He adjusted his wire-framed glasses and gave me a nod.

"Seventeen-year-old female being treated for injuries by the ambo crew," Hopkins said. "She and her best friend, also seventeen, slipped away into the woods to use the bathroom. On their way back, they were attacked. She got away. We're searching the woods, but the best friend is still missing."

I smelled the heavy scent of woodsmoke in the air. Over the officers' shoulders, I could see the remnants of a bonfire in the center of the clearing. Glowing red ashes danced in the air above it like snowflakes. Flashlight beams lit up the woods around us. I could hear police officers shouting for the missing girl. Her name was Mallory.

"She say how many attackers?" Frank asked.

Hopkins shook his head. "She didn't say much, and we didn't want to push her. We left that for you guys."

"I was first on the scene," Mackleson said. "I'm pretty sure the girl was in shock."

"What type of injuries?" I asked.

The deputy flipped open a small spiral notepad. "Deep scratches on her face, chest, and arms. A pretty nasty gouge on her back. I used a towel to stop the bleeding. And..." He hesitated before continuing. "...what resembles some kind of bite mark on her left shoulder."

"Bite mark?" I wasn't sure I'd heard him correctly.

Mackleson shrugged. "Yes, sir. That's what it looked like to me, so I wrote it down. Anyway, I gave the bloody towel to forensics so they would have it for comparison. They're working on the girl now."

From where I was standing, I could see Shelly Sunderland and her two-man crew gathered at the rear of the ambulance. Several portable light-stands had been set up around them.

"Once we showed up," Hopkins said, "most of the kids took off running or on ATVs. Best estimate is forty or fifty of them. This is the only road in or out wide enough for cars, but..." He pointed at the tree line on the opposite side of the clearing. "...there's a whole network of trails back there. Most of them come out behind the high school, which is where they probably parked. We have names and addresses for over a dozen kids who are still here, including the missing girl's ex-boyfriend. Everyone's been cooperative so far." He pointed again. "There's a Jeep and a pickup over there that are unaccounted for. We ran the plates." He handed over a folded sheet of paper.

"Good job," Frank said, scanning the information. "Both of you."

Detective Frank Logan rarely gave out compliments, but when he did, you knew he meant it. Both Hopkins and Mackleson were standing a little taller when we left them a minute later.

On our way to the ambulance, we walked past a group of teenagers sitting on a scattering of tree stumps arranged in a rough circle around the fire. I counted eight boys and six girls, most of them dressed in Halloween costumes. The only one I recognized was the killer from the *Scream* movies. The boy's Ghostface mask was pushed high atop his head; the face beneath it looked all of fifteen years old. All of the kids looked scared or worried. And that was before Frank flashed them his Clint Eastwood bad-cop glare: eyes narrowed, lips pursed, neck muscles tensed.

Once we were safely past them, he broke into a grin and asked, "You want to take Shelly and the girl? I'll talk to the kids?"

I thought about it before answering. "If it's okay with you, let's stick together. I have a weird feeling about this one."

He looked at me. "How come?"

"Not really sure." I glanced around. A bloated orange moon had swam free of the clouds. The treetops overhead were brushed in its luminesce. The branches swayed back and forth in the autumn breeze, rattling together like the dusty bones of bygone giants. Shadows cavorted around us. Far off in the distance, I could hear a dog barking. "Something doesn't feel right. I can't put my finger on it yet. Something just feels...off."

"Off."

I nodded.

"You been watching too many scary movies."

"Maybe."

"Don't know why you and the wife waste your time. Don't you get enough horror stories on the job?"

"That's just it," I said. "Movies are different. Kind of like riding a rollercoaster. A quick thrill-ride, and then it's over." I shook my head. "Nothing like the job."

"If you say so." And then under his breath: "I hate rollercoasters."

The injured girl's name was Valerie Berry. She was a junior at North Harford High School. Her brother, Lonnie, was a year ahead of her and the quarterback of the varsity football team. He hadn't attended the bonfire tonight. Instead, he'd gone to dinner and a movie in Fallston with his girlfriend. Although she was no longer wearing her costume—Shelly Sunderland and her crew had tagged and bagged it shortly after their arrival—Valerie had dressed for the occasion as a witch. Black corduroy skirt over black-and-white striped leggings and old-fashioned saddle-shoes. A bright orange, baggy sweater. Lipstick-red lips and dark eyeshadow topped off with a pointy, black hat. For the first part of the evening, she'd carried around a broomstick. But at some point, she'd misplaced it. She swore she hadn't had anything to drink the entire night.

Mallory Collins was a different story. Valerie estimated that her best friend had downed three or four beers and a couple of wine coolers. She may have also smoked some weed; Valerie wasn't certain about that.

A week earlier, Mallory had shocked her closest friends by breaking up with her longtime boyfriend, a senior named Todd Robinson—and that'd been only the first of many drastic changes. A few days later, she'd abruptly quit the field hockey team. The next morning, she'd shown up at homeroom with nearly ten inches of her beautiful blond hair chopped off. She'd also begun talking about getting her septum pierced and a tattoo on her ankle. Despite the chilly temperature, she'd shown up at tonight's bonfire dressed as a sexy Snow White in a black leather miniskirt, a flimsy red bustier, and thigh-high leather boots. Her newly shorn hair had been dyed midnight black.

To our surprise, Frank and I managed to gather all of this information directly from Valerie Berry. After speaking with Hopkins and Mackleson, we'd expected to find a young girl mute with terror in the back of the ambulance. Instead, according to Shelly Sunderland, Miss Berry had started talking a few minutes before our arrival, and now they couldn't get her to shut up.

"We were scraping her fingernails for trace evidence," Shelly told us, "and it was like a switch was suddenly flipped. One minute she was just sitting there, hunched over, head leaning to the side, eyes all glassy, and the next, she was bright eyed and bubbly. I've seen people come out of shock before, but never quite like that."

"She could very well still be in shock," one of the paramedics said, lowering his voice. "Her vitals are stable, but she needs stitches on her chest and shoulder and x-rays on that arm. We don't get moving soon, her parents are liable to beat us to the hospital."

"Just one more question," Frank said, "and you can take her." He didn't wait for the paramedic's approval.

"Valerie, what can you tell us about Mallory's ex-boyfriend?"

"Todd?" She stared at Frank for a moment before continuing, eyes squinting in the harsh lights. "He's a good guy. They've been dating forever. No one understands why she broke up with him."

"She never offered an explanation?"

Valerie shook her head. "Not really. Nothing that made any kind of sense."

"What exactly did she tell you?"

Valerie rolled her eyes, and for a breathless moment I thought she was going to faint. But then she was leaning forward and talking a mile a minute. "Something about feeling claustrophobic. And needing space. They *did* spend a lot of time together."

Frank scribbled in his notepad and snapped it closed. "You've been very brave, Valerie. My partner and I'll stop by the hospital in the morning to talk with you again. In the meantime, get some rest." He turned and started walking away.

I started to follow, then stopped and turned around. I knew I should leave it alone for now, but I couldn't stop myself. "Can you tell me one more time what you saw in the woods?"

The paramedic gave me some serious side-eye, which I ignored. But I could feel Shelly Sunderland glaring at me, and that bothered me.

"Like I said, I didn't really see much. I *heard* something. A flapping sound. Like wind against the side of a tent. Then the bushes moved right in front of us." She shivered, and I immediately felt guilty for pushing so hard. "And then a shadow swooped over us. A big...dark shadow. That's the only way I can describe it. I got knocked to the ground. I could feel blood on my face and chest. I heard Mallory scream. Just once, and then she was quiet. I was up and running by then. I heard branches breaking behind me. It was chasing me. I could feel its breath on the back of my neck and..."

She broke down sobbing then, and I got out of there.

"Jesus, Ben."

"Save it. I already feel terrible for making her cry."

"That's not what I was gonna say." He glanced back at the ambulance. The doors were closed, and it was pulling away, lights flashing. "Did you see her eyes? Hear how fast she was talking? Bet you ten bucks her blood test comes back positive for *something*."

I watched the ambulance disappear into the darkness. "She said, '*It* was chasing me.' *It*. Not 'he.'"

"She never saw her attacker. Probably figures it was an animal. I read an article in *The Aegis* last year. Mountain lion sightings in Rocks State Park. That's only three or four miles from—"

"You get a good look at her shoulder?"

Frank nodded. "Messy as hell, but it looked like a bite wound to me."

"Me too."

"Not big enough for an animal, though."

"I thought the same thing."

"What's bothering you? We've had biters before."

I shrugged but didn't say anything.

"Lemme guess." He arched his eyebrows. "Something about it feels *off*."

I answered him with my middle finger and walked away.

Fourteen pairs of eyes stared nervously back at us. The teenagers had abandoned their tree stumps around the fire and were now standing in a group not far from the wood's edge. They huddled close together in the flickering shadows, their reasoning clear: there was safety in numbers.

"My name's Detective Frank Logan. This is my partner, Ben Richards. Let's get this out of the way up front. We're not here to bust your balls for holding a bonfire without a permit or shotgunning a couple of beers. We just want to find your friend, Mallory Collins."

No one moved. No one said anything.

"In other words," Frank went on, "just relax. You're not in any kind of trouble."

That seemed to do the trick. Facial expressions loosened. Arms uncrossed. Hands came out of pockets. Even the wind whispered a sigh of relief.

"Is Val okay?" a young blond girl asked.

"A few stitches and she'll be as good as new," Frank said. "You can all go visit her tomorrow."

"What about Mallory?" asked the kid in the *Scream* mask. "Why haven't they found her yet?"

Frank put up his hands. "Tell you what. Let us ask our questions first, and then we'll do our best to answer yours." He turned and gave me a look. *Your* turn.

I stepped forward. Cleared my throat. "So, did anyone see or hear anything unusual tonight? Either on the walk or drive over here, or once the party got started?"

Silence hung thick in the air. Eyes stared down at the ground. Expensive sneakers and cowboy boots kicked at the dirt.

A girl dressed all in black with her mascara running finally spoke up. "Like what?"

"Anything you can think of," I said. "Maybe a strange noise coming from the woods. Or a glimpse of something from the corner of your eye."

"Any strangers at the party tonight?" Frank asked.

More silence. This was why we preferred to speak to witnesses one-on-one. People tended to talk more when they didn't have an audience. But there wasn't enough time for that right now, and we knew it.

"C'mon, don't be afraid to speak up," I said. "Detective Logan and I've worked together for a long time. We've heard it all, and if there's anything we've learned, it's that the devil is in the details. You might think it's unimportant or insignificant, but let us decide that."

The kids looked around at each other, and then all at once it was like a dam burst.

"—*Joey, didn't you say you hea*—"
"—*isn't it weird that Hank didn't sho*—"
"—*no, I told him that was an owl*—"
"—*he's sick, dumba*—"
"—*you didn't tell me shi*—"
"—*that's why he didn't on Friday*—"
"—*who was wearing the grim reaper*—"
"—*are there more crickets out tonig*—"
"—*Val said Lonnie was pis*—"
"—*I thought I saw*—"
"—*haven't seen a damn thing.*"

"Whoa, whoa, whoa." Frank raised his hands in the air again. "Slow down! One at a time!"

The girl with the runny mascara went first. "I thought I saw something when we were walking on the path, but it was too dark to tell what it was."

"I saw it, too," the girl standing next to her said. "It had to have been some type of animal. I could see its eyes glowing."

Next, a boy wearing a Cal Ripken jersey claimed he'd heard a noise up in the trees. The sound had given him goose bumps. Before he could elaborate, his buddy shouldered his way to the front of the group.

"I heard it, too," he said. "It was just a barn owl. I hear 'em all the time cuz I live out here. Joey's from Joppatowne. He don't have a clue what an owl sounds like."

"Hank" turned out to be a popular classmate, one who rarely missed out on a night of adolescent debauchery. He hadn't been at school today because he was home in bed with the flu.

"I heard he had the runs and a one hundred two temperature," a skinny boy with a face full of freckles said. "My brother dropped off a...a, uh, six-pack of Gatorade earlier tonight to help him stay hydrated."

Frank glanced at me, smirking, and I could read his mind: *Gatorade, my ass.*

"How about Valerie Berry and Mallory Collins?" he asked. "Either of them been hanging around new people lately? Any sudden changes in routine? Been involved in any recent fights or feuds?"

No one answered right away, but several of the kids glanced at the tallest boy in the group. Standing in the back, wearing a faded tan hunting jacket, he had messy dark hair, bushy sideburns, and the beginning of a beard. His brown eyes locked on mine. I met his gaze, and he looked away first.

"Val's as straight as an arrow," a girl wrapped in a blanket said. "Junior class president. National Honor Society. Latin Club. She finally kissed a boy last spring. It was a guy she was tutoring in math, and it happened on a *Wednesday afternoon,* for Godsake."

Nervous laughter rippled through the group.

"Mallory's...different," the girl continued. "She changed."

"Changed in what way?" I asked.

"In pretty much every way," another boy answered.

An uneasy murmur of agreement passed amongst the teenagers.

The girl in the blanket went on. "Most of our parents would say that we're *all* changing, going through phases, I know mine would." She glanced at the runny mascara girl dressed all in black. "But for some of us, it's more than just a phase."

Mascara girl flashed her classmate a hurt look and stared down at the ground.

"Yeah," the shortest boy in the crowd said, "but most of the other chicks just stop wearing bras and start listening to My Chemical Romance. Mallory Collins cut off all her hair and told Mr. Cliff to eat a *dick!*"

"Mr. Cliff's an asshole."

"I didn't say I disagreed with her...but I guess you had to be there. Everyone was pretty freaked out. When would the old Mallory ever have said something like that?"

"Never."

"Not until earlier this month."

"She's always been a drama queen, but nothing like that."

"Did anything specific happen earlier this month?" Frank asked. "Some kind of trigger?"

"Not that we know of," one of the other girls answered. "I mean, we've all talked about it, and everyone pretty much agrees. She showed up at school one morning, and it was like she'd become a different person."

"When was this?" Frank asked, flipping open his notepad. "Does anyone know exactly when it started?"

The tall boy in the faded hunting jacket stepped forward. "I do."

It was half-past midnight, and the three of us were standing next to what was left of the bonfire. As the remnants of burned timbers collapsed upon each other, the flames snapped and crackled and popped, tossing showers of sparks into the air, like miniature fireworks. The warmth felt good.

Frank and I had been talking with Mallory Collins' ex-boyfriend, Todd Robinson, for the past ten minutes, and I think it was fair to say that we both liked him. Some people, without even trying, made a good first impression. Todd was one of those people. Polite and well-spoken, he was clearly authentic and comfortable in his own skin. Rare for a guy his age. Hell, rare for folks of most any age.

This was what we'd learned so far:

Todd Robinson turned eighteen two weeks earlier. He worked at the Sunoco gas station at the corner of River Road and Industry Lane. B student. Mother worked at Edgewood Arsenal. Father died in a trucking accident when Todd was fourteen. He helped coach his younger brother's rec soccer team. Wanted to start his own landscaping business after graduation. He fell in love with Mallory Collins in middle school and worked up the courage to ask her out the summer after his freshman year in high school. She said yes, and they went to a movie and played minigolf on their first date. His mother drove them. They'd been boyfriend and girlfriend ever since. Homecomings and proms. Church services on Sunday mornings and family lunches at Mallory's house right after. They went to each other's games and did homework together. They rarely fought and spoke often about getting married when they were older.

Until, that is...everything changed.

As Todd began to explain that Mallory's personality shift started during the first weekend of October, I thought I saw something moving in the treetops. A shadow set beneath all the others, dark and slippery amongst the branches. My eyes tried to track it, but after losing sight of the shape, I convinced myself that it was probably just a trick of the wind and shadows. An illusion cast by the autumn moon. Frank was right; I'd managed to give myself a serious case of the willies. It wasn't like me.

The rest of the teenagers were gathered at the mouth of the unpaved road that led to the clearing. Their parents were starting to show up. I watched as a handful of uniformed officers patiently brought them up to speed. There were plenty of concerned faces and tears. All of this while flashlight beams and muffled shouts continued to pierce the darkness within the woods. I sighed and returned my attention to the conversation at hand. It was going to be a long night.

Todd Robinson shrugged and showed his palms to the moon. "...and then our good night calls started getting shorter and shorter. We already didn't text as much as we used to. She'd told me she was trying to cut back on her cell phone and be more present. I thought that was admirable and told her so. But then she stopped asking to make plans after school. No more doing homework together or taking her dog for hikes. I work all day on Saturday, so that just left Sundays. All of the sudden, we were barely seeing each other."

"And when you were together..." I asked. "What was she like?"

He thought about it for a moment. "Distant. Like she was preoccupied or worried about something."

"Did you ask her what was wrong?"

"Yes, sir. All the time, but she never really gave me a straight answer. More than once, I asked if there was someone else, if she wanted to take a break. She insisted there wasn't."

Now it was Frank's turn. "Did the two of you ever argue about it?"

He shook his head. "She got mad at me once when I mentioned that I'd spoken with her parents. They were worried about her, too. But that was the only time."

"I know you don't want to get her into trouble, but any chance she's using drugs? I'm not talking about weed."

"I don't think so," Todd said. "I mean, I guess anything's possible, but I'm pretty sure I would've noticed. We saw each other every day until we broke up. She wasn't too high or low or spaced out. She was just different."

"And you have no idea at all what might've been bothering her?"

"I know she wasn't getting along with her mom, and she was stressed about being recruited for field hockey. She'd always wanted to play at a good college. Mallory's one of the best players in the county. At least she was before she quit."

"Did she give a reason for quitting the team?"

"She said she was tired of playing, that it wasn't fun anymore. But it sure seemed to come out of nowhere. Her mother told me she came straight home from school every afternoon and locked herself inside her bedroom. What's fun about that?"

The question was out of my mouth before I could stop it: "Did you ever get the idea that she was frightened of something?"

Nodding slowly, Todd said, "Now that you mention it, yeah, I kind of did feel that way sometimes."

"Can you give us an example of one of those times?"

"On the way home from church a couple of weeks ago, she kept looking behind us like someone was following us."

"And were they?"

"I must've checked a half dozen times, but I didn't see anyone."

"Anything else?"

"Her father would kill me if he found out...but sometimes I would sneak in after dark and spend the night in Mallory's room. The next morning, I'd wake up early and jog home before my mother woke up."

Frank scribbled in his notebook. "And you're sure her parents didn't know?"

"Positive," he said. "They're real religious and strict. We never would've heard the end of it."

"You were talking about Mallory being afraid," I said, trying not to sound impatient.

He nodded. "She started closing her curtains at night."

I stayed quiet and waited for him to continue.

"Ever since she was a kid, Mallory loved waking up to the sunrise...right up until she didn't."

"And you think she started doing that because she was scared?"

"That was how it felt."

"Did she ever offer an explanation?"

"No, sir. And I didn't push it. To be honest, I was just happy to be over there."

"And all of this started..." Frank consulted his notepad. "The first weekend of October?"

Todd gave a sad nod. "Yes, sir. That's when..." His voice trailed off, his eyes scanning the dark woods surrounding us.

"That's when what?" I asked.

"It's probably nothing," he said.

"Go ahead, tell us, just in case," Frank said, and I could tell by the tone of my partner's voice that he was thinking the same thing I was: *The devil is in the details.*

"Mallory and her family go camping three or four times a year. They have an old travel trailer that they haul up and down the East Coast. Cape Hatteras and Virginia Beach in the summer. New England in the fall. Even Canada once in a while. I've gone with them a bunch of times, and it's usually a lot of fun. It was, anyway.

"At the beginning of October—we get a four-day weekend for fall break—they went to West Virginia. Out in the middle of nowhere, according to Mallory. Their last night there, Mallory got lost in the woods just as it was getting dark. Mal's an experienced hiker, but she said that somehow she got turned around and confused. Once it was full dark and her parents couldn't find her, they freaked out and called the local police. The cops organized a search party to look for her. It took Mallory almost four hours to find her way back to camp, and by then she was dehydrated and bruised and bleeding from hiking off-trail. She was really embarrassed and upset by the whole thing. Later that night, she FaceTimed me from the campsite. She was crying and her face was all scratched up. She had bandages on both of her arms. When I asked her what happened, she said she couldn't remember most of it. She'd gone off-trail to check out the river and couldn't find her way back. She said she tried walking, with the sound of the water behind her, figuring that she'd eventually run into the trail. Only she never did. She must've skipped right over it and kept on going. At some point, she turned around and tried to find the river again, but it was gone. She remembered crossing over a creek and seeing an old stone well in a field, but that was about it. Other than the moon."

"The moon?"

"She said it was following her. She ended up breaking the number one rule for when you get lost. She panicked and started running. That's how she got all scratched up. But she swore the moon chased her all the way back to camp."

"That's...odd."

"I picked her up that Sunday night after she got home, and we went out for pizza. She was quieter than usual, but she seemed okay. Not looking forward to school the next day, but happy to be home.

"We got ice cream cones after dinner and took the long way back to her house. It gets pretty dark on Pyle's Road, and just as we rounded the bend right before the old wooden bridge, she sat up and started pointing at something up in the woods ahead of us.

"I didn't see anything, so at first I thought she was just pulling my leg. Trying to spook me. We did that to each other sometimes. But then her hand started shaking and her eyes went as wide as silver dollars. She started crying and kept trying to say something, but nothing would come out.

"I started to pull over, but she shook her head and took hold of my arm so tight I had bruises in the shape of her fingers the next day. So I kept on driving, and after a few minutes, she finally began to calm down.

"I asked her a couple more times what was wrong, but she wouldn't answer me. Rest of the way home, we just held hands and listened to the radio. But then in the driveway, right before she got out, I heard her whisper something to herself."

"What was it?"

"*'It followed me,'* she said. *'It followed me home.'*"

"Did you ask her what she meant?" My voice sounded funny. I cleared my throat.

"No, sir, I didn't. I was afraid to upset her again, and I wasn't a hundred percent sure I'd heard her right. I'm still not sure. I just walked her to the door and said good night."

"And the two of you never talked about it again?"

He shook his head. "I picked her up for school the next morning, and I could feel it right away. The way she looked at me, talked to me, even her touch...it was all different."

"How was it different?" Frank asked.

He thought about it. "It's hard to describe."

"Take your time and try."

"Everything about her...felt *off*."

Frank and I exchanged a look—and waited for him to continue.

"That's really the only way I can explain it."

Todd stared at us for a long moment, and for the first time

tonight, he looked like he'd just woken up from a bad dream. His eyes looked very young and very lost.

"Anyway, that's how it started."

"Last question." I didn't think Todd was going to break down in tears the way Valerie had, but I wasn't taking any chances. "Frank and I really appreciate all your help."

He nodded, turned his eyes to the lonely moon above, and said, "I still love her, Detective. Probably always will."

Just focus and finish, I told myself. "Did Mallory and Valerie ever get into fights or arguments?"

"Not really," he said, shaking his head. "I mean, once in a while they got annoyed with each other, but nothing serious. They've always been really close. Like sisters. Ever since grade school."

"Even since Mallory began to change?"

"As far as I know," he said. "Wait...do you think Valerie might've done something to Mallory?"

"No, no." I put up my hands. "That's not what I was saying."

And then he got it—and his entire body went rigid.

"You think...you think Mallory attacked Valerie and took off?"

Frank closed his notepad and returned it to his pocket. "So what do you make of all that?"

"I think he's telling the truth." I watched as Todd Robinson climbed into the back seat of his parents' Subaru. "Not so sure about everyone else, including Mallory Collins."

"*Especially* Mallory Collins."

"What I don't get is—"

"There you are," Shelly Sunderland said from behind us. "I was looking for you guys."

Frank immediately sucked in his gut and straightened his posture. In addition to being a first-rate forensics investigator, Shelly Sunderland was a pretty redhead in her mid-forties and newly single. Frank hadn't had a date in six months.

"Sorry about before," I said. "I should've waited."

She waved a hand at me. "If I had a nickel for every time a detective made a witness cry..." She shrugged her shoulders. "I'd have a helluva lot of nickels."

It was easy to see why Frank had a crush on her.

"Anyway," she said. "You guys wanted to know about the wound on Valerie Berry's shoulder."

"Is it a bite mark?" I asked.

"It is," she said, nodding. "An unusual one."

"How so?" Frank's voice sounded a tone deeper than it had just minutes earlier. I resisted the urge to bust his chops.

"There are clear impressions for only four teeth. Two upper and two lower. The remaining flesh is torn rather than punctured."

"She was wearing a heavy sweater," I said.

"Yes, and that could explain the lack of precise markings. We've seen that hundreds of times before."

"But?"

"But...the four puncture marks are of an unusual shape and size and remarkably deep. I believe they reached to the bone."

"Are they human?" I asked.

"In all likelihood. I'll know more once I get back to the lab."

"We'll stop by sometime tomorrow," Frank said. "I'll make sure to call first."

"Sounds good," she said. "I'll be around for a couple more hours if you need me." She started to walk away, then stopped and turned around. "Is that a new cologne you're wearing, Frank?"

My partner blushed. "It is. Chanel Bleu. It was on sale at Macy's."

"I like it."

And she walked away.

"Don't you dare say a word."

We were making our way down a winding, dirt path in the woods, both of us carrying flashlights. I was trying my best not to laugh and failing miserably.

"*Chanel Bleu. I got it on sale at Macy's.* You sure have a way with words, partner."

"I got nervous."

"I think she likes you, Frank."

"You're an idiot."

"No, I'm serious."

"Why do you say that?"

"She mentioned your cologne. I'm pretty sure that means something."

"I'm pretty sure it means you're an idiot."

"That makes no—"

Suddenly, there was a blinding light shining in our faces. "Detectives Logan and Richards?"

"That's right," Frank said. "Would you mind getting your goddamn flash outta my eyes?"

"I'm sorry, sir." The light went away, and the Maryland State Trooper standing in front of us looked like he wanted to disappear. "Sergeant Hopkins radioed and told me to meet you here."

"You're supposed to take us to the crime scene."

"Yes, sir," he said, turning around and leading the way. "It's not much of a crime scene, I'm afraid. Some trampled down leaves. A couple broken branches."

"No blood trail?"

He shook his head. "No, sir."

We walked another thirty or forty yards in silence. Frank belched, and I could smell the pepperoni and sausage from the Sicilian pizza we'd shared a couple hours earlier. The state trooper tripped over a tree root, twice, and almost fell. It was not his night. Finally, we arrived at the scene.

A half dozen light-stands had been erected around a sloping stretch of trail and the surrounding woods, maybe twenty yards long and half as wide. The immediate area was daytime bright, which made the encroaching darkness that much deeper. It reminded me of an underwater scene from a movie. A second trooper stood off to the side, watching one of Shelly's technicians take photographs. The man was pointing the camera at an overhead section of tree trunk approximately ten or twelve feet off the ground. There was a gnarled section where narrow strips of bark had been carved away. I stepped closer for a better look. It resembled a claw mark.

"It's too quiet out here."

It was a quarter past one in the morning but felt hours later. I was starting to get cold and hungry. I didn't bother to ask Frank; he was always hungry. The pair of state troopers and Shelly Sunderland's guy had left five minutes earlier. Deputy Hopkins was due any minute, but for now it was just the two of us.

"I like the quiet," Frank said.

I looked around and shivered. It felt like the lights were losing their power and darkness was closing in on us. "Even the crickets have stopped chirping."

Frank ignored me. "Let's go over this one more time." He walked a ways down the path and stopped. "So we think the two girls were initially attacked here." He gazed up and down the path, glanced up at the moon through the trees, and then turned around. "We have no idea what happened to Mallory, but it appears that Valerie was knocked to the ground here." He gestured to a patch of trampled brush just off the path. It was marked with a yellow evidence placard. "She managed to scramble to her feet and run in this direction." He started walking. When he was a couple of strides past me on the trail, he halted again. "The skid marks in the dirt tell us she was most likely knocked down a second time somewhere around here, and that's probably when she was bitten." He spun in a slow circle. "But no drag marks in the brush anywhere. No trace blood. No torn clothing. It's like Mallory Collins just up and disappeared."

"There's one thing I don't get," I said.

"Only one?"

I looked over my shoulder at the direction from which we'd originally came. "If the girls had to pee, why did they walk so far into the woods?"

"That's a fair question."

"They could've gone a tenth of the distance, and no one would've seen them."

"It's almost like they were up to something."

"Maybe."

"Take a look at this." He started down the trail. I followed. He stopped next to the patch of trampled brush and weeds. I did, too. Frank took a deep breath and said, "Look up."

At first, I didn't see anything out of the ordinary. A gap in the foliage, yet another window through which the pensive orange moon could judge our incompetence.

Then I saw it—and the breath caught in my throat.

"Jesus," I whispered once I was able to.

"Pretty much my reaction when I noticed it a few minutes ago."

High up in the treetops, at least sixty feet off the forest floor, where neighboring branches met and intertwined in the star-speckled sky, there was a dangling web of broken limbs and torn vines. It was as if something had plummeted from high above the earth, smashing a hole through the forest ceiling as it screamed toward the surface.

Something big.

Farther off the trail. Just outside the reach of the spotlights. Frank stopped walking and steadied his flash at the patch of forest floor in front of us. "Take a look."

Surrounding a deep crater was a circular area of broken branches, singed brush, and rocks, as well as a scattering of splintered tree trunks. The hole in the ground was empty.

"Looks like an impact zone and a debris field."

"Exactly," Frank said, hoisting a branch from the ground. It was at least six inches in diameter. He held it up to the moonlight. "See the break?"

Jagged splinters as long as rulers poked from the edges. Most of the bark had been stripped away. The limb hadn't just snapped; it had *exploded*.

I shook my head. "It's like the man in the moon hurled a bowling ball at someone."

"The who?"

"The man in the moon. You know how sometimes it looks like there's a face on the surface."

Frank lifted his eyes to the ragged opening in the foliage. His fleshy cheeks shone a deep red from the chill night air. Squinting, he said, "I don't see any damn face."

I glanced up at the bloated moon. He was right. There was nothing there. Just a fat orange blob that resembled an uncarved pumpkin missing its stem.

And then I saw something in the broken treetops.

A dark, angular shadow, midnight black, sitting perfectly still amongst the swaying limbs.

Gooseflesh rose on my arms, and I felt the tiny hairs on the back of my neck stiffen.

Whatever it was, it was staring right at me.

The wind picked up. The trees danced, and I heard that awful sound again, like dry bones scraping against each other.

"What're you staring at, Ben?" My partner nudged me in the ribs. "You're starting to give me the creeps."

"Nothing," I whispered, and I was telling the truth. Whatever had been there moments earlier was gone.

"You hungry?"

I'd been waiting for Frank to ask. "I could eat. You?"

"Starving." He glanced at his wristwatch. "Where the hell we gonna go at this hour?"

It was three a.m., and we were back in the clearing. Not long ago, the breeze had grown steady, clouds had rolled in, and it'd started to rain.

"There's always IHOP on Bel Air Road."

"I could go for some pancakes."

The bonfire had burned itself out before the rain arrived. There was nothing left except for a pyramid of smoldering ash. Tendrils of gray smoke rose high into the air and dissipated like ghosts in a cemetery. All of the kids were gone. I pictured them at home now, hair wet from a shower, dressed in their night clothes, perched on living room and den sofas, explaining what had transpired tonight to anxious mothers and fathers.

Mallory Collins' parents had shown up a couple of hours earlier and caused quite a scene. Trooper Hopkins spoke with them first, then Frank and I gave it our best go, before Lieutenant Patterson, who was officially in charge of the search, finally showed up. Talking to someone in charge seemed to do the trick, and now the Collinses were waiting back at the high school where a command center had been established in the commuter parking lot.

"Don't have to tell me twice," I said and started for the car.

We were halfway across the clearing and discussing our IHOP orders when Deputy Mackleson called out to us from the tree line. "Detectives!"

"Just keep walking," Frank said. "Pretend we don't hear him."

"Detective Richards! Detective Logan!"

I stopped walking and turned around.

The deputy was running across the field, chasing after us.

"Goddamn it," Frank muttered under his breath.

Deputy Mackleson slid to a stop on the wet grass in front of us. "We just...got a call...on the radio." Trying to catch his breath. "Couple of officers...stumbled upon a homeless man living in the woods behind the old post office. They found...Mallory Collins' skirt and one of her boots...inside his tent. There's blood on the skirt."

"Any sign of the girl?"

He shook his head. "Negative. But the search has shifted in that direction, so hopefully soon." He hurried to his cruiser. "I'll see you there."

Frank and I stood side-by-side in the rain, watching the cruiser's taillights fade away in the distance.

"Jesus, was I ever that green?"

"Doubtful," I said. "Pretty sure you were born old."

"Guess we don't have time for pancakes."

"Guess not."

A strong gust of wind rattled the treetops. Somewhere, hidden, an owl called out. We stared up at the sky, waiting for something to answer. When it didn't, we climbed into our car. I started the engine and turned the heater on HIGH.

"Couple of drowned rats," Frank complained.

"At least you smell good."

"Shut up, Ben."

"Whatever you say, Frank."

ABOUT THE AUTHORS

L.P. Hernandez is an author of horror and speculative fiction. His stories have been featured in anthologies from Cemetery Dance, Dark Matter Ink, and Cemetery Gates Media among others. He is a regular contributor to The NoSleep Podcast and has released two short story collections. His third collection will be published by Cemetery Dance in 2024. His novella, *Stargazers,* was published under the My Dark Library banner. When not writing, L.P. serves as a medical administrator in the U.S. Air Force. He is a husband, father, and a dedicated metalhead. Find out more about L.P. at www.lphernandez.com.

G. Nicholas Miranda lives in Dayton, Ohio where he writes during his lunch breaks. His story, "Cemetery Lake," was previously published in *If I Die Before I Wake – Tales of the Dark Deep (The Better Off Dead Series, Vol. 6)*. Other works have appeared in *Strange Aeons: 2021: Orbital Lovecraft* and the *Books of Horror Community Anthology, Vol. 2 & 3*, with more set to appear very soon.

Kevin M. Folliard is a Chicagoland writer whose fiction has been collected by The Horror Tree, The Dread Machine, Demain Publishing, Dark Owl Publishing, and more. His recent publications include his horror anthology *The Misery King's Closet*, his YA fantasy adventure novel *Grayson North: Frost-Keeper of the Windy City*, and his 2022 dinosaur adventure novel *Carnivore Keepers*. Kevin currently resides in the western suburbs of Chicago, IL, where he enjoys his day job in academia and membership in the La Grange Writers Group. Find out more about Kevin at www.kevinfolliard.com.

Mike Marcus is a horror and dark fantasy author living in Pittsburgh, PA, with his wife, Amy, and German Shepherd–mutt, Tucker.

This is Mike's third appearance in a Sinister Smile Press anthology, with stories previously appearing in *A Pile of Bodies, A Pile of Heads: Let the Bodies Hit the Floor Vol. 1* and the limited-edition *Dead Hookers in Gas Station Bathrooms: Road Trip Horror*. Mike has published nearly a dozen short stories in anthologies in the five years he's been writing fiction, with stories in *The Jewish Book of Horror* from Denver Horror Collective, *Dark Nature* from Macabre Ladies Publishing, and *The Modern Deity's Guide to Surviving Humanity* from Zombies Need Brains, Inc.

Mike is a US Army veteran and graduate of Frostburg State University, in Frostburg, MD.

Find out more about Mike at www.mikemarcusauthor.com, or follow him on Facebook at mikemarcus.author, and on Twitter at @mikemarcus77.

Bryan Holm grew up in Minnesota and currently lives in St. Louis Park with his wife and dog. He once toured the Coen brothers' childhood home under the pretense of purchasing it, in hopes he could absorb whatever alchemy led to their genius. It didn't work. He is a photographer by day who spends his nights writing and consuming all things horror. His short fiction has been published in numerous anthologies, and his screenplay was featured on the Bloodlist as a Fresh Blood Selects. His debut novella is being released in 2024 by D&T Publishing. Find out more about Bryan at www.bryanholm.com.

Jason A. Wyckoff is the author of two short story collections published by Tartarus Press, *Black Horse and other Strange Stories* (2012) and *The Hidden Back Room* (2016). His work has appeared in anthologies from Haverhill House, Plutonian Press, and Siren's Call Publications, as well as the journals *Nightscript*, *Weirdbook*, and *Turn* *to Ash*, among others. He lives in Columbus, Ohio, USA. Married, with cats. Find out more about Jason at www.jasonawyckoff.weebly.com.

Alexandr Bond has been writing since he was nine years old and has a love for fantasy, the supernatural, and cosmic horror. His work has been published in *Cosmic Horror Monthly* and Sinister Smile Press as well as a number of NaNoWriMo anthologies.

He is legally blind and albino and has received his BA in English/Creative Writing from Southern New Hampshire University. When not writing, he spends his time reading and learning; most recently, he is learning how to speak Deutsch and Japanese. He has traveled throughout the continental United States but currently resides in North Carolina with his family, including six lazy cats and a fifteen-year-old dog.

Find out more about Alexandr at alexandrbond.wordpress.com; his Amazon Author page: Alexandr Bond; and his Facebook page: Alexandr Bond – Author.

David Anthony was born and raised in Southwest Michigan where he currently resides with his wife and daughter. Having been a fan of dark fiction all his life, he now writes horror, sci-fi, and fantasy of the darker varieties. His stories can be found in various magazines and anthologies, including "The Thing in the Corner," published in *Lovecraft eZine*, issue 36, and "Outrun the Wolves," published in *If I Die Before I Wake, Vol. 7: Tales of Savagery and Slaughter*. Find out more about David and his work at www.davidaanthony.wordpress.com.

David Rider celebrated All Hallows' Eve during his formative years on the streets of Calumet City, Illinois. Like most feral Gen Xers of the time, his Halloween nights were unsupervised, and curfews were ignored. The last time he trick-or-treated, non-costumed punks his own age snatched his full candy bag. He responded with the witty rejoinder, "Hey!" and permanently hung up his costume after that. He now lives with his wife, kids, and dogs in a rural Midwestern town that forces children to stop begging for their sugar fixes by 7 p.m. on October 31.

He is a member of the Horror Writers Association. His stories have appeared in various anthologies from Sinister Smile Press, and another by Grendel Press. He has published two novels, *We Are Van Helsing* Books One and Two. A third novel, *Anca's Undead Playlist*, is coming soon. Find out more about David at www.davidriderauthor.com.

Sarah Cannavo is a writer haunting southern New Jersey. Her work has appeared in *The Cryptid Chronicle*s, DBND Publishing's *Halloween Horror Volume 3*, *JOURN-E*, and *Pulp Modern*, among others. Her poetry was nominated for the 2020, 2021, and 2023 Rhysling and 2022 Dwarf Stars Awards. Her story "Unreality" and novella "Wolf of the Pines" are available on Amazon. She's been rumored to post on her site The Moody Muse at www.moodilymusing.blogspot.com, and has occasionally been sighted Tweeting @moodilymusing. If you listen closely on moonless nights, you may be able to hear her screaming "DAENERYS DESERVED BETTER" into the darkness. Find out more about Sarah at www.moodilymusing.blogspot.com.

DW Milton is a pen name. The author has a day job but would rather be writing speculative fiction with short stories recently published in HellBound Books' *Anthology of Splatterpunk*, *Hyphen-Punk,* and *BOMBFIRE* magazines and Raven Tale Publishing's *We're Infested* anthology. Upcoming pieces are headed for HorrorAddicts.net's Manor of Frights anthology, Black Ink Fictions Home Sweet Horror anthology, SavagePlanets magazine, and Theaker's Quarterly Fiction UNSPLATTERPUK! 6. Find out more about DW at www.dwmilton.com.

Scotty Milder is a writer, filmmaker, and film educator living in Albuquerque, New Mexico. He received his MFA in Screenwriting from Boston University, and his award-winning short films have screened at festivals all over the world, including Cinequest, the Dead By Dawn Festival of Horror, HollyShorts, and the H.P. Lovecraft Film Festival, and CthulhuCon. His independent feature film *Dead Billy* is available to stream on Amazon.com and Google Play.

His short fiction has appeared or will appear in such magazines as *Dark Matter Magazine, Cosmic Horror Monthly, Dark Moon Digest*, and anthologies from Dark Moon Books, HellBound Books, Dark Peninsula Press, Sinister Smile Press, Dark Ink Books, and others.

He teaches screenwriting and film production at Santa Fe Community College. He is also host of the Horror From the High Desert podcast and co-host of The Weirdest Thing history podcast with actor/theatre artist Amelia Ampuero.

Find out more about Scotty at www.scottymilder.com or www.facebook.com/scottymilderwrites.

Richard Chizmar is the *New York Times* bestselling author of the *Gwendy Trilogy* (with Stephen King), as well as *Chasing the Boogeyman, Widow's Point*, and many other books. *Becoming the Boogeyman* will be published by Simon & Schuster/Gallery Books in October 2023.

He is the founder/publisher of *Cemetery Dance* magazine and the Cemetery Dance Publications book imprint. He has edited more than 35 anthologies, and his short fiction has appeared in dozens of publications, including multiple editions of *Ellery Queen's Mystery Magazine* and *The Year's 25 Finest Crime and Mystery Stories*. He has won two World Fantasy awards, four International Horror Guild awards, and the HWA's Board of Trustees' award.

Chizmar (in collaboration with Johnathon Schaech) has also written screenplays and teleplays for United Artists, Sony Screen Gems, Lions Gate, Showtime, NBC, and many other companies.

He has adapted the works of many bestselling authors including Stephen King, Peter Straub, and Bentley Little.

Chizmar's work has been translated into more than fifteen languages throughout the world, and he has appeared at numerous conferences as a writing instructor, guest speaker, panelist, and guest of honor. Find out more about Richard at www.richardchizmar.com.

W.H. Chizmar is a writer and filmmaker from Bel Air, Maryland. He is the author of numerous short stories and essays. His work has appeared in various anthologies alongside legendary storytellers such as Ray Bradbury and Stephen King. In 2018, he co-wrote the novella *Widow's Point* with his father, Richard Chizmar, and soon after it was adapted into a feature film.

The father-and-son duo also joined forces to write and direct several short horror films, including 2019's *Trapped*, based on a story idea by Stephen King. Chizmar currently contributes monthly original content for his Patreon page and also works at Cemetery Dance Publications. When he's not at his desk, you can probably find him wandering the woods with his dog, J.J.

More from Sinister Smile Press

ANTHOLOGIES

If I Die Before I Wake:
The Better Off Dead Series
Volumes 1-8

A Pile of Bodies, A Pile of Heads
Let the Bodies Hit the Floor Series
Volumes 1 & 2

Screaming in the Night:
Sinister Supernatural Stories
Volume 1

Institutionalized:
Tales of Demented and Deranged

Just a Girl

Evil Little Fucks

COLLECTIONS

Devil's Gulch:
A Collaborative Horror Experience

Lethal Lords and Ladies of the Night
Volumes 1 & 2

Strange Frequencies
Richard Clive

Dark Days
Steven Pajak

Everything Went to Shit
R.E. Sargent

NOVELS

By Mike Duke
The Book of Smarba

By Steven Pajak
Project Hindsight
Wolves Among Sheep
Nowere to Run

By R.E. Sargent
The Karen Carter Trilogy
One-Star Review
Becoming Karen Carter
A Review to Die For

By James Watts
Them
Shadows of the Damned
Beasts of Sorrow

By EV Knight
Partum

Visit our website for
full list of publications
www.sinistersmilepress.com